Shane

SHANE

The Critical Edition

Jack Schaefer

Edited by James C. Work
Foreword by
Marc Simmons

University of
Nebraska Press
Lincoln and London

7/1984
Eng.

Copyright 1984
by the University
of Nebraska Press
Acknowledgments for
the use of copyrighted
material appear on p. xvii.

First Bison Book printing: 1984
Most recent printing indicated
by the first digit below:
1 2 3 4 5 6 7 8 9 10

The text of *Shane* is
reprinted from the
original 1949 edition.
Shane is available in
hardcover from Houghton
Mifflin Company, 2 Park Street,
Boston, Massachusetts 02108,
and in a low-price paperback
edition from Bantam Books,
666 Fifth Avenue,
New York, New York 10103.

**Library of Congress Cataloging
in Publication Data**
Schaefer, Jack, 1907–
Shane: the critical edition.
Bibliography: p.
1. Schaefer, Jack, 1907–.
Shane—Addresses, essays,
lectures. I. Work, James C. II. Title.
PS3537.C223S5   1984   813'.54   83–25948
ISBN 0-8032-4145-3
ISBN 0-8032-9142-6 (pbk.)

Contents

The Film: Essays in Criticism

Marc Simmons

Foreword

By any standard of measurement, Jack Schaefer's *Shane* rates as a classic in the literature of the American West. Since its publication in 1949 it has gained a worldwide readership, appearing in more than seventy editions and thirty foreign languages. *Shane* received a boost in 1953 when director George Stevens produced an award-winning film version that continues to charm viewers on late-night television. And I think it is safe to declare that today the many men and boys (and even a few girls) who are graced with the given name of Shane bear witness to the influence that Schaefer's hero exerted upon their parents.

For the fact is that *Shane,* the novel, addressed an entire generation: post-World War II Americans who did not quite comprehend, during the unsettling 1950s, that one age was crumbling around them and a new, tense, faster-paced time was at hand. Schaefer wrote of people—of Shane and the Starrett family—cut from noble cloth. They were strong, hardworking, brave, self-disciplined, responsible, honest; ungalled by self-doubt or any sense of inferiority. In short, they possessed those virtues that, by the mid-twentieth century, were increasingly being dismissed as outdated or unattainable.

The film provided my own introduction to *Shane*. That first viewing, as an impressionable youngster, left me shaken. I could not have explained why, then, but *Shane* drew me back to the movie theater again and again throughout grade school and high school. Embarrassing as it is to admit now, I saw it more than thirty times. Only later did I meet people who confessed they had seen it nearly as often. If Shane had redirected the course of my life, the same had happened to them, or so they claimed.

By a strange turning of fate, I came afterward to northern New Mexico, where I gained the friendship of Jack Schaefer. Our first meeting was in the proper spirit of the Old West. On a borrowed Indian horse, I rode thirty miles from Cochiti Pueblo, crossing the Rio Grande and ascending the thousand-foot lava escarpment known as La Bajada, to Schaefer's ranch south of Santa Fe.

Dismounting at the gate, I rang a small mission bell, and Schaefer came out into the courtyard. He had been at the typewriter, laboring over a new novel, *Monte Walsh*.

From my old cavalry saddlebags, I drew a worn and much-thumbed copy of the first paperback edition of *Shane*. When I handed it to Schaefer for autographing, he expressed astonishment at seeing the early Bantam edition with its twenty-five-cent price tag. We sat for an hour against an adobe wall talking about Shane and Monte and a host of other persons, fictional and real, who fill the pages of Schaefer's books.

For me, *Shane* has been an almost lifelong companion. I return to it whenever I need a bit of inspiration or a boost of energy. The book's messages are as deep and vital as the man it describes; and it addresses, in symbolic fashion, the central problems of our existence.

Now that may be too much for many people to swallow, for after all, they say, *Shane* is merely another bullets-and-blood western, though several cuts above the average. Schaefer himself has disavowed any intention of creating symbols or treating philosophical issues in his book. But in the late-night hours when he was composing *Shane*, a deeper level of meaning seems to have crept into his prose, unawares.

As analytical psychologists have demonstrated, a piece of writing, especially one recognized as a work of art, can be laden with unconscious symbols. These well up spontaneously, appear unbidden, while the writer is engaged in the creative process. The symbolism, or the extra meaning, taken on by commonplace words and incidents can be discovered by a discerning observer even while remaining hidden from the author. To those doubters who regard this as mere intellectual invention, a quote from the book can be offered. Young Bob Starrett, narrator of the story, speaks of Shane as "the symbol of all the dim, formless imaginings of danger and terror in the untested realm of human potentialities beyond my understanding." That statement not only sets the tone of the book, it signals to the reader that the hero has a higher purpose, that his activities represent somethng more than appears on the surface.

Above all, Shane emerges as an uncommon man—in his personal appearance, his movements, his abilities, his character. He is someone capable of standing up to any crises "in the simple solitude of his own invincible completeness." As an autonomous man, accepting the responsibility of ethical decision and exercising a measure of control over events surrounding him, Shane refuses to drift with the tide. He is the antithesis of modern mass man and of T. S. Eliot's "hollow men," disillusioned and despairing. Experiencing a profound inner conflict the nature of which is never made explicit, Shane in fact is engaged in the difficult task of disciplining himself toward wholeness.

When Bob gets a glimmer of what Shane is and represents, it awakens him to the possibility that man can become what he ought to be. At that moment of perception, Shane "was no longer a stranger. He was a man like father in whom a boy could believe in the simple knowledge that what was beyond comprehension was still clean and solid and right." Therein lies the meaning and the necessity of the heroic exemplar.

The hero has been held up for emulation in the writings of the Greeks, in medieval epics, and in modern literature. *L'uomo universale* has inspired civilized people in all times and places and created in them an awe similar to that felt by Bob in his encounters with Shane. Such models are salutary reminders, for the rest of us, of what is possible in the human equation.

The thesis of Schaefer's book, then, expresses belief in the essential worth of the individual. And it describes the timeless theme of one man's search for himself, of his efforts to tap his latent potentialities. More than that, it is an affirmation that we are not powerless automatons, ruled by environmental, social, or even psychological forces beyond our control.

That message, although buttressed by the weight of truth, is a difficult one to convey in today's world. To the businessman in the pressurized tank of his high-rise office building, to the unionized assembly-line worker in an air-conditioned factory, or to the farmer enmeshed in the debt structure of agribusiness, it is easy to succumb to the false prophets of our age who proclaim that the individual is helpless and ineffectual and that, because of the frailties of our natures, there is little we can do about it. Such a notion would have made no sense at all to Shane and the Starretts.

But they are the products of fiction, declare the cynics and debunkers. Such people never really existed. We all have feet of clay, so there is no such creature as the autonomous, self-contained, confident, moral, and capable man or woman. When a bogus dogma like that is preached, and believed, it can dispirit an entire nation.

I recall attending a showing of *Shane* twenty-five years after its release, during a film classic series on a university campus. I was not surprised that it now appeared a bit dated and that some of its original luster had faded. But I was wholly unprepared for the reaction of the young audience. Throughout, they laughed at serious moments, jeered at Shane's deference toward women, and hooted at Bob's open admiration for his hero. Without making too much of that single incident, it seems to me at the very least that some of our youth have capitulated to the doctrine that the world is without serious purpose, chaos is our destiny, and serious thought is a pointless exercise in futility.

The question remains, however: Is Shane purely the fictional product of his creator, or is he the facsimile of a type of individual that actually exists? The historical literature on America's West, to cite one category of evidence, contains abundant reference to Shane-like persons who left their mark on the developing frontier. More recently, psychologist Abraham Maslow has studied examples of such people — he calls them self-actualizers — and has described their motivation and character in detail in the scientific literature. His definition of a self-actualizing person (one who is self-reliant and maintains an inner consistency) was formulated after Schaefer had written his novel, but as an apt description of Shane's personality it seems almost tailor-made.

I once asked Jack Schaefer if the character of Shane was based upon anyone he had actually known. He replied that he had never considered the matter, but after pondering for a few moments, he was struck with a sudden thought. "Now that you bring it up, I believe that Shane had the qualities of my father. Of course, my father wasn't Shane, but he was that sort of man." Upon reflection, I suspect that most of us could recall persons met along the way who have mirrored at least some of the qualities exemplified by Shane.

The far Wyoming valley where Schaefer's protagonist confronts the rancher Fletcher and his hired gunslinger forms the setting for a simpler time, one in which the line between good and evil and between civilized and primitive life could be clearly drawn. With the complexities of the modern age, the boundaries separating right conduct from wrong have become blurred, and in some quarters they have practically vanished. But if *Shane* has anything to teach us, as we grope our way toward the twenty-first century, it is this: the pursuit of higher values and aspirations, and the quest for self-mastery and a firm sense of identity offer the straightest trail to achievement of the authentic life.

This is pretty heady stuff for a book classed as a "stock Western." But in that lies its universality.

James C. Work

Preface

Western novels either exploit the West or explicate it. Like movie critics, book reviewers tell us whether a particular title of the first kind is worth our money; scholars and literary critics interpret the second kind for us. Once the criticisms have been written, it is possible to bring together in a single edition a good explicative novel and the critical interpretations it has provoked. Obviously, *Shane*'s critics have said almost everything that might be said in this preface: that *Shane* has a surprisingly broad readership, that it suggests unusually complex social themes, that it has literary roots reaching far down into world literary history. Each historian and critic has found something new to add, each offering the reader a new perspective.

Years of critical interest come together in this edition in order to present the reader with intellectual direction and challenge, to perhaps articulate the reader's own unexpressed reactions to the novel. To put it another way, the critical edition is for those who want to study *Shane* rather than merely read it. Under its surface, such a reader will find *Shane* to be like Starrett's stubborn stump. Plenty of roots and meanings exist which, while not fully visible, cannot be ignored. Digging in with the tools of literary scholarship, the essays in this edition allow the reader to get at the roots.

It is customary in a preface to acknowledge the cooperation of the individuals involved in bringing together a book, and such acknowledgment is heartily offered here. But the astonishing and gratifying thing about that cooperation is that the novelist and the contributors all have been so true to the western spirit symbolized by Shane. Jack Schaefer quickly and patiently responded (again) to the dozens of questions an editor has to ask; his assistance was immediate and unmitigated, like Shane's help in the cultivator dispute or the battle with the stump. The reaction of the other contributors was equally generous, quick, and unquestioning. They gave copyright permissions without stint, offered me editorial carte blanche to change their words, and made no demands. Of those whom I asked specifically to write for this edition—Simmons, Marsden, Guthrie, Rankin—not a single one said that he was too busy, or had nothing to offer. Seeing a job of work to be done, they set to it.

As for those editorial changes, they are few. With Jack Schaefer's cooperation, I corrected two minor points in Gerald Haslam's biography (one concerned where Schaefer was working when he wrote *Shane*, and one concerned the origin of the story in *The Canyon*). Parts of Michael Marsden's "The Making of *Shane*" have previously appeared in journals, but the essay was largely written anew for this edition.

Two widely sold hardbound editions of *Shane* are those of 1949 and 1954. Most other editions in English, ranging from the large-type London edition of 1949 to the series of

Bantam editions and reprintings that began in 1950, are
taken from either the 1949 or the 1954 hardbound versions.

One difference between the two editions is, of course,
that the one of 1954 is illustrated by John McCormack.
Except for those illustrations, the 1954 *appears* to be a
photocopy of the 1949; however, in preparing this critical edition, I discovered another important difference.
There are, in the 1949 edition, nineteen variations of the
words "hell" and "damn" that were subsequently censored
for the 1954 version. The publishers, calling this a school
edition, had cleaned up the "rough" language so that
Shane would not offend secondary school boards and
librarians.

Interestingly, whoever edited the offending words
seems to have overlooked two of them—or left them in for
some reason: the 1954 version has a "damned" on page 85
and a "damn it all" on page 90, even though all the other
swearing in the novel has been carefully changed. Those
changes are as follows (top page numbers refer to both
Houghton Mifflin editions; bracketed numbers to the
critical edition):

Page	Edition	
27	1949	"It's what I said. A hundred and ten. Hell, ... "
[87]	1954	"It's what I said. A hundred and ten. I'll ... "
35	1949	"damned well that whether you have a hat on or"
[95]	1954	"right well that whether you have a hat on or"
58	1949	"this way are worth a damn"
[118]	1954	"this way are worth a hoot"
65	1949	"it sets off one hell of a blow-off of trouble"
[125]	1954	"it sets off one mighty big blow-off of trouble"
72	1949	"Well, I'll be damned," said father
[132]	1954	"Well, I'll be blowed," said father

Page	Edition	
92	1949	"What the hell?"
[152]	1954	"What's got into you?"
92	1949	"This is a hell of a country up here"
[152]	1954	"This is a rotten kind of a country"
92	1949	"Hell, " he said to himself
[152]	1954	"Well," he said to himself
94	1949	"Hell, there ain't nobody else standing there"
[154]	1954	"Don't see anybody else standing there"
94	1949	"I'll be damned," flipped Chris
[154]	1954	"Well, look at that," flipped Chris
103	1949	"Helped me, damn them!"
[163]	1954	"Helped me, blast them!"
103	1949	"Damn it, man, I'm beginning to"
[163]	1954	"Man, I'm beginning to"
154	1949	"You're a damn fool, Wright"
[214]	1954	You're a fool, Wright"
154	1949	"you're a God-damned liar!"
[214]	1954	"you're a low-crawling liar!"
156	1949	"But damn it, Joe! A man can't just"
[216]	1954	"Joe! A man can't just go around"
171	1949	"your man would make one hell of a driving"
[231]	1954	"your man would make a top-rank driving"
183	1949	from the table. "Damn it, Shane"
[243]	1954	from the table. "Great Godfrey, Shane"
206	1949	"And there's damn few"
[266]	1954	"And there's mighty few"
207	1949	"I'm a damned poor substitute"
[267]	1954	"I'm a poor substitute"

I shall leave it to more accomplished linguists to discover whether the swear words found their way into the many translations of the novel. This critical edition adheres to the 1949 first edition.

Acknowledgments

Grateful acknowledgment is made for permission to use in this volume the following copyrighted material:

Albright, Charles, Jr. Review of the film *Shane*. Reprinted from *Magill's Survey of Cinema*, English Language Films, 1st ser., 4: 1534–38. By permission of the publisher, Salem Press, Inc. Copyright, 1980, by Frank N. Magill.

Cleary, Michael. "Jack Schaefer: The Evolution of Pessimism," *Western American Literature* 14 (May 1979): 33–47.

Crowther, Bosley. Review of the film *Shane*, © 1953 by the New York Times Company. Reprinted by permission.

Erisman, Fred. "Growing Up with the American West: Fiction of Jack Schaefer," *Popular Press* (Bowling Green State University, 1974).

Folsom, James K. "*Shane* and Hud: Two Stories in Search of a Medium," *Western Humanities Review* 24, no. 4 (Autumn 1970): 359–72.

Haslam, Gerald. *Jack Schaefer*. Boise State University Western Writers Series, no. 20 (1975).

Kael, Paulin. Review of the film *Shane*. In *Kiss Kiss Bang Bang* (Boston: Little, Brown, 1968).

Marsden, Michael T. "Savior in the Saddle: The Sagebrush Testament," which appeared in *Illinois Quarterly* and also in *Focus on the Western* (Englewood Cliffs, N.J.: Prentice-Hall, 1974).

Marsden, Michael T. "*Shane*: From Magazine Serial to American Classic," *South Dakota Review* 15, no. 4 (Winter 1977–78): 59–67, used here in "The Making of *Shane*: A Story for All Media."

Mikkelsen, Robert. "The Western Writer: Jack Schaefer's Use of the Western Frontier," *Western Humanities Review* 8, no. 2 (Spring 1954).

Nuwer, Henry Joseph. "An Interview with Jack Schaefer," *South Dakota Review* (Spring 1973).

Schaefer, Jack. "A New Direction," speech printed in *Western American Literature* (Winter 1976).

Schein, Harry. "The Olympian Cowboy," *American Scholar* 24, no. 3 (Summer 1955). Translated from the Swedish by Ida M. Alcock. Copyright 1955 by the United Chapters of Phi Beta Kappa. By permission of the publishers.

Work, James C. "Settlement Waves and Coordinate Forces in *Shane,*" *Western American Literature* 14 (Fall 1979): 191–200.

Special acknowledgment and gratitude is extended to those who wrote especially for this edition of *Shane*:

A. B. Guthrie, Jr., for remarks on writing the screenplay for the film *Shane*.

Michael T. Marsden for "The Making of *Shane*: A Story for All Media."

Chuck Rankin for "Clash of Frontiers: A Historical Parallel to Jack Schaefer's *Shane*."

Marc Simmons for the Foreword, at Jack Schaefer's suggestion.

Historical and
Biographical
Background

Chuck Rankin

Clash of Frontiers:
A Historical Parallel
to Jack Schaefer's *Shane*

> The cattle kingdom was a forerun-
> ner and an obstacle. It appropriated
> the Great Plains when the farmer
> could not take them, and for a time it
> stood in his way to dispute his com-
> ing.
>
> Walter Prescott Webb,
> *The Great Plains*

> Always it has been the frontier
> which has allured many of our bol-
> dest souls. And always, just back of
> the frontier, advancing, receding,
> crossing it this way and that, suc-
> ceeding and failing, hoping and de-
> spairing—but steadily advancing in
> the net result—has come that por-
> tion of the population which builds
> homes and lives in them, and which
> is not content with a blanket for a
> bed and the sky for a roof.
>
> Emerson Hough,
> *The Passing of the Frontier*

The American farmer faltered when
he reached the Great Plains. His methods, his know-how,
even his tools, were no match for what Stephen H. Long
had called the Great American Desert. In time, the farmer
ventured out onto the plains. In keeping with his innova-
tive nature, he invented new techniques to subdue and
cultivate this "desert." But while the farmer grappled with

new conditions on the eastern edge of the prairies, a cattle-man's empire spread north from Texas across the western plains states. The cattle kingdom adapted so rapidly to the arid, open range that it flourished and came to support a cohesive, entrenched culture within little more than a decade. The homesteading farmer would find the cattle baron another stumbling block when he encountered his empire in the high-plains West.

For the cattle and farming frontiers to have met in this way, the timing had to have been perfect. And it was. The farming frontier had jumped the Mississippi River and was settling Minnesota and eastern Nebraska and Kansas when the Civil War drained it of manpower and impetus. The westward march of homesteading stalled at the frontier line it had reached before the war, advancing little farther during those four bloody years. The Civil War took six hundred thousand lives, the flower of a generation. The farming frontier required time to regain momentum in the aftermath of Appomattox.

If anything could power a new salient into the American frontier it was economics—the oportunity to make money, and to make it quickly. In 1866, a Texas longhorn could be bought in southern Texas for three or four dollars. In the beef-hungry north, the same cow could be sold for ten times that much. All one had to do was get her there. With a scrap of scratch paper and a pencil stub, even a Texas cowpoke could figure a tidy profit when he multiplied those numbers by the one to three thousand head of cattle in the average herd to be driven north.

The conclusion of the Civil War also unleashed the railroads, which built west at a feverish pace in the late 1860s. To meet them, as well as gain open country, dodge Indians, and avoid quarantine laws, the trail drivers swung farther west each year. By 1870, steel rails stretched from Omaha to San Francisco and all the way across Kansas to

Denver. The Cheyenne and Arapaho Indians were chased from eastern Colorado, and scores of men with wagons collected the bones of the great buffalo herds as they were systematically slaughtered for hides on the southern plains. Ranchers and cattle soon replaced Indians and buffalo.

Not all the cattle brought north from Texas could be sold immediately, so cattlemen turned to fattening them on prairie grasses as the early freighters had done with their worn-out oxen. Cattlemen bought small holdings along the myriad small streams that cut the high plains like veins of a leaf. If a man owned the water courses in such a dry region, he could control the lands they drained, and the drainages often stretched for thousands, sometimes millions, of acres. But the cattleman's primary claim to a rangeland empire frequently was based on simply having seen it first. Eastern land laws, designed to carve the land into pieces of 160 acres or less, could easily undermine such a thin pretext to ownership. Fences would consummate the growing number of lawful boundaries.

Inefficiency was also a weakness. Open-range cattle ranching flourished on a vast scale in the American West in the late nineteenth century because its wastefulness could be tolerated—for a while. For almost a century, the more efficient farmer had been moving out the less efficient rancher, forcing him to seek new lands, usually to the west. The farther west the rancher had gone, the more arid the lands had become. The vastness of the Great Plains, coupled with the rancher's ten-year head start over the farmer, allowed the cattleman's empire to spread over unprecedented distances with little or no competition for use of the land. When competition did come, in the form of homesteaders, railroads, and towns, ranchers were forced to become more efficient, and the open-range days became a memory.

Geographical immensity coupled with neglect of the livestock gave the cattle empire its most familiar characteristics. A short supply of labor on the frontier had forced the rancher to abandon any hope for close herding of his stock early on, and the animals had grown increasingly wild.[1] Spaniards had turned cattle loose in southern Texas to fend for themselves as early as the 1500s. By the late 1800s, the obstreperous nature of Texas longhorns was well-known. The wildness of the livestock and the vast distances involved forced the cattleman onto horseback and required him to carry a gun. Thus was born the need for the twin physical accoutrements of plains romance: the horse and the six-shooter.

By the early 1870s, cattle barons had laid claim to much of the southern plains; farther north, however, the last of the Great Plains tribes held tenaciously to their homelands in southern Montana, western Dakota, and northern Wyoming. The Sioux had won their war temporarily against the string of forts the United States Army had built to protect the Bozeman Trail, which wound through central Wyoming on its way to the gold camps of Montana. Ironically, Congress created Wyoming Territory in 1868, the same year government agents concluded the second treaty of Fort Laramie guaranteeing Sioux rights to the northern plains.

In 1876, the Sioux won the battle against Custer, but a year later they lost the war, the treaty, and their rights to most of the northern plains. Cattlemen moved into the vacant grasslands quickly. Within a year of the Black Hills treaty, 375,000 cattle grazed on Wyoming grasses, and by 1880 the United States Census had counted twenty-one thousand residents in Wyoming Territory.

It was the period of the giant spread, cattle drives, roundups, good prices at market, few fences, and fewer homesteaders. Charles Russell was capturing the various scenes in his imagination to record in oils and watercolors in later years; Beadle's dime novels were filling heads back East with pulp paper exaggerations; and Buffalo Bill Cody entertained Americans and Europeans alike with his Wild West Show. Some cattlemen amassed fortunes from the cattle business, others kept track of their herds by "book count"—a loose form of estimating—and most found relaxation at the posh Cheyenne Club.

The Wyoming Stock Growers' Association became synonymous with political power in the Territory. The Association, with a membership of 85 in 1879, boasted 416 members by 1885, along with an annual budget of more than $57,000. The organization obtained approval from the territorial legislature for laws designed to maintain the health of the open-range economy. As cattlemen turned to improved breeding of their stock, for example, the Association pushed through a quarantine law to prevent continued competition from Texas cattle driven north.

In 1884, the Association guided the "maverick law" through the territorial legislature. The name supposedly came from William Maverick, who, legend says, was the only Texas cattleman during the Civil War not to brand his cattle. Animals without a brand were thus called mavericks. Wyoming's maverick law held that all unmarked cattle were to be rounded up and branded with the Wyoming Stock Growers' Association "M." Mavericks were to be sold at auction, with the proceeds going to the Association's treasury to pay for stock inspectors and detectives, who in turn would be employed to prevent "rustling," or stealing of mavericks.

The law reflected the big cattleman's fear that the growing number of small ranchers and homesteaders settling in Wyoming would usurp a major source of his wealth by taking property the cattleman could not effectively control. That property came in two forms: the open range and the maverick calf. The cattleman's way of life was based on free use of the open range—land he did not own out-right—and on the scarcity of competition for its use. The maverick became a focus for his fear that the foundation to his precarious empire could be appropriated with some-one else's lasso. It was for these reasons that Luke Fletcher, the cattle baron in Jack Schaefer's novel *Shane,* could not allow Joe Starrett and homesteaders like him to settle 160-acre pieces of the open range and raise herds of their own.

As the open range became less open, the cattle kings attempted to protect their empires by preventing the small rancher, the homesteader, even their own foremen and cowboys from competing with them. Men like Fletcher were willing to let men like Starrett work for them, but they could not tolerate them if they competed independently. Small farmers and ranchers naturally staked claims to the best land they could get, usually land along a creek or with some other source of water. As Fletcher tells Starrett, "I can't let a bunch of nesters keep coming in here and choke me off from my water rights."[2]

Not all the big cattlemen thought the maverick law so wise. They realized that in a democracy where people often cherished equal opportunity more than liberty, fric-tion was almost certain. Said Emerson Hough, "A certain antipathy now began to arise between the great cattle own-ers and the small ones, especially on the upper ranges, where some rather bitter wars were fought—the cow kings accusing their smaller rivals of rustling cows; the small men accusing the larger operators of having for years done the same thing, and of having grown rich at it."[3] The maverick law symbolized the conflict that would erupt in northern Wyoming in what came to be known as the Johnson County War.

Nature, however, struck the first blow at the open range cattle empires. Dry summers in 1885 and 1886 stretched the ability of the overgrazed ranges to support the more than two million head of cattle spread over them, and set the stage for disaster. Declining prices persuaded cattlemen to keep their herds on the range rather than send them to market, and prompted them to lay off some of their hired hands. Many of the cowboys who found themselves out of work turned to homesteading—Wyoming style. They started small ranches by filing claims on 160 acres under the Homestead Act, and built small herds by "rustling" mavericks.

The winter of 1886–87 is legendary. It killed cattle by the thousands and toppled those open range empires already teetering from mismanagement. Snow and extreme subzero temperatures for forty days that winter purged the high plains of cattle and inefficient investors alike. Some people estimated that up to 90 percent of the herds were lost in what cowboys called "the great die up." Others say losses may not have been higher than 15 percent.[4]

In any event, the catastrophe changed the nature of the open-range cattle industry. It sent so many foreign investors fleeing for the safety of their homelands that by 1889 Wyoming's cattle industry was essentially American.[5] It sent the Wyoming Stock Growers' Association into a period of temporary decline,[6] and it weakened the big cattlemen temporarily. Referring to Fletcher, Schaefer writes: "A series of bad years working up to the dry summer and terrible winter of '86 had cut his herds about the time the first homesteaders moved in and he had not objected too much."[7] The disastrous winter and the subsequent struggle to recover what had been lost also made the cattle barons all the more conscious of how precarious their empires really were, especially in the face of mounting competition from the homesteader and small rancher.

Instead of persuading the cattle kings to change their

ways, however, catastrophe cemented their resolve to protect their way of life. "Many lessons could have been
learned," concluded Harry Sinclair Drago, "but few were.
Perhaps that was because men—many no longer young—
who had lost a fortune and had the grit to make a fresh
start had no room in their single-track minds for anything
else."[8] As many of them rebuilt their empires they reinforced their defensiveness as well.

By the late 1880s, the farming frontier was fast overtak-
ing the cattle empires. As A. S. Mercer notes, the settlers,
who now outnumbered the cattle barons, "thought they
had some rights the cattlemen were bound to respect."[9]
Railroads pushed into north central Wyoming in 1887 and
1888, bringing homesteaders armed with eastern land
laws and the legal right to 160 acres. With their growing
numbers came a shift in political power, especially on the
local level. Local juries promptly acquitted the men the
Association's stock detectives hauled into court for rustling, and some of the few newspapers outside Cheyenne
and Laramie grew increasingly vehement in their protests
against cattle king oppression. The big cattlemen, having
rebuilt their empires, grew nervous.

In July 1889, Albert J. Bothwell, a cattle king, and five
of his neighbors lynched Jim Averell and Averell's alleged
paramour, Ella Watson. Bothwell and others claimed the
two were rustlers and outlaws. The pair's real crime was
having staked claims to Bothwell's open range and,
perhaps more intolerably, to precious stream-front property along the Sweetwater River. If Averell and Watson
could stake homestead claims, others could do so as well,
and Bothwell's control of the surrounding open range
would slip from his grasp.

On a hot summer afternoon, Averell and Watson were
taken at gunpoint from Averell's ranch and hanged from a
scrub pine tree three miles east of Independence Rock,

where three decades earlier thousands of Oregon-bound immigrants had etched their names. "Cattle Kate," as the pro-cattle king press dubbed Watson, was the only woman ever hanged in Wyoming. The six men who did it were named in an arrest warrant but never stood trial. All witnesses for the prosecution disappeared.[10]

Statehood in 1890 helped the Wyoming Stock Growers' Association regain its hold on political power. Hard work and good times had revitalized the cattle industry, and big cattle money could dominate statewide elections just as well as it had influenced territorial appointments made in Washington. Yet the numbers of homesteaders and small ranchers kept growing, and the big cattlemen's obsession with mavericks never subsided.

Johnson County in north central Wyoming, one of the more fertile counties in the state, became a magnet to the new wave of homesteaders. Buffalo, named after the city of New York rather than the plains animal, was its county seat. To Buffalo, says Helena Huntington Smith, "the cowman was a symptom of backwardness along with the Indian. He was a stumbling block in the way of population and progress, and like the Indian he had to go."[11] The town was a source of irritation to the cattlemen. It symbolized a rival way of life whose existence threatened their own.

As juries in Buffalo increasingly turned "rustlers" loose, detectives for the cattlemen's Association increasingly turned to justice at the point of a gun. In Schaefer's *Shane*, a bachelor homesteader is killed in a face-to-face encounter with a gunman in a saloon. In late 1891, two Johnson County men, one a small rancher with a family, were "dry gulched"—shot in the back—along the road south of Buffalo. Though historians have never been able to prove who did it, they strongly imply Association stock detective and hired gunfighter Frank Canton.[12]

The same fall, leading members of the Association made plans for the most notorious vigilante act of Wyoming's history. They hired twenty-three gunfighters, borrowed a cannon from Fort D. A. Russell, boarded a Colorado and Southern train in Cheyenne, and headed for Buffalo. Gunfighters, association men, a doctor, and two newspapermen, they numbered fifty-two in all. Their intention was to invade Johnson County and eliminate up to seventy rustlers and rustler sympathizers whose names appeared on a list compiled by the secretary of the Wyoming Stock Growers' Association.[13]

The "invaders" never made it to Buffalo. They were sidetracked by the temptation to go after two men whose names appeared on their hit list at a small ranch halfway between Casper and Buffalo. The vigilantes surrounded a small cabin where the rustlers were staying and killed the two men during a day-long siege. The delay was costly, however, because it allowed word of their plans to reach Buffalo. Fear quickly turned to anger in the isolated town as it drew support from people who had settled the surrounding northern Wyoming ranges. An estimated two or three hundred people took up arms and subsequently surrounded the invaders at another ranch house fifteen miles south of Buffalo.

Association men got word to the state's two senators in Washington, who in turn persuaded President Benjamin Harrison to call out the army to intervene. The invaders lost two of their Texas gunfighters, who shot themselves accidentally in separate incidents and died of gangrene. Charges were brought against the invaders, but the cases did not come to trial for nine months and were eventually dismissed because Johnson County could not afford to prosecute them. As in the Averell and Watson lynching case, witnesses became scarce.

The Johnson County War had no winners, save the

small, independent rancher. Gone were the days of the
open range and the ruthless plundering of the public do-
main's free grasses for private profit. Gone was the cattle
baron whose whim was law and power unresistible. "Hired
guns" soon packed law degrees instead of six-shooters and
fought legal duels in the courts and the state legislature.
Gone, too, was the threat of the homesteader's range-
destroying intensive agriculture. The farming frontier
never really overran the cattle frontier in Wyoming. Some
isolated incidents of violence occurred in the aftermath of
the Johnson County conflict, but the two sides generally
worked to reconcile differences. "In a small, thinly settled
community where you rub elbows with your neighbors,"
wrote Helena Huntington Smith, "you must either get
along with them or shoot them on sight."[14] Most people
chose the more peaceful alternative.

Historian Edward Everett Dale addressed this theme in
a slightly different way: "At last the cow man realized that
the old order was gone and broken in fortune," he wrote.
"Occasionally one of these men who has not yet accepted
the new order may still be seen. Such an individual stands
like a blackened tree trunk in the midst of plowed fields, a
mute reminder of a bygone era."[15]

Eleven years later, when Schaefer worked a story that
had been serialized earlier in *Argosy* into the novel *Shane,*
he added a dramatic scene in which the book's hero and
homesteader Joe Starrett work feverishly to pull a giant
stump from one of Starrett's fields. Starrett's son, Bob,
who watches the process in awe, explains to the reader:

> That was the one bad spot on our place. It stuck out
> like an old scarred sore in the cleared open space
> back of the barn—a big old stump, all jagged across
> the top, the legacy of some great tree that must have
> died before we came into the valley and finally
> snapped by a heavy windstorm.[16]

Says the elder Starrett to Shane, "That's the millstone around my neck. That's the one fool thing about this place I haven't licked yet."

Referring to the open range cattleman and the special social forces that shaped him, Dale wrote, "One who knows at first hand the story of these men is likely to forget their shortsightedness and poor judgment and to think only of their courage."[17] Referring to the stump, Schaefer's Starrett adds, "You know, Shane, I've been feuding with this thing so long I've worked up a spot of affection for it. It's tough. I can admire toughness. The right kind."[18]

Notes

1. Terry G. Jordan, "The Origin and Distribution of Open Range Cattle Ranching," *Social Science Quarterly* 53 (1972): 113. Jordan goes so far as to say that the tendency to leave "cattle to fend for themselves on the open range led to a kind of 'bovine emancipation.' Referring to Frederick Jackson Turner's frontier thesis, Jordan said, 'One need but extend the Turnerian analysis to the realm of domestic animals to explain the self-reliant, belligerent livestock of the open range'" (p. 117).

2. Jack Schaefer, *Shane* (Boston: Houghton Mifflin, 1949), p. 95.

3. Emerson Hough, *The Passing of the Frontier: A Chronicle of the Old West* (New Haven: Yale University Press, 1918), pp. 147–48.

4. W. Turrentine Jackson, "The Wyoming Stock Growers' Association: Its Years of Temporary Decline, 1886–1890, *Agricultural History* 22 (October 1949): 261.

5. Harry Sinclair Drago, *The Great Range Wars: Violence on the Grasslands* (New York: Dodd, Mead, 1970), p. 260.

6. Jackson, "Temporary Decline," pp. 260–70.

7. Schaefer, *Shane*, p. 46.

8. Drago, *Great Range Wars*, p. 255.

9. A. S. Mercer, *Banditti of the Plains: Or the Cattlemen's Invasion of Wyoming in 1892* (Norman: University of Oklahoma Press, p. 12.

10. Harry Sinclair Drago, *Notorious Ladies of the Frontier* (New York: Dodd, Mead, 1969), pp. 223–35. See also Helena Huntington Smith, *The War on Powder River* (New York: McGraw-Hill Book Company, 1966), pp. 121–34.

11. Smith, *War on Powder River*, p. 144.

12. T. A. Larson, *History of Wyoming* (Lincoln: University of Nebraska Press, 1965), p. 272.

13. Drago, *Great Range Wars*, p. 278; Larson, *History of Wyoming*, p. 276.

14. Smith, *War on Powder River*, p. 284.

15. Edward Everett Dale, "The Cow Country in Transition," *Mississippi Valley Historical Review* 24 (June 1937): 19.

16. Schaefer, *Shane*, pp. 12–13.

17. Dale, "Cow Country in Transition," p. 19.

18. Schaefer, *Shane*, p. 13.

Gerald Haslam

Jack Schaefer

In 1945 Jack Schaefer, then a Norfolk, Virginia, newspaper editor, decided to write a story "to prove that there is no reason why an attempt cannot be made to create literature about the west as about the east or the south or any place anywhere." He set his story in a Wyoming valley torn by conflict between pioneer farmers and a resident cattle baron trying to retain the open range. Then he introduced a paladin figure called Shane.

An interest in American history originally diverted Jack Schaefer's attention toward the West. He perceived that, though the region was very important historically, it had been "neglected by historians and writers alike" (Nuwer, "Interview with Jack Schaefer," p. 49). Zeroing in on the trans-Mississippi West as his area of special interest, Schaefer read history, paying little attention to Western fiction. "In fact," he reflected recently, "if I had known of the tremendous amount of bad Western writing that was flooding the market I wouldn't have written anything" (Nuwer, "Interview," p. 50). Schaefer's own fiction certainly reflects historical fact rather than tired Western clichés.

Perhaps more interesting than his reasons for writing the novel is the fact that Schaefer had never been west of Toledo, Ohio, at the time when he wrote *Shane*. As Winfield Townley Scott has observed, Schaefer "is a researcher, a scholar of the [western] history, and his talents are intensely focused to dramatize its truth in fiction, to tell stories about it" ("Introduction," in *The Collected Stories of Jack Schaefer*, p. vii). Schaefer's writing illustrates the fact that a keen mind, solid research, and craftsmanship can go a long way in the creation of art. In any case, his experiences in the West—mainly the experiences he had while he was doing research for a series of articles for *Holiday*—made a profound impression upon him. As a result of his growing interest in the American West, Schaefer and his family moved to New Mexico in the mid-1950s.

The son of Carl and Minnie (Hively) Schaefer, Jack Warner Schaefer was born on November 19, 1907, in Cleveland. Carl Schaefer, a lawyer, was a "Lincoln nut" and a friend of Carl Sandburg. Both parents, he recalls, were readers, so young Jack early developed a taste for books. In high school, Jack edited the campus literary magazine, as his sister had done before him, and he did some public speaking. During his undergraduate years at Oberlin College, his interests lay principally in Greek and Latin classics and in creative writing. He credits his study of Latin with helping him to understand grammar. After graduating in 1929, Schaefer moved to Columbia University for graduate study in English literature, specializing in the Johnsonian period and in a somewhat obscure playwright and actor named Arthur Murphy, although his real favorite was Oliver Goldsmith.

But the world of scholarly minutiae was not for Schaefer, who found the pursuit "a dull and stupid waste of time." He tried to alter his graduate project so that he could study a more dynamic subject: development of motion pictures. "The thesis committee at Columbia just laughed at me. They said that movies were merely cheap reproductions of stage plays" (Nuwer, "Interview," p. 49). So Columbia and Schaefer parted company. Many years later, writing to a Ph.D. candidate in American literature, Schaefer expressed some of his continuing displeasure with what passes for scholarship in many graduate schools, noting especially that scholars, "instead of sweating to dig out and make certain what the writer meant when he wrote, . . . dream up their silly notions of what they think he ought to have meant—then prattle gaily about that." Schaefer especially chided "the silly jargon and critical gobbledygook that flourishes in the literarily snobbish little quarterlies."

After leaving Columbia, Schaefer pursued a career in journalism, accepting editorial jobs in New Haven, Baltimore, and Norfolk. He also worked as assistant director of education at the Connecticut State Reformatory for a spell. But journalism, in particular, left its mark on his literary style. His writing remains direct, detailed, and sensitive. Although he has expressed skepticism about the value of journalism as good training for a writer of fiction, there is no question that his own style reflects many of the best elements of journalistic writing. Schaefer's journalistic experience was somewhat unusual in that it was "98-plus percent editorial," rather than reporting. "In effect I wrote thousands of small essays (some not so small)," he explained in a note dated August 19, 1974, "always spurred by the tradition of those papers and by my own Germanic zeal to try to write well, be literate and direct and concise, express firm conviction based on thorough research and honest reasoning and supported by sound arguments. . . . I'm reasonably certain that if I had done much reporting, I would have ruined myself as a writer."

The opening lines of his first book, *Shane* (1949), illustrate the crispness of expression and the directness of syntax that enliven Schaefer's writing: "He rode into our valley in the summer of '89. I was a kid then, barely topping the backboard of father's old chuck-wagon. I was on the upper rail of our small corral, soaking in the late afternoon sun, when I saw him far down the road where it swung into the valley from the open plain beyond" (*The Short Novels of Jack Schaefer*, p. 5).

One salient characteristic of Schaefer's prose is its clarity. Because the central account in almost all of his works is crisp and seemingly simple, it appeals to widely different audiences. In an article in *English Journal,* Lynn Dieter quite aptly points out that "*Shane* is at an easy reading level for high school freshmen" (p. 1258). But *Shane* is also a book rich in such literary devices as complex point of view, counterpoint, and understatement, besides its mythical and historical roots. Virtually all of Schaefer's published work has the same clarity of expression, which is united with complexity of vision. Comparing Schaefer's style with that of Stephen Crane, Winfield Townly Scott praises Schaefer's "clear, functional writing, authentic dialogue, and a speed of narrative enclosed within a thoughtfulness of tone" (Scott, "Introduction," p. ix).

In any case, Schaefer favors the active voice and often counterpoints simple, unexpanded sentences with longer, more complex, and strongly evocative units. In the following lines from a short story, "The Old Man," Schaefer brackets a relatively simple sentence with two complex units, and thus uses conjoining and embedding as technical devices:

And suddenly he knew, knew in real knowing not just as an idea taught in class, that other men had come first, men who didn't stick to roads and who knew Indians and fought them and sometimes even lived with them and could bring in eleven hundred buffalo hides in a single season. The wind drifting in from the west was not just the wind anymore. Maybe that wind blowing against his cheek came from way off, beyond this Minnesota, from beyond the far Black Hills near the Devil's Tower where the old man had killed a mountain lion once or even up in the real mountains themselves where Boone Helm lay buried with a rope-broken neck. (*The Collected Stories of Jack Schaefer,* 1966, p. 443)

It is unlikely that Schaefer consciously intended to balance conjoined with embedded units. It is more likely that, with his ear for the rhythms of language, he created the necessary balance in order to provide the effect he sought, neither introducing unnecessary complications nor avoiding complexity. He has been especially effective in his use of sentence fragments.

His is, in fact, a style that often borders on the oral tradition. This is a style that distills techniques and makes much use of *skaz,* which is the technique of including an oral narrator and his tale within a story. This technique allows the author to achieve the strength of the oral tradition and of more formal styles as well. Such a blend typifies the style of much that Jack Schaefer has written, and in his own assessment of himself as a writer, he recognizes that he has employed a mixed style.

In answer to a question some years ago, Schaefer wrote in a letter: "I'm an aging old-fashioned person (pre-T. S. Eliot and the New and then the Newer Criticism not so much by actual years as by deliberate choice) who thinks and writes in the direct old-fashioned manner and who likes to believe that he is bumbling along in the ancient tradition of tale-tellers and has profound contempt for most modern writing particularly the symbol-laden psychological - probing crawl - inside - your - characters'-

minds pretentious nonsense that is so popular with critics these days."

On the surface, Schaefer's attitude seems extremely anti-intellectual or anti-what-passes-for-intellectualism-these-days. Yet it is not. In harking back to the tale-telling tradition, he places primary importance squarely where it belongs—upon the teller-listener-subject triad, and upon the responsibility of the artist, who must find important material and then present it as honestly and as powerfully as possible. Schaefer found his own special material on America's western frontier.

In his preface to *The Big Range* (1953), Schaefer explains in part why the West fascinates him:

The cast is various: rancher, sheepherder, homesteader, town settler, soldier, miner, cowboy. Yet the essential purpose (for a writer) is the same throughout: to establish a distinct and individual major character and pit him against a specific human problem and show how he rose to meet it. And all of them, the characters and stories that evolve from them, are conditioned by the wide open spaces of the old West, in which the energies and capabilities of men and women, for good or for evil, were unleashed on an individual basis as they had rarely been before or elsewhere in human history. (p. 1)

Further, in his Editor's Note to *Out West* (1955), Schaefer amplifies his reasons for considering the West a particularly rich source for literature. Here he mentions first "bigness, open bigness, violent bigness—and the right moment in history," and then he stresses the idea that "this West itself was not merely indifferent, difficult, imposing hardship conditions; it was often actively hostile" (p. v). "The result of combining people with such an environment," he noted in a recent letter, "was to unleash human energies, to throw into sharp focus human strengths and weaknesses, as rarely before in any period or place and never before on any comparable scale."

One major problem for writers of Westerns has been a popular tendency for people to think of Western writing exclusively in terms of that simple code which first appeared in dime novels, which was honed by Owen Wister, and which was adopted pervasively by Hollywood. When a writer develops his material with depth and complexity, he often finds that the critics are unwilling or unable to evaluate it realistically. As Wallace Stegner observes: "Critics rarely approach it from the near, or literary side. They mount it from the right . . . and ride it hard as myth."

Schaefer's writing, for all its apparent straightforward quality, has often been interpreted in terms of symbol and myth. The writer himself says in a letter, "I do not think in terms of allegory and myth." Yet any artist—any tale teller on a street corner as well as any novelist—is aware of the collective secrets of his culture, and he will stir the stew at greater depth than his consciousness controls. Schaefer is aware of this problem, too. Discussing *Shane* in another letter, Schaefer explains that he "tried to make it classical in form—stripped to the absolute essentials, starting and moving in a straight line to an inevitable conclusion. Other layers of meaning crept in," he acknowledges, "but did not interfere with the straight-line story."

All writers manipulate symbols to some extent, and Jack Schaefer does also. In *Shane* the author employs complex narrative devices to present a "straight-line story" as well as to make it inevitable that deeper interpretation will be necessary. The story is told by Bob Starrett, who was a boy at the time of the action, but who is a man when he spins his yarn. This is an effective fictional device, for it allows Schaefer to "throw Shane up larger than life, extra-heroic, etc., without the story degenerating into outright melodrama," as the author explains. It is precisely the integration of the "extra-heroic" elements into the mundane but desperate struggle that makes *Shane* a remarkable book. Physical descriptions of Shane fade into connotative associations: "not a man but a clearly visualized symbol of all the dim, formless imaginings of danger and terror in the untested realm of human understanding" (*Short Novels*, p. 99). Even though Shane may be only a fictional character, he is a character whose essential qualities are created by the subjective responses of the reader. These responses are in turn the result of Schaefers' mode of presenting the character.

Perhaps the most remarkable fact about *Shane* is that it is a first novel. Schaefer began writing fiction in order to relax, and he began with a short story about "the basic legend of the West." It was 1945, when Schaefer was working as associate editor of the *Norfolk Virginian–Pilot*. The short story grew into a short novel. Schaefer submitted it to *Argosy*, and that magazine published it in 1946 as a three-part serial titled "Rider from Nowhere." Schaefer recalls that his name was misspelled on the cover when the first installment appeared. Houghton Mifflin released the novel in book form in 1949, and since then it has gone through more than seventy editions in some thirty languages.

Shane opens when Bob, the boy-turned-man narrator, sees a figure riding into a Wyoming valley and on through its tiny town toward his father's farm. "There seemed nothing remarkable about him, just another stray horseman riding up the road toward the cluster of frame buildings that our town. Then I saw a pair of cowhands, loping past him, stop and stare after him with a curious intentness" (p. 5). With this opening scene, Schaefer has already planted seeds of mystery and suspense.

When the stranger reaches the Starrett farm, Bob is struck first by the man's worn but elegant clothing—duds unlike those commonly sported by locals. But the "impact of the man himself" is even more impressive, and Bob "could read the endurance in the lines of that dark figure and the quiet power in it." The man's eyes were fixed in "habitual alertness," and looking into these searching eyes, the boy felt a strange chill. The man moved easily, "yet even in this easiness was a suggestion of tension. It was the easiness of a coiled spring, of a trap set" (p. 6).

In only a page and a half, Schaefer suggests a number of important questions concerning the stranger. Moreover, the author begins the slow process of forcing his readers into creating their own Shane, who, as James K. Folsom so well sums it up, "becomes visualized then not in actuality upon the external stage but retrospectively upon the internal landscape of the reader's mind" ("*Shane* and *Hud*: Two Stories in Search of a Medium," p. 363). Why did the cowboys pay special attention to Shane when he rode through town? Why are his clothes dark and worn, but elegant? Why is he so alert, so searching? After Bob's father, Joe Starrett, invites the stranger to spend the night with them, they exchange names, the horseman saying only, "Call me Shane."

After establishing this mysterious quality of Shane—a quality reinforced throughout the tale by Bob's description of the man—Schaefer quickly but subtly introduces elements of the plot. The renewed attempts of Fletcher, a cattleman, to roust homesteaders off what had been open range, and the rallying of the settlers around the powerful earthy figure of Joe Starrett, are counterpointed by a growing friendship, a growing love, between Bob and Shane, who accepts a job with the Starretts. This latter bond involves Shane in the conflict, and Fletcher is troubled.

On Shane's first morning with the Starretts, just after breakfast, he and Joe Starrett attack a huge old stump that has resisted the farmer's efforts to remove it, and the central symbolic scene of the novel comes into focus. The stump's roots, as big around as Bob's waist, twist "down into the ground like they would hold there for eternity and past." Observes Starrett: "Yes. . . . That's the millstone round my neck. That's the one fool thing about this place I haven't licked yet" (p. 16).

Following a brief incident with a peddler, a scene that illustrates Starrett's respect for Shane, the quiet stranger attacks the stump that, like Fletcher, resists the will of the farmers. Shane first begins chopping at a root by himself, while Bob and his father watch. But then Joe Starrett joins the fray: "Their eyes met over the top of the stump and held and neither one of them said a word. Then they swung up their axes and both of them said plenty to that old stump." With Bob looking on awestruck, Mrs. Starrett joins the group. She wears a hat newly altered as Shane had suggested, and she thereby reveals her infatuation with the new man.

The two men work all day on the massive stump, only to discover that a large, nearly inaccessible taproot still binds it to the earth. Saying nothing, Starrett braces himself and lifts the stump slightly so that Shane, who is not as big as Starrett, can attack the root. Together, the two men defeat the stump and all it represents. When Marian Starrett suggests that the men "use some sense" and let a team of horses pull the old stump from the ground, her husband shouts, "Horses! . . . No! We started this with manpower and, by Godfrey, we'll finish it with manpower!" (p. 27).

Schaefer's writing makes it clear that symbolic interpretation is necessary in evaluating the scene; indeed, the author becomes somewhat heavy-handed in his language, a fault which he avoids in his later books. For example, after the men have completed their ritual defeat of the stump, and after the chopping and their own sounds of exertion have ceased, the narrator describes "an old stump on its side with root ends making a strange pattern against the glow of the sun sinking behind the far mountains and two men looking over it into each other's eyes" (p. 26). This scene, like many others in the novel, is clearly written to evoke something of the drama, or the melodrama, which carries so many code Westerns. In this connection it seems remarkable that Schaefer could venture so close to banality without succumbing to the banal. In *Shane* the incipient banality can be charged to Schaefer's inexperience as a novelist, just as his ultimate avoidance of the banal can be considered a clue to his special strengths as a writer of fiction.

Unlike the endless code Westerns that use similar plots, *Shane* does not immediately and outrageously introduce a robber-baron cattleman who bullies homesteaders. Working subtly, Schaefer provides ample evidence that Fletcher, the cattleman, is one of these characters. But he does so only as one aspect of Shane's increasing involvement with the Starretts and with the other farmers. Moreover, the narrator hints that Fletcher himself is a victim of history. Like Shane, the cattleman represents a dying force on the frontier. He is a man prepared to use violence to solve a dilemma, and as such a man he cannot be all villain.

When at length Fletcher resorts to physical force, Shane is also forced to react in ways that reveal his true strength. Shane has been quietly working with Joe Starrett on the farm; and as Fletcher begins pressing for all the land in the valley, he more and more resents the presence of this stranger. The cattle baron sends two men to the settlement with orders to beat Shane and to run him out of the valley.

Accompanying a group of farmers into the village for supplies, Shane ventures into the saloon next to the general store. Fletcher's men follow Shane there and gaze through the window at him. One of them stiffens when he

sees Shane, and immediately climbs back onto his horse.
The other cowpoke, Chris, startled by his partner's action,
asks him:

"What's got into you?"

"I'm leaving."

"Huh? I don't get it."

"I'm leaving. Now. For good."

"Hey, listen. Do you know that guy?"

"I didn't say that. There ain't nobody can claim I
said that. I'm leaving, that's all. You can tell Fletcher.
This is a rotten kind of country up here anyhow." (p.
50)

Shane's aura is intensified once more when he declines
to fight the bold Chris. Telling the cowpoke to have Fletcher "send a man next time," Shane leaves the saloon. While
the elated Chris gloats, Grafton, the owner of the saloon,
mutters, "That boy's a fool." Then, of Shane, he observes:
"He wasn't afraid of Chris. He was afraid of himself"
(p. 53).

When Shane is at last goaded into action—more angry
at the complaints of his fellow farmers than at the cowboy's
foolish behavior—he systematically disables Chris, beating him and breaking his arm. The full capabilities of
Shane's mysterious potency are now unmistakable. So is
Schaefer's ability to write fight scenes, for both this battle
and those that follow are in most respects superior. These
are startling, exciting descriptions that make full use of the
heightened senses and the shattered perceptions of actual
fighting. After his destruction of Chris, Shane eyes the
whining homesteaders—who had been particularly troubled when Chris called them "pigfarmers"—and says
coldly, "Your pigs are dead and buried" (p. 57). It is clear
that Shane's allegiance belongs to Joe Starrett, who has
supported him all along, not to the farmers as a group.

The fight scene begins heating up the action. Another

battle, in which the small, efficient Shane and the large, powerful Starrett trounce five of Fletcher's men, brings matters to a head. Fletcher can no longer control the farmers with his own men; so he imports a gunfighter, Stark Wilson, to frighten the homesteaders. Though Fletcher is himself a victim of change, the moment he resorts to violence his actions are no more justified than is the violence of those without cause. Moreover, his own destruction resides in his first act of violence.

Like a minor chord, a second thread of tension hovers in the background of the story and adds complications to its interrelationships. This accelerating complication is Marian Starrett's growing infatuation with Shane. Joe Starrett's dogged acceptance of his wife's feelings suggests the possibility that the odd triangle might have Shane rather than Marian at its apex. Schaefer realistically uses farmers as frontiersmen, and he subtly introduces a woman's perception of the developing circumstances, thereby creating an unusually complex picture of human relationships.

Hearing of Wilson's arrival, Shane warns Starrett to keep the farmers out of town, but his warning comes too late to save Ernie Wright, whom Wilson goads into a fight and kills. Starrett is the man whom Fletcher most wants to be rid of, for he knows that Starrett is the farmers' strength. After first trying to buy Starrett and Shane, Fletcher turns matters over to Wilson. By nature Starrett cannot refuse a challenge when it implies a sexual threat: "Yes, Starrett. Think it over. You wouldn't like someone else to be enjoying this place of yours—that woman there in the window." The sexual tension of the novel—never overt, yet always just beneath the surface—illustrates the basic humanity of the characters in a historically accurate situation where an abundance of men seek the attention of only a few women.

One of Schaefer's most important accomplishments in *Shane* is that the background seems to be a real frontier and the people real people. Fletcher, for example, recognizes that the settlers, especially the villagers, are turning against him when he brings in a gunfighter. A growing social order is replacing the rampant individualism of Fletcher's day. Moreover, the characters are keenly aware of the significance of the land, which is the setting of their drama. The environment itself is a dynamic force to which the characters must respond and within the framework of which they must interact. Indeed it sometimes appears that the interaction occurs as much between character and environment as between character and character. Even in this, his first book, the author justifies Robert Mikkelsen's conclusion that Schaefer's "achievement is a sensitive re-construction of the Western Frontier." ("The Western Writer: Jack Schaefer's Use of the Western Frontier," p. 155). In *Shane*, that frontier serves largely as backdrop for a classic confrontation. Yet the credibility of Schaefer's treatment of the frontier as backdrop helps to raise the story above other novels of its kind.

A confrontation is inevitable when Joe Starrett pre-pares to go to town and to die in order to kill Wilson and to rid the valley of Fletcher. "Fletcher'll be done," he tells his wife. "The town'll see to that." Starrett is "desperate with inner torment," but he has determined that he must make this sacrifice. He feels certain that Shane will care for his family. But Shane has other ideas.

Dressed in the sinister garments he wore when he first entered the story, his weapon "distinct against the dark material," Shane intervenes. "Belt and holster and gun . . . were part of him, part of the man, of the full sum of the integrate force that was Shane" (p. 95). To the assertion that the coming fight is Starrett's business, Shane says, "This is my business. My kind of business." Then Shane wins a violent fight with Starrett and makes an emotional break from Marian. He saddles his horse, an animal as mysterious and powerful as its rider. "The horse came out of the pasture, its hooves making no noise in the deep grass, a dark and powerful shape etched in the moonlight drifting across the field straight to the man" (p. 98).

Shane meets Wilson in Grafton's saloon. Wilson is at first uninterested in him, since Starrett is his target. Shane, however, is interested in Wilson.

> Wilson's face sobered and his eyes glinted coldly.
> "I've no quarrel with you," he said flatly. . . .
> "What you want, Wilson, and what you'll get are two different things. Your killing days are done."
> Wilson had it now. You could see him grasp the meaning. (p. 103)

Although Shane has not worn a gun since early in the novel, his efficiency at everything he does makes it clear that Wilson is in more trouble than he realizes. There is a sudden blur of action; both guns roar. Shane stands firm while Wilson sprawls, "bitter disbelief twisting his features." "'I gave him his chance,' murmurs Shane out of the depths of a great sadness." (p. 104)

Bob, the boy narrator, notices that Shane has been hit, but before anything can be said about it, Fletcher shoots at Shane from the balcony of the saloon. Shane kills the cattleman and says, "I expect that finishes it!"

Throughout the novel, the reader's perception of events is colored by the essential innocence of Bob, the narrator. This device is a variation upon what may be Schaefer's dominant theme: growing up. Again and again in his fiction, the author places characters in difficult situations and shows how they have to grow and develop during the process of meeting their problems. In *Shane*, the statement of growth is at times a bit heavyhanded. Bob asks tearfully for assurance that Wilson could never have been fast enough to wound Shane if Shane had been "in practice." Shane gives the assurance, but then he continues: "A man is what he is, Bob, and there's no breaking the mold. I've tried that and I've lost" (p. 106).

Then Shane rides away on the horse that has come to seem mythic, and his mysterious path disappears into historic darkness: "He was riding away. . . . The big horse, patient and powerful, was already settling into the steady pace that had brought him into our valley, and the two, the man and the horse, were a single dark shape in the road as they passed beyond the reach of the light from the windows" (p. 113).

A remarkably strong first novel, *Shane* is nonetheless burdened in places by hyperbolic symbolism, whether it is intended or not. The presence of symbolism is particularly noticeable because Schaefer's prose is, in general, spare and understated. But the author's use of point of view justifies what could be the negative effects of overwritten passages, for these passages may be defined as attempts to record Bob's distorted memories. Schaefer's persistent theme of individual growth and self-realization in the West is explicitly stated by Shane himself when he says to Chris, "There's only one thing really wrong with you. You're young. That's one thing time can always cure" (p. 62). Another of the themes is directly out of Frederick Jackson Turner via Ray Allen Billington: herdsmen roaming ahead of the line of settlement, pioneering unwittingly for the very farmers who would drive them from their lands. So pervasive are these themes in Schaefer's work, that in league with Schaefer's historic bent, they have prompted Fred Erisman to suggest that "Schaefer seems almost to be treating the West as a microcosm of the United States" ("Growing Up With the American West: Fiction of Jack Schaefer," pp. 711/67, 711/68). Erisman's suggestion helps explain why *Shane* also examines the role of the individual in a frontier society.

Shane gained a wider audience when, in 1953, Paramount Studios released George Stevens' motion picture version of the novel. Reviews were excellent, with more than a few reviewers suggesting that here, indeed, was a classic movie. They committed themselves to this complimentary stance despite their acknowledgment of Paramount's poor judgment in converting the film to a widescreen epic, physically trimming the frames, and altering much of the best photographic composition. The use of cutting shears was not the only change wrought in converting *Shane* to a new medium (as James K. Folsom has ably demonstrated; see "*Shane* and *Hud:* Two Stories in Search of a Medium"). A great many subtle touches within the novel could not be graphically transferred to film, but the plot remained the same, thanks to the screenplay written by A. B. Guthrie, Jr. Some of the characters were superbly depicted, especially Jack Palance's Stark Wilson and Ben Johnson's Chris.

If reviewers considered the film to be several cuts above the average Western, critics have been somewhat more troubled. Pauline Kael, in *Kiss Kiss Bang Bang,* found it necessary to analyze the film in terms of myth: "Here's Galahad on the range, in one of those elaborately simple epics American directors love to make," she asserts; "superficially, this type of film is a Western, and thus salable, but those trained in the New Criticism will recognize it as the creation of myth . . . the western was better off before it became so self-importantly self-conscious" (p. 347). George Fenin and William Everson in *The Western: From Silents to the Seventies* show a better historic grasp of the subject in naming *Shane* one of the two finest Westerns of the fifties, the other being *From Hell to Texas.* They further noted that the harsh realism of the film and its "ending of sheer pathos" harked back to such great Westerns as William S. Hart's *The Toll Gate* (1920).

Despite Leslie Fiedler's claim in *Return of the Vanishing*

American (p. 143) that *Shane* is an example of the kind of movie which proves to be better than the novel on which it is based, most of the strengths of the film are derived from the novel, while most of its weaknesses are unequivocally those of the film itself. Indeed, the major flaw of the motion picture lies in its inability to translate into a different medium the complex point of view and the nostalgia upon which much of the novel depends for its strength. For the subtle power of the combined narrative techniques in the novel, the film substitutes only color photography. It is a fair gauge of the quality of the novel that the film remains an acknowledged classic.

The four years after the publication of *Shane* were especially productive for Schaefer. He had quit his newspaper job in 1949 in order to write full-time, and he had spent a period on short rations while trying to peddle that first novel to a book publisher. He wrote many short stories during the next four years, as well as a good short novel, *First Blood* (1953). But the major work emerging from that period was another short novel called *The Canyon* (1953).

The circumstances leading to the creation of *The Canyon* are interesting, not only because the book itself has real merit, but because the circumstances of production provide some important insights into the author's response to his predicament. in a letter dated December 8, 1967, Schaefer opens by saying, "I have a special fondness for that one." His "special fondness" for *The Canyon* is partly the result of a clash between his immediate vision of popular success and his growing sense of its inadequacy. The almost blinding success of *Shane,* in both book and movie versions, had brought to Schaefer monetary rewards, a pleasantly secure reputation as an author, and the adulation of many readers. But as promoters and publishers beset him with all kinds of offers, he found himself considering an altogether different option. As soon as he was sure, he acted decisively. "I simply said 'no' all around," he declares farther on in a letter of December 8, 1967,

> and sat down at my old portable and wrote *The Canyon* in the serene assurance that it would have no commercial success. But would be a book I wanted to write.
>
> What I mean is: It was with *The Canyon* that I made my decision to keep right on with the furrow I had started to plow — to keep on with my somewhat lonesome attempt to prove that there is no reason why the attempt at least cannot be made to create literature out of western material, to write only what I wanted to write and to please myself alone and not to fall into the trap of repeating myself, of doing the same kind of thing over and over just because a first one had been successful.

The Canyon is both a further exploration of the growing-up theme, the theme of self-realization, and of the man-alone motif. The Little Bear "legend" is wholly Schaefer's creation; he obtained his Cheyenne background information in the George Bird Grinnell collection at the Yale University Library. Schaefer contends that "the Amerindians in general (with some exceptions) were truly civilized and . . . we whites, better or ahead or whatever you want to call it only in our deadly emphasis on technology, were the invading barbarians." In *America's Frontier Heritage* (1966), historian Ray Allen Billington writes that the common frontier attitude toward Indians was based upon a belief in Manifest Destiny: "The red men could be pushed aside, or assigned to the barren wastes of Western reservation, for they had abandoned all rights to justice by hindering the march of progress" (p. 202). But before, during, and after the imposition of white "progress," Indians shared the human dilemmas that exist for most people.

Little Bear, protagonist of *The Canyon,* is a Cheyenne warrior who opposes war. "A convinced pacifist in a nation that lived for warfare," wrote Oliver La Farge in a review, "Little Bear revolted against the basis of his people's culture" (*New York Times Book Review,* November 8, 1953, p. 28). By extension, he is Everyman caught in a struggle between his personal values and those of his culture. After consulting an elder, a young man goes away from his people onto the plains to fast and, he hopes, to communicate with spirits that might direct him. This quest is an ancient custom among the Cheyenne. Fasting and smoking until mysterious contact is made, "at last his mind emptied itself of all thinking" (*The Short Novels of Jack Schaefer,* p. 241). Little Bear's spirit quest is successful: "And the Maiyun of the hills emerged like smoke from their homes in the far rock bluffs and clustered around him" (p. 241).

The spirits are not pleased with this strange one with stubby legs who "fights a festering within him and is afraid." Little Bear's quest is complex, for his world view is sacred rather than profane. Listening to voices in the wind, he wanders over the night-darkened prairie and falls into a secret canyon, breaking his leg. He has no weapon save a knife.

The early part of the novel is concerned with Little Bear's attempts to survive with a broken leg. Confined to the canyon, he finds animals and hunts rabbits to sustain himself. He fights pain and his human limitations to kill a buffalo. He battles and defeats a cougar. But the most important animal is a badger that he finds in a talus pile.

> He came around a clump of bushes and saw the badger. Its short-legged broad body was stretched out on a low flat stone. It was sleeping in the sun. . . .
>
> Quietly he sat down cross-legged on the ground. Time passed and the badger opened its eyes. It saw him. It looked at him with its black shining eyes. "Oh badger," he said. "Speak to me." It jumped from the stone and was gone. (pp. 259–60)

Little Bear brings the badger a piece of meat each day,

sitting quietly before the animal's den, and filling his mind with thoughts which the badger may read. On the fourth day of this ritual, Little Bear is rewarded:

> The badger looked at him and its eyes became very bright. It spoke. "Big Brother," it said, "Why do you feel that this canyon is a cage?" The eyes of the badger dimmed and closed and after a time they opened again and were very bright. "All men live in cages," it said. . . . "Stones piled upon stones rise upward. Rock striking on rock chips away small pieces." (p. 261)

Here Schaefer drops into the drowsy consciousness of Little Bear just as he does in his earlier communication with the Maiyun. The mystical conversation with the badger, intensely real for Little Bear, need not be real for the reader. The author allows room for rational or supra-rational explanations, but the point is that Little Bear obeys the badger's instructions, beginning the slow process of cutting niches in a wall of the canyon and piling stones upon stones to build a way out. It is important for the reader to notice that the author evokes the sacred world view of Little Bear.

During the long days which he spends working his way out of his "cage," Little Bear has time to reflect upon and to really see the canyon. "Oh badger. It is a good cage" (p. 275).

The badger advised him once more: "'There is much,' it said, 'But there is something lacking. There is no warmth of body to body in the shelter at night'"(p. 278). Looking for a mate, Little Bear returns to his people and finds Spotted Turtle. "She was not beautiful but there was a warm wisdom and an understanding on her face and she was beautiful to him and she was very womanly." He takes her to his canyon.

Soon Spotted Turtle is pregnant. After a mild winter,

their boy-child is born. They name him Little Fox. But the following spring is cruel; rain and fog keep everything damp. "And their little-slim-person, their small-fuzzy-one, their Little Fox, caught a cough that would not leave him" (p. 311). Spotted Turtle keeps the baby warm, and nurses him when he will eat,

> but he would eat only a little and after a time none at
> all. He was very weak and sick.
> She would not leave the small one for a moment.
> She held him in her arms and rocked him in them
> and leaned her head over him and nothing would
> stop the coughing. It was a small sound with no
> strength in it, yet it filled the lodge with big fear. (p.
> 311)

Faced with an enemy he cannot fight, let alone defeat, Little Bear is helpless. The small, hacking cough is killing his son. In depicting this scene, Schaefer's prose remains simple, almost sere, presenting the impact of the baby's death honestly and with little maudlin appeal:

> He laid the small bundle on the ledge, inside the
> cave. Carefully he pointed it eastward toward the ris-
> ing sun. He took the things that had been the things
> of the small one from her and laid them about the
> bundle. And a fresh sadness gripped him. There was
> no painted pony to be killed by the grave so that the
> spirit of the small one could ride the spirit of the pony
> and travel fast along the path where all footprints go
> the same way. There was no old man of the tribe to
> sing a death song passed down from the forefathers
> to cheer the small spirit on the path. There was only a
> grieving father who could not speak and behind him
> yet not with him a grieving mother who would not
> speak. (p. 313)

In grief, Spotted Turtle cuts the middle finger from her left hand. Their loss has opened a gap between her and

Little Bear, and now she is apart from him. But Little Bear cannot cut off one of his own fingers—a man must have whole, strong hands—so he draws his knife twice across his chest, saying nothing, allowing his blood to speak his mourning. Spotted Turtle can now begin to accept him once more.

But a bitter thought tortures Little Bear, and here Schaefer introduces a deeper exploration of one of the themes first presented in *Shane*—the relationship of the individual to society. Much of *The Canyon* examines Little Bear's adjustment to himself when he is removed from the mores and dynamics of Cheyenne culture. Now, with the death of his son, he asks himself: "'If there had been other women here, they would have known what to do. . . . If there had been a man skilled in medicines'" (p. 128). The canyon has allowed Little Bear to avoid tribal obligations.

Now he realizes that when he quit the tribe he had abandoned positive things as well as negative. Little Bear tells Spotted Turtle that they must return. His wife replies: "I would not take you from the place that is yours." And he replies, "You are not taking me out of this place. I am taking myself and my woman where we belong as a man must" (p. 133).

In a letter dated April 5, 1965, the author explains that Little Bear at last accepts "the fact that no man is an island unto himself, that the very act of living brings with it debts and obligations to others, and doing what seemed to him the right thing to do." Little Bear's is a spirit quest for wholeness, and at length he realizes the complexity of fulfillment.

The Canyon is a superb parable of the quest for individualism in a dynamic society. Fred Erisman is justified in asserting that, in Schaefer's mind, true independence requires that the individual must be able to make his peace with himself and his society simultaneously ("Growing up with the American West," p. 713/71). Mulls Little Bear: "One man cannot change a tribe. But one man can live with a tribe and not let it change him too much."

The author is less disdainful of symbolic interpretations of *The Canyon* than of the same approach to most of his other books, saying he regards it "to some extent as a parable for all men, only in terms of a Cheyenne Indian. But again, in the writing, it was to me simply a straightforward tale presented with a few minor technical tricks of form" (letter dated April 6, 1965). In a review, H. L. Davis claimed that "Little Bear is not an Indian at all, but a suburban American thrown into a place and time to which his values are not suited. The basis of the whole story is the contrast of periods" (*New York Herald Tribune,* December 6, 1953, p. 26). Davis also perceived precisely what Schaefer intended to convey to his readers. By means of a quest, observes Davis, Little Bear learns that an act of sacrifice for his woman is in itself an emotional fulfillment and a form of adjustment to his world. Ultimately, Little Bear emerges as a vastly different kind of man from the typical suburban American, if only because his basis for understanding himself and his world is essentially a sacred one.

Two other books by Schaefer were published by Houghton Mifflin in 1953. *First Blood* is a tense short novel concerning a young man's decision about what is right. The book explores growth, both in the protagonist and in his town. Jess Harker must choose between a boy's hero-worship and an adult's growing knowledge that the rule of law is necessary, and his decision represents the continuing move toward stability and orderly processes in the West. *"Maybe,* I thought, *maybe I've got my full growth at last. . . . If this is being a man, I don't like it. But I can't change it"* (pp. 115–16). And the town, by its acceptance of Jess after he has stopped a lynching, demonstrates that it too has matured. *First Blood* is hardly more than a novella—as were

Shane and *The Canyon*—so Houghton Mifflin fleshed out the 116 pages by adding a short story, "Jacob."

The other volume which Schaefer published in 1953 was a collection of short stories, *The Big Range,* which Hoffman Birney asserted in the *New York Times Book Review* "earns a double A rating" (July 5, 1953, p. 13). By 1953 Schaefer had clearly demonstrated that he was a master of the novella, but he was also an accomplished short story writer, his tales having appeared in *Argosy, Bluebook, Boy's Life, Colliers, Fresco, Gunsmoke, Holiday,* and the *Saturday Evening Post.* At this point in his career, *The Big Range* provided an interesting and effective example of the high quality of fiction that Schaefer had been able to make out of his keen interest in the unique way of life in the real West. In another review, Seth Agnew observed: "Primarily, Mr. Schaefer is concerned with the people of this new West and with the environment and new way of life which was to become the West of today" (*Saturday Review of Literature,* August 8, 1953, p. 17).

A year later, in 1954, *The Pioneers* was released. It is a collection of personal stories dealing with the pioneering life. In 1959, *The Kean Land, and Other Stories* appeared. The title piece is either a very long short story or a novella. *The Plainsmen* was published in 1963. As time passed, Schaefer wrote fewer short stories, and as he concedes, "the early ones were probably the best."

Which of his stories does Schaefer prefer? He answered that question in a letter dated July 24, 1974:

"Cooter James" is the one which gives me the most satisfaction—in this sense: usually in going through any of them I note small things I would like to change. I would not change one word in "Cooter." Of the tall tale kind of thing, I particularly like "Leander Frailey" and "My Town." For sheer straight fun, I like "Cat Nipped" and "Nate Bartlett's Store." In a serious vein I've always like "Jeremy Rodock," but I think "Something Lost" and "Stalemate" are better stories — probably because of my current (1974) interest in animals and how lousily we treat them. Take your own pick. I like 'em all — and usually because each does manage to convey something of what in each case I was trying to say about the human species.

The range of Schaefer's stories is indeed wide. He chooses as subjects the kinds of western people whom other writers have largely ignored. In "The Coup of Long Lance," for example, an aging warrior counts a final coup and claims a youthful warrior's reward. "Hugo Kertchak, Builder" movingly presents an immigrant carpenter, the kind of person who made the frontier habitable. Schaefer tells a strong story about the kind of man who builds houses and barns and coffins, and whose work parallels the growth of communities in the West. Hugo Kertchak exemplifies the independence which Schaefer favors: "This America owes me nothing at all," Hugo tells a social worker. "It gave what a man needs. A home without fear. Good friends. A chance to work. Freedom to work right. If there is owing, it is for me. To take care of myself" (*Collected Stories,* p. 314). The same fierce independence appears in various ways in "Old Anse," "Salt of the Earth," and "Kittura Remsburg."

"Cooter James" tells of a loner cowhand who, beset by an unscratchable itch, tries town life, and a boarding house, and clerking, and living alone, only to find that a widow-woman offers the necessary abrasive. There is equally keen humor in "Nate Bartlett's Store" and "Cat Nipped," both of which also feature interesting story-telling devices from oral literature. Reading Schaefer's tales, people sometimes feel as though some old coot is regaling them personally.

Commenting upon *The Kean Land, and Other Stories,* an

anonymous reviewer for *Kirkus* has noticed that "these
odd characters Schaefer likes to collect personalize a fading frontier" (*Kirkus,* January 1, 1959, p. 24). The narrator
of one of Schaefer's stories, "Enos Carr," is more accurate
when he says:

> I'm writing about this Enos Carr character. Not a
> story, not anything like that, because it doesn't have
> any form and hasn't any action and doesn't get any-
> where. Just an account of what we saw of him and
> learned about him. I'm writing it because I collect
> odd characters, like to get them down on paper.
> They're quaint, interesting.They're not important
> because a world made up of odd characters would be
> a weird one to live in and probably couldn't even
> function at all. Matter of fact, studying odd charac-
> ters can help you appreciate the normal everyday
> capable people who keep the world wagging on a
> fairly even keel, a place where most of us can earn a
> decent living and get some enjoyment out of life"
> (*Collected Stories,* pp. 469–70).

Schaefer uses these "characters" to counterpoint the
importance of average folks. For every Enos Carr there
are several Hugo Kertchaks, and this constant and accurate sense of the actual pioneers, whether they are in the
foreground or in the background, makes his frontier stories remarkably complete and compelling. There have
been few better writers of short stories on the West than
Jack Schaefer.

In 1957 Houghton Mifflin published what may be
Schaefer's most underrated novel, *Company of Cowards.* It
is the story of Jared Heath, an officer convicted of cowardice in the Civil War, and of his small command of line
officers, all "busted" for cowardice. Human conflicts
abound when these men are sent to New Mexico to prove
themselves. Unlike the action in *Shane* and *The Canyon,*

Heath's task is approached frontally, and Schaefer's prose is in many places more complex and, paradoxically, more direct than it had been in his previous novels. This change in style caused reviewer F. H. Lyell in a *New York Times* review (August 25, 1957, p. 26), to say that the "Faulknerian rhythm" of the prose is not substantiated by enough depth.

In any case, Heath's story not only explores the ways in which an individual comes to grips with himself, but it also examines the dynamics of how diverse people may be molded into a unit. In accomplishing the latter purpose, Heath proves his own ability to lead, and in the process he is able to explore himself. In the end, all of Heath's men, even the dead, have their commissions restored to them after their battle with Indians. Heath vindicates himself in the eyes of his most demanding critic—himself—and he rides away from the army. "He had the clothes he wore and a horse and a rifle. Only those. And something more. An enduring quietness within" (p. 125).

As a leader, Heath became very strong. One of his men, old Selous, reported "I go to pieces out there again and I'd of been running like——well, I'd of been running, only there was a goddamned heartless bastard of a better man out there who wouldn't let me run. I found out I could follow him" (p. 122).

Some critics have lamented the lack of depth in Schaefer's development of the secondary characters, but as Schaefer explains in a letter, he had set out primarily to tell Heath's story. "I was not attempting to explore situations in depth. I was telling a tale about one man, Jared Heath, and how a bitter happening shook him and his faith in himself and how he carried on until he learned about himself." But even so, some of these critics seem justified, for the book whets one's appetite for a more thorough exploration of both Heath and the other characters. As an adventure yarn, it is first-rate, and it is an effective exploration of Schaefer's continuing themes—individualism and society, and the historic development of the West. Heath "rode West and he became a man akin to the great timeless mountains that he could see marching in their own majestic indifferent serenity along the horizon of his small homestead ranch all the rest of his days" (p. 125).

Company of Cowards, like *Shane,* was converted into a large-budget motion picture, *Advance to the Rear.* It only vaguely resembled the novel, and despite a cast that included Glenn Ford, Stella Stevens, and Melvin Douglas, the movie was less than memorable.

Three years after *Company of Cowards* was published, Schaefer ventured into what was a new literary field for him, and he did so with his customary success. He wrote *Old Ramon* (1960) for a juvenile audience. It is the story of an aging sheepherder who takes care of his patron's son for a summer. But it is also much more than this. Reviewers were unanimous in their favorable judgment of the book. "Unusually fine writing," said *Library Journal* (May 15, 1960, p. 2043); "a lyrical little gem," wrote Robert Hood in the *New York Times Book Review* (April 10, 1960, p. 38); and M. S. Libby, writing in the New York *Herald Tribune Book Review* (May 8, 1960, p. 4), said, "This is a little masterpiece written with power and restraint. It will linger in anyone's mind."

The book is indeed a gem. It illustrates again Schaefer's use of brisk, understated prose to carry a parable-like tale. Once more, the central concerns are the closely related themes of growing up and independence. The boy learns. Through his relationship with Old Ramon and Sanche and Pedro the sheepdogs, through his trials on a great desert, through his frights from rattlesnakes and wolves, through his coping with sandstorms and stampedes, he learns something of what it means to be a man. When Sanche foolishly tackles a wolf and is killed, "The boy's breath

caught in a sob." "Let the tears come," said Old Ramon
softly. "They are good for you. And the dog will know. The
spirit of the dog will know" (p. 92).

Old Ramon is a gentle, persuasive book. "To be brave is a
fine thing. But it is not enough. One must be wise too," the
sheepherder tells the boy after Sanche is buried. "In a
way," lamented a reviewer (M. M. R.) in the Chicago *Sunday Tribune*, "it is a shame that this may be read only by
young people, for it is so beautifully written many adults
would enjoy it. . . . The telling is neither ponderous nor
preachy but warm and moving and very real" (May 8,
1960, p. 18).

In 1963 Schaefer published his longest, perhaps most
ambitious novel, *Monte Walsh*. Telling the story of a cowpoke from the time of the open-range cattle kingdom
through its demise (and his) early in this century, the book
presents an interesting character and merges him with the
industry he represents. Born in 1856, Monte is a boy who
gravitates toward horses. When he is sixteen years old, a
misunderstanding sends him into the world on his own,
just as the cattle industry has begun to flourish. At eighteen he is told: "You ain't the worse hand I ever had tailin' a
herd" (p. 31). By twenty-one, Monte is "squint-eyed from
wind and sun," and "riding point with a Seven Z herd of
wild woolly longhorns" (p. 35).

After one particularly uproarious night in Dodge City
in 1879, Monte meets another young cowpoke, Chet Rollins, and between them a lifelong friendship begins.
Theirs is a young man's world, without ties and with the
possibility of adventure hovering beyond every chore.
They drift to the Northern Plains, for the cattle industry is
growing.

"Let's make tracks," Monte suggests.

"Anywheres," said Chet. "What the hell. Anywheres at all."

"I've heard there's a good cattle country opening

down in New Mexico," said Monte. "You ever been
there?"

"Looks like I will be," said Chet. (p. 62)

Early in the novel it becomes clear that Monte and Chet
are complementary parts of a single whole. Though
Monte is impulsive ("always into something") and well able
to take care of himself, Chet is likely to be "a jump ahead,
figuring a better way." Ultimately, these characteristics are
to play vital roles in determining which of the two men can
adjust to changing times, and which of them finds the
world drifting away from what he is prepared to be.

Reviewer Orville Prescott observes that "there is really
no way of escaping the cowboy myth. . . . As long as our
country survives, the cowboy myth will survive too — and
seldom in pleasanter form than in *Monte Walsh*" (*New York
Times,* September 9, 1975, section L, p. 5). But the *cowboy
myth* is not examined in Schaefer's book. Rather the cowboy himself is portrayed with a sense of authenticity that is
worthy of Andy Adams or of Gene Rhodes. Moreover,
Schaefer uses a superior narrative technique that breathes
life not only into Monte but also into Chet and into several
other peripheral characters as well. What Prescott actually
perceives is his own — and perhaps most readers' — inability to accept *Monte Walsh* without reference to the national
cowboy fantasy. Schaefer counters the inaccuracy of myth
by means of spare prose, solid research, and a story that is
intensely human.

Monte and Chet are not men of leisure, as figures in
code Westerns seem to be. They are working cowboys.
Even though Schaefer does not seem to have consciously
set out to debunk the cowboy myth, he has demonstrated
that there is a drama in the epic of the short-lived cattle
kingdom, without gunfighters and Indian battles and
tack-room romances. But one vital and realistic force does
impose itself. This force is *change,* the encroachment of

civilization, for *Monte Walsh* is set during the time of massive transition, when much of the West is becoming civilized. Monte's cattle kingdom was but one small step in that complex process.

The protagonist drifts from ranch to range and from village to town, toting his bedroll and his considerable abilities. He punches for the Slash Y that Cal Brennan put together before the consolidated Cattle Company engulfed it. Old Cal describes his crew, summing up Monte in the telling: "Good boys. . . . But footloose." Monte's work is single men's work. A family has no place in it. Douglas Branch in *The Cowboy and His Interpreters* long ago observed: "The family, the pillar of society-that rooted and stabilized the civilization that came with the passing of the range, was of little influence in shaping the society of the cow-country" (p. 156). Monte's experiences help to validate this argument.

But in Monte Walsh's day the range country was being transformed. Families were establishing themselves, and Monte's world was slowly passing. As early as 1879 he had noted changes at Dodge: "Three times he had been here and each time the town surprised him with its growth. It was not as wide open as it had been last year or the year before, but still there was plenty to keep a man occupied while he got rid of his hard earned pay" (p. 38).

In an intense, complex episode, Monte's death is presaged by the death of a man named Powder Kent in 1888. By analogy, this episode anticipates the death of the frontier which both men loved. Two malcontent mustangers start a range fire on Slash Y land. While Monte and company fight the blaze, Powder Kent spots the mustangers and trails them. From surrounding ranches and the nearby hamlet of Harmony, communal help that would not have been available years before joins the Slash Y men fighting the fire. Monte rides inside the fire line pulling a carcass drag, and his lungs are seared by the intense heat, an injury that will plague him to the grave. At the same time, Powder Kent confronts the mustangers and is killed in the ensuing battle.

In as fine a show of Western machismo as one is apt to find, the badly hurt Monte refuses to acknowledge the seriousness of his condition: "Ain't there . . . any whiskey . . . around?" (p. 303). But it takes more than whiskey to reverse lung damage.

When Powder Kent's body is returned to the ranch house, his fellow waddies bury him. At the head of his grave they put a cross, with the Slash Y brand at the top of the upright. On the crosspiece they carefully carve this legend:

WILLIAM (POWDER) KENT
1847–1888
A Good Man With a Gun

A special horse named Hellfire figures prominently in Monte's story. He is a Slash Y colt foaled by a Slash Y mare, and at first he is virtually unrideable. Eventually he is ridden and brutalized and nearly sold for glue. As with all wild things, civilization must break him or kill him. But Monte sets him free to spend his last days in the badlands.

The Hellfire section of the novel contains one of the important themes of the book: the fact that civilization is unwilling to tolerate wildness, whether the wildness is in Hellfire or in Monte. This chapter is also a good example of the episodic structure of the novel, for it is composed of a number of related tales, generally in chronological order and tied together by italicized passages. Though there may be some formal objections to the structure of this narrative, it is nonetheless effective as a story.

So the separate tales go, with the years passing. In an almost unnoticed but relentless erosion of Monte's way of life, his special world becomes ever narrower and more precarious. Near the turn of the century, the death of Monkey Face, his dun horse, seems to him the cruelest of all possible blows. Monte looks down upon the "limp body lying in a trodden dust and on back into the miles and the years of a long long trail with a good horse under him" (p. 370).

Chet Rollins has married and settled down. He is a successful businessman, for unlike Monte he has adjusted to the new Southwest. The two men remain the closest of friends. But Chet's wife, who is his own link with the growing domesticity of the cattle country, does not share her husband's regard for "an old saddle bum who looks older than he is and smells of liquor half the time" (p. 397).

The remarks of a young range manager, a businessman, provide a good survey of the changes that have overtaken the cattle industry during Monte's lifetime. The young manager does not like oldtime cowhands. He has learned to stay clear of them. "Too set in their ways. Too damn independent. Why last month I had one quit me just because I sold a horse out of his string. Too good a price to miss" (p. 387).

To the end, Monte remains his own man, and what is perhaps more important, he makes it clear that, however uncommonly such situations occur in changing cow country, there are still times when a good man on a horse is the best answer. After riding and crawling from a remote mine in the midst of a storm in order to fetch a doctor for others, Monte is fatally stricken. His much-used body and scorched lungs falter. "I can't understand it," the doctor tells Chet Rollins. "Exposure yes. Bruised and banged, yes. And pneumonia. Yes. All that's understandable. But a man like that ought to be able to fight it. He's made of gristle and rawhide. It's inside. His lungs" (p. 438). Then Chet remembers and understands.

Just before dying, Monte reaffirms the integrity of his

way of life: "no goddamned . . . autymobile . . . could of . . . done it." The next day Chet buries him, having a stone erected over the grave with a Slash Y brand and this inscription:

MONTE WALSH

1856–1913

A Good Man With a Horse

First the gunman has passed. Now the horseman is no more. Chet Rollins, survivor, goes back to fill his seat in the state legislature.

Taking it as a whole, Schaefer's most ambitious novel, *Monte Walsh,* is a success. Without relying upon popular myths, it manages to capture the quality of life in the cattle country. It is a book so rich in substance that Orville Prescott has said, "the wonder is how much vitality, vigor and humor Mr. Schaefer has been able to crowd into his long book" (*New York Times,* September 9, 1963, p. 25). For the author has not stretched a thin plot. Though the structure of the story might raise some questions, there is no doubt that Schaefer has written a thoroughly fleshed-out novel. In it he has made variations upon his persistent themes: problems of growth, the symbiotic relationship between individuals and society, and the injunction to "know thyself." In the judgment of David Otis Kelley, "this is not just another Western. It is worthy of a place alongside the writing of Will James and Eugene Manlove Rhodes" (*Library Journal,* September 15, 1963, p. 3226).

Perhaps the most apt comment on the novel appears in Walter C. Clapham's *Western Movies.* Discussing the big-budget motion picture version of the story, Clapham says: "Blessed with the best of beginnings, a novel by Jack Schaefer, . . . this moody, impressive picture is a requiem for the cowboy" (p. 123). It is indeed a fine film, featuring solid performances by Jack Palance and by Lee Marvin, who plays Monte. But it does not truly follow or in any way equal the novel.

In 1965, Schaefer published a controversial book of nonfiction sketches, *Heroes Without Glory: Some Goodmen of the Old West,* which has ruffled the feathers of some reviewers, especially easterners. Schaefer flouts popular notions when he asserts that even though "the cult of the old-time western badman flourishes like the green bay tree," the villains are in fact "Outclassed. Right across the board. By the goodmen" (Introduction, p. x).

> Shucks, the average seat-soaked flea-ridden cowhand bringing a trail herd up to a rail head or the northern ranges had more straight courage, the steady, enduring brand, faced obstacles and danger and death more often and more gallantly than any badman on record—and did this day after day without fuss or feathers as part of his job. (p. xi)

But how dare someone suggest that Joe Starrett is more admirable than Stark Wilson? John Greenway scarcely contains his scorn. "Schaefer's introductory contention is wrong," he writes. "So his book falls flat on its face. . . . It is admirable how he contrives, goodman after goodman, to stretch nothing into not much" (*Book Week,* April 11, 1965, p. 9). Sadly, Greenway does not burden himself with evidence to refute the author's contention. Moreover, a close reading of the book strongly validates Schaefer's claim. In his accounts of such men as John A. Thompson, the phenomenal postman of the Sierras; or Wash-A-Kie, the astute Shoshone leader; or John S. Chism, the tough Texan who pioneered the cattle industry; or Elfego Baca, the gritty New Mexican lawman who made believers out of more than a few erstwhile outlaws, Schaefer justifies his contention. The major weakness of the book is its form. The brief sketches necessarily produce thin characters, if fascinating ones.

The publication of *Mavericks* in 1967 marks Schaefer's last major work of fiction, or so he claims. In a letter dated

August 19, 1974, he calls this short novel "some kind of epitaph." It has this particular relevance to his own life, he says, because, "Like Old Jake I had come to realize that I was a part of the whole damnable process of so-called civilization which was ruining this world in which we live."

If *Mavericks* is an epitaph, it is a magnificent one. Like *Old Ramon*, it is written for younger readers, and like *Old Ramon*, it has earned raves from reviewers. *Horn Book* calls it a "superb . . . magnificent tribute to a vanishing breed of men and horses" (December 1967, p. 760). And A. R. Bosworth plays a variation upon the same theme: "An excellent book . . . a colorful, sometimes even poetic story" (*Book World,* January 14, 1968, p. 14).

Jake Hanlon, the protagonist of *Mavericks,* is an old man who is sitting "still and quiet as a wrinkled lizard on a sun-warmed stone," looking out into an immense open plain covered with Yucca and cactus. Out of that vast southwestern plain, memories sweep the old man, especially memories of mustangs "with the look of eagles in their eyes." Jake himself sees with the eyes of experience.

Schaefer captures the old man's slow, sensitive manner of life—reading footprints at a water hole, preparing a leisurely breakfast, carefully shaving—just as he recreates Jake's adventures in an everpresent past. Jimmie Dunn, Jake's horse, is a prominent part of the living memories in this past-present continuum. Especially persistent is the memory of the 530-mile race which the man and the horse had won against all comers.

A stray horse wanders in to drink at Jake's water. Its small saddle, its broken rein, and a trail of small boot tracks tell the old man a story, quickly moving him from his old adventures into a new one. He finds the lost boy and reunites him with his family, and that experience recalls another: the memory of Jake in the act of releasing penned mustangs from the Martinez corral. The old man watches them flee, gasping: "Go—it. They—ain't—

goin'—to make—dogfood—out—of—you" (p. 157).

Old Jake has realized before his death that he has been part of the process that has ruined the mustangs. In this sense he has helped to destroy their habitat and eventually the mustangs themselves. As Jake is the last of his breed, so the mustangs are the last of theirs. Jake rebels at the thought that the mustangs will be confined to reservations, but he is an integral part of a historical paradox. Like Daniel Boone and Leatherstocking, his very existence among the wild things he loves must doom them at last to the effects of civilization. When asked what can be done for the few remaining wild horses if reservations are not established, he can only reply: "We can remember 'em, I reckon that's all we've left ourselves able to do" (p. 170).

Mavericks forces us to the bitter realization of what civilization has meant to the Southwest. This realization is, in turn, a product of the author's genius as a story teller. "Never again could I write of people with the same 'innocence' of past years," he wrote in a letter. "If I was writing them [the stories] now, I would have difficulty seeing them as I saw them when originally writing them. How, for example, could I present Shane as heroic in the situation he confronted even though seeing him and it through the eyes of a boy, when in my own mind, I would be seeing him as part of that 'deadly conquest called civilization?'" Schaefer says that his growing perceptions of the excesses of civilization have culminated "quite chronologically and logically in what Old Jake came to realize in my final people-book, *Mavericks*."

Most recently, Schaefer has finished his work on a labor of love: a detailed southwestern bestiary that has just been published by Houghton Mifflin. In his introduction, Schaefer tells his readers that, in his development from eastern newspaper man to Western fictioneer, he eventually gained a special insight that led him to turn from people to beasts:

Always I was writing about people, about us feather-
less bipeds who sum ourselves by genus and species
as *Homo sapiens*. Any other creatures who crept in
were merely stage furniture for the human drama.
And then, as a writer, I came to a full stop. I had lost
my innocence. I had become ashamed of my species
and myself. I understood at last in full consequence
that despite whatever dodges of motive and intent
and personal activities I might cite . . . I was a contributing part of the heedless human onrush that was
ruining the land I loved and forcing toward extinction ever more of my fellow creatures whose companion right to continued existence ought to be respected.

As a result of this revelation, he has been forced to accept
the fact that: "bedded deep in me is the conviction that a
world inhabited only by us humans and those others we
decide are useful to us would be a barren and lonesome
place." If, as Fred Erisman has argued, growing up with
the American West has been Schaefer's special theme, one
must argue also that *Mavericks* represents a crotchety old
age. Rather than preaching endlessly about human failings, Schaefer has turned to animals, about which he can
still write with vigor and freshness.

Ultimately, Jack Schaefer's roots are in the tale-telling
tradition that demands entertainment along with depth,
and in the tradition that abjures pontificating. There has
been a tendency to see Schaefer as a latter-day Mary Hal-
lock Foote or Owen Wister or Helen Hunt Jackson, since
they are all easterners who have found satisfying literary
material in the West. But Schaefer seems to be a writer who
found the West in himself, and then himself in the West. In
many of his short stories, and in novels like *Shane*, *The Canyon*, and *Monte Walsh*, he has explored western experiences with the skill and depth of one who is a part of his
own subject matter.

Moreover, he has managed to capture both a popular and a critical audience. His books have sold remarkably well. As he has observed, he has written no best-sellers: "My books just keep on going quite steadily in their modest ways. They seem to be rather durable." Durable they are, and important. Jack Schaefer has found his material and has presented it honestly, illuminating the recesses of an otherwise dimly seen time and place, and of the people who inhabit that time and place. In doing so, he has raised himself above the horde of Western authors who have been satisfied with far less than this.

References

Clapham, Walter C. *Western Movies.* London: Octopus Books, 1974.

Branch, Douglas. *The Cowboy and His Interpreters.* New York: Appleton, 1926.

Dieter, Lynn. "Behavioral Objectives in the English Classroom: A Model." *English Journal,* 59 (December 1970: 1258–62, 1271.

Erisman, Fred. "Growing Up With the American West: Fiction of Jack Schaefer." In *The Popular Western,* Richard W. Etulain and Michael T. Marsden. Bowling Green, Ohio: Bowling Green University Popular Press, 1974.

Fenin, George, and William Everson. *The Western: From Silents to the Seventies.* New York: Grossman, 1973.

Fiedler, Leslie. *The Return of the Vanishing American.* New York: Stein and Day, 1969.

Folsom, James K. "*Shane and Hud:* Two Stories in Search of a Medium." *Western Humanities Review,* 24 (Autumn 1970): 359–72.

Haslam, G. W. "Jack Schaefer's Frontier: The West as Human Testing Ground." *Rocky Mountain Review,* 4 (1967): 59–71.

———. "Jack Schaefer." *Western American Writers,* cassette lecture series. Deland, Florida: Everett/Edwards, 1974.

————. "Shane: Twenty-five Years Later." *Western American Literature*, 9 (Fall 1974): 215–16.

Johnson, Dorothy M. "Jack Schaefer's People." In *The Short Novels of Jack Schaefer*. Boston: Houghton Mifflin, 1967. Pp. vii–x.

Kael, Pauline. *Kiss Kiss Bang Bang*. Boston: Little Brown, 1968.

Mikkelsen, Robert. "The Western Writer: Jack Schaefer's Use of the Western Frontier." *Western Humanities Review*, 6 (Spring 1954): 151–55.

Nuwer, Henry. "An Interview With Jack Schaefer," *South Dakota Review*, 11 (Spring 1973): 48–58.

Oliva, Leo E. "The American Indian in Recent Historical Fiction: A Review Essay," *The Prairie Scout*, 1 (1973): 95–120.

Schaefer, Jack. *The Short Novels of Jack Schaefer*. Boston: Houghton Mifflin, 1967.

Scott, Winfield Townley. "Introduction." In *The Collected Stories of Jack Schaefer*. Boston: Houghton Mifflin, 1966. Pp. vii–xi.

Shor, Rachel. "Jack Schaefer." *Wilson Library Bulletin*, 35 (February 1961): 471.

Simmons, Marc. "A Salute to *Shane*." *The Roundup*, 22 (May 1974): 1–2, 9, 11.

SHANE
by Jack Schaefer

I

HE RODE INTO OUR VALLEY in the summer of '89. I was a kid then, barely topping the backboard of father's old chuck-wagon. I was on the upper rail of our small corral, soaking in the late afternoon sun, when I saw him far down the road where it swung into the valley from the open plain beyond.

In that clear Wyoming air I could see him plainly, though he was still several miles away. There seemed nothing remarkable about him, just another stray horseman riding up the road toward the cluster of frame buildings that was our town. Then I saw a pair of cowhands, loping past him, stop and stare after him with a curious intentness.

He came steadily on, straight through the town without slackening pace, until he reached the fork a half-mile below our place. One branch turned left across the river ford and on to Luke Fletcher's big spread. The other bore ahead along the right bank where we homesteaders had pegged our claims in a row up the valley. He hesitated briefly, studying the choice, and moved again steadily on our side.

As he came near, what impressed me first was his clothes. He wore dark trousers of some serge material tucked into tall boots and held at the waist by a wide belt, both of a soft black leather tooled in intricate design. A coat of the same dark material as the trousers was neatly folded and strapped to his saddle-roll. His shirt was finespun linen, rich brown in color. The handkerchief knotted loosely around his throat was black silk. His hat was not the familiar Stetson, not the familiar gray or muddy tan. It was a plain black, soft in texture, unlike any hat I had ever seen, with a creased crown and a wide curling brim swept down in front to shield the face.

All trace of newness was long since gone from these things. The dust of distance was beaten into them. They were worn and stained and several neat patches showed on the shirt. Yet a kind of magnificence remained and with it a hint of men and manners alien to my limited boy's experience.

Then I forgot the clothes in the impact of the man himself. He was not much above medium height, almost slight in build. He would have looked frail alongside father's square, solid bulk. But even I could read the endurance in the lines of that dark figure and the quiet power in its effortless, unthinking adjustment to every movement of the tired horse.

He was clean-shaven and his face was lean and hard and burned from high forehead to firm, tapering chin. His eyes seemed hooded in the shadow of the hat's brim. He came closer, and I could see that this was because the brows were drawn in a frown of fixed and habitual alertness. Beneath them the eyes were endlessly searching from side to side and forward, checking off every item in view, missing nothing. As I noticed this, a sudden chill, I could not have told why, struck through me there in the warm and open sun.

He rode easily, relaxed in the saddle, leaning

his weight lazily into the stirrups. Yet even in this easiness was a suggestion of tension. It was the easiness of a coiled spring, of a trap set.

He drew rein not twenty feet from me. His glance hit me, dismissed me, flicked over our place. This was not much, if you were thinking in terms of size and scope. But what there was was good. You could trust father for that. The corral, big enough for about thirty head if you crowded them in, was railed right to true sunk posts. The pasture behind, taking in nearly half of our claim, was fenced tight. The barn was small, but it was solid, and we were raising a loft at one end for the alfalfa growing green in the north forty. We had a fair-sized field in potatoes that year and father was trying a new corn he had sent all the way to Washington for and they were showing properly in weedless rows.

Behind the house mother's kitchen garden was a brave sight. The house itself was three rooms — two really, the big kitchen where we spent most of our time indoors and the bedroom beside it. My little lean-to room was added back of the kitchen. Father was planning, when he could get around to it, to build mother the parlor she wanted.

We had wooden floors and a nice porch across the front. The house was painted too, white with green trim, rare thing in all that region, to remind her, mother said when she made father do it, of her native New England. Even rarer, the roof was shingled. I knew what that meant. I had helped father split those shingles. Few places so spruce and well worked could be found so deep in the Territory in those days.

The stranger took it all in, sitting there easily in the saddle. I saw his eyes slow on the flowers mother had planted by the porch steps, then come to rest on our shiny new pump and the trough beside it. They shifted back to me, and again, without knowing why, I felt that sudden chill. But his voice was gentle and he spoke like a man schooled to patience.

"I'd appreciate a chance at the pump for myself and the horse."

I was trying to frame a reply and choking on it, when I realized that he was not speaking to me but past me. Father had come up behind me and was leaning against the gate to the corral.

"Use all the water you want, stranger."

Father and I watched him dismount in a single flowing tilt of his body and lead the horse over to the trough. He pumped it almost full and let the horse sink its nose in the cool water before he picked up the dipper for himself.

He took off his hat and slapped the dust out of it and hung it on a corner of the trough. With his hands he brushed the dust from his clothes. With a piece of rag pulled from his saddle-roll he carefully wiped his boots. He untied the handkerchief from around his neck and rolled his sleeves and dipped his arms in the trough, rubbing thoroughly and splashing water over his face. He shook his hands dry and used the handkerchief to remove the last drops from his face. Taking a comb from his shirt pocket, he smoothed back his long dark hair. All his movements were deft and sure, and with a quick precision he flipped down his sleeves, reknotted the handkerchief, and picked up his hat.

Then, holding it in his hand, he spun about and strode directly toward the house. He bent low and snapped the stem of one of mother's petunias and tucked this into the hatband. In another moment the hat was on his head, brim swept down in swift, unconscious gesture, and he was swinging gracefully into the saddle and starting toward the road.

I was fascinated. None of the men I knew were proud like that about their appearance. In that short time the kind of magnificence I had noticed had emerged into plainer view. It was in the very air of him. Everything about him showed the effects of long use and hard use, but showed too the strength of quality and competence. There was no chill on me now. Already I was imagining myself in hat and belt and boots like those.

He stopped the horse and looked down at us. He was refreshed and I would have sworn the tiny wrinkles around his eyes were what with him would be a smile. His eyes were not restless when he looked at you like this. They were still and steady and you knew the man's whole attention was concentrated on you even in the casual glance.

"Thank you," he said in his gentle voice and was turning into the road, back to us, before father spoke in his slow, deliberate way.

"Don't be in such a hurry, stranger."

I had to hold tight to the rail or I would have fallen backwards into the corral. At the first sound of father's voice, the man and the horse, like a

single being, had wheeled to face us, the man's
eyes boring at father, bright and deep in the shadow of the hat's brim. I was shivering, struck
through once more. Something intangible and
cold and terrifying was there in the air between
us.

I stared in wonder as father and the stranger
looked at each other a long moment, measuring
each other in an unspoken fraternity of adult
knowledge beyond my reach. Then the warm sun·
light was flooding over us, for father was smiling
and he was speaking with the drawling emphasis
that meant he had made up his mind.

"I said don't be in such a hurry, stranger. Food
will be on the table soon and you can bed down
here tonight."

The stranger nodded quietly as if he too had
made up his mind. "That's mighty thoughtful of
you," he said and swung down and came toward
us, leading his horse. Father slipped into step
beside him and we all headed for the barn.

"My name's Starrett," said father. "Joe Starrett. This here," waving at me, "is Robert Mac-
Pherson Starrett. Too much name for a boy. I
make it Bob."

The stranger nodded again. "Call me Shane,"

he said. Then to me: "Bob it is. You were watching me for quite a spell coming up the road."

It was not a question. It was a simple statement. "Yes . . ." I stammered. "Yes. I was."

"Right," he said. "I like that. A man who watches what's going on around him will make his mark."

A man who watches . . . For all his dark appearance and lean, hard look, this Shane knew what would please a boy. The glow of it held me as he took care of his horse, and I fussed around, hanging up his saddle, forking over some hay, getting in his way and my own in my eagerness. He let me slip the bridle off and the horse, bigger and more powerful than I had thought now that I was close beside it, put its head down patiently for me and stood quietly while I helped him curry away the caked dust. Only once did he stop me. That was when I reached for his saddle-roll to put it to one side. In the instant my fingers touched it, he was taking it from me and he put it on a shelf with a finality that indicated no interference.

When the three of us went up to the house, mother was waiting and four places were set at the table. "I saw you through the window," she said

and came to shake our visitor's hand. She was a
slender, lively woman with a fair complexion
even our weather never seemed to affect and a
mass of light brown hair she wore piled high to
bring her, she used to say, closer to father's size.

"Marian," father said, "I'd like you to meet Mr.
Shane."

"Good evening, ma'am," said our visitor. He
took her hand and bowed over it. Mother stepped
back and, to my surprise, dropped in a dainty
curtsy. I had never seen her do that before. She
was an unpredictable woman. Father and I would
have painted the house three times over and in
rainbow colors to please her.

"And a good evening to you, Mr. Shane. If Joe
hadn't called you back, I would have done it myself. You'd never find a decent meal up the valley."

She was proud of her cooking, was mother.
That was one thing she learned back home, she
would often say, that was of some use out in this
raw land. As long as she could still prepare a
proper dinner, she would tell father when things
were not going right, she knew she was still civilized and there was hope of getting ahead. Then
she would tighten her lips and whisk together her

special most delicious biscuits and father would watch her bustling about and eat them to the last little crumb and stand up and wipe his eyes and stretch his big frame and stomp out to his always unfinished work like daring anything to stop him now.

We sat down to supper and a good one. Mother's eyes sparkled as our visitor kept pace with father and me. Then we all leaned back and while I listened the talk ran on almost like old friends around a familiar table. But I could sense that it was following a pattern. Father was trying, with mother helping and both of them avoiding direct questions, to get hold of facts about this Shane and he was dodging at every turn. He was aware of their purpose and not in the least annoyed by it. He was mild and courteous and spoke readily enough. But always he put them off with words that gave no real information.

He must have been riding many days, for he was full of news from towns along his back trail as far as Cheyenne and even Dodge City and others beyond I had never heard of before. But he had no news about himself. His past was fenced as tightly as our pasture. All they could learn was that he was riding through, taking each day as it came, with nothing particular in mind except maybe seeing a part of the country he had not been in before.

Afterwards mother washed the dishes and I dried and the two men sat on the porch, their voices carrying through the open door. Our visitor was guiding the conversation now and in no time at all he had father talking about his own plans. That was no trick. Father was ever one to argue his ideas whenever he could find a listener. This time he was going strong.

"Yes, Shane, the boys I used to ride with don't see it yet. They will some day. The open range can't last forever. The fence lines are closing in. Running cattle in big lots is good business only for the top ranchers and it's really a poor business at that. Poor in terms of the resources going into it. Too much space for too little results. It's certain to be crowded out."

"Well, now," said Shane, "that's mighty interesting. I've been hearing the same quite a lot lately and from men with pretty clear heads. Maybe there's something to it."

"By Godfrey, there's plenty to it. Listen to me, Shane. The thing to do is pick your spot, get your land, your own land. Put in enough crops to carry you and make your money play with a small herd, not all horns and bone, but bred for meat and fenced in and fed right. I haven't been at it long, but already I've raised stock that averages three hundred pounds more than that long-legged stuff Fletcher runs on the other side of the river and it's better beef, and that's only a beginning.

"Sure, his outfit sprawls over most of this valley and it looks big. But he's got range rights on a lot more acres than he has cows and he won't even have those acres as more homesteaders move in. His way is wasteful. Too much land for what he gets out of it. He can't see that. He thinks we small fellows are nothing but nuisances."

"You are," said Shane mildly. "From his point of view, you are."

"Yes, I guess you're right. I'll have to admit that. Those of us here now would make it tough for him if he wanted to use the range behind us on this side of the river as he used to. Altogether we cut some pretty good slices out of it. Worse still, we block off part of the river, shut the range off from the water. He's been grumbling about that off and on ever since we've been here. He's worried that more of us will keep coming and settle on the other side too, and then he will be in a fix."

The dishes were done and I was edging to the

door. Mother nailed me as she usually did and
shunted me off to bed. After she had left me in
my little back room and went to join the men on
the porch, I tried to catch more of the words. The
voices were too low. Then I must have dozed, for
with a start I realized that father and mother were
again in the kitchen. By now, I gathered, our visitor was out in the barn in the bunk father had
built there for the hired man who had been with
us for a few weeks in the spring.

"Wasn't it peculiar," I heard mother say, "how
he wouldn't talk about himself?"

"Peculiar?" said father. "Well, yes. In a way."

"Everything about him is peculiar." Mother
sounded as if she was stirred up and interested.
"I never saw a man quite like him before."

"You wouldn't have. Not where you come
from. He's a special brand we sometimes get out
here in the grass country. I've come across a few.
A bad one's poison. A good one's straight grain
clear through."

"How can you be so sure about him? Why, he
wouldn't even tell where he was raised."

"Born back east a ways would be my guess. And
pretty far south. Tennessee maybe. But he's been
around plenty."

"I like him." Mother's voice was serious. "He's so nice and polite and sort of gentle. Not like most men I've met out here. But there's something about him. Something underneath the gentleness . . . Something . . ." Her voice trailed away.

"Mysterious?" suggested father.

"Yes, of course. Mysterious. But more than that. Dangerous."

"He's dangerous all right." Father said it in a musing way. Then he chuckled. "But not to us, my dear." And then he said what seemed to me a curious thing. "In fact, I don't think you ever had a safer man in your house."

2

IN THE MORNING I slept late and stumbled into the kitchen to find father and our visitor working their way through piles of mother's flapjacks. She smiled at me from over by the stove. Father slapped my rump by way of greeting. Our visitor nodded at me gravely over his heaped-up plate.

"Good morning, Bob. You'd better dig in fast or I'll do away with your share too. There's magic in your mother's cooking. Eat enough of these flannel cakes and you'll grow a bigger man than your father."

"Flannel cakes! Did you hear that, Joe?" Mother came whisking over to tousle father's hair. "You must be right. Tennessee or some such place. I never heard them called that out here."

Our visitor looked up at her. "A good guess, ma'am. Mighty close to the mark. But you had a husband to help you. My folks came out of Mississippi and settled in Arkansas. Me, though — I was fiddle-footed and left home at fifteen. Haven't had anything worth being called a real flannel cake since." He put his hands on the table edge and leaned back and the little wrinkles at the corners of his eyes were plainer and deeper. "That is, ma'am, till now."

Mother gave what in a girl I would have called a giggle. "If I'm any judge of men," she said, "that means more." And she whisked back to the stove.

That was how it was often in our house, kind of jolly and warm with good feeling. It needed to be this morning because there was a cool grayness in the air and before I had even begun to slow on my second plate of flapjacks the wind was rushing down the valley with the rain of one of our sudden summer storms following fast.

Our visitor had finished his breakfast. He had eaten so many flapjacks that I had begun to wonder whether he really would cut into my share. Now he turned to look out the window and his lips tightened. But he pushed back from the table and started to rise. Mother's voice held him to his chair.

"You'll not be traveling in any such weather. Wait a bit and it'll clear. These rains don't last long. I've another pot of coffee on the stove."

Father was getting his pipe going. He kept his eyes carefully on the smoke drifting upward. "Marian's right. Only she doesn't go far enough. These rains are short. But they sure mess up the road. It's new. Hasn't settled much yet. Mighty soggy when wet. Won't be fit for traveling till it drains. You better stay over till tomorrow."

Our visitor stared down at his empty plate as if it was the most important object in the whole room. You could see he liked the idea. Yet he seemed somehow worried about it.

"Yes," said father. "That's the sensible dodge. That horse of yours was pretty much beat last night. If I was a horse doctor now, I'd order a day's rest right off. Hanged if I don't think the same prescription would do me good too. You stick here the day and I'll follow it. I'd like to take you around, show you what I'm doing with the place."

He looked pleadingly at mother. She was surprised and good reason. Father was usually so set on working every possible minute to catch up on his plans that she would have a tussle making him ease some once a week out of respect for the Sabbath. In bad weather like this he usually would fidget and stomp about the house as if he thought it was a personal insult to him, a trick to keep him from being out and doing things. And here he was talking of a whole day's rest. She was puzzled. But she played right up.

"You'd be doing us a favor, Mr. Shane. We don't get many visitors from outside the valley. It'd be real nice to have you stay. And besides —" She crinkled her nose at him the way she did when she would be teasing father into some new scheme of hers. "And besides — I've been waiting for an excuse to try a deep-dish apple pie I've heard tell of. It would just be wasted on these other two. They eat everything in sight and don't rightly know good from poor."

He was looking up, straight at her. She shook a finger at him. "And another thing. I'm fair bubbling with questions about what the women are wearing back in civilization. You know, hats and such. You're the kind of man would notice them. You're not getting away till you've told me."

Shane sat back in his chair. A faint quizzical

expression softened the lean ridges of his face. "Ma'am, I'm not positive I appreciate how you've pegged me. No one else ever wrote me down an expert on ladies' millinery." He reached out and pushed his cup across the table toward her. "You said something about more coffee. But I draw the line on more flannel cakes. I'm plumb full. I'm starting in to conserve space for that pie."

"You'd better!" Father was mighty pleased about something. "When Marian puts her mind to cooking, she makes a man forget he's got any limits to his appetite. Only don't you go giving her fancy notions of new hats so she'll be sending off to the mail-order house and throwing my money away on silly frippery. She's got a hat."

Mother did not even notice that. She knew father was just talking. She knew that whenever she wanted anything real much and said so, father would bust himself trying to get it for her. She whisked over to the table with the coffee pot, poured a fresh round, then set it down within easy reach and sat down herself.

I thought that business about hats was only a joke she made up to help father persuade our visitor to stay. But she began almost at once, pester-

ing him to describe the ladies he had seen in
Cheyenne and other towns where the new styles
might be. He sat there, easy and friendly, telling
her how they were wearing wide floppy-brimmed
bonnets with lots of flowers in front on top and
slits in the brims for scarves to come through and
be tied in bows under their chins.

Talk like that seemed foolish to me to be coming from a grown man. Yet this Shane was not
bothered at all. And father listened as if he
thought it was all right, only not very interesting.
He watched them most of the time in a good-
natured quiet, trying every so often to break in
with his own talk about crops and steers and giving up and trying again and giving up again with
a smiling shake of his head at those two. And the
rain outside was a far distance away and meaningless because the friendly feeling in our kitchen
was enough to warm all our world.

Then Shane was telling about the annual stock
show at Dodge City and father was interested and
excited, and it was mother who said: "Look, the
sun's shining."

It was, so clear and sweet you wanted to run out
and breathe the brilliant freshness. Father must
have felt that way because he jumped up and fair-

ly shouted, "Come on, Shane. I'll show you what
this hop-scotch climate does to my alfalfa. You
can almost see the stuff growing."

Shane was only a step behind him, but I beat
them to the door. Mother followed and stood
watching awhile on the porch as we three started
out, picking our path around the puddles and the
taller clumps of grass bright with the raindrops.
We covered the whole place pretty thoroughly,
father talking all the time, more enthusiastic
about his plans than he had been for many weeks.
He really hit his stride when we were behind the
barn where we could have a good view of our little
herd spreading out through the pasture. Then he
stopped short. He had noticed that Shane was not
paying much attention. He was quiet as could be
for a moment when he saw that Shane was looking
at the stump.

That was the one bad spot on our place. It
stuck out like an old scarred sore in the cleared
space back of the barn — a big old stump, all
jagged across the top, the legacy of some great tree
that must have died long before we came into the
valley and finally been snapped by a heavy wind-
storm. It was big enough, I used to think, so that
if it was smooth on top you could have served
supper to a good-sized family on it.

But you could not have done that because you could not have got them close around it. The huge old roots humped out in every direction, some as big about as my waist, pushing out and twisting down into the ground like they would hold there to eternity and past.

Father had been working at it off and on, gnawing at the roots with an axe, ever since he finished poling the corral. The going was slow, even for him. The wood was so hard that he could not sink the blade much more than a quarter inch at a time. I guess it had been an old burr oak. Not many of those grew that far up in the Territory, but the ones that did grew big and hard. Ironwood we called it.

Father had tried burning brushpiles against it. That old stump just jeered at fire. The scorching seemed to make the wood harder than ever. So he was fighting his way around root by root. He never thought he had much time to spare on it. The rare occasions he was real mad about something he would stomp out there and chew into another root.

He went over to the stump now and kicked the nearest root, a smart kick, the way he did every time he passed it. "Yes," he said. "That's the millstone round my neck. That's the one fool

thing about this place I haven't licked yet. But I
will. There's no wood ever grew can stand up to
a man that's got the strength and the will to keep
hammering at it."

He stared at the stump like it might be a person sprouting in front of him. "You know, Shane,
I've been feuding with this thing so long I've
worked up a spot of affection for it. It's tough. I
can admire toughness. The right kind."

He was running on again, full of words and sort
of happy to be letting them out, when he noticed
again that Shane was not paying much attention,
was listening to some sound in the distance. Sure
enough, a horse was coming up the road.

Father and I turned with him to look toward
town. In a moment we saw it as it cleared the
grove of trees and tall bushes about a quarter-mile
away, a high-necked sorrel drawing a light buckboard wagon. The mud was splattering from its
hooves, but not bad, and it was stepping free and
easy. Shane glanced sideways at father.

"Not fit for traveling," he said softly. "Starrett,
you're poor shakes as a liar." Then his attention
was on the wagon and he was tense and alert,
studying the man upright on the swaying seat.

Father simply chuckled at Shane's remark.

"That's Jake Ledyard's outfit," he said, taking the lead toward our lane. "I thought maybe he'd get up this way this week. Hope he has that cultivator I've been wanting."

Ledyard was a small, thin-featured man, a peddler or trader who came through every couple of months with things you could not get at the general store in town. He would pack in his stock on a mule-team freighter driven by an old, white-haired Negro who acted like he was afraid even to speak without permission. Ledyard would make deliveries in his buckboard, claiming a hard bargain always and picking up orders for articles to bring on the next trip. I did not like him, and not just because he said nice things about me he did not mean for father's benefit. He smiled too much and there was no real friendliness in it.

By the time we were beside the porch, he had swung the horse into our lane and was pulling it to a stop. He jumped down, calling greetings. Father went to meet him. Shane stayed by the porch, leaning against the end post.

"It's here," said Ledyard. "The beauty I told you about." He yanked away the canvas covering from the body of the wagon and the sun was bright on a shiny new seven-pronged cultivator lying on its side on the floor boards. "That's the best buy I've toted this haul."

"Hm-m-m-m," said father. "You've hit it right. That's what I've been wanting. But when you start chattering about a best buy that always means big money. What's the tariff?"

"Well, now." Ledyard was slow with his reply. "It cost me more than I figured when we was talking last time. You might think it a bit steep. I don't. Not for a new beauty like that there. You'll make up the difference in no time with the work you'll save with that. Handles so easy even the boy here will be using it before long."

"Pin it down," said father. "I've asked you a question."

Ledyard was quick now. "Tell you what, I'll shave the price, take a loss to please a good customer. I'll let you have it for a hundred and ten."

I was startled to hear Shane's voice cutting in, quiet and even and plain. "Let you have it? I reckon he will. There was one like that in a store in Cheyenne. List price sixty dollars."

Ledyard shifted part way around. For the first time he looked closely at our visitor. The surface smile left his face. His voice held an ugly undertone. "Did anyone ask you to push in on this?"

"No," said Shane, quietly and evenly as before. "I reckon no one did." He was still leaning against the post. He did not move and he did not say anything more. Ledyard turned to father, speaking rapidly.

"Forget what he says, Starrett. I've spotted him now. Heard of him half a dozen times along the road up here. No one knows him. No one can figure him. I think I can. Just a stray wandering through, probably chased out of some town and hunting cover. I'm surprised you'd let him hang around."

"You might be surprised at a lot of things," said father, beginning to bite off his words. "Now give it to me straight on the price."

"It's what I said. A hundred and ten. Hell, I'll be out money on the deal anyway, so I'll shave it to a hundred if that'll make you feel any better." Ledyard hesitated, watching father. "Maybe he did see something in Cheyenne. But he's mixed up. Must have been one of those little makes — flimsy and barely half the size. That might match his price."

Father did not say anything. He was looking at Ledyard in a steady, unwavering way. He had

not even glanced at Shane. You might have believed he had not even heard what Shane had
said. But his lips were folding in to a tight line
like he was thinking what was not pleasant to
think. Ledyard waited and father did not say
anything and the climbing anger in Ledyard
broke free.

"Starrett! Are you going to stand there and let
that — that tramp nobody knows about call me a
liar? Are you going to take his word over mine?
Look at him! Look at his clothes! He's just a
cheap, tinhorn — "

Ledyard stopped, choking on whatever it was
he had meant to say. He fell back a step with a
sudden fear showing in his face. I knew why
even as I turned my head to see Shane. That
same chill I had felt the day before, intangible
and terrifying, was in the air again. Shane was
no longer leaning against the porch post. He was
standing erect, his hands clenched at his sides, his
eyes boring at Ledyard, his whole body alert and
alive in the leaping instant.

You felt without knowing how that each teetering second could bring a burst of indescribable
deadliness. Then the tension passed, fading in
the empty silence. Shane's eyes lost their sharp

focus on Ledyard and it seemed to me that reflected in them was some pain deep within him.

Father had pivoted so that he could see the two of them in the one sweep. He swung back to Ledyard alone.

"Yes, Ledyard, I'm taking his word. He's my guest. He's here at my invitation. But that's not the reason." Father straightened a little and his head went up and he gazed into the distance beyond the river. "I can figure men for myself. I'll take his word on anything he wants to say any day of God's whole year."

Father's head came down and his voice was flat and final. "Sixty is the price. Add ten for a fair profit, even though you probably got it wholesale. Another ten for hauling it here. That tallies to eighty. Take that or leave that. Whatever you do, snap to it and get off my land."

Ledyard stared down at his hands, rubbing them together as if they were cold. "Where's your money?" he said.

Father went into the house, into the bedroom where he kept our money in a little leather bag on the closet shelf. He came back with the crumpled bills. All this while Shane stood there, not moving, his face hard, his eyes following

father with a strange wildness in them that I
could not understand.

Ledyard helped father heave the cultivator to
the ground, then jumped to the wagon seat and
drove off like he was glad to get away from our
place. Father and I turned from watching him
into the road. We looked around for Shane and
he was not in sight. Father shook his head in
wonderment. "Now where do you suppose — "
he was saying, when we saw Shane coming out of
the barn.

He was carrying an axe, the one father used
for heavy kindling. He went directly around the
corner of the building. We stared after him and
we were still staring when we heard it, the clear
ringing sound of steel biting into wood.

I never could have explained what that sound
did to me. It struck through me as no single
sound had ever done before. With it ran a
warmth that erased at once and forever the feelings of sudden chill terror that our visitor had
evoked in me. There were sharp hidden hard-
nesses in him. But these were not for us. He
was dangerous as mother had said. But not to us
as father too had said. And he was no longer a

stranger. He was a man like father in whom a boy could believe in the simple knowing that what was beyond comprehension was still clean and solid and right.

I looked up at father to try to see what he was thinking, but he was starting toward the barn with strides so long that I had to run to stay close behind him. We went around the far corner and there was Shane squared away at the biggest uncut root of that big old stump. He was swinging the axe in steady rhythm. He was chewing into that root with bites almost as deep as father could drive.

Father halted, legs wide, hands on hips. "Now lookahere," he began, "there's no call for you — "

Shane broke his rhythm just long enough to level a straight look at us. "A man has to pay his debts," he said and was again swinging the axe. He was really slicing into that root.

He seemed so desperate in his determination that I had to speak. "You don't owe us anything," I said. "Lots of times we have folks in for meals and — "

Father's hand was on my shoulder. "No, Bob. He doesn't mean meals." Father was smiling, but he was having to blink several times together and

I would have sworn that his eyes were misty. He stood in silence now, not moving, watching Shane.

It was something worth seeing. When father worked on that old stump, that was worth seeing too. He could handle an axe mighty well and what impressed you was the strength and will of him making it behave and fight for him against the tough old wood. This was different. What impressed you as Shane found what he was up against and settled to it was the easy way the power in him poured smoothly into each stroke. The man and the axe seemed to be partners in the work. The blade would sink into the parallel grooves almost as if it knew itself what to do and the chips from between would come out in firm and thin little blocks.

Father watched him and I watched the two of them and time passed over us, and then the axe sliced through the last strip and the root was cut. I was sure that Shane would stop. But he stepped right around to the next root and squared away again and the blade sank in once more.

As it hit this second root, father winced like it had hit him. Then he stiffened and looked away from Shane and stared at the old stump. He began to fidget, throwing his weight from one foot to the other. In a short while more he was walking around inspecting the stump from different angles as if it was something he had never seen before. Finally he gave the nearest root a kick and hurried away. In a moment he was back with the other axe, the big double-bladed one that I could hardly heft from the ground.

He picked a root on the opposite side from Shane. He was not angry the way he usually was when he confronted one of those roots. There was a kind of serene and contented look on his face. He whirled that big axe as if it was only a kid's tool. The striking blade sank in maybe a whole half-inch. At the sound Shane straightened on his side. Their eyes met over the top of the stump and held and neither one of them said a word. Then they swung up their axes and both of them said plenty to that old stump.

3

IT WAS EXCITING at first watching them. They were hitting a fast pace, making the chips dance. I thought maybe each one would cut through a root now and stop. But Shane finished his and looked over at father working steadily away and with a grim little smile pulling at his mouth he moved on to another root. A few moments later father smashed through his with a blow that sent the axe head into the ground beneath. He wrestled with the handle to yank the head loose and he too tackled another root without even waiting to wipe off the dirt. This began to look like a long session, so I started to wander away. Just as I headed around the corner of the barn, mother came past the corner.

She was the freshest, prettiest thing I had ever seen. She had taken her hat and stripped the old ribbon from it and fixed it as Shane had told her. Some of the flowers by the house were in a small bouquet in front. She had cut slits in the brim and the sash from her best dress came around the crown and through the slits and was tied in a perky bow under her chin. She was stepping along daintily, mighty proud of herself.

She went up close to the stump. Those two choppers were so busy and intent that even if they were aware she was there they did not really notice her.

"Well," she said, "aren't you going to look at me?"

They both stopped and they both stared at her.

"Have I got it right?" she asked Shane. "Is this the way they do it?"

"Yes, ma'am," he said. "About like that. Only their brims are wider." And he swung back to his root.

"Joe Starrett," said mother, "aren't you at least going to tell me whether you like me in this hat?"

"Lookahere, Marian," said father, "you know damned well that whether you have a hat on or whether you don't have a hat on, you're the nicest thing to me that ever happened on God's green earth. Now stop bothering us. Can't you see we're busy?" And he swung back to his root.

Mother's face was a deep pink. She pulled the bow out and the hat from her head. She held it swinging from her hand by the sash ends. Her hair was mussed and she was really mad.

"Humph," she said. "This is a funny kind of resting you're doing today."

Father set the axe head on the ground and leaned on the handle. "Maybe it seems funny to you, Marian. But this is the best resting I've had for about as long as I can remember."

"Humph," said mother again. "You'll have to quit your resting for a while anyhow and do what I suppose you'll call work. Dinner's hot on the stove and waiting to be served."

She flounced around and went straight back to the house. We all tagged her in and to an uncomfortable meal. Mother always believed you should be decent and polite at mealtime, particularly with company. She was polite enough now. She was being special sweet, talking enough for the whole table of us without once saying a word about her hat lying where she had thrown it on the chair by the stove. The trouble was that she was too polite. She was trying too hard to be sweet.

As far as you could tell, though, the two men were not worried by her at all. They listened absently to her talk, chiming in when she asked them direct questions, but otherwise keeping quiet. Their minds were on that old stump and whatever it was that old stump had come to mean to them and they were in a hurry to get at it again.

After they had gone out and I had been helping mother with the dishes awhile, she began humming low under her breath and I knew she was not mad any more. She was too curious and puzzled to have room for anything else.

"What went on out there, Bob?" she asked me. "What got into those two?"

I did not rightly know. All I could do was try to tell her about Ledyard and how our visitor had called him on the cultivator. I must have used the wrong words, because, when I told her about Ledyard talking mean and the way Shane acted, she got all flushed and excited.

"What do you say, Bob? You were afraid of him? He frightened you? Your father would never let him do that."

"I wasn't frightened of him," I said, struggling

to make her see the difference. "I was — well, I was just frightened. I was scared of whatever it was that might happen."

She reached out and rumpled my hair. "I think I understand," she said softly. "He's made me feel a little that way too." She went to the window and stared toward the barn. The steady rhythm of double blows, so together they sounded almost as one, was faint yet clear in the kitchen. "I hope Joe knows what he's doing," she murmured to herself. Then she turned to me. "Skip along out, Bob. I'll finish myself."

It was no fun watching them now. They had eased down to a slow, dogged pace. Father sent me once for the hone, so they could sharpen the blades, and again for a spade so he could clear the dirt away from the lowest roots, and I realized he might keep me running as long as I was handy. I slipped off by myself to see how mother's garden was doing after the rain and maybe add to the population in the box of worms I was collecting for when I would go fishing with the boys in town.

I took my time about it. I played pretty far afield. But no matter where I went, always I could hear that chopping in the distance. You could not help beginning to feel tired just to hear it, to think how they were working and staying at it.

Along the middle of the afternoon, I wandered into the barn. There was mother by the rear stall, up on a box peering through the little window above it. She hopped down as soon as she heard me and put a finger to her lips.

"I declare," she whispered. "In some ways those two aren't even as old as you are, Bob. Just the same — " She frowned at me in such a funny, confiding manner that I felt all warm inside. "Don't you dare tell them I said so. But there's something splendid in the battle they're giving that old monster." She went past me and toward the house with such a brisk air that I followed to see what she was going to do.

She whisked about the kitchen and in almost no time at all she had a pan of biscuits in the oven. While they were baking, she took her hat and carefully sewed the old ribbon into its old place. "Humph," she said, more to herself than to me. "You'd think I'd learn. This isn't Dodge City. This isn't even a whistle stop. It's Joe Starrett's farm. It's where I'm proud to be."

Out came the biscuits. She piled as many as

she could on a plate, popping one of the leftovers into her mouth and giving me the rest. She picked up the plate and marched with it out behind the barn. She stepped over the cut roots and set the plate on a fairly smooth spot on top of the stump. She looked at the two men, first one and then the other. "You're a pair of fools," she said. "But there's no law against me being a fool too." Without looking at either of them again, she marched away, her head high, back toward the house.

The two of them stared after her till she was out of sight. They turned to stare at the biscuits. Father gave a deep sigh, so deep it seemed to come all the way from his heavy work shoes. There was nothing sad or sorrowful about it. There was just something in him too big to be held tight in comfort. He let his axe fall to the ground. He leaned forward and separated the biscuits into two piles beside the plate, counting them even. One was left on the plate. He set this by itself on the stump. He took up his axe and reached it out and let it drop gently on the lone biscuit exactly in the middle. He rested the axe against the stump and took the two halves of the biscuit and put one on each pile.

He did not say a word to Shane. He pitched

into one pile and Shane did into the other, and
the two of them faced each other over the last uncut roots, munching at those biscuits as if eating
them was the most serious business they had ever
done.

Father finished his pile and dabbled his fingers
on the plate for the last crumbs. He straightened
and stretched his arms high and wide. He seemed
to stretch and stretch until he was a tremendous
tower of strength reaching up into the late afternoon sun. He swooped suddenly to grab the plate
and toss it to me. Still in the same movement he
seized his axe and swung it in a great arc into the
root he was working on. Quick as he was, Shane
was right with him, and together they were talking again to that old stump.

I took the plate in to mother. She was peeling
apples in the kitchen, humming gaily to herself.
"The woodbox, Bob," she said, and went on humming. I carried in stove-lengths till the box would
not hold any more. Then I slipped out before she
might think of more chores.

I tried to keep myself busy down by the river
skipping flat stones across the current all muddy
still from the rain. I was able to for a while. But

that steady chopping had a peculiar fascination. It was always pulling me toward the barn. I simply could not grasp how they could stick at it hour after hour. It made no sense to me, why they should work so when routing out that old stump was not really so important. I was wavering in front of the barn, when I noticed that the chopping was different. Only one axe was working.

I hurried around back. Shane was still swinging, cutting into the last root. Father was using the spade, was digging under one side of the stump, bringing the dirt out between the cut roots. As I watched, he laid the spade aside and put his shoulder to the stump. He heaved against it. Sweat started to pour down his face. There was a little sucking sound and the stump moved ever so slightly.

That did it. Of a sudden I was so excited that I could hear my own blood pounding past my eardrums. I wanted to dash to that stump and push it and feel it move. Only I knew father would think I was in the way.

Shane finished the root and came to help him. Together they heaved against the stump. It angled up nearly a whole inch. You could begin to see an open space in the dirt where it was ripping loose. But as soon as they released the pressure, it fell back.

Again and again they heaved at it. Each time it would angle up a bit farther. Each time it would fall back. They had it up once about a foot and a half, and that was the limit. They could not get past it.

They stopped, breathing hard, mighty streaked now from the sweat rivulets down their faces. Father peered underneath as best he could. "Must be a taproot," he said. That was the one time either of them had spoken to the other, as far as I knew, the whole afternoon through. Father did not say anything more. And Shane said nothing. He just picked up his axe and looked at father and waited.

Father began to shake his head. There was some unspoken thought between them that bothered him. He looked down at his own big hands and slowly the fingers curled until they were clenched into big fists. Then his head stopped shaking and he stood taller and he drew a deep breath. He turned and backed in between two cut root ends, pressing against the stump. He pushed his feet into the ground for firm footholds. He bent his knees and slid his shoulders down the stump and wrapped his big hands around the root ends. Slowly he began to straighten. Slowly that huge old stump began to rise. Up it came, inch by inch, until the side was all the way up to the limit they had reached before.

Shane stooped to peer under. He poked his axe into the opening and I heard it strike wood. But the only way he could get in position to swing the axe into the opening was to drop on his right knee and extend his left leg and thigh into the opening and lean his weight on them. Then he could bring the axe sweeping in at a low angle close to the ground.

He flashed one quick glance at father beside and behind him, eyes closed, muscles locked in that great sustained effort, and he dropped into position with the whole terrible weight of the stump poised above nearly half of his body and sent the axe sweeping under in swift powerful strokes.

Suddenly father seemed to slip. Only he had not slipped. He had straightened even further. The stump had leaped up a few more inches. Shane jumped out and up and tossed his axe aside. He grabbed one of the root ends and helped father ease the stump down. They both were blowing like they had run a long way. But they would not stay more than a minute before they were heaving again at the stump. It came up more easily now and the dirt was tearing loose all around it.

I ran to the house fast as I could. I dashed into the kitchen and took hold of mother's hand. "Hurry!" I yelled. "You've got to come!" She did not seem to want to come at first and I pulled at her. "You've got to see it! They're getting it out!" Then she was excited as I was and was running right with me.

They had the stump way up at a high angle. They were down in the hole, one on each side of it, pushing up and forward with hands flat on the under part reared before them higher than their heads. You would have thought the stump was ready to topple over clear of its ancient foundation. But there it stuck. They could not quite push it the final inches.

Mother watched them battling with it. "Joe," she called, "why don't you use some sense? Hitch up the team. Horses will have it out in no time at all."

Father braced himself to hold the stump still.

He turned his head to look at her. "Horses!" he shouted. All the pent silence of the two of them that long afternoon through was being shattered in the one wonderful shout. "Horses! Great jumping Jehosaphat! No! We started this with manpower and, by Godfrey, we'll finish it with manpower!"

He turned his head to face the stump once more and dropped it lower between his humped shoulders. Shane, opposite him, stiffened, and together they pushed in a fresh assault. The stump quivered and swayed a little — and hung fixed at its crazy high angle.

Father grunted in exasperation. You could see the strength building up in his legs and broad shoulders and big corded arms. His side of the upturned stump rocked forward and Shane's side moved back and the whole stump trembled like it would twist down and into the hole on them at a grotesque new angle.

I wanted to shout a warning. But I could not speak, for Shane had thrown his head in a quick sideways gesture to fling his hair from falling over his face and I had caught a glimpse of his eyes. They were aflame with a concentrated cold fire. Not another separate discernible movement did he make. It was all of him, the whole man, pulsing in the one incredible surge of power. You could fairly feel the fierce energy suddenly burning in him, pouring through him in the single coordinated drive. His side of the stump rocked forward even with father's and the whole mass of the stump tore loose from the last hold and toppled away to sprawl in ungainly defeat beyond them.

Father climbed slowly out of the hole. He walked to the stump and placed a hand on the rounded bole and patted it like it was an old friend and he was perhaps a little sorry for it. Shane was with him, across from him, laying a hand gently on the old hard wood. They both looked up and their eyes met and held as they had so long ago in the morning hours.

The silence should have been complete. It was not because someone was shouting, a high-pitched, wordless shout. I realized that the voice was mine and I closed my mouth. The silence was clean and wholesome, and this was one of the things you could never forget whatever time might do to you in the furrowing of the years, an old stump on its side with root ends making a strange pattern against the glow of the sun sinking behind the far mountains and two men looking over it into each other's eyes.

I thought they should join the hands so close on the bole of the stump. I thought they should at least say something to each other. They stood quiet and motionless. At last father turned and came toward mother. He was so tired that the weariness showed in his walk. But there was no weariness in his voice. "Marian," he said, "I'm rested now. I don't believe any man since the world began was ever more rested."

Shane too was coming toward us. He too spoke only to mother. "Ma'am, I've learned something today. Being a farmer has more to it than I ever thought. Now I'm about ready for some of that pie."

Mother had been watching them in a wide-eyed wonder. At his last words she let out a positive wail. "Oh-h-h — you — you — men! You made me forget about it! It's probably all burned!" And she was running for the house so fast she was tripping over her skirt.

The pie was burned all right. We could smell it when we were in front of the house and the men were scrubbing themselves at the pump-trough. Mother had the door open to let the kitchen air out. The noises from inside sounded as if she might be throwing things around. Kettles were banging and dishes were clattering. When we went in, we saw why. She had the table set and was putting supper on it and she was grabbing the things from their places and putting them down on the table with solid thumps. She would not look at one of us.

We sat down and waited for her to join us. She put her back to us and stood by the low shelf near the stove staring at her big pie tin and the burned stuff in it. Finally father spoke kind of sharply. "Lookahere, Marian. Aren't you ever going to sit down?"

She whirled and glared at him. I thought maybe she had been crying. But there were no tears on her face. It was dry and pinched-looking and there was no color in it. Her voice was sharp like father's. "I was planning to have a deep-dish apple pie. Well, I will. None of your silly man foolishness is going to stop me."

She swept up the big tin and went out the door with it. We heard her on the steps, and a few seconds later the rattle of the cover of the garbage pail. We heard her on the steps again. She came

in and went to the side bench where the dishpan
was and began to scrub the pie tin. The way she
acted, we might not have been in the room.

Father's face was getting red. He picked up his
fork to begin eating and let it drop with a little
clatter. He squirmed on his chair and kept taking
quick side looks at her. She finished scrubbing
the tin and went to the apple barrel and filled her
wooden bowl with fat round ones. She sat by the
stove and started peeling them. Father fished in
a pocket and pulled out his old jackknife. He
moved over to her, stepping softly. He reached
out for an apple to help her.

She did not look up. But her voice caught him
like she had flicked him with a whip. "Joe Starrett, don't you dare touch a one of these apples."

He was sheepish as he returned to his chair.
Then he was downright mad. He grabbed his
knife and fork and dug into the food on his plate,
taking big bites and chewing vigorously. There
was nothing for our visitor and me to do but follow his example. Maybe it was a good supper. I
could not tell. The food was only something to
put in your mouth. And when we finished, there
was nothing to do but wait because mother was
sitting by the stove, arms folded, staring at the
wall, waiting herself for her pie to bake.

We three watched her in a quiet so tight that it hurt. We could not help it. We would try to look away and always our eyes would turn back to her. She did not appear to notice us. You might have said she had forgotten we were there.

She had not forgotten because as soon as she sensed that the pie was done, she lifted it out, cut four wide pieces, and put them on plates. The first two she set in front of the two men. The third one she set down for me. The last one she laid at her own place and she sat down in her own chair at the table. Her voice was still sharp.

"I'm sorry to keep you men waiting so long. Your pie is ready now."

Father inspected his portion like he was afraid of it. He needed to make a real effort to take his fork and lift a piece. He chewed on it and swallowed and he flipped his eyes sidewise at mother and back again quickly to look across the table at Shane. "That's prime pie," he said.

Shane raised a piece on his fork. He considered it closely. He put it in his mouth and chewed on it gravely. "Yes," he said. The quizzical expression on his face was so plain you could not possibly miss it. "Yes. That's the best bit of stump I ever tasted."

What could a silly remark like that mean? I had

no time to wonder, for father and mother were acting so queer. They both stared at Shane and their mouths were sagging open. Then father snapped his shut and he chuckled and chuckled till he was swaying in his chair.

"By Godfrey, Marian, he's right. You've done it, too."

Mother stared from one to the other of them. Her pinched look faded and her cheeks were flushed and her eyes were soft and warm as they should be, and she was laughing so that the tears came. And all of us were pitching into that pie, and the one thing wrong in the whole world was that there was not enough of it.

4

THE SUN was already well up the sky when I awakened the next morning. I had been a long time getting to sleep because my mind was full of the day's excitement and shifting moods. I could not straighten out in my mind the way the grown folks had behaved, the way things that did not really matter so much had become so important to them.

I had lain in my bed thinking of our visitor out in the bunk in the barn. It scarce seemed possible that he was the same man I had first seen, stern and chilling in his dark solitude, riding up our road. Something in father, something not of words or of actions but of the essential substance of the human spirit, had reached out and spoken

to him and he had replied to it and had unlocked
a part of himself to us. He was far off and unap-
proachable at times even when he was right there
with you. Yet somehow he was closer, too, than
my uncle, mother's brother, had been when he
visited us the summer before.

I had been thinking, too, of the effect he had on
father and mother. They were more alive, more
vibrant, like they wanted to show more what they
were, when they were with him. I could appreciate that because I felt the same way myself. But
it puzzled me that a man so deep and vital in his
own being, so ready to respond to father, should
be riding a lone trail out of a closed and guarded
past.

I realized with a jolt how late it was. The door
to my little room was closed. Mother must have
closed it so I could sleep undisturbed. I was frantic that the others might have finished breakfast
and that our visitor was gone and I had missed
him. I pulled on my clothes, not even bothering
with buttons, and ran to the door.

They were still at the table. Father was fussing
with his pipe. Mother and Shane were working
on a last round of coffee. All three of them were
subdued and quiet. They stared at me as I burst
out of my room.

"My heavens," said mother. "You came in here like something was after you. What's the matter?"

"I just thought," I blurted out, nodding at our visitor, "that maybe he had ridden off and forgotten me."

Shane shook his head slightly, looking straight at me. "I wouldn't forget you, Bob." He pulled himself up a little in his chair. He turned to mother and his voice took on a bantering tone. "And I wouldn't forget your cooking, ma'am. If you begin having a special lot of people passing by at mealtimes, that'll be because a grateful man has been boasting of your flannel cakes all along the road."

"Now there's an idea," struck in father as if he was glad to find something safe to talk about. "We'll turn this place into a boarding house. Marian'll fill folks full of her meals and I'll fill my pockets full of their money. That hits me as a mighty convenient arrangement."

Mother sniffed at him. But she was pleased at their talk and she was smiling as they kept on playing with the idea while she stirred me up my breakfast. She came right back at them, threatening to take father at his word and make him spend all his time peeling potatoes and washing dishes. They were enjoying themselves even though I

could feel a bit of constraint behind the easy joshing. It was remarkable, too, how natural it was to
have this Shane sitting there and joining in almost like he was a member of the family. There
was none of the awkwardness some visitors always brought with them. You did feel you ought
to be on your good behavior with him, a mite
extra careful about your manners and your speech.
But not stiffly so. Just quiet and friendly about
it.

He stood up at last and I knew he was going to
ride away from us and I wanted desperately to
stop him. Father did it for me.

"You certainly are a man for being in a hurry.
Sit down, Shane. I've a question to ask you."

Father was suddenly very serious. Shane,
standing there, was as suddenly withdrawn into a
distant alertness. But he dropped back into his
chair.

Father looked directly at him. "Are you running away from anything?"

Shane stared at the plate in front of him for a
long moment. It seemed to me that a shade of
sadness passed over him. Then he raised his eyes
and looked directly at father.

"No. I'm not running away from anything.
Not in the way you mean."

"Good." Father stooped forward and stabbed at the table with a forefinger for emphasis. "Look, Shane. I'm not a rancher. Now you've seen my place, you know that. I'm a farmer. Something of a stockman, maybe. But really a farmer. That's what I decided to be when I quit punching cattle for another man's money. That's what I want to be and I'm proud of it. I've made a fair start. This outfit isn't as big as I hope to have it some day. But there's more work here already than one man can handle if it's to be done right. The young fellow I had ran out on me after he tangled with a couple of Fletcher's boys in town one day." Father was talking fast and he paused to draw breath.

Shane had been watching him intently. He moved his head to look out the window over the valley to the mountains marching along the horizon. "It's always the same," he murmured. He was sort of talking to himself. "The old ways die hard." He looked at mother and then at me, and as his eyes came back to father he seemed to have decided something that had been troubling him. "So Fletcher's crowding you," he said gently.

Father snorted. "I don't crowd easy. But I've got a job to do here and it's too big for one man, even for me. And none of the strays that drift up this way are worth a damn."

"Yes?" Shane said. His eyes were crinkling again, and he was one of us again and waiting.

"Will you stick here awhile and help me get things in shape for the winter?"

Shane rose to his feet. He loomed up taller across the table than I had thought him. "I never figured to be a farmer, Starrett. I would have laughed at the notion a few days ago. All the same, you've hired yourself a hand." He and father were looking at each other in a way that showed they were saying things words could never cover. Shane snapped it by swinging toward mother. "And I'll rate your cooking, ma'am, wages enough."

Father slapped his hands on his knees. "You'll get good wages and you'll earn 'em. First off, now, why don't you drop into town and get some work clothes. Try Sam Grafton's store. Tell him to put it on my bill."

Shane was already at the door. "I'll buy my own," he said, and was gone.

Father was so pleased he could not sit still. He jumped up and whirled mother around. "Marian, the sun's shining mighty bright at last. We've got ourselves a man."

"But, Joe, are you sure what you're doing? What kind of work can a man like that do? Oh, I know he stood right up to you with that stump. But that was something special. He's been used to good living and plenty of money. You can tell that. He said himself he doesn't know anything about farming."

"Neither did I when I started here. What a man knows isn't important. It's what he is that counts. I'll bet you that one was a cowpuncher when he was younger and a tophand too. Anything he does will be done right. You watch. In a week he'll be making even me hump or he'll be bossing the place."

"Perhaps."

"No perhapsing about it. Did you notice how he took it when I told him about Fletcher's boys and young Morley? That's what fetched him. He knows I'm in a spot and he's not the man to leave me there. Nobody'll push him around or scare him away. He's my kind of a man."

"Why, Joe Starrett. He isn't like you at all. He's smaller and he looks different and his clothes are different and he talks different. I know he's lived different."

"Huh?" Father was surprised. "I wasn't talking about things like that."

Shane came back with a pair of dungaree pants, a flannel shirt, stout work shoes, and a good, serviceable Stetson. He disappeared into the barn and emerged a few moments later in his new clothes, leading his horse unsaddled. At the pasture gate he slipped off the halter, turned the horse in with a hearty slap, and tossed the halter to me.

"Take care of a horse, Bob, and it will take care of you. This one now has brought me better than a thousand miles in the last few weeks." And he was striding away to join father, who was ditching the field out past the growing corn where the ground was rich but marshy and would not be worth much till it was properly drained. I watched him swinging through the rows of young corn, no longer a dark stranger but part of the place, a farmer like father and me.

Only he was not a farmer and never really could be. It was not three days before you saw that he could stay right beside father in any kind of work. Show him what needed to be done and he could do it, and like as not would figure out a better way of getting it done. He never shirked the meanest task. He was ever ready to take the hard end of any chore. Yet you always felt in some indefinable fashion that he was a man apart.

There were times when he would stop and look off at the mountains and then down at himself and any tool he happened to have in his hands as if in wry amusement at what he was doing. You had no impression that he thought himself too good for the work or did not like it. He was just different. He was shaped in some firm forging of past circumstance for other things.

For all his slim build he was plenty rugged. His slenderness could fool you at first. But when you saw him close in action, you saw that he was solid, compact, that there was no waste weight on his frame just as there was no waste effort in his smooth, flowing motion. What he lacked alongside father in size and strength, he made up in quickness of movement, in instinctive coordination of mind and muscle, and in that sudden fierce energy that had burned in him when the old stump tried to topple back on him. Mostly this last slept in him, not needed while he went easily through the day's routine. But when a call came, it could flame forward with a driving intensity that never failed to frighten me.

I would be frightened, as I had tried to explain to mother, not at Shane himself, but at the suggestion it always gave me of things in the human equation beyond my comprehension. At such times there would be a concentration in him, a singleness of dedication to the instant need, that seemed to me at once wonderful and disturbing. And then he would be again the quiet, steady man who shared with father my boy's allegiance.

I was beginning to feel my oats about then, proud of myself for being able to lick Ollie Johnson at the next place down the road. Fighting, boy style, was much in my mind.

Once, when father and I were alone, I asked him: "Could you beat Shane? In a fight, I mean."

"Son, that's a tough question. If I had to, I might do it. But, by Godfrey, I'd hate to try it. Some men just plain have dynamite inside them, and he's one. I'll tell you, though. I've never met a man I'd rather have more on my side in any kind of trouble."

I could understand that and it satisfied me. But there were things about Shane I could not understand. When he came in to the first meal after he agreed to stay on with us, he went to the chair that had always been father's and stood beside it waiting for the rest of us to take the other places. Mother was surprised and somewhat annoyed. She started to say something. Father quieted her with a warning glance. He walked to the chair across from Shane and sat down like this was the right and natural spot for him and afterwards he and Shane always used these same places.

I could not see any reason for the shift until the first time one of our homestead neighbors knocked on the door while we were eating and came straight on in as most of them usually did. Then I suddenly realized that Shane was sitting opposite the door where he could directly confront anyone coming through it. I could see that was the way he wanted it to be. But I could not understand why he wanted it that way.

In the evenings after supper when he was talking lazily with us, he would never sit by a window. Out on the porch he would always face the road. He liked to have a wall behind him and not just to lean against. No matter where he was, away from the table, before sitting down he would swing his chair into position, back to the nearest wall, not making any show, simply putting it there and bending into it in one easy motion. He did not even seem to be aware that this was unusual. It was part of his fixed alertness. He always wanted to know everything happening around him.

This alertness could be noted, too, in the watch he kept, without appearing to make any special effort, on every approach to our place. He knew first when anyone was moving along the road and he would stop whatever he was doing to study carefully any passing rider.

We often had company in the evenings, for the other homesteaders regarded father as their leader and would drop in to discuss their affairs with him. They were interesting men in their own fashions, a various assortment. But Shane was not anxious to meet people. He would share little in their talk. With us he spoke freely enough. We were, in some subtle way, his folks. Though we had taken him in, you had the feeling that he had adopted us. But with others he was reserved; courteous and soft-spoken, yet withdrawn beyond a line of his own making.

These things puzzled me and not me alone. The people in town and those who rode or drove in pretty regularly were all curious about him. It was a wonder how quickly everyone in the valley, and even on the ranches out in the open country, knew that he was working with father.

They were not sure they liked having him in their neighborhood. Ledyard had told some tall tale about what happened at our place that made them stare sharply at Shane whenever they had a chance. But they must have had their own measure of Ledyard, for they did not take his story too straight. They just could not really make up their minds about Shane and it seemed to worry them.

More than once, when I was with Ollie Johnson on the way to our favorite fishing hole the other side of town, I heard men arguing about him in front of Mr. Grafton's store. "He's like one of these here slow-burning fuses," I heard an old mule-skinner say one day. "Quiet and no sputtering. So quiet you forget it's burning. Then it sets off one hell of a blow-off of trouble when it touches powder. That's him. And there's been trouble brewing in this valley for a long spell now. Maybe it'll be good when it comes. Maybe it'll be bad. You just can't tell." And that puzzled me too.

What puzzled me most, though, was something it took me nearly two weeks to appreciate. And yet it was the most striking thing of all. Shane carried no gun.

In those days guns were as familiar all through

the Territory as boots and saddles. They were not used much in the valley except for occasional hunting. But they were always in evidence. Most men did not feel fully dressed without one.

We homesteaders went in mostly for rifles and shotguns when we had any shooting to do. A pistol slapping on the hip was a nuisance for a farmer. Still every man had his cartridge belt and holstered Colt to be worn when he was not working or loafing around the house. Father buckled his on whenever he rode off on any trip, even just into town, as much out of habit, I guess, as anything else.

But this Shane never carried a gun. And that was a peculiar thing because he had a gun.

I saw it once. I saw it when I was alone in the barn one day and I spotted his saddle-roll lying on his bunk. Usually he kept it carefully put away underneath. He must have forgotten it this time, for it was there in the open by the pillow. I reached to sort of feel it — and I felt the gun inside. No one was near, so I unfastened the straps and unrolled the blankets. There it was, the most beautiful-looking weapon I ever saw. Beautiful and deadly-looking.

The holster and filled cartridge belt were of the same soft black leather as the boots tucked under the bunk, tooled in the same intricate design. I knew enough to know that the gun was a single-action Colt, the same model as the Regular Army issue that was the favorite of all men in those days and that oldtimers used to say was the finest pistol ever made.

This was the same model. But this was no Army gun. It was black, almost due black, with the darkness not in any enamel but in the metal itself. The grip was clear on the outer curve, shaped to the fingers on the inner curve, and two ivory plates were set into it with exquisite skill, one on each side.

The smooth invitation of it tempted your grasp. I took hold and pulled the gun out of the holster. It came so easily that I could hardly believe it was there in my hand. Heavy like father's, it was somehow much easier to handle. You held it up to aiming level and it seemed to balance itself into your hand.

It was clean and polished and oiled. The empty cylinder, when I released the catch and flicked it, spun swiftly and noiselessly. I was surprised to see that the front sight was gone, the barrel smooth right down to the end, and that the hammer had been filed to a sharp point.

Why should a man do that to a gun? Why

should a man with a gun like that refuse to wear it and show it off? And then, staring at that dark and deadly efficiency, I was again suddenly chilled, and I quickly put everything back exactly as before and hurried out into the sun.

The first chance I tried to tell father about it. "Father," I said, all excited, "do you know what Shane has rolled up in his blankets?"

"Probably a gun."

"But — but how did you know? Have you seen it?"

"No. That's what he would have."

I was all mixed up. "Well, why doesn't he ever carry it? Do you suppose maybe it's because he doesn't know how to use it very well?"

Father chuckled like I had made a joke. "Son, I wouldn't be surprised if he could take that gun and shoot the buttons off your shirt with you awearing it and all you'd feel would be a breeze."

"Gosh agorry! Why does he keep it hidden in the barn then?"

"I don't know. Not exactly."

"Why don't you ask him?"

Father looked straight at me, very serious. "That's one question I'll never ask him. And don't you ever say anything to him about it. There are some things you don't ask a man. Not if you respect him. He's entitled to stake his claim to what he considers private to himself alone. But you can take my word for it, Bob, that when a man like Shane doesn't want to tote a gun you can bet your shirt, buttons and all, he's got a mighty good reason."

That was that. I was still mixed up. But whenever father gave you his word on something, there was nothing more to be said. He never did that except when he knew he was right. I started to wander off.

"Bob."

"Yes, father."

"Listen to me, son. Don't get to liking Shane too much."

"Why not? Is there anything wrong with him?"

"No-o-o-o. There's nothing wrong about Shane. Nothing you could put that way. There's more right about him than most any man you're ever likely to meet. But — " Father was throwing around for what to say. "But he's fiddle-footed. Remember. He said so himself. He'll be moving on one of these days and then you'll be all upset if you get to liking him too much."

That was not what father really meant. But that was what he wanted me to think. So I did not ask any more questions.

5

THE WEEKS went rocking past, and soon it did not seem possible that there ever had been a time when Shane was not with us. He and father worked together more like partners than boss and hired man. The amount they could get through in a day was a marvel. The ditching father had reckoned would take him most of the summer was done in less than a month. The loft was finished and the first cutting of alfalfa stowed away.

We would have enough fodder to carry a few more young steers through the winter for fattening next summer, so father rode out of the valley and all the way to the ranch where he worked once and came back herding a half-dozen more. He was gone two days. He came back to find that Shane, while he was gone, had knocked out the end of the corral and posted a new section making it half again as big.

"Now we can really get going next year," Shane said as father sat on his horse staring at the corral like he could not quite believe what he saw. "We ought to get enough hay off that new field to help us carry forty head."

"Oho!" said father. "So we can get going. And we ought to get enough hay." He was pleased as could be because he was scowling at Shane the way he did at me when he was tickled silly over something I had done and did not want to let on that he was. He jumped off his horse and hurried up to the house where mother was standing on the porch.

"Marian," he demanded right off, waving at the corral, "whose idea was that?"

"Well-l-l," she said, "Shane suggested it." Then she added slyly, "But I told him to go ahead."

"That's right." Shane had come up beside him. "She rode me like she had spurs to get it done by today. Kind of a present. It's your wedding anniversary."

"Well, I'll be damned," said father. "So it is."
He stared foolishly at one and then the other of
them. With Shane there watching, he hopped
on the porch and gave mother a kiss. I was embarrassed for him and I turned away — and
hopped about a foot myself.

"Hey! Those steers are running away!"

The grown folks had forgotten about them.
All six were wandering up the road, straggling
and separating. Shane, that soft-spoken man, let
out a whoop you might have heard halfway to
town and ran to father's horse, putting his hands
on the saddle and vaulting into it. He fairly
lifted the horse into a gallop in one leap and that
old cowpony of father's lit out after those steers
like this was fun. By the time father reached the
corral gate, Shane had the runaways in a compact
bunch and padding back at a trot. He dropped
them through the gateway neat as pie.

He was tall and straight in the saddle the few
seconds it took father to close the gate. He and
the horse were blowing a bit and both of them
were perky and proud.

"It's been ten years," he said, "since I did anything like that."

Father grinned at him. "Shane, if I didn't

know better, I'd say you were a faker. There's still a lot of kid in you."

The first real smile I had seen yet flashed across Shane's face. "Maybe. Maybe there is at that."

I think that was the happiest summer of my life.

The only shadow over our valley, the recurrent trouble between Fletcher and us homesteaders, seemed to have faded away. Fletcher himself was gone most of those months. He had gone to Fort Bennett in Dakota and even on East to Washington, so we heard, trying to get a contract to supply beef to the Indian agent at Standing Rock, the big Sioux reservation over beyond the Black Hills. Except for his foreman, Morgan, and several surly older men, his hands were young, easygoing cowboys who made a lot of noise in town once in a while but rarely did any harm and even then only in high spirits. We liked them — when Fletcher was not there driving them into harassing us in constant shrewd ways. Now, with him away, they kept to the other side of the river and did not bother us. Sometimes, riding in sight on the other bank, they might even wave to us in their rollicking fashion.

Until Shane came, they had been my heroes. Father, of course, was special all to himself. There could never be anyone quite to match him. I wanted to be like him, just as he was. But first I wanted, as he had done, to ride the range, to have my own string of ponies and take part in an all-brand round-up and in a big cattle drive and dash into strange towns with just such a rollicking crew and with a season's pay jingling in my pockets.

Now I was not so sure. I wanted more and more to be like Shane, like the man I imagined he was in the past fenced off so securely. I had to imagine most of it. He would never speak of it, not in any way at all. Even his name remained mysterious. Just Shane. Nothing else. We never knew whether that was his first name or last name or, indeed, any name that came from his family. "Call me Shane," he said, and that was all he ever said. But I conjured up all manner of adventures for him, not tied to any particular time or place, seeing him as a slim and dark and dashing figure coolly passing through perils that would over-come a lesser man.

I would listen in what was closely akin to wor-ship while my two men, father and Shane, argued

long and amiably about the cattle business. They
would wrangle over methods of feeding and
bringing steers up to top weight. But they were
agreed that controlled breeding was better than
open range running and that improvement of
stock was needed even if that meant spending big
money on imported bulls. And they would speculate about the chances of a railroad spur ever
reaching the valley, so you could ship direct without thinning good meat off your cattle driving
them to market.

It was plain that Shane was beginning to enjoy
living with us and working the place. Little by
little the tension in him was fading out. He was
still alert and watchful, instinct with that unfail-
ing awareness of everything about him. I came to
realize that this was inherent in him, not learned
or acquired, simply a part of his natural being.
But the sharp extra edge of conscious alertness,
almost of expectancy of some unknown trouble
always waiting, was wearing away.

Yet why was he sometimes so strange and
stricken in his own secret bitterness? Like the
time I was playing with a gun Mr. Grafton gave
me, an old frontier model Colt with a cracked
barrel someone had turned in at the store.

I had rigged a holster out of a torn chunk of oilcloth and a belt of rope. I was stalking around near the barn, whirling every few steps to pick off a skulking Indian, when I saw Shane watching me from the barn door. I stopped short, thinking of that beautiful gun under his bunk and afraid he would make fun of me and my sorry old broken pistol. Instead he looked gravely at me.

"How many you knocked over so far, Bob?"

Could I ever repay the man? My gun was a shining new weapon, my hand steady as a rock as I drew a bead on another one.

"That makes seven."

"Indians or timber wolves?"

"Indians. Big ones."

"Better leave a few for the other scouts," he said gently. "It wouldn't do to make them jealous. And look here, Bob. You're not doing that quite right."

He sat down on an upturned crate and beckoned me over. "Your holster's too low. Don't let it drag full arm's length. Have it just below the hip, so the grip is about halfway between your wrist and elbow when the arm's hanging limp. You can take the gun then as your hand's coming up and there's still room to clear the holster without having to lift the gun too high."

"Gosh agorry! Is that the way the real gunfighters do?"

A queer light flickered in his eyes and was gone. "No. Not all of them. Most have their own tricks. One likes a shoulder holster; another packs his gun in his pants belt. Some carry two guns, but that's a show-off stunt and a waste of weight. One's enough, if you know how to use it. I've even seen a man have a tight holster with an open end and fastened on a little swivel to the belt. He didn't have to pull the gun then. Just swung up the barrel and blazed away from the hip. That's mighty fast for close work and a big target. But it's not certain past ten or fifteen paces and no good at all for putting your shot right where you want it. The way I'm telling you is as good as any and better than most. And another thing — "

He reached and took the gun. Suddenly, as for the first time, I was aware of his hands. They were broad and strong, but not heavy and fleshy like father's. The fingers were long and square on the ends. It was funny how, touching the gun, the hands seemed to have an intelligence all their own, a sure movement that needed no guidance of thought.

His right hand closed around the grip and you knew at once it was doing what it had been created for. He hefted the old gun, letting it lie loosely in the hand. Then the fingers tightened and the thumb toyed with the hammer, testing the play of it.

While I gaped at him, he tossed it swiftly in the air and caught it in his left hand and in the instant of catching, it nestled snugly into this hand too. He tossed it again, high this time and spinning end over end, and as it came down, his right hand flicked forward and took it. The forefinger slipped through the trigger guard and the gun spun, coming up into firing position in the one unbroken motion. With him that old pistol seemed alive, not an inanimate and rusting metal object, but an extension of the man himself.

"If it's speed you're after, Bob, don't split the move into parts. Don't pull, cock, aim, and fire. Slip back the hammer as you bring the gun up and squeeze the trigger the second it's up level."

"How do you aim it, then? How do you get a sight on it?"

"No need to. Learn to hold it so the barrel's

right in line with the fingers if they were out straight. You won't have to waste time bringing it high to take a sight. Just point it, low and quick and easy, like pointing a finger."

Like pointing a finger. As the words came, he was doing it. The old gun was bearing on some target over by the corral and the hammer was clicking at the empty cylinder. Then the hand around the gun whitened and the fingers slowly opened and the gun fell to the ground. The hand sank to his side, stiff and awkward. He raised his head and the mouth was a bitter gash in his face. His eyes were fastened on the mountains climbing in the distance.

"Shane! Shane! What's the matter?"

He did not hear me. He was back somewhere along the dark trail of the past.

He took a deep breath, and I could see the effort run through him as he dragged himself into the present and a realization of a boy staring at him. He beckoned to me to pick up the gun. When I did, he leaned forward and spoke earnestly.

"Listen, Bob. A gun is just a tool. No better and no worse than any other tool, a shovel — or an axe or a saddle or a stove or anything. Think of it always that way. A gun is as good — and as bad — as the man who carries it. Remember that."

He stood up and strode off into the fields and I knew he wanted to be alone. I remembered what he said all right, tucked away unforgettably in my mind. But in those days I remembered more the way he handled the gun and the advice he gave me about using it. I would practice with it and think of the time when I could have one that would really shoot.

And then the summer was over. School began again and the days were growing shorter and the first cutting edge of cold was creeping down from the mountains.

6

MORE THAN THE SUMMER was over. The season of friendship in our valley was fading with the sun's warmth. Fletcher was back and he had his contract. He was talking in town that he would need the whole range again. The homesteaders would have to go.

He was a reasonable man, he was saying in his smooth way, and he would pay a fair price for any improvements they had put in. But we knew what Luke Fletcher would call a fair price. And we had no intention of leaving. The land was ours by right of settlement, guaranteed by the government. Only we knew, too, how faraway the government was from our valley way up there in the Territory.

The nearest marshal was a good hundred miles away. We did not even have a sheriff in our town.

There never had been any reason for one. When folks had any lawing to do, they would head for Sheridan, nearly a full day's ride away. Our town was small, not even organized as a town. It was growing, but it was still not much more than a roadside settlement.

The first people there were three or four miners who had come prospecting after the blow-up of the Big Horn Mining Association about twenty years before, and had found gold traces leading to a moderate vein in the jutting rocks that partially closed off the valley where it edged into the plain. You could not have called it a strike, for others that followed were soon disappointed. Those first few, however, had done fairly well and had brought in their families and a number of helpers.

Then a stage and freighting line had picked the site for a relay post. That meant a place where you could get drinks as well as horses, and before long the cowboys from the ranches out on the plain and Fletcher's spread in the valley were drifting in of an evening. With us homesteaders coming now, one or two more almost every season, the town was taking shape. Already there were several stores, a harness and blacksmith shop, and nearly a dozen houses. Just the year be-

fore, the men had put together a one-room school-
house.

Sam Grafton's place was the biggest. He had a
general store with several rooms for living quarters back of it in one half of his rambling building, a saloon with a long bar and tables for cards
and the like in the other half. Upstairs he had
some rooms he rented to stray drummers or anyone else stranded overnight. He acted as our post-
master, an elderly man, a close bargainer but
honest in all his dealings. Sometimes he served as
a sort of magistrate in minor disputes. His wife
was dead. His daughter Jane kept house for him
and was our schoolteacher when school was in
session.

Even if we had had a sheriff, he would have
been Fletcher's man. Fletcher was the power in
the valley in those days. We homesteaders had
been around only a few years and the other
people still thought of us as there by his suffer-
ance. He had been running cattle through the
whole valley at the time the miners arrived,
having bought or bulldozed out the few small
ranchers there ahead of him. A series of bad
years working up to the dry summer and terrible
winter of '86 had cut his herds about the time the
first of the homesteaders moved in and he had not

objected too much. But now there were seven of
of us in all and the number rising each year.

It was a certain thing, father used to say, that
the town would grow and swing our way. Mr.
Grafton knew that too, I guess, but he was a careful man who never let thoughts about the future
interfere with present business. The others were
the kind to veer with the prevailing wind.
Fletcher was the big man in the valley, so they
looked up to him and tolerated us. Led to it, they
probably would have helped him run us out.
With him out of the way, they would just as will-
ingly accept us. And Fletcher was back, with a
contract in his pocket, wanting his full range
again.

There was a hurried counsel in our house soon
as the news was around. Our neighbor toward
town, Lew Johnson, who heard it in Grafton's
store, spread the word and arrived first. He was
followed by Henry Shipstead, who had the place
next to him, the closest to town. These two had
been the original homesteaders, staking out their
hundred and eighties two years before the
drought and riding out Fletcher's annoyance
until the cut in his herds gave him other worries.

They were solid, dependable men, old-line farmers who had come West from Iowa.

You could not say quite as much for the rest, straggling in at intervals. James Lewis and Ed Howells were two middle-aged cowhands who had grown dissatisfied and tagged father into the valley, coming pretty much on his example. Lacking his energy and drive, they had not done too well and could be easily discouraged.

Frank Torrey from farther up the valley was a nervous, fidgety man with a querulous wife and a string of dirty kids growing longer every year. He was always talking about pulling up stakes and heading for California. But he had a stubborn streak in him, and he was always saying, too, that he'd be damned if he'd make tracks just because some big-hatted rancher wanted him to.

Ernie Wright, who had the last stand up the valley butting out into the range still used by Fletcher, was probably the weakest of the lot. Not in any physical way. He was a husky, likable man, so dark-complected that there were rumors he was part Indian. He was always singing and telling tall stories. But he would be off hunting when he should be working and he had a quick temper that would trap him into doing fool things without taking thought.

He was as serious as the rest of them that night. Mr. Grafton had said that this time Fletcher meant business. His contract called for all the beef he could drive in the next five years and he was determined to push the chance to the limit.

"But what can he do?" asked Frank Torrey. "The land's ours as long as we live on it and we get title in three years. Some of you fellows have already proved up."

"He won't really make trouble," chimed in James Lewis. "Fletcher's never been the shooting kind. He's a good talker, but talk can't hurt us." Several of the others nodded. Johnson and Shipstead did not seem to be so sure. Father had not said anything yet and they all looked at him.

"Jim's right," he admitted. "Fletcher hasn't ever let his boys get careless thataway. Not yet anyhow. That ain't saying he wouldn't, if there wasn't any other way. There's a hard streak in him. But he won't get real tough for a while. I don't figure he'll start moving cattle in now till spring. My guess is he'll try putting pressure on us this fall and winter, see if he can wear us down. He'll probably start right here. He doesn't like any of us. But he doesn't like me most."

"That's true." Ed Howells was expressing the

unspoken verdict that father was their leader. "How do you figure he'll go about it?"

"My guess on that," father said — drawling now and smiling a grim little smile like he knew he was holding a good hole card in a tight game — "my guess on that is that he'll begin by trying to convince Shane here that it isn't healthy to be working with me."

"You mean the way he — " began Ernie Wright.

"Yes." Father cut him short. "I mean the way he did with young Morley."

I was peeping around the door of my little room. I saw Shane sitting off to one side, listening quietly as he had been right along. He did not seem the least bit surprised. He did not seem the least bit interested in finding out what had happened to young Morley. I knew what had. I had seen Morley come back from town, bruised and a beaten man, and gather his things and curse father for hiring him and ride away without once looking back.

Yet Shane sat there quietly as if what had happened to Morley had nothing to do with him. He simply did not care what it was. And then I understood why. It was because he was not Morley. He was Shane.

Father was right. In some strange fashion the feeling was abroad that Shane was a marked man. Attention was on him as a sort of symbol. By taking him on father had accepted in a way a challenge from the big ranch across the river. What had happened to Morley had been a warning and father had deliberately answered it. The long unpleasantness was sharpened now after the summer lull. The issue in our valley was plain and would in time have to be pushed to a showdown. If Shane could be driven out, there would be a break in the homestead ranks, a defeat going beyond the loss of a man into the realm of prestige and morale. It could be the crack in the dam that weakens the whole structure and finally lets through the flood.

The people in town were more curious than ever, not now so much about Shane's past as about what he might do if Fletcher tried any move against him. They would stop me and ask me questions when I was hurrying to and from school. I knew that father would not want me to say anything and I pretended that I did not know what they were talking about. But I used to watch Shane closely myself and wonder how all the slow-climbing tenseness in our valley could be so focused on one man and he seem to be so in-different to it.

For of course he was aware of it. He never missed anything. Yet he went about his work as usual, smiling frequently now at me, bantering mother at mealtimes in his courteous manner, arguing amiably as before with father on plans for next year. The only thing that was different was that there appeared to be a lot of new activity across the river. It was surprising how often Fletcher's cowboys were finding jobs to do within view of our place.

Then one afternoon, when we were stowing away the second and last cutting of hay, one fork of the big tongs we were using to haul it up to the loft broke loose. "Have to get it welded in town," father said in disgust and began to hitch up the team.

Shane stared over the river where a cowboy was riding lazily back and forth by a bunch of cattle. "I'll take it in," he said.

Father looked at Shane and he looked across the way and he grinned. "All right. It's as good a time as any." He slapped down the final buckle and started for the house. "Just a minute and I'll be ready."

"Take it easy, Joe." Shane's voice was gentle,

but it stopped father in his tracks. "I said I'll take it in."

Father whirled to face him. "Damn it all, man. Do you think I'd let you go alone? Suppose they —" He bit down on his own words. He wiped a hand slowly across his face and he said what I had never heard him say to any man. "I'm sorry," he said. "I should have known better." He stood there silently watching as Shane gathered up the reins and jumped to the wagon seat.

I was afraid father would stop me, so I waited till Shane was driving out of the lane. I ducked behind the barn, around the end of the corral, and hopped into the wagon going past. As I did, I saw the cowboy across the river spin his horse and ride rapidly off in the direction of the ranch-house.

Shane saw it, too, and it seemed to give him a grim amusement. He reached backwards and hauled me over the seat and sat me beside him.

"You Starretts like to mix into things." For a moment I thought he might send me back. Instead he grinned at me. "I'll buy you a jackknife when we hit town."

He did, a dandy big one with two blades and a corkscrew. After we left the tongs with the black-smith and found the welding would take nearly

an hour, I squatted on the steps on the long porch
across the front of Grafton's building, busy whit-
tling, while Shane stepped into the saloon side
and ordered a drink. Will Atkey, Grafton's thin,
sad-faced clerk and bartender, was behind the bar
and several other men were loafing at one of the
tables.

It was only a few moments before two cowboys
came galloping down the road. They slowed to a
walk about fifty yards off and with a show of non-
chalance ambled the rest of the way to Grafton's,
dismounting and looping their reins over the rail
in front. One of them I had seen often, a young
fellow everyone called Chris, who had worked
with Fletcher several years and was known for a
gay manner and reckless courage. The other was
new to me, a sallow, pinch-cheek man, not much
older, who looked like he had crowded a lot of
hard living into his years. He must have been
one of the new hands Fletcher had been bringing
into the valley since he got his contract.

They paid no attention to me. They stepped
softly up on the porch and to the window of the
saloon part of the building. As they peered
through, Chris nodded and jerked his head
toward the inside. The new man stiffened. He
leaned closer for a better look. Abruptly he

turned clear about and came right down past me and went over to his horse.

Chris was startled and hurried after him. They were both so intent they did not realize I was there. The new man was lifting the reins back over his horse's head when Chris caught his arm.

"What the hell?"

"I'm leaving."

"Huh? I don't get it."

"I'm leaving. Now. For good."

"Hey, listen. Do you know that guy?"

"I didn't say that. There ain't nobody can claim I said that. I'm leaving, that's all. You can tell Fletcher. This is a hell of a country up here anyhow."

Chris was getting mad. "I might have known," he said. "Scared, eh. Yellow."

Color rushed into the new man's sallow face. But he climbed on his horse and swung out from the rail. "You can call it that," he said flatly and started down the road, out of town, out of the valley.

Chris was standing still by the rail, shaking his head in wonderment. "Hell," he said to himself, "I'll brace him myself." He stalked up on the porch, into the saloon.

I dashed into the store side, over to the opening between the two big rooms. I crouched on a box just inside the store where I could hear everything and see most of the other room. It was long and fairly wide. The bar curved out from the opening and ran all the way along the inner wall to the back wall, which closed off a room Grafton used as an office. There was a row of windows on the far side, too high for anyone to look in from outside. A small stairway behind them led up to a balcony-like across the back with doors opening into several little rooms.

Shane was leaning easily with one arm on the bar, his drink in his other hand, when Chris came to perhaps six feet away and called for a whiskey bottle and a glass. Chris pretended he did not notice Shane at first and bobbed his head in greeting to the men at the table. They were a pair of mule-skinners who made regular trips into the valley freighting in goods for Grafton and the other shops. I could have sworn that Shane, studying Chris in his effortless way, was somehow disappointed.

Chris waited until he had his whiskey and had gulped a stiff shot. Then he deliberately looked Shane over like he had just spotted him.

"Hello, farmer," he said. He said it as if he did not like farmers.

Shane regarded him with grave attention. "Speaking to me?" he asked mildly and finished his drink.

"Hell, there ain't nobody else standing there. Here, have a drink of this." Chris shoved his bottle along the bar. Shane poured himself a generous slug and raised it to his lips.

"I'll be damned," flipped Chris. "So you drink whiskey."

Shane tossed off the rest in his glass and set it down. "I've had better," he said, as friendly as could be. "But this will do."

Chris slapped his leather chaps with a loud smack. He turned to take in the other men. "Did you hear that? This farmer drinks whiskey! I didn't think these plow-pushing dirt-grubbers drank anything stronger than soda pop!"

"Some of us do," said Shane, friendly as before. Then he was no longer friendly and his voice was like winter frost. "You've had your fun and it's mighty young fun. Now run home and tell Fletcher to send a grown-up man next time." He turned away and sang out to Will Atkey. "Do you have any soda pop? I'd like a bottle."

Will hesitated, looked kind of funny, and

scuttled past me into the store room. He came back right away with a bottle of the pop Grafton kept there for us school kids. Chris was standing quiet, not so much mad, I would have said, as puzzled. It was as though they were playing some queer game and he was not sure of the next move. He sucked on his lower lip for a while. Then he snapped his mouth and began to look elaborately around the room, sniffing loudly.

"Hey, Will!" he called. "What's been happening in here? It smells. That ain't no clean cattleman smell. That's plain dirty barnyard." He stared at Shane. "You, farmer. What are you and Starrett raising out there? Pigs?"

Shane was just taking hold of the bottle Will had fetched him. His hand closed on it and the knuckles showed white. He moved slowly, almost unwillingly, to face Chris. Every line of his body was as taut as stretched whipcord, was alive and somehow rich with an immense eagerness. There was that fierce concentration in him, filling him, blazing in his eyes. In that moment there was nothing in the room for him but that mocking man only a few feet away.

The big room was so quiet the stillness fairly hurt. Chris stepped back involuntarily, one pace, two, then pulled up erect. And still nothing happened. The lean muscles along the sides of Shane's jaw were ridged like rock.

Then the breath, pent in him, broke the stillness with a soft sound as it left his lungs. He looked away from Chris, past him, over the tops of the swinging doors beyond, over the roof of the shed across the road, on into the distance where the mountains loomed in their own unending loneliness. Quietly he walked, the bottle forgotten in his hand, so close by Chris as almost to brush him yet apparently not even seeing him, through the doors and was gone.

I heard a sigh of relief near me. Mr. Grafton had come up from somewhere behind me. He was watching Chris with a strange, ironic quirk at his mouth corners. Chris was trying not to look pleased with himself. But he swaggered as he went to the doors and peered over them.

"You saw it, Will," he called over his shoulder. "He walked out on me." Chris pushed up his hat and rolled back on his heels and laughed. "With a bottle of soda pop too!" He was still laughing as he went out and we heard him ride away.

"That boy's a fool," Mr. Grafton muttered.

Will Atkey came sidling over to Mr. Grafton.

"I never pegged Shane for a play like that," he said.

"He was afraid, Will."

"Yeah. That's what was so funny. I would've guessed he could take Chris."

Mr. Grafton looked at Will as he did often, like he was a little sorry for him. "No, Will. He wasn't afraid of Chris. He was afraid of himself." Mr. Grafton was thoughtful and perhaps sad too. "There's trouble ahead, Will. The worst trouble we've ever had."

He noticed me, realizing my presence. "Better skip along, Bob, and find your friend. Do you think he got that bottle for himself?"

True enough, Shane had it waiting for me at the blacksmith shop. Cherry pop, the kind I favored most. But I could not enjoy it much. Shane was so silent and stern. He had slipped back into the dark mood that was on him when he first came riding up our road. I did not dare say anything. Only once did he speak to me and I knew he did not expect me to understand or to answer.

"Why should a man be smashed because he has courage and does what he's told? Life's a dirty business, Bob. I could like that boy." And he

turned inward again to his own thoughts and
stayed the same until we had loaded the tongs in
the wagon and were well started home. Then
the closer we came, the more cheerful he was. By
the time we swung in toward the barn, he was the
way I wanted him again, crinkling his eyes at me
and gravely joshing me about the Indians I would
scalp with my new knife.

Father popped out the barn door so quick you
could tell he had been itching for us to return.
He was busting with curiosity, but he would not
come straight out with a question to Shane. He
tackled me instead.

"See any of your cowboy heroes in town?"

Shane cut in ahead of me. "One of Fletcher's
crew chased us in to pay his respects."

"No," I said, proud of my information. "There
was two of them."

"Two?" Shane said it. Father was the one who
was not surprised. "What did the other one do?"

"He went up on the porch and looked in the
window where you were and came right back
down and rode off."

"Back to the ranch?"

"The other way. He said he was leaving for
good."

Father and Shane looked at each other. Father

was smiling. "One down and you didn't even know it. What did you do to the other?"

"Nothing. He passed a few remarks about farmers. I went back to the blacksmith shop."

Father repeated it, spacing the words like there might be meanings between them. "You — went — back — to — the — blacksmith — shop."

I was worried that he must be thinking what Will Atkey did. Then I knew nothing like that had even entered his head. He switched to me. "Who was it?"

"It was Chris."

Father was smiling again. He had not been there but he had the whole thing clear. "Fletcher was right to send two. Young ones like Chris need to hunt in pairs or they might get hurt." He chuckled in a sort of wry amusement. "Chris must have been considerable surprised when the other fellow skipped. And more when you walked out. It was too bad the other one didn't stick around."

"Yes," Shane said, "it was."

The way he said it sobered father. "I hadn't thought of that. Chris is just cocky enough to take it wrong. That can make things plenty unpleasant."

"Yes," Shane said again, "it can."

7

IT WAS JUST as father and Shane had said. The story Chris told was common knowledge all through the valley before the sun set the next day and the story grew in the telling. Fletcher had an advantage now and he was quick to push it. He and his foreman, Morgan, a broad slab of a man with flattened face and head small in proportion to great sloping shoulders, were shrewd at things like this and they kept their men primed to rowel us homesteaders at every chance.

They took to using the upper ford, up above Ernie Wright's stand, and riding down the road past our places every time they had an excuse for going to town. They would go by slowly, looking everything over with insolent interest and passing remarks for our benefit.

The same week, maybe three days later, a covey of them came riding by while father was putting a new hinge on the corral gate. They acted like they were too busy staring over our land to see him there close.

"Wonder where Starrett keeps the critters," said one of them. "I don't see a pig in sight."

"But I can smell 'em!" shouted another one. With that they all began to laugh and whoop and holler and went tearing off, kicking up a lot of dust and leaving father with a tightness around his mouth that was not there before.

They were impartial with attentions like that. They would hand them out anywhere along the line an opportunity offered. But they liked best to catch father within earshot and burn him with their sarcasm.

It was crude. It was coarse. I thought it silly for grown men to act that way. But it was effective. Shane, as self-sufficient as the mountains, could ignore it. Father, while it galled him, could keep it from getting him. The other homesteaders, though, could not help being irritated and showing they felt insulted. It roughed their nerves and made them angry and restless. They did not know Shane as father and I did. They

were not sure there might not be some truth in
the big talk Chris was making.

Things became so bad they could not go into
Grafton's store without someone singing out for
soda pop. And wherever they went, the conversation near by always snuck around somehow to
pigs. You could sense the contempt building up
in town, in people who used to be neutral, not
taking sides.

The effect showed, too, in the attitude our
neighbors now had toward Shane. They were constrained when they called to see father and Shane
was there. They resented that he was linked to
them. And as a result their opinion of father
was changing.

That was what finally drove Shane. He did not
mind what they thought of him. Since his session
with Chris he seemed to have won a kind of inner
peace. He was as alert and watchful as ever, but
there was a serenity in him that had erased entirely the old tension. I think he did not care
what anyone anywhere thought of him. Except
us, his folks. And he knew that with us he was
one of us, unchangeable and always.

But he did care what they thought of father.
He was standing silently on the porch the night

Ernie Wright and Henry Shipstead were arguing with father in the kitchen.

"I can't stomach much more," Ernie Wright was saying. "You know the trouble I've had with those blasted cowboys cutting my fence. Today a couple of them rode over and helped me repair a piece. Helped me, damn them! Waited till we were through, then said Fletcher didn't want any of my pigs getting loose and mixing with his cattle. My pigs! There ain't a pig in this whole valley and they know it. I'm sick of the word."

Father made it worse by chuckling. Grim, maybe, yet still a chuckle. "Sounds like one of Morgan's ideas. He's smart. Mean, but — "

Henry Shipstead would not let him finish. "This is nothing to laugh at, Joe. You least of all. Damn it, man, I'm beginning to doubt your judgment. None of us can keep our heads up around here any more. Just a while ago I was in Grafton's and Chris was there blowing high about your Shane must be thirsty because he's so scared he hasn't been in town lately for his soda pop."

Both of them were hammering at father now. He was sitting back, saying nothing, his face clouding.

"You can't dodge it, Joe." This was Wright.

"Your man's responsible. You can try explaining all night, but you can't change the facts. Chris braced him for a fight and he ducked out — and left us stuck with those stinking pigs."

"You know as well as I do what Fletcher's doing," growled Henry Shipstead. "He's pushing us with this and he won't let up till one of us gets enough and makes a fool play and starts something so he can move in and finish it."

"Fool play or not," said Ernie Wright. "I've had all I can take. The next time one of those — "

Father stopped him with a hand up for silence. "Listen. What's that?"

It was a horse, picking up speed and tearing down our lane into the road. Father was at the door in a single jump, peering out.

The others were close behind him. "Shane?"

Father nodded. He was muttering under his breath. As I watched from the doorway of my little room, I could see that his eyes were bright and dancing. He was calling Shane names, cursing him, softly, fluently. He came back to his chair and grinned at the other two. "That's Shane," he told them and the words meant more than they seemed to say. "All we can do now is wait."

They were a silent crew waiting. Mother got up from her sewing in the bedroom where she had been listening as she always did and came into the kitchen and made up a pot of coffee and they all sat there sipping at the hot stuff and waiting.

It could not have been much more than twenty minutes before we heard the horse again, coming swiftly and slewing around to make the lane without slowing. There were quick steps on the porch and Shane stood in the doorway. He was breathing strongly and his face was hard. His mouth was a thin line in the bleakness of his face and his eyes were deep and dark. He looked at Shipstead and Wright and he made no effort to hide the disgust in his voice.

"Your pigs are dead and buried."

As his gaze shifted to father, his face softened. But the voice was still bitter. "There's another one down. Chris won't be bothering anybody for quite a spell." He turned and disappeared and we could hear him leading the horse into the barn.

In the quiet following, hoofbeats like an echo sounded in the distance. They swelled louder and this second horse galloped into our lane and pulled to a stop. Ed Howells jumped to the porch and hurried in.

"Where's Shane?"

"Out in the barn," father said.

"Did he tell you what happened?"

"Not much," father said mildly. "Something about burying pigs."

Ed Howells slumped into a chair. He seemed a bit dazed. The words came out of him slowly at first as he tried to make the others grasp just how he felt. "I never saw anything like it," he said, and he told about it.

He had been in Grafton's store buying a few things, not caring about going into the saloon because Chris and Red Marlin, another of Fletcher's cowboys, had hands in the evening poker game, when he noticed how still the place was. He went over to sneak a look and there was Shane just moving to the bar, cool and easy as if the room was empty and he the only one in it. Neither Chris nor Red Marlin was saying a word, though you might have thought this was a good chance for them to cut loose with some of their raw sarcasm. One look at Shane was enough to tell why. He was cool and easy, right enough. But there was a curious kind of smooth flow to his movements that made you realize without being conscious of thinking about it that being quiet was a mighty sensible way to be at the moment.

"Two bottles of soda pop," he called to Will Atkey. He leaned his back to the bar and looked the poker game over with what seemed a friendly interest while Will fetched the bottles from the store. Not another person even twitched a muscle. They were all watching him and wondering what the play was. He took the two bottles and walked to the table and set them down, reaching over to put one in front of Chris.

"The last time I was in here you bought me a drink. Now it's my turn."

The words sort of lingered in the stillness. He got the impression, Ed Howells said, that Shane meant just what the words said. He wanted to buy Chris a drink. He wanted Chris to take that bottle and grin at him and drink with him.

You could have heard a bug crawl, I guess, while Chris carefully laid down the cards in his right hand and stretched it to the bottle. He lifted it in a sudden jerk and flung it across the table at Shane.

So fast Shane moved, Ed Howells said, that the bottle was still in the air when he had dodged, lunged forward, grabbed Chris by the shirtfront and hauled him right out of his chair and over the table. As Chris struggled to get his feet under him, Shane let go the shirt and slapped him, sharp and stinging, three times, the hand flicking back and forth so quick you could hardly see it, the slaps sounding like pistol shots.

Shane stepped back and Chris stood swaying a little and shaking his head to clear it. He was a game one and mad down to his boots. He plunged in, fists smashing, and Shane let him come, slipping inside the flailing arms and jolting a powerful blow low into his stomach. As Chris gasped and his head came down, Shane brought his right hand up, open, and with the heel of it caught Chris full on the mouth, snapping his head back and raking up over the nose and eyes.

The force of it knocked Chris off balance and he staggered badly. His lips were crushed. Blood was dripping over them from his battered nose. His eyes were red and watery and he was having trouble seeing with them. His face, Ed Howells said, and shook a little as he said it, looked like a horse had stomped it. But he drove in again, swinging wildly.

Shane ducked under, caught one of the flying

wrists, twisted the arm to lock it and keep it from bending, and swung his shoulder into the armpit. He yanked hard on the wrist and Chris went up and over him. As the body hurtled over, Shane kept hold of the arm and wrenched it sideways and let the weight bear on it and you could hear the bone crack as Chris crashed to the floor.

A long sobbing sigh came from Chris and that died away and there was not a sound in the room. Shane never looked at the crumpled figure. He was straight and deadly and still. Every line of him was alive and eager. But he stood motionless. Only his eyes shifted to search the faces of the others at the table. They stopped on Red Marlin and Red seemed to dwindle lower in his chair.

"Perhaps," Shane said softly, and the very softness of his voice sent shivers through Ed Howells, "perhaps you have something to say about soda pop or pigs."

Red Marlin sat quiet like he was trying not even to breathe. Tiny drops of sweat appeared on his forehead. He was frightened, maybe for the first time in his life, and the others knew it and he knew they knew and he did not care. And none of them blamed him at all.

Then, as they watched, the fire in Shane smouldered down and out. He seemed to withdraw back within himself. He forgot them all and turned toward Chris unconscious on the floor, and a sort of sadness, Ed Howells said, crept over him and held him. He bent and scooped the sprawling figure up in his arms and carried it to one of the other tables. Gently he set it down, the legs falling limp over the edge. He crossed to the bar and took the rag Will used to wipe it and returned to the table and tenderly cleared the blood from the face. He felt carefully along the broken arm and nodded to himself at what he felt.

All this while no one said a word. Not a one of them would have interfered with that man for a year's top wages. He spoke and his voice rang across the room at Red Marlin. "You'd better tote him home and get that arm fixed. Take right good care of him. He has the makings of a good man." Then he forgot them all again and looked at Chris and went on speaking as if to that limp figure that could not hear him. "There's only one thing really wrong with you. You're young. That's the one thing time can always cure."

The thought hurt him and he strode to the swinging doors and through them into the night.

That was what Ed Howells told. "The whole

business," he finished, "didn't take five minutes. It was maybe thirty seconds from the time he grabbed holt of Chris till Chris was out cold on the floor. In my opinion that Shane is the most dangerous man I've ever seen. I'm glad he's working for Joe here and not for Fletcher."

Father leveled a triumphant look at Henry Shipstead. "So I've made a mistake, have I?"

Before anyone else could push in a word, mother was speaking. I was surprised, because she was upset and her voice was a little shrill. "I wouldn't be too sure about that, Joe Starrett. I think you've made a bad mistake."

"Marian, what's got into you?"

"Look what you've done just because you got him to stay on here and get mixed up in this trouble with Fletcher!"

Father was edging toward being peeved himself. "Women never do understand these things. Lookahere, Marian. Chris will be all right. He's young and he's healthy. Soon as that arm is mended, he'll be in as good shape as he ever was."

"Oh, Joe, can't you see what I'm talking about? I don't mean what you've done to Chris. I mean what you've done to Shane."

8

THIS TIME MOTHER WAS RIGHT. Shane was changed. He tried to keep things as they had been with us and on the surface nothing was different. But he had lost the serenity that had seeped into him through the summer. He would no longer sit around and talk with us as much as he had. He was restless with some far hidden desperation.

At times, when it rode him worst, he would wander alone about our place, and this was the one thing that seemed to soothe him. I used to see him, when he thought no one was watching, run his hands along the rails of the corral he had fastened, test with a tug the posts he had set, pace out past the barn looking up at the bulging loft and stride out where the tall corn was standing in big shocks to dig his hands in the loose soil and lift some of it and let it run through his fingers.

He would lean on the pasture fence and study our little herd like it meant more to him than lazy steers to be fattened for market. Sometimes he would whistle softly, and his horse, filled out now so you could see the quality of him and moving with a quiet sureness and power that made you think of Shane himself, would trot to the fence and nuzzle at him.

Often he would disappear from the house in the early evening after supper. More than once, the dishes done, when I managed to slip past mother, I found him far back in the pasture alone with the horse. He would be standing there, one arm on the smooth arch of the horse's neck, the fingers gently rubbing around the ears, and he would be looking out over our land where the last light of the sun, now out of sight, would be flaring up the far side of the mountains, capping them with a deep glow and leaving a mystic gloaming in the valley.

Some of the assurance that was in him when he came was gone now. He seemed to feel that he needed to justify himself, even to me, to a boy tagging his heels.

"Could you teach me," I asked him, "to throw somebody the way you threw Chris?"

He waited so long I thought he would not answer. "A man doesn't learn things like that," he said at last. "You know them and that's all." Then he was talking rapidly to me, as close to pleading as he could ever come. "I tried. You can see that, can't you, Bob? I let him ride me and I gave him his chance. A man can keep his self-respect without having to cram it down another man's throat. Surely you can see that, Bob?"

I could not see it. What he was trying to explain to me was beyond my comprehension then. And I could think of nothing to say.

"I left it up to him. He didn't have to jump me that second time. He could have called it off without crawling. He could have if he was man enough. Can't you see that, Bob?"

And still I could not. But I said I could. He was so earnest and he wanted me to so badly. It was a long, long time before I did see it and then I was a man myself and Shane was not there for me to tell. . . .

I was not sure whether father and mother were aware of the change in him. They did not talk about it, not while I was around anyway. But one afternoon I overheard something that showed mother knew.

I had hurried home from school and put on my old clothes and started out to see what father and Shane were doing in the cornfield, when I thought of a trick that had worked several times. Mother was firm set against eating between meals. That was a silly notion. I had my mind set on the cookies she kept in a tin box on a shelf by the stove. She was settled on the porch with a batch of potatoes to peel, so I slipped up to the back of the house, through the window of my little room, and tiptoed into the kitchen. Just as I was carefully putting a chair under the shelf, I heard her call to Shane.

He must have come to the barn on some errand, for he was there by the porch in only a moment. I peeped out the front window and saw him standing close in, his hat in his hand, his face tilted up slightly to look at her leaning forward in her chair.

"I've been wanting to talk to you when Joe wasn't around."

"Yes, Marian." He called her that the same as father did, familiar yet respectful, just as he always regarded her with a tenderness in his eyes he had for no one else.

"You've been worrying, haven't you, about what may happen in this Fletcher business? You thought it would just be a case of not letting him scare you away and of helping us through a hard time. You didn't know it would come to what it has. And now you're worried about what you might do if there's any more fighting."

"You're a discerning woman, Marian."

"You've been worrying about something else too."

"You're a mighty discerning woman, Marian."

"And you've been thinking that maybe you'll be moving on."

"And how did you know that?"

"Because it's what you ought to do. For your own sake. But I'm asking you not to." Mother was intense and serious, as lovely there with the light striking through her hair as I had ever seen her. "Don't go, Shane. Joe needs you. More than ever now. More than he would ever say."

"And you?" Shane's lips barely moved and I was not sure of the words.

Mother hesitated. Then her head went up. "Yes. It's only fair to say it. I need you too."

"So-o-o," he said softly, the word lingering on his lips. He considered her gravely. "Do you know what you're asking, Marian?"

"I know. And I know that you're the man to stand up to it. In some ways it would be easier for me, too, if you rode out of this valley and never came back. But we can't let Joe down. I'm counting on you not ever to make me do that. Because you've got to stay, Shane, no matter how hard it is for us. Joe can't keep this place without you. He can't buck Fletcher alone."

Shane was silent, and it seemed to me that he was troubled and hard pressed in his mind. Mother was talking straight to him, slow and feeling for the words, and her voice was beginning to tremble.

"It would just about kill Joe to lose this place. He's too old to start in again somewhere else. Oh, we would get along and might even do real well. After all, he's Joe Starrett. He's all man and he can do what has to be done. But he promised me this place when we were married. He had it in his mind for all the first years. He did two men's work to get the extra money for the things we would need. When Bob was big enough to walk and help some and he could leave us, he came on here and filed his claim and built this house with his own hands, and when he brought us here it was home. Nothing else would ever be the same."

Shane drew a deep breath and let it ease out slowly. He smiled at her and yet, somehow, as I watched him, my heart ached for him. "Joe should be proud of a wife like you. Don't fret any more, Marian. You'll not lose this place."

Mother dropped back in her chair. Her face, the side I could see from the window, was radiant. Then, woman like, she was talking against herself. "But that Fletcher is a mean and tricky man. Are you sure it will work out all right?"

Shane was already starting toward the barn. He stopped and turned to look at her again. "I said you won't lose this place." You knew he was right because of the way he said it and because he said it.

9

ANOTHER PERIOD OF PEACE had settled over our valley. Since the night Shane rode into town, Fletcher's cowboys had quit using the road past the homesteads. They were not annoying us at all and only once in a while was there a rider in view across the river. They had a good excuse to let us be. They were busy fixing the ranch buildings and poling a big new corral in preparation for the spring drive of new cattle Fletcher was planning.

Just the same, I noticed that father was as watchful as Shane now. The two of them worked always together. They did not split any more to do separate jobs in different parts of the farm. They worked together, rode into town together when anything was needed. And father took to wearing his gun all the time, even in the fields. He strapped it on after breakfast the first morning following the fight with Chris, and I saw him catch Shane's eye with a questioning glance as he buckled the belt. But Shane shook his head and father nodded, accepting the decision, and they went out together without saying a word.

Those were beautiful fall days, clear and stir ring, with the coolness in the air just enough to set one atingling, not yet mounting to the bitter cold that soon would come sweeping down out of the mountains. It did not seem possible that in such a harvest season, giving a lift to the spirit to match the wellbeing of the body, violence could flare so suddenly and swiftly.

Saturday evenings all of us would pile into the light work wagon, father and mother on the seat, Shane and I swinging legs at the rear, and go into town. It was the break in routine we looked forward to all week.

There was always a bustle in Grafton's store with people we knew coming and going. Mother would lay in her supplies for the week ahead, taking a long time about it and chatting with the womenfolk. She and the wives of the other homesteaders were great ones for swapping recipes and this was their bartering ground. Father would give Mr. Grafton his order for what he wanted and go direct for the mail. He was always getting catalogues of farm equipment and pamphlets from Washington. He would flip through their pages and skim through any letters, then settle on a barrel and spread out his newspaper. But like as not he would soon be bogged down in an argument with almost any man handy about the best crops for the Territory and it would be Shane who would really work his way into the newspaper.

I used to explore the store, filling myself with crackers from the open barrel at the end of the main counter, playing hide and seek with Mr. Grafton's big and knowing old cat that was a whiz of a mouser. Many a time, turning up boxes, I chased out fat furry ones for her to pounce on. If mother was in the right mood, I would have a bag of candy in my pocket.

This time we had a special reason for staying longer than usual, a reason I did not like. Our schoolteacher, Jane Grafton, had made me take a note home to mother asking her to stop in for a talk. About me. I never was too smart at formal schooling to begin with. Being all excited over the doings at the big ranch and what they might mean to us had not helped any. Miss Grafton, I guess, just sort of endured me under the best of conditions. But what tipped her into being downright annoyed and writing to mother was the weather. No one could expect a boy with any spirit in him to be shut up in a schoolroom in weather like we had been having. Twice that week I had persuaded Ollie Johnson to sneak away with me after the lunch hour to see if the fish were still biting in our favorite pool below town.

Mother finished the last item on her list, looked around at me, sighed a little, and stiffened her shoulders. I knew she was going to the living quarters behind the store and talk to Miss Grafton. I squirmed and pretended I did not notice her. Only a few people were left in the store, though the saloon in the adjoining big room was doing fair businss. She went over to where father was leafing through a catalogue and tapped him.

"Come along, Joe. You should hear this, too. I declare, that boy is getting too big for me to handle."

Father glanced quickly over the store and paused, listening to the voices from the next room. We had not seen any of Fletcher's men all evening and he seemed satisfied. He looked at Shane, who was folding the newspaper.

"This won't take long. We'll be out in a mo. ment."

As they passed through the door at the rear of the store, Shane strolled to the saloon opening. He took in the whole room in his easy, alert way and stepped inside. I followed. But I was supposed not ever to go in there, so I stopped at the entrance. Shane was at the bar, joshing Will Atkey with a grave face that he didn't think he'd have soda pop tonight. It was a scattered group in the room, most of them from around town and familiar to me by sight at least. Those close to Shane moved a little away, eyeing him curiously. He did not appear to notice.

He picked up his drink and savored it, one elbow on the bar, not shoving himself forward into the room's companionship and not withdrawing either, just ready to be friendly if anyone wanted that and unfriendly if anyone wanted that too.

I was letting my eyes wander about, trying to tag names to faces, when I saw that one of the swinging doors was partly open and Red Marlin was peeking in. Shane saw it too. But he could not see that more men were out on the porch, for they were close by the building wall and on the store side. I could sense them through the window near me, hulking shapes in the darkness. I was so frightened I could scarcely move.

But I had to. I had to go against mother's rule. I scrambled into the saloon and to Shane and I gasped: "Shane! There's a lot of them out front!"

I was too late. Red Marlin was inside and the others were hurrying in and fanning out to close off the store opening. Morgan was one of them, his flat face sour and determined, his huge shoulders almost filling the doorway as he came through. Behind him was the cowboy they called Curly because of his shock of unruly hair. He was stupid and slow-moving, but he was thick and powerful, and he had worked in harness with Chris for several years. Two others followed them, new men to me, with the tough, experienced look of old herd hands.

There was still the back office with its outside door opening on a side stoop and the rear alley. My knees were shaking and I tugged at Shane and tried to say something about it. He stopped me with a sharp gesture. His face was clear, his eyes bright. He was somehow happy, not in the pleased and laughing way, but happy that the waiting was over and what had been ahead was here and seen and realized and he was ready for it. He put one hand on my head and rocked it gently, the fingers feeling through my hair.

"Bobby boy, would you have me run away?"

Love for that man raced through me and the warmth ran down and stiffened my legs and I was so proud of being there with him that I could not keep the tears from my eyes. I could see the rightness of it and I was ready to do as he told me when he said: "Get out of here, Bob. This isn't going to be pretty."

But I would go no farther than my perch just inside the store where I could watch most of the big room. I was so bound in the moment that I did not even think of running for father.

Morgan was in the lead now with his men spread out behind him. He came about half the way to Shane and stopped. The room was quiet except for the shuffling of feet as the men by the bar and the nearest tables hastened over to the far wall and some of them ducked out the front doors. Neither Shane nor Morgan gave any attention to them. They had attention only for each other. They did not look aside even when Mr. Grafton, who could smell trouble in his place from any distance, stalked in from the store, planting his feet down firmly, and pushed past Will Atkey behind the bar. He had a resigned expression on his face and he reached under the counter, his hands reappearing with a short-barreled shotgun. He laid it before him on the bar and he said in a dry, disgusted voice: "There will be no gunplay, gentlemen. And all damages will be paid for."

Morgan nodded curtly, not taking his eyes from Shane. He came closer and stopped again little more than an arm's length away. His head was thrust forward. His big fists were clenched at his sides.

"No one messes up one of my boys and gets away with it. We're riding you out of this valley on a rail, Shane. We're going to rough you a bit and ride you out and you'll stay out."

"So you have it all planned," Shane said softly. Even as he was speaking, he was moving. He flowed into action so swift you could hardly believe what was happening. He scooped up his half-filled glass from the bar, whipped it and its contents into Morgan's face, and when Morgan's hands came up reaching or striking for him, he grasped the wrists and flung himself backwards, dragging Morgan with him. His body rolled to meet the floor and his legs doubled and his feet, catching Morgan just below the belt, sent him flying on and over to fall flat in a grotesque spraddle and slide along the boards in a tangle of chairs and a table.

The other four were on Shane in a rush. As they came, he whirled to his hands and knees and leaped up and behind the nearest table, tipping it in a strong heave among them. They scattered, dodging, and he stepped, fast and light, around the end and drove into the tail man, one of the new men, now nearest to him. He took the blows at him straight on to get in close and I saw his knee surge up and into the man's groin. A high scream was literally torn from the man and he collapsed to the floor and dragged himself toward the doors.

Morgan was on his feet, wavering, rubbing a hand across his face, staring hard as if trying to focus again on the room about him. The other three were battering at Shane, seeking to box him between them. They were piling blows into him, crowding in. Through that blur of movement he was weaving, quick and confident. It was incredible, but they could not hurt him. You could see the blows hit, hear the solid chunk of knuckles on flesh. But they had no effect. They seemed only to feed that fierce energy. He moved like a flame among them. He would burst out of the mêlée and whirl and plunge back, the one man actually pressing the three. He had picked the second new man and was driving always directly at him.

Curly, slow and clumsy, grunting in exasperation, grabbed at Shane to grapple with him and hold down his arms. Shane dropped one shoulder and as Curly hugged tighter brought it up under his jaw with a jolt that knocked him loose and away.

They were wary now and none too eager to let him get close to any one of them. Then Red Marlin came at him from one side, forcing him to turn that way, and at the same time the second new man did a strange thing. He jumped high in the air, like a jack rabbit in a spy hop, and lashed out viciously with one boot at Shane's head. Shane saw it coming, but could not avoid it, so he rolled his head with the kick, taking it along the side. It shook him badly. But it did not block the instant response. His hands shot up and seized the foot and the man crashed down to land on the small of

his back. As he hit, Shane twisted the whole leg
and threw his weight on it. The man buckled on
the floor like a snake when you hit it and groaned
sharply and hitched himself away, the leg dragging, the fight gone out of him.

But the swing to bend down on the leg had put
Shane's back to Curly and the big man was plow-
ing at him. Curly's arms clamped around him,
pinning his arms to his body. Red Marlin leaped
to help and the two of them had Shane caught
tight between them.

"Hold him!" That was Morgan, coming forward with the hate plain in his eyes. Even then,
Shane would have broke away. He stomped one
heavy work shoe, heel edged and with all the
strength he could get in quick leverage, on Curly's near foot. As Curly winced and pulled it back
and was unsteady, Shane strained with his whole
body in a powerful arch and you could see their
arms slipping and loosening. Morgan, circling in,
saw it too. He swept a bottle off the bar and
brought it smashing down from behind on Shane's
head.

Shane slumped and would have fallen if they
had not been holding him. Then, as Morgan

stepped around in front of him and watched, the vitality pumped through him and his head came up.

"Hold him!" Morgan said again. He deliberately flung a huge fist to Shane's face. Shane tried to jerk aside and the fist missed the jaw, tearing along the cheek, the heavy ring on one finger slicing deep. Morgan pulled back for another blow. He never made it.

Nothing, I would have said, could have drawn my attention from those men. But I heard a kind of choking sob beside me and it was queer and yet familiar and it turned me instantly.

Father was there in the entranceway!

He was big and terrible and he was looking across the overturned table and scattered chairs at Shane, at the dark purplish bruise along the side of Shane's head and the blood running down his cheek. I had never seen father like this. He was past anger. He was filled with a fury that was shaking him almost beyond endurance.

I never thought he could move so fast. He was on them before they even knew he was in the room. He hurtled into Morgan with ruthless force, sending that huge man reeling across the room. He reached out one broad hand and grabbed Curly by the shoulder and you could see the fingers sink into the flesh. He took hold of Curly's belt with the other hand and ripped him loose from Shane and his own shirt shredded down the back and the great muscles there knotted and bulged as he lifted Curly right up over his head and hurled the threshing body from him. Curly spun through the air, his limbs waving wildly, and crashed on the top of a table way over by the wall. It cracked under him, collapsing in splintered pieces, and the man and the wreckage smacked against the wall. Curly tried to rise, pushing himself with hands on the floor, and fell back and was still.

Shane must have exploded into action the second father yanked Curly away, for now there was another noise. It was Red Marlin, his face contorted, flung against the bar and catching at it to keep himself from falling. He staggered and caught his balance and ran for the front doorway. His flight was frantic, headlong. He tore through the swinging doors without slowing to push them. They flapped with a swishing sound and my eyes shifted quickly to Shane, for he was laughing.

He was standing there, straight and superb, the

blood on his face bright like a badge, and he was laughing.

It was a soft laugh, soft and gentle, not in amusement at Red Marlin or any single thing, but in the joy of being alive and released from long discipline and answering the urge in mind and body. The lithe power in him, so different from father's sheer strength, was singing in every fiber of him.

Morgan was in the rear corner, his face clouded and uncertain. Father, his fury eased by the mighty effort of throwing Curly, had looked around to watch Red Marlin's run and now was starting toward Morgan. Shane's voice stopped him.

"Wait, Joe. The man's mine." He was at father's side and he put a hand on father's arm. "You'd better get them out of here." He nodded in my direction and I noticed with surprise that mother was near and watching. She must have followed father and have been there all this while. Her lips were parted. Her eyes were glowing, looking at the whole room, not at anyone or anything in particular, but at the whole room.

Father was disappointed. "Morgan's more my size," he said, grumbling fashion. He was not worried about Shane. He was thinking of an excuse to take Morgan himself. But he went no further. He looked at the men over by the wall. "This is Shane's play. If a one of you tries to interfere, he'll have me to reckon with." His tone showed that he was not mad at them, that he was not even really warning them. He was simply making the play plain. Then he came to us and looked down at mother. "You wait out at the wagon, Marian. Morgan's had this coming to him for quite a long time now and it's not for a woman to see."

Mother shook her head without moving her eyes now from Shane. "No, Joe. He's one of us. I'll see this through." And the three of us stayed there together and that was right, for he was Shane.

He advanced toward Morgan, as flowing and graceful as the old mouser in the store. He had forgotten us and the battered men on the floor and those withdrawn by the wall and Mr. Grafton and Will Atkey crouched behind the bar. His whole being was concentrated on the big man before him.

Morgan was taller, half again as broad, with a

long reputation as a bullying fighter in the valley. But he did not like this and he was desperate. He knew better than to wait. He rushed at Shane to overwhelm the smaller man with his weight. Shane faded from in front of him and as Morgan went past hooked a sharp blow to his stomach and another to the side of his jaw. They were short and quick, flicking in so fast they were just a blur of movement. Yet each time at the instant of impact Morgan's big frame shook and halted in its rush for a fraction of a second before the momentum carried him forward. Again and again he rushed, driving his big fists ahead. Always Shane slipped away, sending in those swift hard punches.

Breathing heavily, Morgan stopped, grasping the futility of straight fighting. He plunged at Shane now, arms wide, trying to get hold of him and wrestle him down. Shane was ready and let him come without dodging, disregarding the arms stretching to encircle him. He brought up his right hand, open, just as Ed Howells had told us, and the force of Morgan's own lunge as the hand met his mouth and raked upwards snapped back his head and sent him staggering.

Morgan's face was puffy and red-mottled. He

bellowed some insane sound and swung up a chair. Holding it in front of him, legs forward, he rushed again at Shane, who sidestepped neatly. Morgan was expecting this and halted suddenly, swinging the chair in a swift arc to strike Shane with it full on the side. The chair shattered and Shane faltered, and then, queerly for a man usually so sure on his feet, he seemed to slip and fall to the floor.

Forgetting all caution, Morgan dove at him — and Shane's legs bent and he caught Morgan on his heavy work shoes and sent him flying back and against the bar with a crash that shook the whole length of it.

Shane was up and leaping at Morgan as if there had been springs under him there on the floor. His left hand, palm out, smacked against Morgan's forehead, pushing the head back, and his right fist drove straight to Morgan's throat. You could see the agony twist the man's face and the fear widen his eyes. And Shane, using his right fist now like a club and lining his whole body behind it, struck him on the neck below and back of the ear. It made a sickening, dull sound and Morgan's eyes rolled white and he went limp all over, sagging slowly and forward to the floor.

IO

IN THE HUSH that followed Morgan's fall, the big
barroom was so quiet again that the rustle of Will
Atkey straightening from below the bar level was
loud and clear and Will stopped moving, embarrassed and a little frightened.

Shane looked neither at him nor at any of the
other men staring from the wall. He looked only
at us, at father and mother and me, and it seemed
to me that it hurt him to see us there.

He breathed deeply and his chest filled and he
held it, held it long and achingly, and released it
slowly and sighing. Suddenly you were impressed
by the fact that he was quiet, that he was still.
You saw how battered and bloody he was. In the
moments before you saw only the splendor of

movement, the flowing brute beauty of line and power in action. The man, you felt, was tireless and indestructible. Now that he was still and the fire in him banked and subsided, you saw, and in the seeing remembered, that he had taken bitter punishment.

His shirt collar was dark and sodden. Blood was soaking into it, and this came only in part from the cut on his cheek. More was oozing from the matted hair where Morgan's bottle had hit. Unconsciously he put up one hand and it came away smeared and sticky. He regarded it grimly and wiped it clean on his shirt. He swayed slightly and when he started toward us, his feet dragged and he almost fell forward.

One of the townsmen, Mr. Weir, a friendly man who kept the stage post, pushed out from the wall, clucking sympathy, as though to help him. Shane pulled himself erect. His eyes blazed refusal. Straight and superb, not a tremor in him. he came to us and you knew that the spirit in him would sustain him thus alone for the farthest distance and forever.

But there was no need. The one man in our valley, the one man, I believe, in all the world whose help he would take, not to whom he would turn but whose help he would take, was there and ready. Father stepped to meet him and put out a big arm reaching for his shoulders. "All right, Joe," Shane said, so softly I doubt whether the others in the room heard. His eyes closed and he leaned against father's arm, his body relaxing and his head dropping sideways. Father bent and fitted his other arm under Shane's knees and picked him up like he did me when I stayed up too late and got all drowsy and had to be carried to bed.

Father held Shane in his arms and looked over him at Mr. Grafton. "I'd consider it a favor, Sam, if you'd figure the damage and put it on my bill."

For a man strict about bills and keen for a bargain, Mr. Grafton surprised me. "I'm marking this to Fletcher's account. I'm seeing that he pays."

Mr. Weir surprised me even more. He spoke promptly and he was emphatic about it. "Listen to me, Starrett. It's about time this town worked up a little pride. Maybe it's time, too, we got to be more neighborly with you homesteaders. I'll take a collection to cover this. I've been ashamed of myself ever since it started tonight, standing here and letting five of them jump that man of yours."

Father was pleased. But he knew what he wanted to do. "That's mighty nice of you, Weir. But this ain't your fight. I wouldn't worry, was I you, about keeping out of it." He looked down at Shane and the pride was plain busting out of him. "Matter of fact, I'd say the odds tonight, without me butting in, too, was mighty close to even." He looked again at Mr. Grafton. "Fletcher ain't getting in on this with a nickel. I'm paying." He tossed back his head. "No, by Godfrey! We're paying. Me and Shane."

He went to the swinging doors, turning sideways to push them open. Mother took my hand and we followed. She always knew when to talk and when not to talk, and she said no word while we watched father lift Shane to the wagon seat, climb beside him, hoist him to sitting position with one arm around him and take the reins in the other hand. Will Atkey trotted out with our things and stowed them away. Mother and I perched on the back of the wagon, father chirruped to the team, and we were started home.

There was not a sound for quite a stretch except the clop of hooves and the little creakings of the wheels. Then I heard a chuckle up front. It was Shane. The cool air was reviving him and he was sitting straight, swaying with the wagon's motion.

"What did you do with the thick one, Joe? I was busy with the redhead."

"Oh, I just kind of tucked him out of the way." Father wanted to let it go at that. Not mother.

"He picked him up like — like a bag of potatoes and threw him clear across the room." She did not say it to Shane, not to any person. She said it to the night, to the sweet darkness around us, and her eyes were shining in the starlight.

We turned in at our place and father shooed the rest of us into the house while he unhitched the team. In the kitchen mother set some water to heat on the stove and chased me to bed. Her back was barely to me after she tucked me in before I was peering around the door jamb. She got several clean rags, took the water from the stove, and went to work on Shane's head. She was tender as could be, crooning like to herself under her breath the while. It pained him plenty as the warm water soaked into the gash under the matted hair and as she washed the clotted blood from his cheek. But it seemed to pain her more, for her hand shook at the worst moments, and she was the one who flinched while he sat there quietly and smiled reassuringly at her.

Father came in and sat by the stove, watching them. He pulled out his pipe and made a very careful business of packing it and lighting it.

She finished. Shane would not let her try a bandage. "This air is the best medicine," he said. She had to be content with cleaning the cuts thoroughly and making certain all bleeding had stopped. Then it was father's turn.

"Get that shirt off, Joe. It's torn all down the back. Let me see what I can do with it." Before he could rise, she had changed her mind. "No. We'll keep it just like it is. To remember tonight by. You were magnificent, Joe, tearing that man away and — "

"Shucks," said father. "I was just peeved. Him holding Shane so Morgan could pound him."

"And you, Shane." Mother was in the middle of the kitchen, looking from one to the other. "You were magnificent, too. Morgan was so big and horrible and yet he didn't have even a chance. You were so cool and quick and — and dangerous and — "

"A woman shouldn't have to see things like that." Shane interrupted her, and he meant it. But she was talking right ahead.

"You think I shouldn't because it's brutal and nasty and not just fighting to see who is better at it, but mean and vicious and to win by any way, but to win. Of course it is. But you didn't start it. You didn't want to do it. Not until they made you anyway. You did it because you had to."

Her voice was climbing and she was looking back and forth and losing control of herself. "Did ever a woman have two such men?" And she turned from them and reached out blindly for a chair and sank into it and dropped her face into her hands and the tears came.

The two men stared at her and then at each other in that adult knowledge beyond my understanding. Shane rose and stepped over by mother. He put a hand gently on her head and I felt again his fingers in my hair and the affection flooding through me. He walked quietly out the door and into the night.

Father drew on his pipe. It was out and absently he lit it. He rose and went to the door and out on the porch. I could see him there dimly in the darkness, gazing across the river.

Gradually mother's sobs died down. She raised her head and wiped away the tears.

"Joe."

He turned and started in and waited then by the door. She stood up. She stretched her hands toward him and he was there and had her in his arms.

"Do you think I don't know, Marian?"

"But you don't. Not really. You can't. Because I don't know myself."

Father was staring over her head at the kitchen wall, not seeing anything there. "Don't fret yourself, Marian. I'm man enough to know a better when his trail meets mine. Whatever happens will be all right."

"Oh, Joe . . . Joe! Kiss me. Hold me tight and don't ever let go."

WHAT HAPPENED IN OUR KITCHEN that night was beyond me in those days. But it did not worry me because father had said it would be all right, and how could anyone, knowing him, doubt that he would make it so.

And we were not bothered by Fletcher's men any more at all. There might not have been a big ranch on the other side of the river, sprawling up the valley and over on our side above Ernie Wright's place, for all you could tell from our house. They left us strictly alone and were hardly ever seen now even in town. Fletcher himself, I heard from kids at school, was gone again. He went on the stage to Cheyenne and maybe farther, and nobody seemed to know why he went.

Yet father and Shane were more wary than they had been before. They stayed even closer together

and they spent no more time than they had to in
the fields. There was no more talking on the
porch in the evenings, though the nights were so
cool and lovely they called you to be out and
under the winking stars. We kept to the house,
and father insisted on having the lamps well
shaded and he polished his rifle and hung it,
ready loaded, on a couple of nails by the kitchen
door.

All this caution failed to make sense to me. So
at dinner about a week later I asked: "Is there
something new that's wrong? That stuff about
Fletcher is finished, isn't it?"

"Finished?" said Shane, looking at me over his
coffee cup. "Bobby boy, it's only begun."

"That's right," said father. "Fletcher's gone
too far to back out now. It's a case of now or
never with him. If he can make us run, he'll be
setting pretty for a long stretch. If he can't, it'll be
only a matter o' time before he's shoved smack
out of this valley. There's three or four of the
men who looked through here last year ready
right now to sharpen stakes and move in soon as
they think it's safe. I'll bet Fletcher feels he got
aholt of a bear by the tail and it'd be nice to be
able to let go."

"Why doesn't he do something, then?" I asked. "Seems to me mighty quiet around here lately."

"Seems to you, eh?" said father. "Seems to me you're mighty young to be doing much seemsing. Don't you worry, son. Fletcher is fixing to do something. The grass that grows under his feet won't feed any cow. I'd be easier in my mind if I knew what he's up to."

"You see, Bob" — Shane was speaking to me the way I liked, as if maybe I was a man and could understand all he said — "by talking big and playing it rough, Fletcher has made this a straight win or lose deal. It's the same as if he'd kicked loose a stone that starts a rockslide and all he can do is hope to ride it down and hit bottom safe. Maybe he doesn't realize that yet. I think he does. And don't let things being quiet fool you. When there's noise, you know where to look and what's happening. When things are quiet, you've got to be most careful."

Mother sighed. She was looking at Shane's cheek where the cut was healing into a scar like a thin line running back from near the mouth corner. "I suppose you two are right. But does there have to be any more fighting?"

"Like the other night?" asked father. "No,

Marian. I don't think so. Fletcher knows better now."

"He knows better," Shane said, "because he knows it won't work. If he's the man I think he is, he's known that since the first time he sicced Chris on me. I doubt that was his move the other night. That was Morgan's. Fletcher'll be watching for some way that has more finesse — and will be more final."

"Hm-m-m," said father, a little surprised. "Some legal trick, eh?"

"Could be. If he can find one. If not — " Shane shrugged and gazed out the window. "There are other ways. You can't call a man like Fletcher on things like that. Depends on how far he's willing to go. But whatever he does, once he's ready, he'll do it speedy and sure."

"Hm-m-m," said father again. "Now you put it thataway, I see you're right. That's Fletcher's way. Bet you've bumped against someone like him before." When Shane did not answer, just kept staring out the window, he went on. "Wish I could be as patient about it as you. I don't like this waiting."

But we did not have to wait long. It was the

next day, a Friday, when we were finishing supper, that Lew Johnson and Henry Shipstead
brought us the news. Fletcher was back and he
had not come back alone. There was another
man with him.

Lew Johnson saw them as they got off the stage.
He had a good chance to look the stranger over
while they waited in front of the post for horses
to be brought in from the ranch. Since it was beginning to get dark, he had not been able to make
out the stranger's face too well. The light striking through the post window, however, was
enough for him to see what kind of man he was.

He was tall, rather broad in the shoulders and
slim in the waist. He carried himself with a sort
of swagger. He had a mustache that he favored
and his eyes, when Johnson saw them reflecting
the light from the window, were cold and had a
glitter that bothered Johnson.

This stranger was something of a dude about
his clothes. Still, that did not mean anything.
When he turned, the coat he wore matching his
pants flapped open and Johnson could see what
had been half-hidden before. He was carrying
two guns, big capable forty-fives, in holsters hung
fairly low and forward. Those holsters were

pegged down at the tips with thin straps fastened around the man's legs. Johnson said he saw the tiny buckles when the light flashed on them.

Wilson was the man's name. That was what Fletcher called him when a cowboy rode up leading a couple of horses. A funny other name. Stark. Stark Wilson. And that was not all.

Lew Johnson was worried and went into Grafton's to find Will Atkey, who always knew more than anyone else about people apt to be coming along the road because he was constantly picking up information from the talk of men drifting in to the bar. Will would not believe it at first when Johnson told him the name. What would he be doing up here, Will kept saying. Then Will blurted out that this Wilson was a bad one, a killer. He was a gunfighter said to be just as good with either hand and as fast on the draw as the best of them. He came to Cheyenne from Kansas, Will claimed he had heard, with a reputation for killing three men there and nobody knew how many more down in the southwest territories where he used to be.

Lew Johnson was rattling on, adding details as he could think of them. Henry Shipstead was slumped in a chair by the stove. Father was frowning at his pipe, absently fishing in a pocket for a match. It was Shane who shut off Johnson with a suddenness that startled the rest of us. His voice was sharp and clear and it seemed to crackle in the air. You could feel him taking charge of that room and all of us in it.

"When did they hit town?"

"Last night."

"And you waited till now to tell it!" There was disgust in Shane's voice. "You're a farmer all right, Johnson. That's all you ever will be." He whirled on father. "Quick, Joe. Which one has the hottest head? Which one's the easiest to prod into being a fool? Torrey is it? Or Wright?"

"Ernie Wright," father said slowly.

"Get moving, Johnson. Get out there on your horse and make it to Wright's in a hurry. Bring him here. Pick up Torrey, too. But get Wright first."

"He'll have to go into town for that," Henry Shipstead said heavily. "We passed them both down the road riding in."

Shane jumped to his feet. Lew Johnson was shuffling reluctantly toward the door. Shane brushed him aside. He strode to the door himself yanked it open, started out. He stopped, leaning forward and listening.

"Easy, man," Henry Shipstead was grumbling, "what's your hurry? We told them about Wilson. They'll stop here on their way back." His voice ceased. All of us could hear it now, a horse pounding up the road at full gallop.

Shane turned back into the room. "There's your answer," he said bitterly. He swung the nearest chair to the wall and sat down. The fire blazing in him a moment before was gone. He was withdrawn into his own thoughts, and they were dark and not pleasant.

We heard the horse sliding to a stop out front. The sound was so plain you could fairly see the forelegs bracing and the hooves digging into the ground. Frank Torrey burst into the doorway. His hat was gone, his hair blowing wild. His chest heaved like he had been running as hard as the horse. He put his hands on the doorposts to hold himself steady and his voice was a hoarse whisper, though he was trying to shout across the room at father.

"Ernie's shot! They've killed him!"

The words jerked us to our feet and we stood staring. All but Shane. He did not move. You might have thought he was not even interested in what Torrey had said.

Father was the one who took hold of the scene. "Come in, Frank," he said quietly. "I take it we're too late to help Ernie now. Sit down and talk and don't leave anything out." He led Frank Torrey to a chair and pushed him into it. He closed the door and returned to his own chair. He looked older and tired.

It took Frank Torrey quite a while to pull himself together and tell his story straight. He was frightened. The fear was bedded deep in him and he was ashamed of himself for it.

He and Ernie Wright, he told us, had been to the stage office asking for a parcel Ernie was expecting. They dropped into Grafton's for a freshener before starting back. Since things had been so quiet lately, they were not thinking of any trouble even though Fletcher and the new man, Stark Wilson, were in the poker game at the big table. But Fletcher and Wilson must have been watching for a chance like that. They chucked in their hands and came over to the bar.

Fletcher was nice and polite as could be, nodding to Torrey and singling out Ernie for talk.

He said he was sorry about it, but he really needed the land Ernie had filed on. It was the right
place to put up winter windshelters for the new
herd he was bringing in soon. He knew Ernie
had not proved up on it yet. Just the same, he
was willing to pay a fair price.

"I'll give you three hundred dollars," he said,
"and that's more than the lumber in your buildings will be worth to me."

Ernie had more than that of his money in the
place already. He had turned Fletcher down
three or four times before. He was mad, the way
he always was when Fletcher started his smooth
talk.

"No," he said shortly. "I'm not selling. Not
now or ever."

Fletcher shrugged like he had done all he could
and slipped a quick nod at Stark Wilson. This
Wilson was half-smiling at Ernie. But his eyes,
Frank Torrey said, had nothing like a smile in
them.

"I'd change my mind if I were you," he said to
Ernie. "That is, if you have a mind to change."

"Keep out of this," snapped Ernie. "It's none
of your business."

"I see you haven't heard," Wilson said softly.

"I'm Mr. Fletcher's new business agent. I'm handling his business affairs for him. His business with stubborn jackasses like you." Then he said what showed Fletcher had coaxed him to it. "You're a damn fool, Wright. But what can you expect from a breed?"

"That's a lie!" shouted Ernie. "My mother wasn't no Indian!"

"Why, you crossbred squatter," Wilson said, quick and sharp, "are you telling me I'm wrong?"

"I'm telling you you're a God-damned liar!"

The silence that shut down over the saloon was so complete, Frank Torrey told us, that he could hear the ticking of the old alarm clock on the shelf behind the bar. Even Ernie, in the second his voice stopped, saw what he had done. But he was mad clear through and he glared at Wilson, his eyes reckless.

"So-o-o-o," said Wilson, satisfied now and stretching out the word with ominous softness. He flipped back his coat on the right side in front and the holster there was free with the gun grip ready for his hand.

"You'll back that, Wright. Or you'll crawl out of here on your belly."

Ernie moved out a step from the bar, his arms

stiff at his sides. The anger in him held him erect as he beat down the terror tearing at him. He knew what this meant, but he met it straight. His hand was firm on his gun and pulling up when Wilson's first bullet hit him and staggered him. The second spun him halfway around and a faint froth appeared on his lips and all expression died from his face and he sagged to the floor.

While Frank Torrey was talking, Jim Lewis and a few minutes later Ed Howells had come in. Bad news travels fast and they seemed to know something was wrong. Perhaps they had heard that frantic galloping, the sound carrying far in the still night air. They were all in our kitchen now and they were more shaken and sober than I had ever seen them.

I was pressed close to mother, grateful for her arms around me. I noticed that she had little attention for the other men. She was watching Shane, bitter and silent across the room.

"So that's it," father said grimly. "We'll have to face it. We sell and at his price or he slips the leash on his hired killer. Did Wilson make a move toward you, Frank?"

"He looked at me." Simply recalling that

made Torrey shiver through. "He looked at me and he said, 'Too bad, isn't it, mister, that Wright didn't change his mind?' "

"Then what?"

"I got out of there quick as I could and came here."

Jim Lewis had been fidgeting on his seat, more nervous every minute. Now he jumped up, almost shouting. "But damn it, Joe! A man can't just go around shooting people!"

"Shut up, Jim," growled Henry Shipstead. "Don't you see the setup? Wilson badgered Ernie into getting himself in a spot where he had to go for his gun. Wilson can claim he shot in self-defense. He'll try the same thing on each of us."

"That's right, Jim," put in Lew Johnson. "Even if we tried to get a marshal in here, he couldn't hold Wilson. It was an even break and the faster man won is the way most people will figure it and plenty of them saw it. A marshal couldn't get here in time anyway."

"But we've got to stop it!" Lewis was really shouting now. "What chance have any of us got against Wilson? We're not gunmen. We're just a bunch of old cowhands and farmers. Call it anything you want. I call it murder."

"Yes!"

The word sliced through the room. Shane was up and his face was hard with the rock ridges running along his jaw. "Yes. It's murder. Trick it out as self-defense or with fancy words about an even break for a fair draw and it's still murder." He looked at father and the pain was deep in his eyes. But there was only contempt in his voice as he turned to the others.

"You five can crawl back in your burrows. You don't have to worry — yet. If the time comes, you can always sell and run. Fletcher won't bother with the likes of you now. He's going the limit and he knows the game. He picked Wright to make the play plain. That's done. Now he'll head straight for the one real man in this valley, the man who's held you here and will go on trying to hold you and keep for you what's yours as long as there's life in him. He's standing between you and Fletcher and Wilson this minute and you ought to be thankful that once in a while this country turns out a man like Joe Starrett."

And a man like Shane. . . . Were those words only in my mind or did I hear mother whisper them? She was looking at him and then at father and she was both frightened and proud at once. Father was fumbling with his pipe, packing it and making a fuss with it like it needed his whole attention.

The others stirred uneasily. They were reassured by what Shane said and yet shamed that they should be. And they did not like the way he said it.

"You seem to know a lot about that kind of dirty business," Ed Howells said, with maybe an edge of malice to his voice.

"I do."

Shane let the words lie there, plain and short and ugly. His face was stern and behind the hard front of his features was a sadness that fought to break through. But he stared levelly at Howells and it was the other man who dropped his eyes and turned away.

Father had his pipe going. "Maybe it's a lucky break for the rest of us," he said mildly, "that Shane here has been around a bit. He can call the cards for us plain. Ernie might still be alive, Johnson, if you had had the sense to tell us about Wilson right off. It's a good thing Ernie wasn't a family man." He turned to Shane. "How do you rate Fletcher now he's shown his hand?"

You could see that the chance to do something, even just to talk at the problem pressing us, eased the bitterness in Shane.

"He'll move in on Wright's place first thing to-morrow. He'll have a lot of men busy on this side of the river from now on, probably push some cattle around behind the homesteads, to keep the pressure plain on all of you. How quick he'll try you, Joe, depends on how he reads you. If he thinks you might crack, he'll wait and let knowing what happened to Wright work on you. If he really knows you, he'll not wait more than a day or two to make sure you've had time to think it over and then he'll grab the first chance to throw Wilson at you. He'll want it, like with Wright, in a public place where there'll be plenty of witnesses. If you don't give him a chance, he'll try to make one."

"Hm-m-m," father said soberly. "I was sure you'd give it to me straight and that rings right." He pulled on his pipe for a moment. "I reckon, boys, this will be a matter of waiting for the next few days. There's no immediate danger right off anyway. Grafton will take care of Ernie's body tonight. We can meet in town in the morning to fix him a funeral. After that, we'd better stay out of town and stick close home as much as possible. I'd suggest you all study on this and drop in again tomorrow night. Maybe we can figure out something. I'd like to see how the town's taking it before I make up my mind on anything.

They were ready to leave it at that. They were ready to leave it to father. They were decent men and good neighbors. But not a one of them, were the decision his, would have stood up to Fletcher now. They would stay as long as father was there. With him gone, Fletcher would have things his way. That was how they felt as they muttered their goodnights and bunched out to scatter up and down the road.

Father stood in the doorway and watched them go. When he came back to his chair, he walked slowly and he seemed haggard and worn. "Somebody will have to go to Ernie's place tomorrow," he said, "and gather up his things. He's got relatives somewhere in Iowa."

"No." There was finality in Shane's tone. "You'll not go near the place. Fletcher might be counting on that. Grafton can do it."

"But Ernie was my friend," father said simply.

"Ernie's past friendship. Your debt is to the living."

Father looked at Shane and this brought him again into the immediate moment and cheered him. He nodded assent and turned to mother, who was hurrying to argue with him.

"Don't you see, Joe? If you can stay away from any place where you might meet Fletcher and — and that Wilson, things will work out. He can't keep a man like Wilson in this little valley forever."

She was talking rapidly and I knew why. She was not really trying to convince father as much as she was trying to convince herself. Father knew it, too.

"No, Marian. A man can't crawl into a hole somewhere and hide like a rabbit. Not if he has any pride."

"All right, then. But can't you keep quiet and not let him ride you and drive you into any fight?"

"That won't work either." Father was grim, but he was better and facing up to it. "A man can stand for a lot of pushing if he has to. 'Specially when he has his reasons." His glance shifted briefly to me. "But there are some things a man can't take. Not if he's to go on living with himself."

I was startled as Shane suddenly sucked in his breath with a long breaking intake. He was battling something within him, that old hidden desperation, and his eyes were dark and tormented against the paleness of his face. He seemed unable to look at us. He strode to the door and went out. We heard his footsteps fading toward the barn.

I was startled now at father. His breath, too, was coming in long, broken sweeps. He was up and pacing back and forth. When he swung on mother and his voice battered at her, almost fierce in its intensity, I realized that he knew about the change in Shane and that the knowing had been cankering in him all the past weeks.

"That's the one thing I can't stand, Marian. What we're doing to him. What happens to me doesn't matter too much. I talk big and I don't belittle myself. But my weight in any kind of a scale won't match his and I know it. If I understood him then as I do now, I'd never have got him to stay on here. But I didn't figure Fletcher would go this far. Shane won his fight before ever he came riding into this valley. It's been tough enough on him already. Should we let him lose just because of us? Fletcher can have his way. We'll sell out and move on."

I was not thinking. I was only feeling. For

some strange reason I was feeling Shane's fingers
in my hair, gently rocking my head. I could not
help what I was saying, shouting across the room.
"Father! Shane wouldn't run away! He wouldn't
run away from anything!"

Father stopped pacing, his eyes narrowed in
surprise. He stared at me without really seeing
me. He was listening to mother.

"Bob's right, Joe. We can't let Shane down."
It was queer, hearing her say the same thing to
father she had said to Shane, the same thing with
only the name different. "He'd never forgive us
if we ran away from this. That's what we'd be
doing. This isn't just a case of bucking Fletcher
any more. It isn't just a case of keeping a piece
of ground Fletcher wants for his range. We've
got to be the kind of people Shane thinks we are.
Bob's right. He wouldn't run away from anything like that. And that's the reason we can't."

"Lookahere, Marian, you don't think I want
to do any running? No. You know me better
than that. It'd go against everything in me. But
what's my fool pride and this place and any plans
we've had alongside of a man like that?"

"I know, Joe. But you don't see far enough."
They were both talking earnestly, not breaking

in, hearing each other out and sort of groping
to put their meaning plain. "I can't really explain it, Joe. But I just know that we're bound
up in something bigger than any one of us, and
that running away is the one thing that would
be worse than whatever might happen to us.
There wouldn't be anything real ahead for us,
any of us, maybe even for Bob, all the rest of our
lives."

"Humph," said father. "Torrey could do it.
And Johnson. All the rest of them. And it
wouldn't bother them too much."

"Joe! Joe Starrett! Are you trying to make
me mad? I'm not talking about them. I'm talking about us."

"Hm-m-m," said father softly, musing like to
himself. "The salt would be gone. There just
wouldn't be any flavor. There wouldn't be much
meaning left."

"Oh, Joe! Joe! That's what I've been trying
to say. And I know this will work out some way.
I don't know how. But it will, if we face it and
stand up to it and have faith in each other. It'll
work out. Because it's got to."

"That's a woman's reason, Marian. But you're
part right anyway. We'll play this game through.

It'll need careful watching and close figuring. But maybe we can wait Fletcher out and make him overplay his hand. The town won't take much to this Wilson deal. Men like that fellow Weir have minds of their own."

Father was more cheerful now that he was beginning to get his thoughts straightened out. He and mother talked low in the kitchen for a long time after they sent me to bed, and I lay in my little room and saw through the window the stars wheeling distantly in the far outer darkness until I fell asleep at last.

THE MORNING SUN brightened our house and everything in the world outside. We had a good breakfast, father and Shane taking their time because they had routed out early to get the chores done and were waiting to go to town. They saddled up presently and rode off, and I moped in front of the house, not able to settle to any kind of playing.

After she bustled through the dishes, mother saw me standing and staring down the road and called me to the porch. She got our tattered old parchesi board and she kept me humping to beat her. She was a grand one for games like that. She would be as excited as a kid, squealing at the big numbers and doubles and counting proudly out loud as she moved her markers ahead.

When I had won three games running, she put the board away and brought out two fat apples and my favorite of the books she had from the time she taught school. Munching on her apple, she read to me and before I knew it the shadows were mighty short and she had to skip in to get dinner and father and Shane were riding up to the barn.

They came in while she was putting the food on the table. We sat down and it was almost like a holiday, not just because it was not a work day, but because the grown folks were talking lightly, were determined not to let this Fletcher business spoil our good times. Father was pleased at what had happened in town.

"Yes, sir," he was saying as we were finishing dinner. "Ernie had a right good funeral. He would have appreciated it. Grafton made a nice speech and, by Godfrey, I believe he meant it. That fellow Weir had his clerk put together a really fine coffin. Wouldn't take a cent for it. And Sims over at the mine is knocking out a good stone. He wouldn't take a cent either. I was surprised at the crowd, too. Not a good word for Fletcher among them. And there must have been thirty people there."

"Thirty-four," said Shane. "I counted 'em. They weren't just paying their respects to Wright, Marian. That wouldn't have brought in some of those I checked. They were showing their opinion of a certain man named Starrett, who made a pretty fair speech himself. This husband of yours is becoming quite a respected citizen in these parts. Soon as the town gets grown up and organized, he's likely to start going places. Give him time and he'll be mayor."

Mother caught her breath with a little sob. "Give . . . him . . . time," she said slowly. She looked at Shane and there was panic in her eyes. The lightness was gone and before anyone could say more, we heard the horses turning into our yard.

I dashed to the window to peer out. It struck me strange that Shane, usually so alert, was not there ahead of me. Instead he pushed back his chair and spoke gently, still sitting in it. "That will be Fletcher, Joe. He's heard how the town is taking this and knows he has to move fast. You take it easy. He's playing against time now, but he won't push anything here."

Father nodded at Shane and went to the door.

He had taken off his gunbelt when he came in and now passed it to lift the rifle from its nails on the wall. Holding it in his right hand, barrel down, he opened the door and stepped out on the porch, clear to the front edge. Shane followed quietly and leaned in the doorway, relaxed and watchful. Mother was beside me at the window, staring out, crumpling her apron in her hand.

There were four of them, Fletcher and Wilson in the lead, two cowboys tagging. They had pulled up about twenty feet from the porch. This was the first time I had seen Fletcher for nearly a year. He was a tall man who must once have been a handsome figure in the fine clothes he always wore and with his arrogant air and his finely chiseled face set off by his short-cropped black beard and brilliant eyes. Now a heaviness was setting in about his features and a fatty softness was beginning to show in his body. His face had a shrewd cast and a kind of reckless determination was on him that I did not remember ever noticing before.

Stark Wilson, for all the dude look Frank Torrey had mentioned, seemed lean and fit. He was sitting idly in his saddle, but the pose did not fool you. He was wearing no coat and the two

guns were swinging free. He was sure of himself,
serene and deadly. The curl of his lip beneath
his mustache was a combination of confidence in
himself and contempt for us.

Fletcher was smiling and affable. He was certain he held the cards and was going to deal them
as he wanted. "Sorry to bother you, Starrett, so
soon after that unfortunate affair last night. I
wish it could have been avoided. I really do.
Shooting is so unnecessary in these things, if only
people would show sense. But Wright never
should have called Mr. Wilson here a liar. That
was a mistake."

"It was," father said curtly. "But then Ernie
always did believe in telling the truth." I could
see Wilson stiffen and his lips tighten. Father
did not look at him. "Speak your piece, Fletcher,
and get off my land."

Fletcher was still smiling. "There's no call for
us to quarrel, Starrett. What's done is done. Let's
hope there's no need for anything like it to be
done again. You've worked cattle on a big ranch
and you can understand my position. I'll be
wanting all the range I can get from now on.
Even without that, I can't let a bunch of nesters
keep coming in here and choke me off from my
water rights."

"We've been over that before," father said. "You know where I stand. If you have more to say, speak up and be done with it."

"All right, Starrett. Here's my proposition. I like the way you do things. You've got some queer notions about the cattle business, but when you tackle a job, you take hold and do it thoroughly. You and that man of yours are a combination I could use. I want you on my side of the fence. I'm getting rid of Morgan and I want you to take over as foreman. From what I hear your man would make one hell of a driving trail boss. The spot's his. Since you've proved up on this place, I'll buy it from you. If you want to go on living here, that can be arranged. If you want to play around with that little herd of yours, that can be arranged too. But I want you working for me."

Father was surprised. He had not expected anything quite like this. He spoke softly to Shane behind him. He did not turn or look away from Fletcher, but his voice carried clearly.

"Can I call the turn for you, Shane?"

"Yes, Joe." Shane's voice was just as soft, but it, too, carried clearly and there was a little note of pride in it.

Father stood taller there on the edge of the

porch. He stared straight at Fletcher. "And the others," he said slowly. "Johnson, Shipstead, and the rest. What about them?"

"They'll have to go."

Father did not hesitate. "No."

"I'll give you a thousand dollars for this place as it stands and that's my top offer."

"No."

The fury in Fletcher broke over his face and he started to turn in the saddle toward Wilson. He caught himself and forced again that shrewd smile. "There's no percentage in being hasty, Starrett. I'll boost the ante to twelve hundred. That's a lot better than what might happen if you stick to being stubborn. I'll not take an answer now. I'll give you till tonight to think it over. I'll be waiting at Grafton's to hear you talk sense."

He swung his horse and started away. The two cowboys turned to join him by the road. Wilson did not follow at once. He leaned forward in his saddle and drove a sneering look at father.

"Yes, Starrett. Think it over. You wouldn't like someone else to be enjoying this place of yours — and that woman there in the window."

He was lifting his reins with one hand to pull

his horse around and suddenly he dropped them and froze to attention. It must have been what he saw in father's face. We could not see it, mother and I, because father's back was to us. But we could see his hand tightening on the rifle at his side.

"Don't, Joe!"

Shane was beside father. He slipped past, moving smooth and steady, down the steps and over to one side to come at Wilson on his right hand and stop not six feet from him. Wilson was puzzled and his right hand twitched and then was still as Shane stopped and as he saw that Shane carried no gun.

Shane looked up at him and Shane's voice flicked in a whiplash of contempt. "You talk like a man because of that flashy hardware you're wearing. Strip it away and you'd shrivel down to boy size."

The very daring of it held Wilson motionless for an instant and father's voice cut into it. "Shane! Stop it!"

The blackness faded from Wilson's face. He smiled grimly at Shane. "You do need someone to look after you." He whirled his horse and put it to a run to join Fletcher and the others in the road.

It was only then that I realized mother was gripping my shoulders so that they hurt. She dropped on a chair and held me to her. We could hear father and Shane on the porch.

"He'd have drilled you, Joe, before you could have brought the gun up and pumped in a shell."

"But you, you crazy fool!" Father was covering his feelings with a show of exasperation. "You'd have made him plug you just so I'd have a chance to get him."

Mother jumped up. She pushed me aside. She flared at them from the doorway. "And both of you would have acted like fools just because he said that about me. I'll have you two know that if it's got to be done, I can take being insulted just as much as you can."

Peering around her, I saw them gaping at her in astonishment. "But, Marian," father objected mildly, coming to her. "What better reason could a man have?"

"Yes," said Shane gently. "What better reason?" He was not looking just at mother. He was looking at the two of them.

13

I DO NOT KNOW how long they would have stood there on the porch in the warmth of that moment. I shattered it by asking what seemed to me a simple question until after I had asked it and the significance hit me.

"Father, what are you going to tell Fletcher tonight?"

There was no answer. There was no need for one. I guess I was growing up. I knew what he would tell Fletcher. I knew what he would say. I knew, too, that because he was father he would have to go to Grafton's and say it. And I understood why they could no longer bear to look at one another, and the breeze blowing in from the sun-washed fields was suddenly so chill and cheerless.

They did not look at each other. They did not say a word to each other. Yet somehow I realized that they were closer together in the stillness there on the porch than they had ever been. They knew themselves and each of them knew that the other grasped the situation whole. They knew that Fletcher had dealt himself a winning hand, had caught father in the one play that he could not avoid because he would not avoid it. They knew that talk is meaningless when a common knowledge is already there. The silence bound them as no words ever could.

Father sat on the top porch step. He took out his pipe and drew on it as the match flamed and fixed his eyes on the horizon, on the mountains far across the river. Shane took the chair I had used for the games with mother. He swung it to the house wall and bent into it in that familiar unconscious gesture and he, too, looked into the distance. Mother turned into the kitchen and went about clearing the table as if she was not really aware of what she was doing. I helped her with the dishes and the old joy of sharing with her in the work was gone and there was no sound in the kitchen except the drip of the water and the chink of dish on dish.

When we were done, she went to father. She sat beside him on the step, her hand on the wood between them, and his covered hers and the moments merged in the slow, dwindling procession of time.

Loneliness gripped me. I wandered through the house, finding nothing there to do, and out on the porch and past those three and to the barn. I searched around and found an old shovel handle and started to whittle me a play saber with my knife. I had been thinking of this for days. Now the idea held no interest. The wood curls dropped to the barn floor, and after a while I let the shovel handle drop among them. Everything that had happened before seemed far off, almost like another existence. All that mattered was the length of the shadows creeping across the yard as the sun drove down the afternoon sky.

I took a hoe and went into mother's garden where the ground was caked around the turnips, the only things left unharvested. But there was scant work in me. I kept at it for a couple of rows, then the hoe dropped and I let it lie. I went to the front of the house, and there they were sitting, just as before.

I sat on the step below father and mother, between them, and their legs on each side of me made it seem better. I felt father's hand on my head.

"This is kind of tough on you, Bob." He could talk to me because I was only a kid. He was really talking to himself.

"I can't see the full finish. But I can see this. Wilson down and there'll be an end to it. Fletcher'll be done. The town will see to that. I can't beat Wilson on the draw. But there's strength enough in this clumsy body of mine to keep me on my feet till I get him, too." Mother stirred and was still, and his voice went on. "Things could be worse. It helps a man to know that if anything happens to him, his family will be in better hands than his own."

There was a sharp sound behind us on the porch. Shane had risen so swiftly that his chair had knocked against the wall. His hands were clenched tightly and his arms were quivering. His face was pale with the effort shaking him. He was desperate with an inner torment, his eyes tortured by thoughts that he could not escape, and the marks were obvious on him and he did not care. He strode to the steps, down past us and around the corner of the house.

Mother was up and after him, running head-long. She stopped abruptly at the house corner, clutching at the wood, panting and irresolute. Slowly she came back, her hands outstretched as if to keep from falling. She sank again on the step, close against father, and he gathered her to him with one great arm.

The silence spread and filled the whole valley and the shadows crept across the yard. They touched the road and began to merge in the deeper shading that meant the sun was dipping below the mountains far behind the house. Mother straightened, and as she stood up, father rose, too. He took hold of her two arms and held her in front of him. "I'm counting on you, Marian, to help him win again. You can do it, if anyone can." He smiled a strange little sad smile and he loomed up there above me the biggest man in all the world. "No supper for me now, Marian. A cup of your coffee is all I want." They passed through the doorway together.

Where was Shane? I hurried toward the barn. I was almost to it when I saw him out by the pasture. He was staring over it and the grazing steers at the great lonely mountains tipped with the gold of the sun now rushing down behind them. As I watched, he stretched his arms up, the fingers reaching to their utmost limits, grasping and grasping, it seemed, at the glory glowing in the sky.

He whirled and came straight back, striding with long steady steps, his head held high. There was some subtle, new, unchangeable certainty in him. He came close and I saw that his face was quiet and untroubled and that little lights danced in his eyes.

"Skip into the house, Bobby boy. Put on a smile. Everything is going to be all right." He was past me, without slowing, swinging into the barn.

But I could not go into the house. And I did not dare follow him, not after he had told me to go. A wild excitement was building up in me while I waited by the porch, watching the barn door.

The minutes ticked past and the twilight deepened and a patch of light sprang from the house as the lamp in the kitchen was lit. And still I waited. Then he was coming swiftly toward me and I stared and stared and broke and ran into the house with the blood pounding in my head.

"Father! Father! Shane's got his gun!"

He was close back of me. Father and mother barely had time to look up from the table before he was framed in the doorway. He was dressed as he was that first day when he rode into our lives, in that dark and worn magnificence from the black hat with its wide curling brim to the soft black boots. But what caught your eye was the single flash of white, the outer ivory plate on the grip of the gun, showing sharp and distinct against the dark material of the trousers. The tooled cartridge belt nestled around him. riding above the hip on the left, sweeping down on the right to hold the holster snug along the thigh, just as he had said, the gun handle about halfway between the wrist and elbow of his right arm hanging there relaxed and ready.

Belt and holster and gun . . . These were not things he was wearing or carrying. They were part of him, part of the man, of the full sum of the integrate force that was Shane. You could see now that for the first time this man who had been living with us, who was one of us, was complete, was himself in the final effect of his being.

Now that he was no longer in his crude work clothes, he seemed again slender, almost slight, as he did that first day. The change was more than that. What had been seeming iron was again steel. The slenderness was that of a tempered blade and a razor edge was there. Slim and dark in the doorway, he seemed somehow to fill the whole frame.

This was not our Shane. And yet it was. I remembered Ed Howells' saying that this was the most dangerous man he had ever seen. I remembered in the same rush that father had said he was the safest man we ever had in our house. I realized that both were right and that this, this at last, was Shane.

He was in the room now and he was speaking to them both in that bantering tone he used to have only for mother. "A fine pair of parents you are. Haven't even fed Bob yet. Stack him full of a good supper. Yourselves, too. I have a little business to tend to in town."

Father was looking fixedly at him. The sudden hope that had sprung in his face had as quickly gone. "No, Shane. It won't do. Even your thinking of it is the finest thing any man ever did for me. But I won't let you. It's my stand. Fletcher's making his play against me. There's no dodging. It's my business."

"There's where you're wrong, Joe," Shane said

gently. "This is my business. My kind of business. I've had fun being a farmer. You've shown me new meaning in the word, and I'm proud that for a while maybe I qualified. But there are a few things a farmer can't handle."

The strain of the long afternoon was telling on father. He pushed up from the table. "Damn it, Shane, be sensible. Don't make it harder for me. You can't do this."

Shane stepped near, to the side of the table, facing father across a corner. "Easy does it, Joe. I'm making this my business."

"No. I won't let you. Suppose you do put Wilson out of the way. That won't finish anything. It'll only even the score and swing things back worse than ever. Think what it'll mean to you. And where will it leave me? I couldn't hold my head up around here any more. They'd say I ducked and they'd be right. You can't do it and that's that."

"No?" Shane's voice was even more gentle, but it had a quiet, inflexible quality that had never been there before. "There's no man living can tell me what I can't do. Not even you, Joe. You forget there is still a way."

He was talking to hold father's attention. As

he spoke the gun was in his hand and before father could move he swung it, swift and sharp, so the barrel lined flush along the side of father's head, back of the temple, above the ear. Strength was in the blow and it thudded dully on the bone and father folded over the table and as it tipped with his weight slid toward the floor. Shane's arm was under him before he hit and Shane pivoted father's loose body up and into his chair and righted the table while the coffee cups rattled on the floor boards. Father's head lolled back and Shane caught it and eased it and the big shoulders forward till they rested on the table, the face down and cradled in the limp arms.

Shane stood erect and looked across the table at mother. She had not moved since he appeared in the doorway, not even when father fell and the table teetered under her hands on its edge. She was watching Shane, her throat curving in a lovely proud line, her eyes wide with a sweet warmth shining in them.

Darkness had shut down over the valley as they looked at each other across the table and the only light now was from the lamp swinging ever so slightly above them, circling them with its steady glow. They were alone in a moment that was all their own. Yet, when they spoke, it was of father.

"I was afraid," Shane murmured, "that he would take it that way. He couldn't do otherwise and be Joe Starrett."

"I know."

"He'll rest easy and come out maybe a little groggy but all right. Tell him, Marian. Tell him no man need be ashamed of being beat by Shane."

The name sounded queer like that, the man speaking of himself. It was the closest he ever came to boasting. And then you understood that there was not the least hint of a boast. He was stating a fact, simple and elemental as the power that dwelled in him.

"I know," she said again. "I don't need to tell him. He knows, too." She was rising, earnest and intent. "But there is something else I must know. We have battered down words that might have been spoken between us and that was as it should be. But I have a right to know now. I am part of this, too. And what I do depends on what you tell me now. Are you doing this just for me?"

Shane hesitated for a long, long moment. "No, Marian." His gaze seemed to widen and encompass us all, mother and the still figure of father and

me huddled on a chair by the window, and somehow the room and the house and the whole place.
Then he was looking only at mother and she was
all that he could see.

"No, Marian. Could I separate you in my
mind and afterwards be a man?"

He pulled his eyes from her and stared into the
night beyond the open door. His face hardened,
his thoughts leaping to what lay ahead in town.
So quiet and easy you were scarce aware that he
was moving, he was gone into the outer darkness.

NOTHING COULD HAVE KEPT ME there in the house
that night. My mind held nothing but the driving desire to follow Shane. I waited, hardly daring
to breathe, while mother watched him go. I
waited until she turned to father, bending over
him, then I slipped around the doorpost out to
the porch. I thought for a moment she had
noticed me, but I could not be sure and she did
not call to me. I went softly down the steps and
into the freedom of the night.

Shane was nowhere in sight. I stayed in the
darker shadows, looking about, and at last I saw
him emerging once more from the barn. The
moon was rising low over the mountains, a clean,
bright crescent. Its light was enough for me to

see him plainly in outline. He was carrying his saddle and a sudden pain stabbed through me as I saw that with it was his saddle-roll. He went toward the pasture gate, not slow, not fast, just firm and steady. There was a catlike certainty in his every movement, a silent, inevitable deadliness. I heard him, there by the gate, give his low whistle and the horse came out of the shadows at the far end of the pasture, its hooves making no noise in the deep grass, a dark and powerful shape etched in the moonlight drifting across the field straight to the man.

I knew what I would have to do. I crept along the corral fence, keeping tight to it, until I reached the road. As soon as I was around the corner of the corral with it and the barn between me and the pasture, I started to run as rapidly as I could toward town, my feet plumping softly in the thick dust of the road. I walked this every school day and it had never seemed long before. Now the distance stretched ahead, lengthening in my mind as if to mock me.

I could not let him see me. I kept looking back over my shoulder as I ran. When I saw him swinging into the road, I was well past Johnson's, almost past Shipstead's, striking into the last open stretch to the edge of town. I scurried to the side of the road and behind a clump of bullberry bushes. Panting to get my breath, I crouched there and waited for him to pass. The hoofbeats swelled in my ears, mingled with the pounding beat of my own blood. In my imagination he was galloping furiously and I was positive he was already rushing past me. But when I parted the bushes and pushed forward to peer out, he was moving at a moderate pace and was only almost abreast of me.

He was tall and terrible there in the road, looming up gigantic in the mystic half-light. He was the man I saw that first day, a stranger, dark and forbidding, forging his lone way out of an unknown past in the utter loneliness of his own immovable and instinctive defiance. He was the symbol of all the dim, formless imaginings of danger and terror in the untested realm of human potentialities beyond my understanding. The impact of the menace that marked him was like a physical blow.

I could not help it. I cried out and stumbled and fell. He was off his horse and over me before I could right myself, picking me up, his grasp strong and reassuring. I looked at him, tearful and afraid, and the fear faded from me. He was no stranger. That was some trick of the shadows. He was Shane. He was shaking me gently and smiling at me.

"Bobby boy, this is no time for you to be out. Skip along home and help your mother. I told you everything would be all right."

He let go of me and turned slowly, gazing out across the far sweep of the valley silvered in the moon's glow. "Look at it, Bob. Hold it in your mind like this. It's a lovely land, Bob. A good place to be a boy and grow straight inside as a man should."

My gaze followed his, and I saw our valley as though for the first time and the emotion in me was more than I could stand. I choked and reached out for him and he was not there.

He was rising into the saddle and the two shapes, the man and the horse, became one and moved down the road toward the yellow squares that were the patches of light from the windows of Grafton's building a quarter of a mile away. I wavered a moment, but the call was too strong. I started after him, running frantic in the middle of the road.

Whether he heard me or not, he kept right on. There were several men on the long porch of the building by the saloon doors. Red Marlin's hair made him easy to spot. They were scanning the road intently. As Shane hit the panel of light from the near big front window, the store window, they stiffened to attention. Red Marlin, a startled expression on his face, dived quickly through the doors.

Shane stopped, not by the rail but by the steps on the store side. When he dismounted, he did not slip the reins over the horse's head as the cowboys always did. He left them looped over the pommel of the saddle and the horse seemed to know what this meant. It stood motionless, close by the steps, head up, waiting, ready for whatever swift need.

Shane went along the porch and halted briefly, fronting the two men still there.

"Where's Fletcher?"

They looked at each other and at Shane. One of them started to speak. "He doesn't want — " Shane's voice stopped him. It slapped at them, low and with an edge that cut right into your mind. "Where's Fletcher?"

One of them jerked a hand toward the doors

and then, as they moved to shift out of his way, his voice caught them.

"Get inside. Go clear to the bar before you turn."

They stared at him and stirred uneasily and swung together to push through the doors. As the doors came back, Shane grabbed them, one with each hand, and pulled them out and wide open and he disappeared between them.

Clumsy and tripping in my haste, I scrambled up the steps and into the store. Sam Grafton and Mr. Weir were the only persons there and they were both hurrying to the entrance to the saloon, so intent that they failed to notice me. They stopped in the opening. I crept behind them to my familiar perch on my box where I could see past them.

The big room was crowded. Almost everyone who could be seen regularly around town was there, everyone but our homestead neighbors. There were many others who were new to me. They were lined up elbow to elbow nearly the entire length of the bar. The tables were full and more men were lounging along the far wall. The big round poker table at the back between the stairway to the little balcony and the door to Grafton's office was littered with glasses and chips. It seemed strange, for all the men standing, that there should be an empty chair at the far curve of the table. Someone must have been in that chair, because chips were at the place and a half-smoked cigar, a whisp of smoke curling up from it, was by them on the table.

Red Marlin was leaning against the back wall, behind the chair. As I looked, he saw the smoke and appeared to start a little. With a careful show of casualness he slid into the chair and picked up the cigar.

A haze of thinning smoke was by the ceiling over them all, floating in involved streamers around the hanging lamps. This was Grafton's saloon in the flush of a banner evening's business. But something was wrong, was missing. The hum of activity, the whirr of voices, that should have risen from the scene, been part of it, was stilled in a hush more impressive than any noise could be. The attention of everyone in the room, like a single sense, was centered on that dark figure just inside the swinging doors, back to them and touching them.

This was the Shane of the adventures I had

dreamed for him, cool and competent, facing that room full of men in the simple solitude of his own invincible completeness.

His eyes searched the room. They halted on a man sitting at a small table in the front corner with his hat on low over his forehead. With a thump of surprise I recognized it was Stark Wilson and he was studying Shane with a puzzled look on his face. Shane's eyes swept on, checking off each person. They stopped again on a figure over by the wall and the beginnings of a smile showed in them and he nodded almost imperceptibly. It was Chris, tall and lanky, his arm in a sling, and as he caught the nod he flushed a little and shifted his weight from one foot to the other. Then he straightened his shoulders and over his face came a slow smile, warm and friendly, the smile of a man who knows his own mind at last.

But Shane's eyes were already moving on. They narrowed as they rested on Red Marlin. Then they jumped to Will Atkey trying to make himself small behind the bar.

"Where's Fletcher?"

Will fumbled with the cloth in his hands. "I — I don't know. He was here awhile ago." Frightened at the sound of his own voice in the stillness, Will dropped the cloth, started to stoop for it, and checked himself, putting his hands to the inside rim of the bar to hold himself steady.

Shane tilted his head slightly so his eyes could clear his hatbrim. He was scanning the balcony across the rear of the room. It was empty and the doors there were closed. He stepped forward, disregarding the men by the bar, and walked quietly past them the long length of the room. He went through the doorway to Grafton's office and into the semi-darkness beyond.

And still the hush held. Then he was in the office doorway again and his eyes bored toward Red Marlin.

"Where's Fletcher?"

The silence was taut and unendurable. It had to break. The sound was that of Stark Wilson coming to his feet in the far front corner. His voice, lazy and insolent, floated down the room.

"Where's Starrett?"

While the words yet seemed to hang in the air, Shane was moving toward the front of the room. But Wilson was moving, too. He was crossing toward the swinging doors and he took his stand just to the left of them, a few feet out from the wall. The position gave him command of the wide aisle running back between the bar and the tables and Shane coming forward in it.

Shane stopped about three quarters of the way forward, about five yards from Wilson. He cocked his head for one quick sidewise glance again at the balcony and then he was looking only at Wilson. He did not like the setup. Wilson had the front wall and he was left in the open of the room. He understood the fact, assessed it, accepted it.

They faced each other in the aisle and the men along the bar jostled one another in their hurry to get to the opposite side of the room. A reckless arrogance was on Wilson, certain of himself and his control of the situation. He was not one to miss the significance of the slim deadliness that was Shane. But even now, I think, he did not believe that anyone in our valley would deliberately stand up to him.

"Where's Starrett?" he said once more, still mocking Shane but making it this time a real question.

The words went past Shane as if they had not been spoken. "I had a few things to say to Fletcher," he said gently. "That can wait. You're a pushing man, Wilson, so I reckon I had better accommodate you."

Wilson's face sobered and his eyes glinted coldly. "I've no quarrel with you," he said flatly, "even if you are Starrett's man. Walk out of here without any fuss and I'll let you go. It's Starrett I want."

"What you want, Wilson, and what you'll get are two different things. Your killing days are done."

Wilson had it now. You could see him grasp the meaning. This quiet man was pushing him just as he had pushed Ernie Wright. As he measured Shane, it was not to his liking. Something that was not fear but a kind of wondering and baffled reluctance showed in his face. And then there was no escape, for that gentle voice was pegging him to the immediate and implacable moment.

"I'm waiting, Wilson. Do I have to crowd you into slapping leather?"

Time stopped and there was nothing in all the world but two men looking into eternity in each other's eyes. And the room rocked in the sudden blur of action indistinct in its incredible swiftness and the roar of their guns was a single sustained blast. And Shane stood, solid on his feet as a rooted oak. and Wilson swayed, his right arm hanging useless, blood beginning to show in a small stream from under the sleeve over the hand, the gun slipping from the numbing fingers.

He backed against the wall, a bitter disbelief twisting his features. His left arm hooked and the second gun was showing and Shane's bullet smashed into his chest and his knees buckled, sliding him slowly down the wall till the lifeless weight of the body toppled it sideways to the floor.

Shane gazed across the space between and he seemed to have forgotten all else as he let his gun ease into the holster. "I gave him his chance," he murmured out of the depths of a great sadness. But the words had no meaning for me, because I noticed on the dark brown of his shirt, low and just above the belt to one side of the buckle, the darker spot gradually widening. Then others noticed, too, and there was a stir in the air and the room was coming to life.

Voices were starting, but no one focused on them. They were snapped short by the roar of a shot from the rear of the room. A wind seemed to whip Shane's shirt at the shoulder and the glass of the front window beyond shattered near the bottom.

Then I saw it.

It was mine alone. The others were turning to stare at the back of the room. My eyes were fixed on Shane and I saw it. I saw the whole man move, all of him, in the single flashing instant. I saw the head lead and the body swing and the driving power of the legs beneath. I saw the arm leap and the hand take the gun in the lightning sweep. I saw the barrel line up like — like a finger pointing — and the flame spurt even as the man himself was still in motion.

And there on the balcony Fletcher, impaled in the act of aiming for a second shot, rocked on his heels and fell back into the open doorway behind him. He clawed at the jambs and pulled himself forward. He staggered to the rail and tried to raise the gun. But the strength was draining out of him and he collapsed over the rail, jarring it loose and falling with it.

Across the stunned and barren silence of the room Shane's voice seemed to come from a great distance. "I expect that finishes it," he said. Unconsciously, without looking down, he broke out the cylinder of his gun and reloaded it. The stain on his shirt was bigger now, spreading fanlike above the belt, but he did not appear to know or care. Only his movements were slow, retarded by an unutterable weariness. The hands were sure and steady, but they moved slowly and the gun dropped into the holster of its own weight.

He backed with dragging steps toward the swinging doors until his shoulders touched them. The light in his eyes was unsteady like the flickering of a candle guttering toward darkness. And then, as he stood there, a strange thing happened.

How could one describe it, the change that came over him? Out of the mysterious resources of his will the vitality came. It came creeping, a tide of strength that crept through him and fought and shook off the weakness. It shone in his eyes and they were alive again and alert. It welled up in him, sending that familiar power surging through him again until it was singing again in every vibrant line of him.

He faced that room full of men and read them all with the one sweeping glance and spoke to them in that gentle voice with that quiet, inflexible quality.

"I'll be riding on now. And there's not a one of you that will follow."

He turned his back on them in the indifference

of absolute knowledge they would do as he said. Straight and superb, he was silhouetted against the doors and the patch of night above them. The next moment they were closing with a soft swish of sound.

The room was crowded with action now. Men were clustering around the bodies of Wilson and Fletcher, pressing to the bar, talking excitedly. Not a one of them, though, approached too close to the doors. There was a cleared space by the doorway as if someone had drawn a line marking it off.

I did not care what they were doing or what they were saying. I had to get to Shane. I had to get to him in time. I had to know, and he was the only one who could ever tell me.

I dashed out the store door and I was in time. He was on his horse, already starting away from the steps.

"Shane," I whispered desperately, loud as I dared without the men inside hearing me. "Oh, Shane!"

He heard me and reined around and I hurried to him, standing by a stirrup and looking up.

"Bobby! Bobby boy! What are you doing here?"

"I've been here all along," I blurted out. "You've got to tell me. Was that Wilson — "

He knew what was troubling me. He always knew. "Wilson," he said, "was mighty fast. As fast as I've ever seen."

"I don't care," I said, the tears starting. "I don't care if he was the fastest that ever was. He'd never have been able to shoot you, would he? You'd have got him straight, wouldn't you — if you had been in practice?"

He hesitated a moment. He gazed down at me and into me and he knew. He knew what goes on in a boy's mind and what can help him stay clean inside through the muddled, dirtied years of growing up.

"Sure. Sure, Bob. He'd never even have cleared the holster."

He started to bend down toward me, his hand reaching for my head. But the pain struck him like a whiplash and the hand jumped to his shirt front by the belt, pressing hard, and he reeled a little in the saddle.

The ache in me was more than I could bear. I stared dumbly at him, and because I was just a boy and helpless I turned away and hid my face against the firm, warm flank of the horse.

"Bob."

"Yes, Shane."

"A man is what he is, Bob, and there's no breaking the mold. I tried that and I've lost. But I reckon it was in the cards from the moment I saw a freckled kid on a rail up the road there and a real man behind him, the kind that could back him for the chance another kid never had."

"But — but, Shane, you — "

"There's no going back from a killing, Bob. Right or wrong, the brand sticks and there's no going back. It's up to you now. Go home to your mother and father. Grow strong and straight and take care of them. Both of them."

"Yes, Shane."

"There's only one thing more I can do for them now."

I felt the horse move away from me. Shane was looking down the road and on to the open plain and the horse was obeying the silent command of the reins. He was riding away and I knew that no word or thought could hold him. The big horse, patient and powerful, was already settling into the steady pace that had brought him into our valley, and the two, the man and the horse, were a single dark shape in the road as they passed beyond the reach of the light from the windows.

I strained my eyes after him, and then in the moonlight I could make out the inalienable out-line of his figure receding into the distance. Lost in my loneliness, I watched him go, out of town, far down the road where it curved out to the level country beyond the valley. There were men on the porch behind me, but I was aware only of that dark shape growing small and indistinct along the far reach of the road. A cloud passed over the moon and he merged into the general shadow and I could not see him and the cloud passed on and the road was a plain thin ribbon to the horizon and he was gone.

I stumbled back to fall on the steps, my head in my arms to hide the tears. The voices of the men around me were meaningless noises in a bleak and empty world. It was Mr. Weir who took me home.

15

FATHER AND MOTHER were in the kitchen, almost as I had left them. Mother had hitched her chair close to father's. He was sitting up, his face tired and haggard, the ugly red mark standing out plain along the side of his head. They did not come to meet us. They sat still and watched us move into the doorway.

They did not even scold me. Mother reached and pulled me to her and let me crawl into her lap as I had not done for three years or more. Father just stared at Mr. Weir. He could not trust himself to speak first.

"Your troubles are over, Starrett."

Father nodded. "You've come to tell me," he said wearily, "that he killed Wilson before they got him. I know. He was Shane."

"Wilson," said Mr. Weir. "And Fletcher."

Father started. "Fletcher, too? By Godfrey, yes. He would do it right." Then father sighed and ran a finger along the bruise on his head. "He let me know this was one thing he wanted to handle by himself. I can tell you, Weir, waiting here is the hardest job I ever had."

Mr. Weir looked at the bruise. "I thought so. Listen, Starrett. There's not a man in town doesn't know you didn't stay here of your own will. And there's damn few that aren't glad it was Shane came into the saloon tonight."

The words broke from me. "You should have seen him, father. He was — he was — " I could not find it at first. "He was — beautiful, father. And Wilson wouldn't even have hit him if he'd been in practice. He told me so."

"He told you!" The table was banging over as father drove to his feet. He grabbed Mr. Weir by the coat front. "My God, man! Why didn't you tell me? He's alive?"

"Yes," said Mr. Weir. "He's alive all right. Wilson got to him. But no bullet can kill that man." A puzzled, faraway sort of look flitted across Mr. Weir's face. "Sometimes I wonder whether anything ever could."

Father was shaking him. "Where is he?"

"He's gone," said Mr. Weir. "He's gone, alone and unfollowed as he wanted it. Out of the valley and no one knows where."

Father's hands dropped. He slumped again into his chair. He picked up his pipe and it broke in his fingers. He let the pieces fall and stared at them on the floor. He was still staring at them when new footsteps sounded on the porch and a man pushed into our kitchen.

It was Chris. His right arm was tight in the sling, his eyes unnaturally bright and the color high in his face. In his left hand he was carrying a bottle, a bottle of red cherry soda pop. He came straight in and righted the table with the hand holding the bottle. He smacked the bottle on the top boards and seemed startled at the noise he made. He was embarrassed and he was having trouble with his voice. But he spoke up firmly.

"I brought that for Bob. I'm a damned poor substitute, Starrett. But as soon as this arm's healed, I'm asking you to let me work for you."

Father's face twisted and his lips moved, but no words came. Mother was the one who said it. "Shane would like that, Chris."

And still father said nothing. What Chris and

Mr. Weir saw as they looked at him must have shown them that nothing they could do or say would help at all. They turned and went out together, walking with long, quick steps.

Mother and I sat there watching father. There was nothing we could do either. This was something he had to wrestle alone. He was so still that he seemed even to have stopped breathing. Then a sudden restlessness hit him and he was up and pacing aimlessly about. He glared at the walls as if they stifled him and strode out the door into the yard. We heard his steps around the house and heading into the fields and then we could hear nothing.

I do not know how long we sat there. I know that the wick in the lamp burned low and sputtered awhile and went out and the darkness was a relief and a comfort. At last mother rose, still holding me, the big boy bulk of me, in her arms. I was surprised at the strength in her. She was holding me tightly to her and she carried me into my little room and helped me undress in the dim shadows of the moonlight through the window. She tucked me in and sat on the edge of the bed, and then, only then, she whispered to me: "Now, Bob. Tell me everything. Just as you saw it happen."

I told her, and when I was done, all she said in a soft little murmur was "Thank you." She looked out the window and murmured the words again and they were not for me and she was still looking out over the land to the great gray mountains when finally I fell asleep.

She must have been there the whole night through, for when I woke with a start, the first streaks of dawn were showing through the window and the bed was warm where she had been. The movement of her leaving must have wakened me. I crept out of bed and peeked into the kitchen. She was standing in the open outside doorway.

I fumbled into my clothes and tiptoed through the kitchen to her. She took my hand and I clung to hers and it was right that we should be together and that together we should go find father.

We found him out by the corral, by the far end where Shane had added to it. The sun was beginning to rise through the cleft in the mountains across the river, not the brilliant glory of midday but the fresh and renewed reddish radiance of early morning. Father's arms were folded on the top rail, his head bowed on them. When he turned to face us, he leaned back against the rail as if he needed the support. His eyes were rimmed and a little wild.

"Marian, I'm sick of the sight of this valley and all that's in it. If I tried to stay here now, my heart wouldn't be in it any more. I know it's hard on you and the boy, but we'll have to pull up stakes and move on. Montana, maybe. I've heard there's good land for the claiming up that way."

Mother heard him through. She had let go my hand and stood erect, so angry that her eyes snapped and her chin quivered. But she heard him through.

"Joe! Joe Starrett!" Her voice fairly crackled and was rich with emotion that was more than anger. "So you'd run out on Shane just when he's really here to stay!"

"But, Marian. You don't understand. He's gone."

"He's not gone. He's here, in this place, in this place he gave us. He's all around us and in us, and he always will be."

She ran to the tall corner post, to the one Shane had set. She beat at it with her hands. "Here, Joe. Quick. Take hold. Pull it down."

Father stared at her in amazement. But he did as she said. No one could have denied her in that moment. He took hold of the post and pulled at it. He shook his head and braced his feet and strained at it with all his strength. The big muscles of his shoulders and back knotted and bulged till I thought this shirt, too, would shred. Creakings ran along the rails and the post moved ever so slightly and the ground at the base showed little cracks fanning out. But the rails held and the post stood.

Father turned from it, beads of sweat breaking on his face, a light creeping up his drawn cheeks.

"See, Joe. See what I mean. We have roots here now that we can never tear loose."

And the morning was in father's face, shining in his eyes, giving him new color and hope and understanding.

~~~~~~ 16 ~~~~~~

I GUESS THAT IS ALL there is to tell. The folks in town and the kids at school liked to talk about Shane, to spin tales and speculate about him. I never did. Those nights at Grafton's became legends in the valley and countless details were added as they grew and spread just as the town, too, grew and spread up the river banks. But I never bothered, no matter how strange the tales became in the constant retelling. He belonged to me, to father and mother and me, and nothing could ever spoil that.

For mother was right. He was there. He was there in our place and in us. Whenever I needed him, he was there. I could close my eyes and he would be with me and I would see him plain and hear again that gentle voice.

I would think of him in each of the moments that revealed him to me. I would think of him most vividly in that single flashing instant when he whirled to shoot Fletcher on the balcony at Grafton's saloon. I would see again the power and grace of a coordinate force beautiful beyond comprehension. I would see the man and the weapon wedded in the one indivisible deadliness. I would see the man and the tool, a good man and a good tool, doing what had to be done.

And always my mind would go back at the last to that moment when I saw him from the bushes by the roadside just on the edge of town. I would see him there in the road, tall and terrible in the moonlight, going down to kill or be killed, and stopping to help a stumbling boy and to look out over the land, the lovely land, where that boy had a chance to live out his boyhood and grow straight inside as a man should.

And when I would hear the men in town talking among themselves and trying to pin him down to a definite past, I would smile quietly to myself. For a time they inclined to the notion, spurred by the talk of a passing stranger, that he was a certain

Shannon who was famous as a gunman and gambler way down in Arkansas and Texas and dropped from sight without anyone knowing why or where. When that notion dwindled, others followed, pieced together in turn from scraps of information gleaned from stray travelers. But when they talked like that, I simply smiled because I knew he could have been none of these.

He was the man who rode into our little valley out of the heart of the great glowing West and when his work was done rode back whence he had come and he was Shane.

THE END

The Novel: Essays
in Evaluation
and Interpretation

Henry Joseph Nuwer

An Interview with
Jack Schaefer:
May 1972

NUWER: I understand that you were born in Cleveland and attended eastern colleges at Oberlin and Columbia University. Were your initial interests in literature in other areas than that of Western writing?

SCHAEFER: Well, when I was a kid I read more Tarzan stories by Edgar Rice Burroughs than anything else. Later I read Dickens, Thackeray, and Trollope. I guess I used to read everything. I started with the classics, both Greek and Latin writers. Before I was through with college though, I had more than enough of Greek. I loved and still enjoy Latin though.

I switched to English literature while at Columbia doing graduate work. I specialized in eighteenth-century literature of the Johnsonian period.

NUWER: Who were you particularly interested in?

SCHAEFER: Arthur Murphy. Are you familiar with him?

NUWER: No, I'm afraid not. Who was he?

SCHAEFER: Well, actually, he was perhaps best known as an actor. He was a player well known to Johnson and Gold-smith. But I soon got off of that. Scholarship strikes me as a dull and stupid waste of time. All that piling up of detail! And for what purpose? While I was at Columbia I had what I thought was a bright idea for my thesis. I wanted to do research on the development of motion pictures. At that time I had an aunt who reviewed films ready to assist me. Besides that I had a tremendous interest in films. The thesis committee at Columbia just laughed at me. They said that movies were merely cheap reproductions of stage plays. After that I left Columbia. I have never been back and have never regretted leaving at all.

NUWER: How did you acquire such an interest in Westerns?

SCHAEFER: My first book, *Shane*, was written in Norfolk, Virginia. I had never been west of Toledo, Ohio, at that time. Those were Depression years. I worked the equivalent of two full-time jobs. I taught nights in a prison; mornings and afternoons I worked for a newspaper and edited a small weekly magazine. Sixteen hours a day! Anyway, when I was through working I read books on American history to relax. You know, nothing that I took in college ever helped me with my work. I'd say that the value of a college education is that it teaches one *how* to learn. My readings in American history were chronological ones. I was getting books to review, and I was happiest and felt most at home west of the Mississippi River. Out here it is so neglected—one of the greatest periods in history—neglected by historians and by writers alike. It is neglected despite its being a distinctive era in history.

I was not reading Western stories then. I read history. I only read a few of the better Westerns. In fact, if I had known of the tremendous amount of bad Western writings that was flooding the market I wouldn't have written anything. This was 1945; I was acting editor of the Norfolk paper. I'd come home very late at night. We had a problem getting any kind of men to staff the paper at that time.

Primarily as a means of relaxation I started writing fiction late at night. I began writing a short story about the basic legend of the West. It kept growing and wound up being a novella. I didn't know what to do with it. Finally I sent it to *Argosy*. This is a story in itself. I didn't know anything about markets and selling a manuscript. I had only one copy of this Western novella and that was single-spaced. I didn't even include a return envelope. Nowadays if there's no return envelope it means the wastebasket for a story. Months passed without a word from *Argosy* but I was pretty busy during those years and just forgot about it. It wasn't until a long time later that Rogers Terrill, the publisher of publishers, told me what a damn fool I had been.

When the manuscript for *Shane* came in, it was just tossed on a desk. One weekend, however, heading out for some relaxation in Connecticut, the editor put some stuff in his briefcase and somehow my manuscript slipped in also. I was lucky. I've always been fortunate with my writing. Instead of being tossed into a wastebasket as it would have been back in the office, *Shane* was given a look. He kept on reading and decided *Argosy* would use it. It first appeared as a three-part serial. They put my name on the cover of the first issue—with my name misspelled! It's been my curse to have people add another "f" to Schaefer when they spell it.

In 1946 they used it. I went on being a newspaper editor. In 1949, after talking it over with my wife Louise, I quit newspaper work. We were in New York without a cent with me selling a pint of blood every now and then. Went into the stumping business with *Shane*. This is the addition which really made *Shane* into a novel. I took it to four different publishing houses. It came back unsold two weeks later.

Knew the name of one literary agent. He had to get suckers. He had William Somerset Maugham and Sinclair

Lewis leave him because of his selling them down the river. Anyway, it was one week later when he called and said *Shane* was sold. Later I was lucky enough to get Don Congdon, the best agent in the business, from the Harold Matson Company. He is thorough, honest, and competent. He likes to comb the small publications as much as the top-paying ones. It was funny one time. I took the only short-short I ever wrote and sent it to Don Congdon. He sent it to a newspaper in Canada. They called him from Vancouver and said that they would have loved to use it, but they couldn't for one reason. They had already published it eighteen months before when my old agent had sent it in to them. I had to call him to get my money. In fact, once I called him up after being away from him for ten years and asked him, just for the fun of it, to send me the money he had gotten for a piece in that foreign magazine. The next thing I know, a check for $72 is in my hands. He was honest and always paid his debts—*if* you caught him and asked him hard enough.

Don Congdon was different. He never presses a writer to change a word. He is actually interested in his writers as friends, not just as clients. He gets as much a kick out of selling a poem for fifteen dollars as in selling movie rights for one hundred thousand dollars. Once when he needed a quiet place to stay, he came over by me. While he was visiting he sold two things over the phone. One was a little piece by some young writer for twenty-five dollars; the other was William Styron's *Nat Turner* to Wolper Productions. He spent more on the phone calls than the young writer made, but he got more out of a thrill from selling that than he did from selling the movie rights.

NUWER: Would you suggest then that a young writer send his material directly to an agent? Or, would it be better if he sent a book-length manuscript on to the publisher for the very first time?

SCHAEFFER: That is a tough question. A good agent is thinking of cutting down, not adding. One thing I know. If there is a reading fee, shy away. The good ones don't charge. They don't have to. They get their ten percent. I guess I'd say it is best for a young writer to get started on his own. With a first novel, one should first try to get a publisher interested. Then the author can write to an agent who can get him a better deal. You must almost always get published first. Then you can get an agent. Here again I was lucky. In fact, other writers envy me when I tell them who my agent is.

NUWER: All right. May I ask how your early life prepared you for the writing profession? Did your parents encourage you? In other words, what forces or people moved you enough to take up writing?

SCHAEFER: My parents were both readers. There was always a house full of books. They didn't stop me or try to check my reading habits. I just read everything in sight. Today I would hope that every household might have a *Shane* to interest youngsters in reading. I always had Alexandre Dumas's works around. My dad in particular was a reader. I guess you might call him a Lincoln nut. He was a friend of Carl Sandburg.

NUWER: I assume then that you had *The Prairie Years* handy as reference material.

SCHAEFER: Yes. It was interesting. Father became a lawyer because Lincoln was a lawyer. But, back to the first question. I always had scribbled things down. I was the editor of the high school literary magazine. My sister was also a literary nut and editor of the same magazine before me. When she needed to fill space I would crank out articles for her. In college I was interested in creative writing and debating.

My first real decision came after *Shane* was published. It was not a question of whether or not I wanted to become a professional writer, but rather a question of what direction it was in that I wanted to go. Most people ask, "Why write Westerns. They're one step above comic books." I agreed for a time. I said good-bye to Westerns and started to write an Eastern. It was all it needed to be in form, heavily laden with symbolism, for example. I didn't like it, though. It was just hard work. Somewhere in the middle of writing it I took a week off and wrote a short story about a sheepherder which just came to me. I sent it off to my agent. Then I went back to finish my Easterner, and found out shortly thereafter that the *Saturday Evening Post* had taken the short story. I finished the Easterner, but you know, it has never been published.

NUWER: What was the name of the Easterner? I'm curious.

SCHAEFER: Oh, let me see now. What was her name? It was *Elsa Eberle*. Yes, it has never been published. Been buried for years. I don't even know if it is here in the house. I said the hell with it and began concentrating on markets like the *Saturday Evening Post* and *Colliers*. *Colliers*, incidentally, used to be a pretty fair magazine in its day.

NUWER: Have you ever regretted writing Westerns?

SCHAEFER: No. In fact, I developed a question that I always ask. I'll go into that in a minute. I started going to a lot of those literary affairs. Inevitably someone would come up to me and ask me what it was that I did for a living. Then I would begin to stare intently at my questioner, and with a glazed look in my eye I would shout out, "*I write Westerns!*" Then, in self defense, I would ask the listener a question of my own. I would ask, "Can you give me one good reason why a writer cannot 'write' good literature about the west the same as he could about the east or anywhere else?" And do you know, no one has yet been able to answer me.

NUWER: You echo this viewpoint in your introduction

to *Out West,* a collection of short stories by other writers that you edited. You said that "the writer who has anything to say to his fellow men can say it as effectively in the western story as in any other form of fiction." I had jotted the quote down here in my notes to discuss with you, but you've anticipated my line of questioning. I did want to ask you to name a couple of writers that you believe have exhibited a high degree of skill in Western writing and story telling.

SCHAEFER: I think I would select Walter Van Tilburg Clark, Dorothy Johnson, H. L. Davis, Oliver La Farge—who wrote about Indians and thus may not be considered a "Western" writer by some people—and Mary Austin.

NUWER: Oh yes. Were you very interested in Mary Austin's work?

SCHAEFER: I had perhaps the only complete collection of Mary Austin's works. I gave them intact to the University of New Mexico's library. I think she is great. Up and away she's the best woman writer and equally as good as any man, too. She did write some potboilers, it is true, that are dated, but several other things are perfectly literary.

NUWER: Going back to your own work: how long before you finally got out West?

SCHAEFER: I had written four books about the West and still I had not been out here. Well, one day my agent and Harry Synos, the senior editor up at Holiday Magazine, were having lunch. Don told Harry I had never been west and Harry said it was time that I went and *Holiday* would foot the bill. The first piece was on the Dakotas and I still have a blown-up photo of a buffalo that appeared in the first article. *Holiday* used the pieces with a slant on a series of old-time cowtowns as compared with today, such as Abilene and Dodge City.

When I was finished and headed back out to Connecticut, Louise asked "How soon can we move?" In just two weeks we had a trailer and truck ready. That truck is still around someplace today. We picked Gunnison in Colorado for our first home. I'm glad we're not living there now though because Colorado is becoming too much like the east. Anyway, this was the time of the great floods. In two weeks we had a trailer and a truck ready. Those '55s were solid vehicles. Like I said, that truck is still being driven today. We decided on Gunnison, Colorado, to make our home. I'm kind of glad it didn't work out there as you will see. I've never liked Colorado as much as New Mexico because it tries too hard to be just like the East. Anyway, we got as far as Salida and the Monarch Pass and the weather reports said it was blizzarding up ahead. We wouldn't attempt to drive the car over the pass. In a way though it was exciting to see the West that I had written about all these years explode before me.

NUWER: What did you do then?

SCHAEFER: I knew that in Salida there was a Western writer named Steve Frazee. I called him and told him who I was. Asked him if he could put us in touch with someone who could help us get over the pass. He said "Stay right there!" Fifteen minutes later there came Steve and a neighbor with a jeep. It was a marvelous introduction to the West. Well, they got us over Monarch Pass, waved goodbye, and went back home. We drove on and found out that the town was closed up for the winter. Two motels there had been shut down too; we couldn't find a place to stay. Luckily we were able to contact one of the motel owners and persuade him to give us a cabin. Then my wife had an idea. "Let's go to Santa Fe for the winter." We landed by Cerillos, built a ranch, and have been located here in New Mexico ever since.

NUWER: Thank you. To get back to your writing

Fred Erisman

Growing Up with the American West: Fiction of Jack Schaefer

Despite the variety of topics available to him as a chronicler of the American West, Jack Schaefer (1907–) returns again and again in his fiction to the theme of growing up. Various critics have commented upon his recurring use of the theme,[1] but such studies really are unnecessary. Schaefer's works tell their own tale: *Shane* (1949), for example, with its youthful narrator and retrospective point of view, makes clear its theme of maturation throughout; *First Blood* (1953) identifies its direction in its title; and *Monte Walsh* (1963) opens with its sixteen-year-old protagonist setting out on what is to become a forty-year-long course of development. As these books suggest, the process, in Schaefer's hands, is a rich topic, and one peculiarly suited to the western settings of his novels.

Schaefer's repeated treatments of the topic, however, take on additional significance when one relates them to the fuller scope of the novels in which they appear. He sets his tales of growing up squarely within the context of the "classical" Western story, which, as John G. Cawelti has pointed out, is almost automatically limited to the period in United States history from 1865 to 1910.[2] This period is a turbulent one, embracing years in which the United States itself was growing up, changing from an idealistic experiment in popular government to a sophisticated, if unwilling, world power. It is a period the history of which suggestively parallels the themes of Schaefer's novels.

These novels, when read with a full awareness of their historical overtones, become more than simple, blood-and-thunder tales of the frontier. They are, to be sure, stories of maturation, but they go beyond human maturation to comment upon national maturation. Indeed, in his accounts of life in the American West, Schaefer seems almost to be treating the West as a microcosm of the United States. He tests his characters with the same tests that one uses to determine the progress of a country toward nationhood, and comments upon the maturing of a nation as he describes the maturing of its people.

In his study of the growth of American national identity, *The American Quest,* Clinton Rossiter remarks that one of the most obvious characteristics of nationhood is territorial integrity.[3] That is, there must be, if a country is truly to be a nation, a clearly defined body of territory with which all members of its society can identify. This can be a territory defined either naturally, as by a river or a mountain range, or arbitrarily, as by dictatorial fiat or international arbitration. It must, though, be defined. Once such a definition has appeared and been generally accepted, both within the country and without, the land is on its way to nationhood.

Schaefer's characters likewise define themselves and their lives by the territory they embrace. Two homesteaders, Joe Starrett, in *Shane,* and Brent Kean, in *The Kean Land* (1959), are ready examples. Their stories are basically stories of the land. Both see their lives as bounded by their homesteads, both feel a considerable identity with their land, and both are ready to go to any length to protect their claim upon the land.[4] This identity is made all the more intense by the presence of outsiders who want to encroach upon the land—the cattle baron, Luke Fletcher, and the land speculator, Herbert Goss, respectively. From this encroachment comes the major conflict of each story, which contributes in each case to the education of the young narrator.

A more subtle kind of territorial identification, however, comes through the ways in which Shane, himself a gunfighter fleeing his past, reacts to the Starrett farm. At first simply a willing helper, Shane quickly comes to feel the same identification that Starrett does—an identification that provides him with something missing from his life. When the pressures of the clash with Fletcher weigh heavy upon him Shane, young Bob Starrett remarks, "would wander alone about our place, and this was the one thing that seemed to soothe him. I used to see him, when he thought no one was watching, run his hands along the rails of the corral he had fastened, test with a tug the posts he had set, pace out past the barn looking up at the bulging loft and stride out where the tall corn was standing in big shocks to dig his hands in the loose soil and lift some of it and let it run through his fingers."[5] There is more here than a simple paean to the agrarian life. Shane, a footloose and violent man, has found himself in the confines of Starrett's land. It is not just land, but cultivated, defined land that speaks to him. He, like the more obvious Starrett, has found where he belongs; his past, though, prevents him from staying. He can defend Starrett, but not himself. Those whose territory is defined and defensible, Schaefer seems to say, those who are committed to the land, are established—a point he makes explicit when Joe Starrett tries futilely to unearth the corner post of his corral.[6] Both, man and post, have taken root.

A second quality that Rossiter sees as defining nationhood is popular cohesion, the quality that consolidates diverse factions into the people of a single community or nation. Only through such a generalized cohesion, he points out, can the tensions, inherent in diversity be contained. The result of such cohesion is not a loss of individual identity, but rather the achieving of a generalized body of goals and ideals that all can share.[7] When this is done, the country will have cemented its national identity still more firmly.

Concern for a similar growth of community permeates Schaefer's novels. A significant part of *First Blood*, for example, focuses upon the transition from lynch law to judicial law in the Western territories. Popular sentiment in the town of Goshen inclines toward the summary execution of a pair of stage-robbers. The circuit judge insists upon the letter of the law, and only slowly does the youthful narrator come to see the broader implications of the judge's action. One person does not make a populace, but he certainly contributes to it; the lesson that Jess Harker learns is also apparent to other of the citizens, as his acceptance by his employer and his fiancee suggests.[8]

The importance of cohesion to even a small society forms the nucleus of *Company of Cowards* (1957), as Jared Heath, a Union officer convicted of cowardice during the Battle of the Wilderness, is given command of a squad of equally disgraced men. His problem is twofold: to overcome the cowardice of his men, and to mold them into some semblance of a combat unit. This he does, through sheer force of will, until his group redeems itself in an Indian skirmish in the Texas Panhandle. Schaefer's point is clear. Cohesion can come about in many ways, by self-education or by the exertions of an able, charismatic leader. (Heath is the latter, as one of the survivors of the skirmish implies: "A man has to face up to things. I go to pieces. I went to pieces out there and I'd of been running like —— well, I'd of been running, only there was a goddamned heartless bastard of a better man out there too who wouldn't let me run. I found out I could follow him."[9]) But regardless of how the cohesion develops, and whether he speaks of an eight-man military unit or a frontier town with a population of a few hundred, Schaefer speaks often of the need for cohesion—for the intangible sense that holds fragmented individuals together and makes of them a functioning society.

A goal of nationhood more complex than either territoriality or cohesiveness is independence. A nation, obviously, has to be politically independent. More than that, however, it needs also to be economically and culturally independent. That is, not only must its government be free from external political influences, but its economy must be free from reliance upon the economic interests of other countries. As Rossiter points out, "A country whose economy is largely owned and controlled from abroad is grievously defective in a principal mark of nationhood." Moreover, a nation must have some sense of its own peculiar achievements. Even if its cultural achievements are but developments of an older, more established culture, they must have their uniqueness emphasized in a way that calls attention to their source.[10] Thus, for example, though the Puritan poets of seventeenth-century New England were writing after British models, they incorporated into their work materials and attitudes that made it distinctively American.

Schaefer's people seek a similar independence. Whether Shane, the gunfighter trying to find a new life as a farmer, or Monte Walsh, the aging broncobuster trying to come to grips with the acceleration of progress, they strive for a life that is peculiarly their own, even as it is linked to the established life of a community. Of all of Schaefer's works, the one that speaks most clearly to this topic is *The Canyon* (1953). Its central theme is independence, as it tells of Little Bear, a Cheyenne brave who cannot conform to the mores of his tribe. Seeking an answer to his dilemma from the spirits of the Great Plains, Little Bear comes at last to an isolated canyon. Trapped here by an injury, he winters over, growing to learn at last that no person is truly free, and that confinement is but a state of mind.

This knowledge is communicated to him by the spirits, through the mystical agency of a badger. "Big brother," says the badger to Little Bear, "why do you feel that this canyon is a cage? . . . All men live in cages. . . . They are shut in on all sides by rock walls of custom and the desire for the good opinion of their neighbors."[11] Aware finally of the realities of human society, Little Bear returns, content, to his tribe: "What was it the old one meant with his words? A man must be certain that his heart speaks truth to him. . . . One man cannot change a tribe. But one man can live with a tribe and not let it change him too much."[12] This, for Schaefer, is the sign of true independence—the ability of the individual to make his peace with himself and his society simultaneously. Schaefer himself says elsewhere that Little Bear "was finally accepting the fact that no man is an island unto himself, that the very fact of living brings with it debts and obligations to others, and doing what seemed to him the right thing to do."[13] The national implications of such a conclusion are plain, as H.L. Davis's review of *The Canyon* notes.[14] The problems faced by Little Bear are identical with those faced, in a different setting and at a different time, by twentieth-century Americans. The reconciling of individual ideals and societal obligations, necessary in any nation, becomes in a democratic nation imperative. Americans, Schaefer argues, like Little

Bear, must make this reconciliation if they are to survive.

Closely allied to the quality of independence in determining nationhood is that of self-identity. The two are virtually inseparable, for, says Rossiter, "to be a nation the [its inhabitants] must *think* they are a nation." Self-identity, moreover, like independence, is in great part a state of mind. Without it, an emerging nation lacks a sense of its own peculiar worth and importance. It has no inherent, identifying quality that makes it stand out from other nations, and it has a good chance of being engulfed and assimilated by the established nations that surround it.[15] Once possessed of an identity, however, the nation comes into its own.

Not surprisingly, Schaefer's novels concern themselves with the need for self-identity. Their characters repeatedly strive to answer the question, "Who and what am I?" When the answer comes, the individual is at peace. Shane, for example, speaks of this in his usual forthright way. His attempt to remake himself as a farmer has failed; he has been forced to resume his old life as a killer. Though saddened by the outcome, he is not destroyed. He makes this plain in his final words to young Bob Starrett: "A man is what he is, Bob, and there's no breaking the mold. I tried that, and I've lost."[16] With these words, he accepts forever the knowledge of what and who he is, and rides away. He knows his place in the world, and knows also that it is not in the Starretts' Wyoming valley.

Other characters react to the question in other ways, but come to essentially the same conclusion. They are what they are, and, once possessed of the knowledge, achieve stability and permanence. Jess Harker, the brash young hero of *First Blood,* faces up to himself in the last pages of the novel:

> I felt old, not in years but in living and what life could
> do to me. . . . Things were so much easier when I was

young and living was simple and black was black and
white was white without the endless shading grada-
tions between and I was not even aware of the bitter
choices that could be exacted by the passing days, *If
this is being a man,* I thought, *I don't like it. But I can't
change it.* . . . The only thing that made sense was loving someone and doing a job and taking what life gave
without whimpering or running away.[17]

Jared Heath, when asked what his conviction for cowardice has left meaningful for him, replies, simply, "To
know! Just that! For myself! Really know!"[18] He finds the
answer at last, months later, when he is discharged from
the army: "He had the clothes he wore and a horse and a
rifle. Only those. And something more. An enduring
quietness within. He rode West, a man akin to the great
timeless mountains that he would see marching in their
own majestic indifferent serenity along the horizon of his
small homestead ranch all the rest of his days."[19]

The "enduring quietness" that Shane, Heath, and Jess
Harker achieve characterizes all of Schaefer's major figures. They know themselves and their capabilities, and
accept the responsibility of this knowledge. Monte Walsh
is a case in point. Knowing full well that, by the standards
of 1900, he is an anachronism, he drifts undaunted across
the Southwest, "working hard and playing hard and
standing up to the consequences of any act because that is
the way it was and the pattern set by the past."[20] He, like
Schaefer's other individuals, thinks of himself as a separate, unique entity, comprised of bad as well as good.
Accepting what he is, he goes on, within his limits, to make
the most of life, for himself and for those he meets. Like
the inhabitants of Rossiter's hypothetical nation, and like
that nation itself, he is preserved by his self-knowledge.

Though Jack Schaefer is writing largely within the
tradition of the familiar Western novel, his emphasis upon

such qualities as territorial integrity, popular cohesion, independence, and self-identity makes plain his concern with more than just the American cowboy. He is concerned about his characters, to be sure, but he is also concerned about the changing times in which these characters live. Since, as Cawelti notes, the Western requires a frontier, it is suggestive to find that two of Schaefer's novels explicitly involve the postfrontier period (*The Kean Land* is set in 1896, and *Monte Walsh* ends with Walsh's death in 1913), and one, *Shane*, is set in 1889, the year prior to the closing of the frontier.[21] Schaefer is, therefore, writing not only of a time of transition, but of the very years in which the transition became most critical.

In focusing upon a people and a time in transition, Schaefer sets himself a specific goal: "to establish a distinct and individual major character and pit him against a specific human problem and show how he rose to meet it."[22] As he works toward this goal in each of his novels, he sets for his characters problems similar to those that the United States was itself facing. The United States, as a nation, between 1865 and 1910 confronted territorial problems in the Caribbean and the Pacific; problems of cohesiveness reflected variously in Reconstruction and the Populist Party; and problems of economic and cultural independence apparent in tariff legislation, the Depression of 1893, and the White City at Chicago. And, as he demonstrates how his characters respond to their problems, Schaefer suggests how the nation, as well, might respond. For him, specific human problems and specific national problems are the same.

The solution to these problems, human and national, Schaefer argues, is self-knowledge—the fourth attribute of nationhood. It is not an easy solution to achieve; rather, it is an exacting and demanding one. It requires that the individual, person or nation, know who he is, what he wants, and how he proposes to get it within the bounds of established society. It requires, in short, internal security, internal stability, and internal purpose, all qualities largely lost from American life after 1890.[23]

Demanding though the solution is, Schaefer believes that it can be achieved. For evidence of this hopeful belief, one can point to the tribulations that his protagonists suffer, only to survive as they grow to know their own qualities and abilities. The most pointed statement of his optimism, however, Schaefer gives to Shane. After brutally beating one of Fletcher's cowhands in a hand-to-hand fight, the gunfighter says, partly to himself and partly to the younger man's inert form, "There's only one thing really wrong with you. You're young. That's the one thing time can always cure."[24] The inadequacies and misjudgments of youth will always be replaced by the serene wisdom of age, if the individual will but accept the process. Schaefer writes of a succession of young men who find this out, and of older men who have already learned it. In doing so, he writes also of a country, young as nations go, that needs still to learn its lessons. If it sticks to its studies, recognizing its strengths and its limitations, it, too, will endure, growing up, like its people, with serenity, dignity, and worth.

Notes

1. See, for example, G. W. Haslam, "Jack Schaefer's Frontier: The West as Human Testing Ground," *Rocky Mountain Review*, 4 (1967): 59–71; and James K. Folsom, "*Shane and Hud*: Two Stories in Search of a Medium," *Western Humanities Review*, 24 (1970): 359–372.

2. John G. Cawelti, *The Six-Gun Mystique* (Bowling Green: Bowling Green University Popular Press, 1971), pp. 35–39.

3. Clinton Rossiter, *The American Quest, 1790–1860* (New York: Harcourt Brace Jovanovich, 1971), pp. 33–35.

4. Jack Schaefer, *The Kean Land*, in *The Short Novels of Jack Schaefer* (Boston: Houghton Mifflin, 1967), pp. 500, 505–7. Cited hereafter as *Short Novels*.

5. Schaefer, *Shane*, in *Short Novels*, p. 61.

6. Ibid., p. 110.

7. Rossiter, pp. 35–39.

8. Schaefer, *First Blood*, in *Short Novels*, pp. 195–200, 218–19.

9. Schaefer, *Company of Cowards*, in *Short Novels*, p. 453.

10. Rossiter, pp. 30, 31–32.

11. Schaefer, *The Canyon*, in *Short Novels*, p. 261.

12. Ibid., p. 315.

13. Jack Schaefer, quoted in Haslam, p. 69.

14. H. L. Davis, "From the Cheyenne Country," *New York Herald Tribune Book Review*, 30 (6 December 1953), 26.

15. Rossiter, pp. 39, 40–45.

16. Schaefer, *Shane*, in *Short Novels*, p. 106.

17. Schaefer, *First Blood*, in *Short Novels*, pp. 219–20.

18. Schaefer, *Company of Cowards*, in *Short Novels*, p. 363.

19. Ibid., p. 456.

20. Jack Schaefer, *Monte Walsh* (Boston: Houghton Mifflin, 1963), p. 443.

21. Cawelti, pp. 35–36.

22. Jack Schaefer, "Author's Note," in *The Big Range* (Boston: Houghton Mifflin, 1953), p. xi.

23. Larzer Ziff, *The American 1890s: Life and Times of a Lost Generation* (1966; repr. New York: Viking-Compass, 1968), p. 214.

24. Schaefer, *Shane*, in *Short Novels*, p. 60.

Robert Mikkelsen

The Western Writer: Jack Schaefer's Use of the Western Frontier

In most popular Western fiction, the West has been reduced to a few conventional stage props. As its title and cover blurb announce, the typical pulp Western story (I would also include in this category the majority of paper-backed Western novels) is concerned almost exclusively with hell-for-leather, smoking-six-gun, boot-hill violence. In order to qualify as "western," this violence must be acted out against such traditional backdrops as piles of greasy poker chips, burning ranches, dust-choked trails full of stampeding cattle, shattered bar glass, rock-walled canyons thick with ricocheting bullets, and false-fronted saloons. A hero dare not take time to enjoy the brilliant coloring of those cliffs or to look analytically at the construction of that saloon. Within the framework of a typical pulp Western the significance of the canyon is not that it is uniquely beautiful, but that it hides a drygulcher; the saloon represents not an example of early western architecture, but the headquarters of a scheming Indian agent. And the hero must keep his mind solely on these realities; neither he nor his author has time to reflect on the westernness of his environment.

The authors of Western stories in "slick" publications are no less superficial in their use of the West. To the conventional actions and scenes they add merely a more polished style and a well-developed romantic motif. On her perilous crossing of the plains, beautiful, sophisticated Kate will not at first respond to what she feels to be the crude advances of an Indian scout. But in the midst of an Indian raid, when her burning wagon train threatens to scorch her lace-trimmed petticoats, she realizes that the buckskinned arms which sweep her to safety throb with the hormones her Eastern suitors lacked. And when she sees his bloodstained hand gently tousle the hair of a little child, she knows at last that he is not only strong but good—in the hearty, raw-boned way of the old West.

It is refreshing to turn to the modern writers of popular fiction who have broken away from such stereotyped use of the western scene, and among them Jack Schaefer deserves attention for his consistent artistic use of the Western frontier. In his preface to *The Big Range* (1953), a collection of short stories, Schaefer outlines his method of fictionalizing the Western frontier.

The cast [of *The Big Range*] is various: rancher, sheepherder, homesteader, town settler, soldier, miner, cowboy. Yet the essential purpose is the same throughout: to establish a distinct and individual major character and pit him against a specific human problem and show how he rose to meet it. And all of them, the characters and the stories that evolve from them, are conditioned by the wide open spaces of the old West, in which the energies and capabilities of men and women, for good or for evil, were unleashed on an individual basis as they had rarely been before or elsewhere in human history.

Historians have long regarded this individualism as a frontier characteristic. One of the frontier "intellectual traits of profound importance," wrote Turner, was "that dominant individualism, working for good or evil." Bernard DeVoto also has seen the frontier as a stimulus to individualism, though he has viewed collective action, such as that of the fur-trapping brigade or the emigrant wagon train, as a far more vital force in shaping western history. However, neither the moral ambiguity of individualism nor its uncertain position in western history is the immediate concern of Schaefer: in acting for good or evil his characters are not demonstrating the good or evil inherent in individualism itself, but the good or evil within themselves and, by extension, in the portion of the American milieu which produced them and which they have carried with them into the West. The parts they play reveal the basic kinds of human action possible in an isolated environment, not necessarily the relation of that action or its environment to Western history.

By vigorously sustaining his method, Schaefer gives his work the two qualities which characterize it and distinguish it from run-of-the-mill popular fiction: use of the frontier to reveal men's true natures and fresh description of that frontier.

A short story called "Jeremy Rodock" illustrates what Schaefer means by "energies and capabilities" which are "unleased on an individual basis," and how he freshens commonplace elements of the western scene.

Rodock is a rancher who raises horses for stagecoach lines, and who has a reputation for lynching horse thieves. One day he and the narrator of the story ride out to bring in a replacement for a horse with a pulled tendon. Their ride takes them into a valley where a large herd of mares and foals are supposed to be grazing. They are missing; the two find their trail, guess rightly that rustlers have driven them off, and follow them. They find the horses in a remote valley, with their front hooves rasped to the quick to prevent them from wandering off. Rodock cannot forget the cruelty of this act, and he lives only to redress it in his own way. The climax occurs when Rodock and the narrator ride back to the valley to await the return of the rustlers (Rodock assumes that they will return for the colts as soon as sufficient time has elapsed to allow their hooves to grow out). The three rustlers are surprised and taken alive. At this point Rodock shows his individuality, which takes an almost sadistic bent. Instead of hanging the three, Rodock forces them to begin a fifty-mile walk in their stocking feet to a hangman's noose. But Rodock does not enjoy his revenge as much as he had anticipated. Their suffering is disturbingly acute, and their leader determines to wipe away his sense of guilt by forcing himself to endure the pain without flinching. One and then another of the rustlers collapse, but the leader keeps on. When he can no longer walk he crawls. Rodock soon has enough of this and releases them. His desire to revenge the rustlers' cruelty has been satisfied and replaced by a Christian sense of his own cruelty. The leader has atoned for his guilt and won the admiration of Rodock and the narrator. Thus in this situation, which develops completely apart from influences outside of the characters' own consciences, two men find an opportunity to assert their integrity.

The Wyoming territory which forms the setting of "Jeremy Rodock" is more, however, than an environment in which characters are free to act for good or evil: it is also a generous slice of the western frontier accurately portrayed. Though the action moves rapidly, Schaefer effectively weaves into it concrete descriptions of the land, the men, and the livestock. The narrator's reaction to the crippled horses is a good example of what Schaefer does with traditional elements of the western scene. He says:

> A good horse is a fine looking animal. But it isn't the appearance that gets into you and makes something

> reach out and respond to him. It's the way he moves
> . . . the clean-stepping speed and competence of him
> that's born in him and is what he is and is his reason
> for being. Take that away from him and he's a pitiful
> thing. And somewhere there were three men who
> had done that to those mares.

Schaefer puts new feeling into the affection which exists in all Western fiction between the cowboy and his horse, but which is seldom as believably articulated as it is here.

In *First Blood,* a novel, Schaefer again uses the assertion of individuality theme of "Jeremy Rodock" and shows the same sensitivity in describing the western frontier. Jess Harker, a cocky young stagecoach driver, is in the awkward, self-conscious process of becoming a man. The men whom he strives to equal are Tom Davisson, a cooly competent sheriff, and Race Crim, a worldly gunman proud of his bloody, unbroken record as a stagecoach guard. Until the climax at the end of the novel, Harker overtly imitates and admires Crim, but unconsciously patterns his behavior after Davisson, whose combination of manliness and integrity he finally achieves. The central incident of the novel occurs when Crim and Harker, who is temporarily promoted from branch-line to main-line stagecoach driving, ride into an ambush while carrying a special shipment of gold. (Crim has talked too much and accidentally betrayed the time and route of the shipment.) Their accompanying guard is killed; Crim, driven by thoughts of his now broken record and the realization that he is responsible for the death of his fellow guard, rides off to revenge himself on the holdup men; and Harker, though wounded, drives the empty stage on to its next station. This incident reveals the intrinsic merit of both Crim and Harker: Crim yields to his selfish desire to regain his lost prestige and salve his conscience, and Harker, though still too flippant and self-confident, behaves maturely.

Crim persists in masking his guilt and smarting pride

behind his frenzied efforts to hunt down the bandits. Harker, feeling that he has proved himself a man, sulks and refuses to go back to driving a branch-line stagecoach. The climax develops when the last of the bandits is taken alive—the others are killed, mostly by Crim—and held for trial in Davisson's jail. Crim leads a lynching party in an assault on the jail at a time when Harker has been deputized and, in Davisson's absence, given the responsibility of protecting the prisoner against a lynch-hysterical mob. Harker chooses between duty and expediency and kills Crim. By so doing he at last achieves his manhood.

All the chief characters in *First Blood* choose freely their own courses of action. As the sheriff of an isolated community quick to execute its own laws, Davisson does not have to insist on due process of law. Crim could purge himself of his vicious self-interest and attain the manliness of Davisson by admitting, if only to himself, that his zeal to kill the holdup men is feigned. Harker could give in to the lynch mob and, in their eyes, assume the stature of his idol, Crim. And for any of them, at any time, there is the frontiersman's alternative to facing unpleasant situations: to move on and begin anew.

While narrating this action, young Harker looks closely at the details of his environment and describes them authentically. His account of driving his first mainline stagecoach away from its station is typical:

the tenders let go the bridles and jumped aside and I shook out Russ Thorp's whip in my hand and cracked the tip like a pistol snapping and those six horses settled like one into the traces and our wheels were rolling free.

What it felt like to drive a stagecoach is described here with immediacy, and this quality, occurring as it does throughout his writing, gives Schaefer's representation of the West a tangibility rarely experienced in Western fiction.

In theme and handling of the western frontier, two of

Schaefer's other novels—*The Canyon* and *Shane*—and his many short stories closely resemble *First Blood* and "Jeremy Rodock." Characters encounter situations demanding both moral and physical action, and their frontier environment allows them to act independently, guided by their senses of justice and decency. Shane returns unwillingly to the raw life of a gunfighter because he knows he can protect the Starrett family only by so doing; Little Bear, the Cheyenne hero of *The Canyon*, returns to the frustrations of tribal life because he knows he cannot fulfill all of his responsibilities as husband and father in his isolated canyon paradise. And pervading all Schaefer's work is his feeling for the men and the country.

His achievement is a sensitive reconstruction of the western frontier.

James C. Work

Settlement Waves and Coordinate Forces in *Shane*

In his discussion of the frontier's influence on American character, Frederick Jackson Turner quotes from *A New Guide to the West* (1836) by John Mason Peck, who saw the westward movement as a series of waves. It is an interesting coincidence that Jack Schaefer would also use the wave metaphor—more than a hundred years later—in describing the western experience. And in describing effects of the western experience upon American character, Schaefer echoes Turner as well: "The best aspects of the American heritage were worked out in the West—America was worked out on the frontier."[1]

It is even more significant that Schaefer's *Shane* is a dramatic corollary to Peck's metaphor. Moreover, *Shane* works out an answer to the question of what happens when two of Peck's waves collide: a new force is born.

It is important to the understanding of *Shane* that we see the novel as a dramatization of Peck's wave metaphor; the novel not only gives concrete referents for the metaphor by providing well-drawn characters as examples of the various waves, but goes beyond the metaphor to provide an answer to the question of what happened when one west-ward-moving wave overran one preceding it. To illustrate, I would first like to discuss the "waves of settlement" idea, then examine Fletcher, the Starretts, and Shane as representations of two "waves." I intend to conclude that in the crucible of frontier conflict a new American character was formed.

Turner quotes that part of Peck's *A New Guide to the West* which identifies three classes of settlers that moved in waves across the frontier regions of America. The metaphor negates the usual notion of the western settlement as a fairly smooth stream of pioneers moving in to occupy the land permanently.

Peck characterizes the first wave as the pioneer type who depends upon free range, unrestricted hunting, and crude agriculture for his living. Such an individual (and his family, if he has one) opens the land a little, clears it a little, but actually does little development. He seldom buys the land, nor does he occupy it for long; he is a pioneer who homesteads and then sells out when the free range becomes depleted or overcrowded, when hunting becomes difficult, or when other log-cabin settlers of the first wave build too close to him. He markets his improvements for whatever they will bring and moves on to settle again in the wilder lands to the west. There his settlement will again be temporary.

Typically, the next wave of settlement is composed of people who buy the land, clear it to permit more efficient agriculture, put up good fences and bridges, spend more time building comfortable cabins and houses, and who sometimes stay to establish such symbols of permanence as orchards, schools, mills, and courthouses. Villages begin during this wave.

This second wave is semi-permanent, however, since it is generally willing to sell out at a profit and move further on to reestablish. The third wave arrives, the people of "capital and enterprise," who come to build in brick and dressed lumber. They put up churches, schools, courts, and homes. Elegance and luxuries appear in abundance during this last wave, and the log-cabin site which had become a settlement and then had become a village now becomes a city. Some of the first-wave pioneers or second-wave settlers may stay behind to enjoy civilization's full establishment, but enough of them go looking for the middle border that the waves of settlement are kept moving.

In his editorial introduction to the anthology *Out West* (1955), Jack Schaefer employs the same metaphor of waves, stressing the diversity of the frontier people and the challenge of the conditions they met:

> escape into the west in actual physical terms of expansion and opportunity and the freeing of men's energies was for nearly three centuries a major part of the American-dream-being-made-reality as the waves of migration lapped ever westward. . . . And the West of the western story caught that dream, that social process, that historical movement, at its full and final peak.[2]

When the waves of settlement broke past the Mississippi, slow at first, then faster and after the Civil War with driving impetus, they took with them people from all the eastern states, people from all the European countries, people of many diverse cultures, people of many diverse social and economic classes and backgrounds. These people were not primitives developing slowly with a land. They were people of assorted civilized traditions swarming into a new land to be developed—into a land in which settlement constantly outran law and the only major restraints upon them were self-imposed or forced by physical fact. They were an amazingly various people pushing forward into a wide arena of freedom of action, confronted with conditions that drew upon their full personal resources, that compelled them again and again to act as independent individuals.[3]

Schaefer sees the West as a rich source of material for the serious novelist who can catch "that dream, that social process, that historical movement." At the time he wrote *Shane*, Schaefer tells us, his knowledge of the West was that of an amateur historian. He was not writing a Western, but rather a book about the West. "I don't read westerns, I never have read westerns—except those by a few friends of mine."[4] It is reasonable to assume from all this that *Shane* is a good deal more history than Western, and that the wave metaphor plays a part in it.

Casual readers of *Shane* may see the central conflict of the novel only as the timeless sodbuster vs. cattleman clash, but the actual confrontation is more serious when regarded as one settlement wave following too closely upon one before it. In the first sort of conflict, things are settled by the death or relocation of one of the principals—as frequently demonstrated in formula Westerns. Such simplicity is hardly true to history, however. But if waves in conflict did not produce a sea of dead settlers, what *did* happen in the collision? Schaefer's answer to that is both complex and plausible.

Before getting to Schaefer's answer, though, we need to establish that *Shane* is indeed a story of two waves—the pioneer opportunist of Peck's first wave and the civilizing agriculturalist of his third wave.

The pioneer is Fletcher, a cattleman who uses the land as he found it, running his cattle over the native grass and making little effort to either improve or limit his range. But progress pushing from the East and the lure of cheap land drawing from the West bring in the fence-building legal "squatters" who in their turn will subdue the wild range, clear the land, and generally "civilize" the area for the establishment of steady commerce, education, churches, and law.

Fletcher has, in effect, stayed behind as his wave has moved on, and is on the way to becoming part of the second wave. There are other members of the first wave in *Shane,* but they have not been on the land as long as has Fletcher, and they are not given major roles in the story. We see these gathered at a meeting of individuals who are discussing how to deal with Fletcher. Two men at the meeting are described as "original homesteaders" who "staked out" their places and have survived by simply enduring Fletcher's irritation. They even understand Fletcher's antagonism; he is, after all, clearly more "original" than they are. Two others at the meeting are cowhands who have become homesteaders, a pair of bachelor "ranchers" working on a shoestring and more intent on staying alive than on making a profit or establishing civilization. Then there is Frank Torrey, who, true to Peck's description, "was always talking about pulling up stakes and heading for California."[5] Another character who fits Peck's definition is Ernie Wright, who prefers hunting to making farm improvements.

The second wave is weak. Some of the members will move on and some will stay to become part of the third movement, as Peck predicts. The third wave, on the other hand, is quite strong. It is as resourceful and as determined as the first wave that it will replace. It relies on an inherited system of law, as the first wave relies upon freedom from law. Joe and Marian Starrett, with their shingled and painted home, their white fence, and with only one stump remaining between them and a "real farm," are obvious representatives of the third wave.

Marian Starrett is essential to the progress of the plot;

indeed, without her it is highly probable that there would not be a plot. At the simplest level she functions as a symbol of what Joe is working for—family, home, love, mother-hood, stability, order. On a more subtle level she is in-teresting as a married woman who finds herself attracted to a transient stranger. It is a significant attraction: Shane is powerfully magnetic. Strong, unique, quiet, compli-mentary of her cooking and homemaking, Shane seems for a time to be the force that will split the family and spoil the chances of a permanent household. Marian smiles more when he is there. She cooks more. She even modifies her millinery in order to be more in step with the women of fashion whom Shane has seen.

"I like him." Mother's voice was serious. "He's so nice and polite and sort of gentle. Not like most men I've met out here. But there's something about him. Something underneath the gentleness. . . . Some-thing . . . ." Her voice trailed away.

"Mysterious?" suggested father.

"Yes, of course. Mysterious. But more than that. Dangerous."

"He's dangerous, all right." Father said it in a mus-ing way. Then he chuckled. "But not to us, my dear." (p. 10)

Marian's function as a part of the love triangle is secon-dary, however, to her appearance as the powerful domes-tic force of the third wave, an expression of civilized life facing conditions at the frontier.

Schaefer chooses food as the central means of iden-tification for the New England-bred Marian: "As long as she could still prepare a proper dinner, she would tell father when things were not going right, she knew she was still civilized and there was hope of getting ahead" (p. 7). Like Father Vaillant in *Death Comes for the Archbishop*, Ma-rian identifies proper eating with being civilized. She is pleased when Shane remarks that her "flannel cakes" remind him of a settled home he had left at fifteen. When the men are hard at work on that stump, the last obstacle, Marian brings them not drink but biscuits. Then, fascinated by watching "in a wide-eyed wonder" as the two men throw aside their tools and attack the stump like two uncivilized bare-handed aboriginals, she allows a pie to burn in the oven. The extremity of her irritation over this incident stems from something deeper than the waste of food: she has yielded, momentarily, to the fascination of the brute and uncivilized. She determinedly remakes the pie, partly to reassure herself that she could still do it, that what she has seen of raw force cannot overcome her determination to be civilized.

At the point in the novel when the decision is made to stand up to Fletcher—a decision that means the men are about to use primitive forces again—Marian's response is first to see that young Bob is provided with a nice fat apple and then to prepare a meal that is "almost like a holiday" (p. 108). On the evening of the showdown, Joe refuses his supper as if finally putting aside the civilized aspect of his life to accept the violent methods represented by Shane. Shane, however, is more accustomed to using violence and is further from being part of a civilized world; he is therefore able to use violence decisively—a blow to the head—to prevent Joe from taking any action.

In view of Marian's use of "proper dinners" to combat the threatening forces of primitive problem solving, it is significant that she fails to prepare food, or even mention it, on the evening *following* the final showdown with Fletcher's gunmen. Even on the following morning there is no mention made of preparing breakfast for the men, who have not eaten since early the previous day. Either she has lost the sense of "still being civilized and hope of getting ahead," or she is now so certain that civilized life has become permanent—as she demonstrates by making Joe try to dislodge the post Shane has set—that her cooking now has become a natural part of that life rather than a symbol of the struggle to attain it. It is clear that her wave of settlement is established.

The symbols of Joe Starrett's civilizing tendencies are so obvious that they need only be barely mentioned. The farm is one, of course, with the paint and shingles and fences and well-cleared fields. His resentment of the stump is a major indicator. The purchase of the "shiny new cultivator" is another.

Joe, like Marian, is fascinated by Shane, but for different reasons. He sees in Shane a capability for forceful action which he lacks. Shane's contribution of that force to the farm brings out a fresh liveliness in Joe's wife, settles the dispute over the cultivator purchase, inspires the boy, and completes the removal of the stump. It is clear that Shane embodies a sort of unrestrained or lawless life, a more primitive standard of behavior; and it is equally clear that he embodies something that Joe, coming from a region where law and technology have obviated the personal capacity for raw force, has not yet developed in proportion to his needs.

Each of the four principal characters becomes aware of something that reflects on Joe's handicap. Marian is attracted by that "something dangerous" in Shane, a certain attitude she does not find in her husband. Young Bob is fascinated by Shane's coolness and his skill with a gun—two attributes he never mentions in connection with his father. Shane obviously perceives that Joe is not yet fully prepared to meet the primitive forces represented by Fletcher's gunfighter, for he physically prevents Joe from it. Joe welcomes the change Shane represents, and accepts the opportunity to add Shane's strength to his own. And in the end he feels incomplete without Shane, wants to abandon the farm to search for the departed gunman.

The Starretts are clearly members of the third wave in Peck's categories. They have come from a law-based civilized region, have met with an obstacle which in their original region would have been dealt with by civil means, and have realized that they are not prepared to settle it by the primitive means evidently required.

Readers of this book are more interested in Shane than in any of the other characters. Who is he? Where does he come from? And where does he go? Is he, as James K. Folsom maintains, a "figure of God's providence in the confusing world of flux"?[6] Such an explanation would hardly take into account Schaefer's concern for history, and would ignore most of the major events in the novel.

Shane is an embodiment of a spirit vital to the first wave of western settlement, just as he is a spirit or force necessary to the success of the third wave. He is, in the words of Turner, a "return to primitive conditions," the momentary rebirth of a force needed at the frontier. Where does he come from? Out of the West, from the first forces of settlement. Shane just happens, in Schaefer's book, to be in human form. In a different version we could as easily have Joe Starrett experience within himself a discovery of new strength. All we really need is the dramatization of the moment described by Turner, when "the bonds of custom are broken and unrestraint is triumphant."[7] Shane triumphs through unrestraint. He is independence, necessary primitive force.

According to Turner, the meeting of the "customary way" and the "primitive condition" results in the formation of a new kind of regional character. Something new is created in a people at that point. If Turner is correct, then it would be inconsistent to merely have Shane appear as a sort of lost, wandering gunman who settles the conflict out of the goodness of his heart and then disappears forever. If Turner is correct, part of Shane must become part of the Starretts.

Schaefer expresses this through the recurring theme of coordinate force. For instance, when the stump needs to be uprooted, it cannot be done by Joe — the civilized force of the third settlement wave — nor by Shane, the first wave primitive force. Neither force has everything it needs to do it alone. They set at it in a coordinated effort and uproot it together. Some readers see the scene as a competition, and others wonder why the men don't get levers or pulleys or animals to help. But Shane and Joe do not chop and dig in a spirit of competition, and they finally get down into the hole and heave up the stump by main force because to bring in any outside force or to be rivals would nullify the whole idea of two forces in coordination.

Joe senses that he and Shane are two equal halves of a single force; his equal division of the biscuits is symbolic enough to convince anyone of that. It is followed by another sign: finishing his half of the last biscuit, there at the stump which symbolizes his role as a civilizing force, "he straightened and stretched his arms high and wide. He seemed to stretch and stretch until he was a tremendous tower of strength reaching up into the late afternoon sun" (p. 27). He is facing west, we assume. Then, later in the book, Shane repeats this gesture. It comes just after he has made his decision to face Fletcher's gunfighter (which symbolizes his role as a primitive force): "I saw him out by the pasture. He was staring over it and the grazing steers at the great lonely mountains tipped with the gold of sun now rushing down behind them. As I watched, he stretched his arms up, the fingers reaching to their utmost limits, grasping and grasping, it seemed, at the glory glowing in the sky" (p. 116).

Just as Joe's stretching seems to gather power from the defeat of the stump, Shane's stretch overreaches anything to do with the farm — such as the pasture and steers — and draws strength from a land further west, a region of more primitive existence. He is attracted, throughout the story, by the good and the civilized (as Joe is drawn to Shane's freedom and power), but he realizes that he is only a "bad" force here. He may realize the good but cannot belong to it in his present form.

The Joe-half of Schaefer's coordinate force fully understands the Shane-half. This is why he does not worry about either Marian or Bob running away with it: it could not let them follow. Joe does not worry (as does Marian) about the danger to Shane. As Bob later realizes, Shane is a manifestation of "the untested realm of human potentialities." When the need for the Shane-half is over, Joe naturally feels guilty about letting it go out of his life. He feels less than a whole man, is suddenly discontented with peace and the farm. This restlessness, of course, is a clear indication that Shane's spirit *has* become part of his own.

Joe's desire to go further west in search of the Shane-half lasts only until Marian demonstrates, with the fence post, that she has at last understood the meaning of the experience. Where does Shane go? Does he die? Marian convinces Joe that "he's all around us, and in us, and he always will be" (p. 135). Bob, too, feels it. That "frontier spirit" described by Turner has happened; a "new American character" has been created through the welding of two forces. The frontier environment demanded that the primitive instinct for survival be present in the people, who at the same time saw the need of more civilized forces of character. For the Starretts, realization of the necessity to let strength do what reason cannot becomes an instrument of their success as surely as the gun is the instrument of Shane's success. "The man and the tool, a good man and a good tool, doing what had to be done . . . a coordinate force beautiful beyond comprehension" (p. 136).

Neither Turner nor Schaefer nor Peck created the "striking characteristics" of the American intellect, and perhaps they did not even discover them. But they have certainly discovered something of its origin—Peck with his waves of settlement, Turner with his essay on "coarseness and strength," and Schaefer with Shane. What is Shane? A necessary part of frontier American intellect and character "shaped in some firm forging of past circumstances" that the boy-turned-man sees as a "thing in the human equation beyond my comprehension . . . a concentration . . . a singleness of dedication to the instant need . . . at once wonderful and disturbing" (p. 40).

Did Shane go away? Did he die? If the "striking characteristics" of the American people are called out by the existence of the frontier, will these traits die out as the frontier disappears? Or will that coordinate force surface again when needed, like Shane, "who rode into our little valley out of the heart of the great glowing West and when his work was done rode back whence he had come"?

Notes

1. Jack Schaefer, "Only a Fool Would Write Westerns," phonotape of a lecture delivered April 16, 1968, in the Lory Student Center Theater under sponsorship of the Fine Arts Series, Colorado State University, Fort Collins, Colorado.

2. Jack Schaefer, "Editor's Note," in *Out West* (London: Transworld Publishers, 1961) I: 8.

3. *Ibid.*, p. 10.

4. Schaefer, "Only a Fool Would Write Westerns."

5. Jack Schaefer, *Shane* (New York: Amsco School Publications, 1949), p. 55. Subsequent references are to this edition.

6. See James K. Folsom, *The American Western Novel* (New Haven: College and University Press, 1966), pp. 126–29.

7. George R. Taylor, ed., *The Turner Thesis concerning the Role of the Frontier in American History*, rev. ed. (Boston: D. C. Heath, 1956), pp. 1–2. Subsequent references are to this edition.

Michael Cleary

Jack Schaefer:
The Evolution
of Pessimism

In his perceptive essay, "Growing Up with the American West: Fiction of Jack Schaefer" Fred Erisman observes that Schaefer's dominant theme of coming of age often goes "beyond human maturation to comment upon national maturation."[1] Erisman traces the progress of Clinton Rossiter's four major characteristics of nationhood in Schaefer's novels: territorial integrity; societal cohesion; political, economical, and cultural independence; and self-knowledge. Erisman concludes that Schaefer's view of America's maturation is optimistic, that although the nation is still young and needs to learn its lessons, it "will endure, growing up, like its people, with serenity, dignity, and worth."[2]

There can be no argument that Schaefer's major theme is that of individual growth—more precisely, the determination of what it means to be a man. In addition, the theme entails the very important consideration of the proper relationship of the individual to society. Erisman's essay is a compelling examination of these ideas as they relate to yet another recurring Schaefer theme, one noted by Gerald Haslam: the historical development of the West.[3] Erisman concludes that Schaefer's interpretation of the settling of the West is uniformly optimistic in all his novels. However, a close textual scrutiny of Schaefer's novels does not support Erisman's contention. It is possible that Erisman's view is in some way reflective of an optimistic element in Rossiter; at any rate, this optimistic attitude toward the development of the West is certainly not the prevailing tone in Schaefer's novels.

I believe that Schaefer's novels exhibit an increasingly pessimistic view of the historical development of the West. Although his early novels are clearly optimistic in this regard, succeeding works reveal a growing skepticism which, in his last novels, leads to a bitter cynicism. In charting Schaefer's interpretation of the history of the frontier, I have chosen to use the more familiar theories of Frederick Jackson Turner rather than those of Rossiter. This would seem to be a reasonable choice, for Schaefer has credited Turner's essay "The Significance of the Frontier in American History" as a major influence on his work.[4] Substituting Turner's definition of national development for Rossiter's should not distort the nature of Erisman's observations, for it is only Erisman's conclusion regarding Schaefer's optimism which is the issue here. I fully concur with his perception of the "national maturation" theme in Schaefer's work, but disagree with his interpretation of that theme. In fact, Turner seems to have anticipated Schaefer's preoccupation with the theme when he wrote:

> The peculiarity of American institutions is the fact that they have been compelled to adapt themselves to the changes of an expanding people . . . involved in crossing a continent, in winning a wilderness, and in developing at each area of this progress out of the primitive economic and political condition of the frontier into the complexity of city life.[5]

In tracing Schaefer's changing attitude toward the taming of the frontier, five novels will be analyzed: *Shane, First Blood, The Kean Land, Monte Walsh,* and *Mavericks*. These works cover the entire spectrum of Schaefer's longer fiction, from his initial publication of *Shane* in 1949 to his final work—*Mavericks*—in 1967. A chronological approach will be helpful in noting the author's shifting sensibilities.

In his best-known novel, *Shane* (1949), Schaefer combines a mythical representation of the romantic West with an optimistic appraisal of the changes brought by civilization. The allegorical figure of Shane is both superior to, and aloof from, the emerging society of 1889 Wyoming. (The date, of course, is one year prior to the census which declared the closing of the frontier and prompted Turner's thesis.) An awareness of encroaching civilization is evident from the first pages of the novel, when Bob describes the Starretts' uncharacteristic house with its white paint and green trim, a reminder to his mother of her New England heritage.[6]

But the historical developments illustrated in *Shane* go beyond the usual East-West dichotomy prevalent from the time of James Fenimore Cooper's *Leatherstocking* novels. Here, the ranching mode of life—not a wilderness retreat—is being overtaken. Joe Starrett is an ex-cowboy who has recognized the imminent demise of the open range. He says that "the boys I used to ride with don't see it yet. They will some day. The open range can't last forever. Running cattle in big lots is . . . poor business. It's certain to be crowded out" (p. 7), and Shane agrees. Joe explains that a combination of farming and small-scale stock management is less wasteful and more productive than the open-range method of the older ranchers such as Fletcher. The ranching, or pastoral, stage of frontier development is the third step of the process of social evolution described by Turner. There are six in all,[7] and it will be

best to list them together, as they will be frequent points of
reference throughout this study:

1. the Indian and hunter
2. the trader, pathfinder of civilization
3. the ranch life
4. the sparsely settled farm community
5. the intensive culture of the denser farm settlement
6. the manufacturing organization with city and
   factory

The conflicts which arise in *Shane* can be traced to the violent transition from ranch life to the next stage of frontier
development: the sparsely settled farm community. As
Joe Starrett says, "the old ways die hard" (p. 32). At this
early stage, governmental guarantees are meaningles ,
the closest marshal is too far away to arrive in time to settle
the violence. This isolation from civilization requires a
personal enforcement of justice decided, ultimately, by
violent expediency.

Although Shane's defense of the Starretts is based on
affection and loyalty, it is understood that the Starretts'
insistence on homesteading rights has a legal basis. Because of this, Shane's actions merely enforce a social order
founded on law; it is more than the rampant justice-by-
force which characterized Fletcher's day.[8] It is ironic that
this fierce individualism is a quality shared by Fletcher and
Shane; both are victims of the changing times, but only
Shane is aware of it. According to Turner, this individualism was necessary and worthwhile, actually a product of
the frontier experience.[9]

In spite of his admiration for such individualism, there
is no doubt where Schaefer's loyalties lie: in terms of frontier evolution, legality, and personal worth, Shane and the
Starretts act appropriately. As John Cawelti points out, the
sacrifice of the hero with savage skills is often a representa-

tion of the enforcement of the ideals of civilization.[10] It is Shane's utilization of his savage skills which simultaneously secures the values of civilization and alienates him from it. *Shane* is one of the few Westerns which carries out "the antithesis between success and honor to its inevitable conclusion: the destruction or exile of the hero from the developing town which can no longer permit the explosions of individual will and aggression."[11]

Underlying Schaefer's obvious respect for the courage and integrity which Shane represents, there is the realization that heroic self-sufficiency is a thing beyond its time. One way this is shown is in the depiction of the changing allegiance of the townspeople, most apparent in the character of Mr. Weir. A minor figure in the novel, Weir weaves in and out of the narrative, and his sporadic appearances serve to remind us that there is more to the town that just Grafton's saloon, the convenient setting for the scenes of violence.

At first aloof and skeptical of the homesteaders, Weir begins to align himself with Starrett after the second fight in Grafton's place. Grafton follows suit, suggesting a break from the ranchers by offering to bill Fletcher, not Starrett, for the damages. Joe is aware of the new allegiance of the townspeople and the homesteaders when he tells Bob: "I can't see the full finish. But I can see this. Wilson down and there'll be an end to it. Fletcher'll be done. The town will see to that" (p. 100). When Ernie Wright, a homesteader, is killed by the gunfighter Wilson, Mr. Weir pays for the coffin, and a local miner makes the headstone. The transition from personal to community responsibility is complete at the close of the novel, when Shane's violent actions assure the safety of the homesteaders even as they demand his exile. As Shane rides off, it is Weir who takes Bob back to the Starrett place. In Turner's scheme of the civilization process, the ranching era is past, and the era of the sparsely settled farm community is moving inexorably toward the next stage—the denser farm settlement: we are told that there are new settlers arriving each year, as well as more townspeople (pp. 46–47).

The conclusion of *Shane* expresses Schaefer's optimistic appraisal of the values of civilization. Temporarily bitter over events, Joe longs to move on to Montana or some other frontier area. Marian's argument is simple and convincing: Shane has sacrificed so that they might put down roots which can never be torn loose (symbolized by the corral post set firmly by Shane). The brief final chapter illustrates how these roots have flourished, for the town has grown and spread up the riverbanks. More important, Bob has been able to "grow straight inside as a man should" (p. 118). The successful maturation of both the town and Bob has been made possible by Shane's defeat of an earlier, less civilized stage of historical development.

First Blood (1953) portrays even more pointedly than *Shane* a moment in frontier history when the enforcement of individual justice is displaced by the civilizing influence of society's laws. Jess Harker is an apprentice freight driver; his job reflects the interaction and interdependence of the towns which have replaced the pastoral (ranching) era of the frontier. The growing need for the freight and stage lines indicates a society which has progressed one step farther than that depicted at the end of *Shane*. This is the society of the denser farm settlements. The towns in *First Blood* are stabilized, not embryonic; they even have names, a feature noticeably absent in *Shane*.

Like young Bob in *Shane*, the teenage Jess Harker of *First Blood* is presented with two role models: the heroic, charismatic Race Crim, a stage guard, and Tom Davisson, a stolid but courageous sheriff. Davisson is the representation of a wave of civilization which was just beginning in the earlier novel. *First Blood* is the depiction of "the drama of the frontier encounter between social order and lawlessness,"[12] just as *Shane* was; but its encounter is placed one step farther along the scale of civilization defined by Turner. The ranching era has been supplanted by the growing towns. Schaefer's depiction of the civilizing influence is shown in the manner in which society achieves justice: the personal brand of enforcement required in *Shane* has been displaced by a formal judicial system whose agent is Tom Davisson. Tom is the legal envoy who was unavailable in the sparsely settled territory of *Shane*. Tom has been a lawman all his life, "watching that people did things right and stuck to regulations."[13] The more populous community cannot depend on the fortuitous arrival of a black-clad stranger to resolve its conflicts; predictably, this reliance on a system's efficacy makes *First Blood* more realistic, less epic than *Shane*.

Jess Harker is poised between the conflicting beliefs of Race and Tom: faith in a personal and immediate brand of justice or the more objective means of legal recourse. In a very real sense, Schaefer illustrates the flaw which was left unexamined in *Shane*. That flaw is portrayed in Walter Van Tilburg Clark's *The Ox-Bow Incident:* that the personal dispensation of justice is acceptable only as long as might and right are perfectly aligned. Race Harker is the equal of Shane in skills such as gunplay, but he lacks Shane's discretion and wisdom. Race is a hothead and a braggart; it is his vain boasts which are responsible for the deaths which occur when his stage is robbed. In trying to capture the outlaws singlehandedly, he shirks his duty to his job and to his fellow townspeople. He even wounds an innocent man, and his vendetta is so obsessive that he leaves the injured man without assistance or comment.

Tom Davisson explains the advantages of a legal system over the subjective enforcement of "right" which previously existed in the earlier stages of the frontier:

This is rough country out here. Rough and new.
We're trying to get some law established because
that's the only way most people can get along
together and be reasonable and decent. . . . I say I'm
the law but I'm only a part of it. Somebody steps out
of line and it's my job to get him and turn him over to
the court to decide is he guilty and what should be
done to him. (p. 50)

Despite his allegiance to the judicial process in *First
Blood,* Schaefer is careful to show that the arrival of a formal legal system is not without its faults. It, too, can be
abused, and it is also complicated, bulky, and awkward.
(Its complex, intricate workings are suggested by the
Judge's name—Webber.) Jess is drawn to Race's quick
and uncomplicated resolution, in spite of knowing that
Race's past actions have been unwise and precipitous. Jess
is attracted to Race's determination to personally punish
the wrongdoers, and not rely on an undependable legal
system. He is not alone in yearning for an earlier time
when solutions were hard and fast; a relocated eastern
schoolteacher explains that, in the end, it is all just a matter
of historical timing:

It could be that the time for Race's way to be right in
this territory is about over and what we need is Tom
Davisson's way, or the judge's, which is the same only
more so. . . . Judge Webber is trying to set a prece-
dent for the benefit of all of us. It could even be for
Race Crim sometime in the future. (pp. 92–93)

The burdensome nature of a system founded on due
process is one price which society extracts for the advance
of civilization. *First Blood* affirms Schaefer's continued
optimism in light of such concessions to historical development, but there is a decided hesitation in his approval
which was not apparent in *Shane.* The retreating figure of
Shane and the sprawling corpse of the avenging Race

Crim mark the demands civilization makes of frontier individualism. Nevertheless, Schaefer is committed to the values of civilization. As Haslam points out, Jess's acceptance by his girl, his boss, and Tom Davisson are indications that his defense of society's method of justice was necessary and right.

In *The Kean Land, and Other Stories* (1959) Schaefer once again analyzes the association of a legal system with the advance of civilization, but with very different results. In this work, Schaefer introduces a character type who reappears in his remaining novels — the old man who has experienced firsthand the different stages of the civilization process. The use of this character type allows a broader scope for his observations about the changing nature of the frontier and the effects of civilization on the frontier spirit.

There are, in fact, two old men in *The Kean Land*. The first is Ben Hammon, who relates a youthful experience much in the vein of the narrators of the other two novels discussed. The contemporary historical perspective is immediately evident, as is Schaefer's considerably altered attitude toward the progress of civilization. Ben Hammon's farm is "an oasis" amid a Colorado city complete with business section and railroad yards and suburbs; Ben is speaking to a young writer of "tales of the American West that was and is no more."[14] The negative effects of Turner's last stage of civilization — the growth of cities — are reflected in Hammon's comments on the ambitions of the real estate people who would like to buy him out and transform his land:

Sure, they'd like to get hold of this piece. One hundred sixty acres good land. What would they do with it? Slap together a couple hundred maybe more of those silly modern shacks they call ranch-houses a real rancher wouldn't live in, and make a lot of

money which seems to be the most important thing
anybody can do nowadays. That's progress. So they
say. (pp. 465–66)

But it is the second old man in *The Kean Land* who is
given major consideration. Brent Kean is over ninety at
the time of the events occurring in 1896. Kean is the product of the first two stages of frontier development described by Turner: the Indian and hunter era and the
trader era. By 1896 the Colorado frontier is moving toward settlements of densely settled farms. As Turner
observed, the advancing civilization brought with it — and
brought about — necessary railroad legislation and laws
regarding the disposition of public land.[15] This development provides the central conflict of *The Kean Land*.

The characters of Brent Kean and Joe Starrett are quite
similar, but Schaefer's perspective is considerably different. Both men have bound themselves to their homesteads and will go to any lengths to protect them; Schaefer
sees both men as justified in opposing the forces which
threaten them. The difference lies in the nature of their
opposition. Whereas Joe Starrett fights against an earlier
era (ranching), Brent Kean battles against a coming era
(the growing towns). In the last analysis, the character of
Brent Kean is more akin to the recalcitrant Fletcher. Both
men defend the ways of the frontier which shaped them,
and both are ground under by the impetus of civilization.
But in *The Kean Land*, for the first time, Schaefer incontest-
ably attacks the civilization process and clearly resents its
effects. The legal system which was seen as essentially ben-
eficial in *First Blood* is now cast in a contemptuous light; the
issue is expressed simply by Kean:

Legal! . . . That's what happens when too many peo-
ple get to crowding in. Everything's got to be legal!
Everybody told what they can do, what they can't do!
A bunch of fools way off in Washington who ain't

ever seen this country, don't know a thing about it,
get to making a lot of silly rules. (p. 487)

Schaefer's shifting attitude toward the law is evident in
the preponderance of "silly rules." Unlike Race Crim,
Brent Kean does all he can to comply with the dictates of
the law, but finally is driven to strike against it. We agree
with him when he observes that "legal foofrawing only
frazzles things till there's no real right or wrong left" (p.
496). Goss, the villainous land-grabber for the railroad,
illustrates a side of the law only glanced at in *First Blood*. He
taunts the sheriff who is constrained by the very rules he
seeks to enforce:

The law is behind us. . . . The trouble with you and
Kean is that you're both old-fashioned, your time is
past and you're just a pair of relics walking around.
. . . Direct action. That's your way. So old-fashioned
you ought to be under a glass in a museum. Manipulating the law is a lot better than manipulating a gun.
Safer. More profitable. (pp. 497–98)

It is this new association of evil intent with legal exploita-
tion which heralds Schaefer's growing pessimism toward
the promise of civilization. In *Shane* and *First Blood*, Joe
Starrett and Tom Davisson act in accordance with the legal
system, and we see the benefits of that system. In *The Kean
Land*, the sheriff (who closely resembles Tom Davisson) is
caught in the machinations of that legal system. Schaefer's
references to "manipulating a gun" and "direct action"
speak to the efficacy of no-nonsense justice meted out in
earlier times. That further progress will bring greater concessions is illustrated by Ben Hammon's evaluation of contemporary times:

Folks crowding in. . . . Too busy making money or
trying to and tearing up and down that highway
there in cars that aren't ever paid for . . . and worrying about meeting installments on all the billy-be-

damned gadgets people think they have to have
nowadays cluttering their houses and getting in the
way of decent living. (p. 466)

The broad historical perspective of *The Kean Land* is
also utilized in *Monte Walsh* (1963). However, instead of
using an aged narrator and a retrospective viewpoint,
Schaefer allows the narrative to unveil the effects of an
encroaching civilization on the frontier. *Monte Walsh* is
Schaefer's most effective attempt to reveal what civilization has extracted from the human spirit. Covering
Monte's life from the age of sixteen in 1872 to his death in
1913, this novel is Schaefer's most ambitious work. As
noted by Haslam, "Walsh is more than just a man. Schaefer's portrait of a working cowboy can also be seen as a symbol of a passing way of life, representing values and integ-
rities which the growing social order is destroying."[16]

The first section of *Monte Walsh* elaborately portrays the
ranching era which was only glimpsed in the earlier
novels. The cowboy life described by Schaefer embodies
the best elements of chivalry, challenge, and self-ful-
fillment in an exciting environment. It is easy to see that
Schaefer's loyalties have changed considerably since
Shane, where the best cowboys were simply high-spirited
rowdies and the worst were bullies and brutes. The young
cowboy Chris gains our sympathy when he leaves the cowboy life to replace Shane on the Starrett farm. In *Monte
Walsh*, young Monte is described in mythic terms, outlined
against our retrospective awareness of a world since jaded:

Another young one was riding north with the trail
herd, with the men and the horses that were taking
the Texas longhorns to the farthest shores of the
American sea of grass, unthinking, uncaring, un-
knowing that he and his kind, compound of ignor-
ance and gristle and guts and something of the deep
hidden decency of the race, would in time ride
straight into the folklore of a weary old world.[17]

The saga of Monte Walsh covers three stages of frontier development: ranching, sparsely settled farm communities, and densely settled farm communities. Through Monte, the reader interprets the changing nature of society; the fact that Monte doesn't change with it is to his benefit, like old Brent Kean and Ben Hammon in *The Kean Land*. Civilization is unwilling to tolerate Monte's kind of wild independence, and the novel shows his world becoming more narrow and precarious.[18] It is also more dull and lifeless, a spiritless world of sameness and complacency.

One of the earliest indications of the foothold of progress on the frontier is when the Consolidated Cattle Company buys up the ranch which is to become the Slash Y. As is so often the case with Schaefer's history, this development has basis in fact. This is the practice described by Douglas Branch in *The Cowboy and His Interpreters:* "The West . . . was becoming the toy of Eastern capital. The code of the West was becoming twisted by alien hands."[19]

As the ranches are transformed into conglomerates, so is the nature of the cowboy's work on the Slash Y. No longer does he work only off the back of a horse working cattle; now he is required to set fence posts, string fence, and—the most unbearable humiliation—tend sheep. As Cal, the ranch manager, says, "hereabout an' nowadays things has changed" (p. 88). Monte's close friend Chet changes with the times, and it is the growing contrast between Chet's adjustment to civilization and Monte's resistance to it which reveals Schaefer's skeptical view of progress.

As Branch observed, there was no place for the family in the cowboy's life, and the role of the cowboy was a solitary one.[20] Chet epitomizes the transition from the era of the open range to the more civilized mode of town life with its emphasis on commerce, law, and politics. He marries, becomes a merchant and a three-term mayor, and at the end of the novel has been elected to the state legislature of the recently admitted state of New Mexico. The emergence of a new state is a larger representation of the growth and change which occur in the town of Harmony, a frequent focal point of the novel. At one point, Monte notices that the town is "no longer quite so little, organized now, beginning to take on some shape. . . . The omens were unmistakable" (p. 382). It is Chet who changes, matures with Harmony and New Mexico; Monte stubbornly retains the life style and values of an earlier time, traveling to increasingly more remote regions where vestiges of the frontier can still be found, and where a totally self-reliant man is still valued.

It is not that Monte is unaware of the changes being undergone in the West, but that he will not accept them. By the close of the novel, Monte is an antiquated eccentric, much like Brent Kean. He looks with disdain on a world where saloons are calling themselves restaurants to attract family trade, new ranchers have been to college, and old ways are looked upon with bemusement. The juxtaposition of Monte's devotion to the old ways and old values with the ravages of progress is Schaefer's way of extolling the virtues of the past. Someone says of Monte, "You can't change that kind. Maybe it's a good thing you can't. They're part of the old days that are sort of fading away. Something's going to be missing from this country when the last of them's gone" (p. 410).

The dominant symbol of progress at the end of the novel is the automobile. Working alone in the mountains, Monte's solitude is invaded by a mining operation and an engineer who maneuvers a car back and forth to the mine. When a mining accident necessitates quick action, it is Monte and his horse, not the "goddamned modern contraptions" which come to the rescue. Monte's dying words testify to Schaefer's preference for the values of the men who conquered the frontier on its own terms: "no goddamned autymobile . . . could of . . . done it" (p. 499).

Mavericks (1967) is Schaefer's last novel. It is a continuation of the polemic nature of his later work which became clearly visible in *The Kean Land*. Again using an older protagonist, the flashbacks are not so much nostalgic reflections of the past as they are mirrors held up to an unsatisfactory present. In fact, the major character, Jake Hanlon, first appeared as a minor character in *Monte Walsh*. And as the automobile became the main symbol of civilization in that novel, the dwindling herds of wild mustangs embody the vanishing frontier in *Mavericks*. Jake is devoted to the destruction of the trucks and planes which attempt to capture and kill the animals which have "the look of eagles."[21] In Jake's recollections of the different mustangs he has owned, Schaefer presents the vitality, integrity, and stubborn endurance which characterize the earlier era. The present times cannot tolerate Old Jake's commitment to action, viewing him as an "old nuisance, a shiftless relic of the past, a lawbreaker, a jailbird, a disgrace to a modern progressive community" (p. 3).

In *Mavericks,* the highway which intrudes across the open land represents the determined progress of civilization. But Schaefer emphasizes the dubious value of change for change's sake. The highway is "the symbol . . . of the relentless onrush of what was called progress, of inevitable indifferent power driving forward regardless of what might be in its path . . . taking over the whole world" (p. 169). It is progress which does not pause long enough to appraise what is being lost. *Mavericks* clearly reveals Schaefer's increasing pessimism toward the civilization process; more specifically, his dissatisfaction is directed at the diminution of human spirit which seems to accompany the society's advance. As Cawelti observes about the Western, it is possible to explore not only the gains of progress, but the losses as well.[22] Cawelti cites these human values which have been destroyed or restricted by the civilization process, and his list is an accurate appraisal of the character of Jake Hanlon and of Schaefer's other frontier survivors: a sense of freedom, spontaneity, personal honor, individual mastery, and the deep camaraderie of men untrammelled by domestic ties.[23]

One way of observing the destruction of values by the growing social order is to look at the effect of civilization on the townspeople. It was seen that business representatives such as Goss were clever, cunning, and unscrupulous in *The Kean Land*. Chet's growing conservatism and deterioration of stern will is directly proportionate to his adjustment to town life in *Monte Walsh*. But Schaefer's most eloquent spokesman against the questionable values of civilization is Henry W. Harper, the friendly patron of Jake Hanlon in *Mavericks*. Henry is the grandson of the respected Hardrock Harper, one of Jake's former employers. Henry W. Harper is plumpish, with soft hands and manicured nails; he lives in a fine big house in town and has abandoned his grandfather's ranch, allowing it to crumble in the desert.

Despite these failings, Henry W. Harper is not a villainous figure; he is the one person who understands Jake's motives and actively strives to protect him. But his means of protection is strictly financial, a superficial measure of personal commitment. This passive figure of the civilized man who tries to place money between the obstinate old men and a threatening world of progress can be traced at least as far back as *The Kean Land*, when Ben Hammon's children promise to bail their father out of jail if he should shoot the troublesome real estate people. In *Monte Walsh*, a Mr. Wilson is a check-writing accountant who admires the reckless life of the cowboys and does what he can to protect them. But it is Henry W. Harper who best expresses how far Schaefer has come in his attitude toward the merits of civilization, and who best defines Schaefer's admittedly anti-civilization feelings:[24]

Times have changed . . . Money's the most important thing nowadays. You have some, you are somebody. I have some and I suppose that makes me
somebody, but I'm not always too sure. I know I'm no
Hardrock, but at least I'm pretty good at signing
checks. . . . I'm a product of money and easy living.
There's about as much firm substance to me as there
is to a pillow. . . . You represent something I haven't
got and wish I had. You stand up to life and spit in its
eye. You believe in a few things . . . and you act on
them. . . . You do the kind of things I'd want to do if I
only had the guts. (pp. 165–66)

James K. Folsom has stated that the burden of Western
fiction is to determine whether the coming of civilization is
good or ill.[25] This study has found that Schaefer's vision of
the merits of civilization has changed markedly since the
heroic figure of Shane rode out of "the heart of the great
glowing West"[26] and left a legacy of frontier independence to increasingly anachronistic successors such as Ben
Hammon, Brent Kean, and Jake Hanlon. This examination of Schaefer's novels shows a progressively more bitter
treatment of the national maturation theme. Schaefer's
view of history contradicts the serenity, dignity, and
worth" which Erisman observes in our national development. Such qualities are discouraged in a society which
finds frontier independence an increasingly unmanage-
able, undesirable obstacle to historical maturation. It is as
if Schaefer began his career in Western fiction with pre-
conceived romantic notions which inspired the elegiac
Shane. But as he pursued his theme in succeeding works,
taking historical developments into the twentieth century,
he was disenchanted by the negative influences of civilization: the reality of the present did not measure up to the
promise of the romantic past. *Mavericks* is Schaefer's last
novel, and he has said that it will serve as his epitaph. Like

Jake Hanlon in that work, Schaefer feels that he has inadvertently helped to destroy what he loved.[27]

A curious thing has thus happened: by looking deeply into the history of western expansion, Schaefer's initial optimism is overcome by a cynical recognition of the demeaning effects of civilization on the human spirit. Schaefer's observations about this evolving pessimism echo the regret and sense of loss so often expressed by his despairing frontier survivors:

> Never again could I write of people with the same "innocence" of past years. . . . If I was writing them now, I would have difficulty seeing them as I saw them . . . originally. . . . How, for example, could I present Shane as heroic in the situation he confronted . . . when in my own mind, I would be seeing him as part of that "deadly conquest called civilization"?[28]

Notes

1. Fred Erisman, "Growing Up with the American West: Fiction of Jack Schaefer," in *The Popular Western: Essays Toward a Definition,* ed. Richard W.Etulain and Michael T.Marsden (Bowling Green, Ohio: Bowling Green University Popular Press, 1974), p. 711/69.

2. Ibid., p. 715/73.

3. Gerald Haslam, *Jack Schaefer* (Boise, Idaho: Boise State University Western Writers Series, no. 20, 1975), 32.

4. Rachel Shor, "Jack Schaefer," *Wilson Library Bulletin,* 35 (1961); 471.

5. Frederick Jackson Turner, "The Significance of the Frontier in American History," in *The Turner Thesis: Concerning the Role of the Frontier in American History,* ed. George Rogers Taylor, 3rd ed. (Lexington, Massachusetts: D. C. Heath, 1972), p. 3.

6. Jack Schaefer, *Shane* (1949; repr. New York: Bantam Books, 1962), p. 3. All further references to this work appear in the text.

7. Turner, p. 9.

8. Haslam, *Jack Schaefer,* p. 17.

9. Turner, p. 23.

10. John G. Cawelti, *The Six-Gun Mystique* (Bowling Green, Ohio: Bowling Green University Popular Press, 1971), p. 49.

11. Ibid., p. 65.

12. Ibid., p. 39.

13. Jack Schaefer, *The Kean Land,* in *The Short Novels of Jack Schaefer* (1959; Boston: Houghton Mifflin Company, 1967), p. 465. All further references to this work appear in the text.

15. Turner, p. 19.

16. G. W. Haslam, "Jack Schaefer's Frontier: The West as Human Testing Ground," *Rocky Mountain Review,* 4 (1967): 70.

17. Jack Schaefer, *Monte Walsh* (Boston: Houghton Mifflin, 1963), p. 29. All further references to this work will appear in the text.

18. Haslam, *Jack Schaefer,* pp. 36–37.

19. Douglas Branch, *The Cowboy and His Interpreters* (1926; repr. New York: Cooper Square Publishers, 1961), p. 118.

20. Ibid., p. 146.

21. Jack Schaefer, *Mavericks* (Boston: Houghton Mifflin, 1967), p. 86. All further references to this work will appear in the text.

22. Cawelti, p. 73.

23. Ibid., p. 52.

24. Haslam, "Jack Schaefer's Frontier," p. 64.

25. James K. Folsom, *The American Western Novel* (New Haven, Connecticut: College and University Press Services, 1966), p. 31.

26. Schaefer, *Shane,* p. 119.

27. Haslam, *Jack Schaefer,* p. 41.

28. Ibid., p. 41.

Michael T. Marsden

**The Making of *Shane:*
A Story for All Media**

Many have praised *Shane* as a
powerful novel, calling it a classic of Western American
literature. But few have attempted to chart and analyze its
remarkable viability as a story form through several different mass media over almost forty years. It is difficult if not
impossible to forget the closing lines of the novel ("he was
the man who rode into our little valley out of the heart of
the great glowing West and when his work was done rode
back whence he had come and he was Shane"), and it is
equally impossible to forget the haunting cries of Joey as
he tries to bring Shane back because the Starretts need
him. The symbols and images of an awesome tree stump,
an innocent bottle of soda pop, a deadly, ivory-handled
six-gun, and a civilized family garden have earned their
permanent places in the American imagination. The power of the *Shane* story does not diminish with the years but
instead seems to become even more effective with each
reading or viewing. The novel, having gone through some
seventy editions in thirty languages,[1] continues to draw
new generations of Americans and non-Americans alike
into the Western American Experience. But the unusual

story of the making and remaking of *Shane* in several mass media is of interest as well.

It still surprises people that Jack Schaefer, who was born in Cleveland, Ohio, had never been west of Toledo, Ohio, when he wrote *Shane*.[2] He moved West only in 1954. *Shane* was probably begun in 1944 and the bulk of it written in 1945, usually late at night when Schaefer's schedule as acting editor of the *Norfolk Virginia Pilot* permitted.[3] It was written in sections over about a year's time on the back of newspaper copy paper as a way for Schaefer to relax and forget the troubles of a war-torn world.

In 1946 Schaefer decided to submit the novel to *Argosy*. He was an unknown and inexperienced novelist, and he forgot to include the return postage for his single-spaced manuscript. It is generally the case with large circulation magazines that unsolicited manuscripts without return postage end up in the wastebasket. In the case of *Shane*, a hurried editor by the name of Rogers Terrill grabbed a bunch of papers from his desk and stuffed them into his briefcase as he prepared to go away for the weekend. Fortunately, *Shane* made the trip with the editor.

Terrill liked what he read of the manuscript that weekend and decided to publish it under the title *Rider from Nowhere* as a three-part serial in the July, September, and October 1946 issues of *Argosy*. As Schaefer rather fondly recalls, the first issue carrying his story contained a misspelling of his name (with two f's) on the cover.

By 1948 Schaefer had left newspaper work and had gone to New York and spent time revising *Shane* and taking it to several publishers. His first agent placed the slim book with Houghton Mifflin within a week after taking on Schaefer as a client. It was published in a hardbound edition in 1949. This was the beginning of a lifelong relationship between Schaefer and Houghton Mifflin. Austin Olney, who was assigned to *Shane* by Houghton Mifflin, is

still Schaefer's editor despite the fact that Schaefer has
shifted subject matter considerably[4] and Olney has moved
up in the company.

Although there are over four million copies of *Shane* in
print today, the book was never really a best-seller. It has
always been a steady seller: it began slowly, benefited from
a few good reviews, and gradually rose in sales. In addition
to its many editions in various languages, there have been
numerous school editions printed, countless excerpts
from the book in various anthologies and textbooks, and
even an edition distributed by the United States Information Agency as an approved export of American culture.
Schaefer notes that the British Broadcasting Corporation
once did a ten-part reading of *Shane*. In addition to the
successful film by George Stevens, a less than successful
television series was based on the novel.

A year after its publication in 1949, *Shane* had sold 6,203
copies. By 1951 it was selling about 8,000 hardbound
copies a year. Bantam brought out a paperback version in
1950 and by 1959 had sold 1,250,000 copies. The Bantam
edition sales have averaged, according to the author's
figures, 120,000 per year.

Schaefer compiled a special list of statistics for the twen-
ty-fifth year of the book's publication (1974) and indicated
that during that year alone Houghton Mifflin had sold
20,647 copies of its textbook edition of the novel and 1,735
copies of the illustrated hardbound edition. During the
same year Bantam sold 96,208 copies of its paperback edition. In England, hardcover and book club sales ac-
counted for another 42,273 copies; and Transworld, a
major foreign distributor, sold yet another 10,276 paperback copies abroad.[6] Clearly, *Shane* has remained a "steady
seller."

It is impossible to gauge accurately the overall influence
of such a novel. Its effect on culture outside the United
States is suggested by its translation into thirty languages.

But there are even further variations—such as a special Japanese edition limited to one thousand English words for the person attempting to learn the language—and these need to be evaluated in determining the novel's overall impact. Schaefer notes with pride that *Shane* found its way into Arthur C. Clarke's *A Fall of Moondust,* where several people are trapped in a submarine-like contraption that is supposed to explode in deep layers of moon dust. While they are waiting to be rescued, they pool their books. Schaefer quotes: "The total haul consisted of assorted lunar guides, including six copies of the official handbook; a current best seller, *The Orange and the Apple,* whose unlikely theme was a romance between Neil Gwynne and Sir Isaac Newton; a Harvard Press edition of *Shane,* with scholarly annotations by a Professor of English . . . ."[7]

Shane's place in American, and perhaps even international, culture seems secure. Its influence, in fact, seems to grow each year as more people are introduced to the stranger who rides in from nowhere and yet everywhere and simply says, "Call me Shane."

Rider from Nowhere, as published in three parts in *Argosy,* was divided into fourteen chapters; the later hardbound edition of the novel contained sixteen chapters. When the magazine serial was revised into a novel in 1948, some new material was added and new chapter divisions were created. The single most important addition to the novel was the stump-pulling sequence toward the beginning, which is powerfully presented in both the novel and in George Stevens's film version.

The first chapters of both the *Argosy* and the novel versions of *Shane* are essentially identical except for minor stylistic changes. Beginning with the second chapter in the *Argosy* version, shifts in plot order and emphasis occur between the magazine and novel versions. For example, in *Argosy,* Shane is sent into town to get "farmer's" clothes almost immediately, whereas the novel allows Shane time to adjust to the prospect of becoming an assistant farmer. It is in the third chapter of the novel that the stump-pulling scene occurs. From that point of the comparison forward, the novel's chapters parallel the magazine's plot sequence except that the emphases are different and the novel is two numerical chapters behind the magazine version. By a re-division of the plot sequences and the addition of the stump-pulling scene, the novel adds two chapters to the original magazine version. But the most important difference is that the last chapter of the novel, the epilogue concerning the legends and myths that have sprung up around the memory of Shane, is separated out and thus given considerably more emphasis. In the novel, the revised chapter divisions seem to sharpen the focus on Shane and to play down the other characters somewhat. They also further emphasize the unusualness of Shane, his almost supernatural qualities. The overall result of the new plot divisions is to provide a more natural flow. For example, in the midst of the huge barroom brawl between Shane and the cowboys before Joe Starrett arrives to aid Shane, the serial version ends the chapter and part one of the serial. The obvious purpose was to keep the reader interested in the story and in purchasing the next issue of the magazine. But the novel provides the entire fight sequence in one chapter, which flows more smoothly because of the change.

Through its use of illustrations and captions, *Argosy* clearly attempts to place *Rider from Nowhere* in the pulp Western tradition. The novel version of *Shane* attempts to refine the original structure so that the story's classic and timeless elements are presented in their most natural rhythms.

The successfulness of the novel cannot, however, be traced solely to its form. Its content is apparently of international, if not universal, appeal; its story is one of human warmth and compassion. From the moment he rides into the valley until the moment he rides out, Shane is presented as something larger than man, perhaps as the very spirit of man. On several occasions Schaefer has stated that he has gone beyond the innocence of *Shane,* and that he could not write such a novel again.[8] Perhaps the novel's appeal is in its basic belief in the ability of the spirit of man to prevail. It seems appropriate that Schaefer's basic story of man's innocence should be placed in the American West and told through the eyes of a man remembering his youth, at the time when he was the future of the country. Although Schaefer had not traveled in the West before he wrote *Shane,* he knew it well through secondary sources, especially western histories, and somehow he was able to synthesize several key shared traditions about the American West which, although they may not have been historically accurate, were culturally accurate as reflections of the beliefs, attitudes, and values of a people.

A specific comment by Schaefer about the background material for *Shane* is noteworthy in this context: "I didn't use any particular book as background for Shane, simply general notions out of years of desultory reading of western material with no notion of ever using any of them in writing of my own. My guess would be that insofar as any book supplied any background for mine, it was *Triggernometry* by Eugene Cunningham. I had that one around in those days."[9] *Triggernometry,* subtitled *A Gallery of Gunfighters with Technical Notes on Leather Slapping as a Fine Art, Gathered from Many a Loose Holstered Expert Over the Years,* is a collection of seventeen folkloristic-biographical sketches of western gunmen and gunfighters (Cunningham suggests that gunmen were less noble in purpose than gunfighters). It was published in 1941 and would have been interesting reading for Jack Schaefer as he sat in a newspaper editor's chair during the early 1940s with *Shane* forming in his mind.

Schaefer's personal love affair with the West began with his readings about it and continued through his travel assignments for *Holiday* in the early 1950s, his move to a ranch near Sante Fe, New Mexico, and his later move to a remodeled adobe home in Albuquerque which was built on the ruins of an Indian cemetery. His own words about the West are sufficient: "The bigness of vast rolling treeless plains and of mountains that rise sheer above the timberline is a bigness that opens outward, that beckons onward, that feeds the imagination with visions of unlimited possibilities."[10]

Schaefer views *Shane* as similar to Greek drama in that it focuses on the tension of the individual versus society,[11] a theme which several critics have indicated dominates Schaefer's overall work. That Schaefer should see the novel in this way is not surprising, for he was a student of Greek literature while at Oberlin College.[12] Gerald Haslam states that Schaefer tried to keep the story of *Shane* classical in form, but that "other layers of meaning crept in"; in Schaefer's opinion, however, these layers of meaning did not interfere with the straight-line story.[13] Schaefer's attempt to link *Shane* with the history of mankind is no more apparent than in the following statement about the Western story: "Perhaps that is because the western story, in its most usual forms, represents the American version of the ever appealing oldest of man legends about himself, that of the sun-god hero . . . and the western story does this in terms of the common man, in simple symbols close to natural experience."[14]

Despite claims to the contrary, such as Gerald Haslam's that "Schaefer's concern, then, is not with 'westerns' as they are popularly—and cheaply conceived,"[15] *Shane* is clearly within the tradition of the popular and well-conceived Western with a story form as indigenous to

America as prairie grass. *Shane's* steady and continually growing success over three decades both as a novel and as a film speaks to its essential popularity as well as to its formulaic purity. It seems to escape time, as does its hero, who rides into the valley to help the forces of civilization against the forces of the wilderness for generation after generation of Americans.

Several critics have noted that the novel is filtered through the innocent eyes of a young boy. But I would suggest that the story is told by an older man looking back at his youth as in a romance. The novel is not just another "coming of age" novel, but rather is structured like a gospel, the Western Good News, as told by the singular, individualistic apostle left behind to grow up straight and tall and honest as a man was meant to. A misreading of the novel's point of view would seem to have led several critics astray, for its message cannot be as easily explained away as only the fabric of a dream.

According to Schaefer, if Shane is modeled on any man, it was his father, a Cleveland, Ohio, lawyer.[16] Despite obvious Christian references scattered throughout the novel, Schaefer denies any Christian influence in his book.[17] Joe and Marian's names, for example, certainly parallel Joseph and Mary; and Shane is depicted as Christ- or Messiah-like in a number of key passages, but as an Old Testament Christ bringing justice, not a New Testament Christ bringing forgiveness![18] Marian's final comments about Shane should satisfy anyone's doubts on the issue: "He's not gone. He's here, in this place, in this place he gave us. He's all around us and in us, and he always will be."[19]

The Christian cross has been replaced by the farmer's stubborn stump, which in turn gives way to the tall corner-post of Joe Starrett's corral which Shane put in and which "grew roots."

It would seem useful to comment briefly on one or two

major points regarding the novel's overall significance which may be found in the lessons that Shane leaves behind for each member of the Starrett family. To Joe he leaves the lessons of self-sacrifice and humility; for to be bested by Shane is nothing to be ashamed of. But to have known Shane and to have worked with and helped Shane is something to be proud of. To Joe he also leaves the lesson that for the true American the future lies not in moving on, as was the "frontiersman's alternative to facing unpleasant situations,"[20] but rather in sinking roots. To Marian he leaves the lessons that human love must give way to spiritual love and that a man must accept what he is and do what he must. To Bob he leaves the entire western tradition which he represents. Although Bob quickly senses the danger in Shane, he also senses the basic rightness of his manner and cause. The specific lesson occurs when Shane teaches Bob that a gun is a tool, perhaps even a good tool in the hands of the right person. The perceptive reader and the matured Bob who reflect back on Shane understand that "the complex of characteristics that the author of a novel can attribute to the benevolent Shane inevitably implies, when visualized, the malevolent Stark Wilson."[21]

The visualization of *Shane* in film form in 1953 is the third step in the evolution of this American classic. With a filmscript by A. B. Guthrie, a musical score by Victor Young, and directed by George Stevens, *Shane* was destined to fill American screens for generations to come. From the opening scenes, as the hero-god descends from the Grand Tetons in the west and into the valley where he will authoritatively announce, "Call me Shane," to the haunting cries of young Joey (Bob) Starrett at the film's end, George Stevens makes it clear to the film audience that he is presenting a god-like hero who comes to bring law and order to a frontier troubled by a rancher-farmer feud that threatens to destroy, allegorically, the country. This is clearly the story of the American Choice.

The additions which the film makes to the story are worthy of consideration. For example, George Stevens has Shane ride down from the Grand Tetons to the west and into the valley at the beginning of the film, which contributes to Shane's aura of supernaturalness.

The image of the fence is another important addition to the story. As Shane rides into the valley, one of his first comments is: "I didn't expect to find any fences here." While the Rykers (Fletchers) want to continue to use the open range for their cattle, families like the Starretts want to fence it in and farm it, making the land a fit place to raise children. The Starretts' garden near the house, which is marked by fragile string, becomes an important symbol in the film when it is ruined by the horses of Ryker and his men. When his men come again to challenge Joe Starrett, they are warned to stay out of the repaired garden. The roots are family deep, and the plants will thrive again no matter what turmoil exists on the surface, for that is the essence of Americanism.

Under Stevens's direction, the stump sequence added to the *Argosy* version of Shane when Schaefer revised it into a novel becomes one of the most powerful in the film, as Shane and Joe struggle with all their human might to unearth the stubborn forces of nature, thus establishing their superiority and dominance over nature. The rhythmic rise and fall of their axes, intercut with the physical images of their struggle with nature, combine to form the overall visual effect of the two men, one a god and one a mortal, merging in their effort to subdue nature. Later in the film, in the fight between Joe and Shane to determine who will go to town to face the gunfighter Wilson, they both stumble over the remains of the stump; nature reasserts itself.

Another addition to the film is the Fourth of July

celebration, which also functions as a celebration of Joe and Marian Starretts' tenth wedding anniversary. The occasion celebrates both the founding of the nation and the basic support for that new nation, the American family. Joe and Marian gave up their individual independence to gain a greater, combined independence; and the suggestion is made on this Fourth of July that the farmers must surrender at least some of their individual independence by working together as a force against the ranchers. The holiday festivities merge with the celebration of the wedding anniversary to form a new civilization in the wilderness.

The film, which received five Academy Award nominations when it opened in 1953 (for best picture, best supporting actor, best director, best screenplay, and best cinematography), is a study in visual and aural balance. As Shane rides into the valley, for example, he is framed by a deer's antlers; it is through the antlers that the camera and then Joey first see Shane. Later, shadows of a deer's antlers frame Joey as he sleeps in the early morning light; in the same scene, they literally frame his bedroom window to the world. The approach to the town is framed by thin, narrow trees, reminiscent in their thinness of the antlers. And of course, Joe and Marian Starrett are framed by branches as they celebrate their wedding anniversary as part of the Fourth of July festivities.

The film's musical score by Victor Young nicely complements A. B. Guthrie's screenplay—as well as Jack Schaefer's novel—in a number of instances in the film, but none more dramatically than during the harmonica rendition of "Beautiful Dreamer," as the farmers gather at the Starrett farm to plan their strategies for survival against rancher Rufe Ryker. The musical piece underscores Marian's warning to Joey not to get to liking Shane too much, because he will be moving on someday. Shortly after this warning, she and Shane share knowing glances and comments as he is framed in Joey's bedroom window just as the deer had been; the difference is that the deer was standing in the morning sunlight and Shane is standing in the night and the rain.

While there are, of course, other changes from the novel to the film, these appear to be the most significant. The film tends to emphasize the ambiguity of the Shane character, the smouldering violence, the capacity for evil as well as for good. What separates Shane from the gunfighter Stark Wilson may be only an alliance with families instead of individualists. The dark side of Shane is the later realization by Schaefer that the outlaws and the open-range ranchers may have been the real heroes because they tried to stop civilization from spreading[22] Schaefer believes, as noted earlier, that he has gone beyond the innocence with which he wrote *Shane* and that he can never return.

On February 22, 1955, a special "Lux Radio Theater" production of *Shane* featured both Alan Ladd and Van Heflin. The "Lux Radio Theater," which had its premier in 1934, had begun by broadcasting adaptations of Broadway dramas. Although it was not initially successful, by 1936 it had shifted emphasis to Hollywood movies, and it became both popular and influential.[23] The program was an important marriage of radio and film, two industries which initially did not perceive themselves as compatible, much less complementary. The major stars would often do full adaptations of their successful movies, thus reinforcing their own successes and the audience's love for movies. These radio adaptations of movies were to the movie audiences of the 1930s, 1940s, and early 1950s what novelizations of screenplays are today. The radio adaptation of *Shane* was remarkably true to the film, deleting rather than changing scenes to fit the one-hour format.

The radio broadcast served to reinforce the importance, in the words of the announcer, of "George Stevens's *Shane*, . . . which received an Academy Award nomination for best picture in 1954," for American culture.

In the aftermath of the great rush of Westerns to the television screen in the late 1950s and early 1960s, the American Broadcasting Companies and Paramount Pictures launched an hour-long television series starring David Carradine and Jill Ireland which was loosely based on *Shane*. It ran for seventeen episodes, aired on Saturday evenings from September 10 through December 31, 1966.[24] The series, produced by Herbert Brodkin, made several major changes in the plot of both the novel and the film, rendering Marian a widow, introducing a grandfather for Joey, and getting Shane to stay on the farm.

It may well have been that the audience felt the plots were too much like other Western offerings on the air and not enough like *Shane*. For example, although the more expected confrontations between the ranchers and the farmers occurred, in a number of the episodes, in the second episode Shane thinks he sees what seem to be ghosts even though he does not believe in them. In the sixth episode, a man and a woman ride into the valley bearing a deadly disease. And in the eighth, Marian's old beau, now a state senator, arrives from the East and rekindles old flames. In the final episode, Ryker seeks Marian's hand in marriage![25]

Or, the audience may not have cared for David Carradine's acting style, which he developed further in his later, successful television series, "Kung Fu." Concerning his acting style in *Shane*, he noted: "But after a couple of weeks, I suddenly realized these people had hired me to do Shane my own way—whatever I could do was what they wanted. 'You've got to tell us,' they said. 'No one knows anything near as much about Shane as you do.'"[26] Carra-

dine left a co-starring role in a Broadway play to act in the
Shane series because he had been intrigued by the movie
ever since he had first seen it; he felt that Shane was "the
first folk-rock cowboy."[27] Anyway, the audience apparently was not intrigued with Carradine's version of the
classic hero, and ABC moved "The Dating Game" and a
new program, "The Newlywed Game," into Shane's one-
hour time slot at the beginning of 1967.

Through several mass media versions of varying degrees of commercial and artistic success over almost four
decades, *Shane* has moved through American culture and
has become a permanent part of it. In 1975 Jack Schaefer
was presented with the Distinguished Achievement A-
ward by the Western Literature Association in Durango,
Colorado. After explaining his conviction that our "species, taken as a whole . . . is more ignoble than noble, more
contemptible than admirable, is a dangerous evolutionary
experiment, a menace to all important forms of life including itself on this spaceship, earth,"[28] he added: "I am a
hopeless case. Incurable. Despite all the downbeat conclusions to which my species sapience drives me, it must be
that my small furry flying friend, my bat, with his ultimate
faith in mankind, asserts the upbeat hope that remains
hidden somewhere intact within me."[29]

Schaefer, then, still believes in the message of that
volume he wrote almost forty years ago, "lost innocence"
or not. He can still believe in it because America believes in
it. *Shane* will always be with us because it speaks not of man
merely enduring, but of the spirit of man prevailing. *Shane*
remains a story with a message as large as the green promise of a new world.

Notes

1. Gerald Haslam, *Jack Schaefer* (Boise, Idaho: Boise State University Western Writers Series, 1975), p. 12.

2. Interview with Jack Schaefer in Albuquerque, New Mexico, February 23, 1973.

3. This and a significant amount of the information which follows is taken from a letter from Jack Schaefer dated May 29, 1975.

4. In 1975 he published his *American Bestiary,* on which he was working when I first interviewed him early in 1973.

5. Clarence Petersen, *The Bantam Story: Thirty Years of Paperback Publishing* (New York: Bantam Books, 1975), p. 77.

6. Letter from Jack Schaefer dated May 29, 1975.

7. Ibid.

8. This point was most effectively presented during my second interview with Jack Schaefer in Albuquerque, New Mexico, on August 11, 1974.

9. Letter from Jack Schaefer dated December 7, 1974.

10. Jack Schaefer, *Out West* (Boston: Houghton Mifflin, 1955), p. ix.

11. Interview with Jack Schaefer, February 23, 1973.

12. Ibid.

13. Haslam, *Jack Schaefer,* p. 11.

14. Schaefer, *Out West,* p. viii.

15. G. W. Haslam, "Jack Schaefer's Frontier: The West As Human Testing Ground," *Rocky Mountain Review,* 4 (1967): 60.

16. Letter from Jack Schaefer dated April 8, 1974.

17. On this topic, Schaefer writes in a letter dated April 8, 1974: "I doubt if there is much if any Christian influence in my book even sneaking in out of the cellar of my mind. My Shane may qualify as a 'savior,' but not as a Christian one — much more, and this deliberately, as a universal, a human, an all-mankind one. Insofar as he had any model, that model was my father — in basic character, that is, not in actions and kind of life — and to my knowledge my father never belonged to any church. . . . There is a sound and more authentic background for what Shane did in the biological background of *homo sapiens* than there is in any religious tradition. He is more an alpha primate male fulfilling

his genetically ingrained obligation to his kind than he is a repetition of a Christ-tradition. He goes deeper than any particular religious meaning. And that was what was somewhat in my mind as I was writing a story which seemed to me might be worth reading."

18. I present my case for this interpretation in my article. "Savior in the Saddle: The Sagebrush Testament," *Illinois Quarterly*, 36, no. 2 (December 1973): 5–15 (repr. in *Focus On The Western*, Jack Nachbar [Englewood Cliffs, N.J.: Prentice-Hall, 1974]).

19. Jack Schaefer, *Shane* (New York: Bantam Books, 1966), p. 117.

20. Robert Mikkelsen, "The Western Writer: Jack Schaefer's Use of the Western Frontier," *Western Humanities Review*, 8, no. 2 (Spring 1954): 154.

21. James K. Folsom, "*Shane* and *Hud*: Two Stories in Search of a Medium," *Western Humanities Review*, 24, no. 4 (Autumn 1970): 365.

22. Interview with Jack Schaefer, August 11, 1974.

23. J. Fred MacDonald, *Don't Touch That Dial: Radio Programming in American Life* (Chicago: Nelson-Hall, 1979), p. 52.

24. I should like to thank Professor J. Fred MacDonald of the Department of History at Northeastern Illinois University for forwarding background information on this television series and for directing my attention to the "Lux Radio Theater" version of *Shane*.

25. These plot summaries were taken from back issues of *TV Guide*. An unsuccessful attempt was made to secure the episodes of *Shane* from Paramount Pictures Corporation for study.

26. Robert De Rous, "David Carradine Rides the New Wave," *TV Guide*, December 17, 1966, p. 24.

27. De Rous, p. 24.

28. Jack Schaefer, "A New Direction," *Western American Literature*, 10, no. 4 (Winter 1976): 267 (a reprint of this talk, given on October 11, 1975).

29. Ibid., p. 272.

The Film:
Essays in Criticism

Introduction

One mile north of Kelly, Wyoming, near the road leading from Jackson to the giant Teton range, a flat, empty sagebrush plain sprawls in the shadow of those jutting peaks. Not many folks live in Kelly any more, but some who do can still remember the time thirty years ago when the "movie people" came and built a western town and built a western ranch and filmed a western movie on this expanse of sage. And when the cameras were finished, the movie people took all the town's shops and houses and all the ranch's fence rails and corral posts back to Hollywood with them, and the sagebrush flats were once again empty. Kelly's view of the Tetons was again unbroken.

Nothing today remains. Nothing but a few strips of celluloid coiled up in cans labeled "Shane." But in those cans the novel, the screenplay, and the film remain a powerful influence. Few, very few, American novels have ever had such an impact upon the celluloid media as has *Shane*. The screenplay was written by A. B. Guthrie, Jr., who reminisced about it in 1983:

I had never written a screenplay at the time my Hollywood agent called to ask if I would write one. I took a breath. The agent went on to say the producer-director would be George Stevens. The name meant nothing to me. I hemmed and hawed. The book from which I would work, I was told, was a story called *Shane* by Jack Schaefer. I had read the story and promptly said yes, I would tackle the job.

Which may say enough about my regard for Schaefer's work. I'll just add that I admired his prose and the flowing movement he effected.

Shane was short for a screenplay and hence called for additions. I made them carefully, mindful of the merits of the book, fearful that I might do violence to it. I hope nothing I did has bothered Schaefer.

Since 1953, the movie *Shane* has been reviewed in hundreds of newspapers and magazines, large and small, and analyzed by domestic and foreign scholars alike. The essays here are only a tiny fraction of that critical interest, but they offer a great deal of insight into both the movie and the novel.

Bosley Crowther (April 24, 1953)

SHANE:
New York Times
Film Review

Shane, screenplay by A.B.Guthrie Jr., based on the novel by Jack Schaefer with additional dialogue by Jack Sher; directed and produced by George Stevens for Paramount Pictures. At the Radio City Music Hall.

Shane	Alan Ladd
Mrs. Starrett	Jean Arthur
Mr. Starrett	Van Heflin
Joey Starrett	Brandon De Wilde
Wilson	Jack Palance
Chris	Ben Johnson
Lewis	Edgar Buchanan
Ryker	Emile Meyer
Torrey	Elisha Cook Jr.
Mr. Shipstead	Douglas Spencer
Morgan	John Dierkes
Mrs. Torrey	Ellen Corby
Grafton	Paul McVey
Atkey	John Miller
Mrs. Shipstead	Edith Evanson
Wright	Leonard Strong
Johnson	Ray Spiker
Susan Lewis	Janice Carroll
Howells	Martin Mason
Mrs. Lewis	Helen Brown
Mrs. Howells	Nancy Kulp

With *High Noon* so lately among us, it scarcely seems possible that the screen should so soon again come up with another great Western film. Yet that is substantially what has happened in the case of George Stevens's *Shane* which made a magnificent appearance at the Music Hall yesterday. Beautifully filmed in Technicolor in the great Wyoming outdoors, under the towering peaks of the Grand Tetons, and shown on a larger screen that enhances the scenic panorama, it may truly be said to be a rich and dramatic mobile painting of the American frontier scene.

For *Shane* contains something more than beauty and the grandeur of the mountains and plains, drenched by the brilliant western sunshine and the violent, torrential, black-browed rains. It contains a tremendous comprehension of the bitterness and passion of the feuds that existed between the new homesteaders and the cattlemen on the open range. It contains a disturbing revelation of the savagery that prevailed in the hearts of the old gunfighters, who were simply legal killers under the frontier code. And it also contains a very wonderful understanding of the spirit of a little boy amid all the tensions and excitements and adventures of a frontier home.

As a matter of fact, it is the concept and the presence of this little boy as an innocent and fascinated observer of the brutal struggle his elders wage that permits a refreshing viewpoint on material that's not exactly new. For it's this youngster's frank enthusiasms and naive reactions that are made the solvent of all the crashing drama in A. B. Guthrie Jr.' script. And it's his youthful face and form, contributed by the precocious young Brandon De Wilde, that Mr. Stevens as director has most creatively worked with through the film.

There is tempestuous violence in a fistfight that a stranger and the youngster's father wage against a gang of cattlemen hoodlums in a plain-board frontier saloon, but the fight has a freshness about it because it is watched by the youngster from under a door. And there's novelty and charm in this stranger because he is hero-worshipped by the boy. Most particularly, there's eloquence and greatness in a scene of a frontier burial on a hill, but it gets its keenest punctuation when the boy wanders off to pet a colt.

The story Mr. Stevens is telling is simply that of the bold and stubborn urge of a group of modest homesteaders to hold on to their land and their homes against the threats and harassments of a cattle baron who implements his purpose with paid thugs. And it is brought to its ultimate climax when the stranger, who seeks peace on one of the farms, tackles an ugly gunfighter imported from Cheyenne to do a job on the leader of the homesteaders, the father of the boy.

This ultimate gunfight, incidentally, makes a beautiful, almost classic scene as Mr. Stevens has staged it in the dismal and dimly lit saloon, with characters slinking in the background as the antagonists, Alan Ladd and Jack Palance, face off in frigid silence before the fatal words fly and the guns blaze. It is a scene which, added to the many that Mr. Stevens has composed in this film, gives the whole thing the quality of a fine album of paintings of the frontier.

And in many respects the characters that Mr. Stevens's actors have drawn might be considered portraits of familiar frontier types. Van Heflin as the leading homesteader is outstanding among those played by Douglas Spencer, Elisha Cook Jr., Edgar Buchanan, and Leonard Strong. Mr. Ladd, though slightly swashbuckling as a gunfighter wishing to retire, does well enough by the character, and Jean Arthur is good as the homesteader's wife. Mr. Palance as the mean, imported gunman; Emile Meyer as the cattleman boss and Paul McVey as the frontier storekeeper give fine portrayals, too. But it is Master De Wilde with his bright face, his clear voice, and his resolute boyish ways who steals the affections ot the audience and clinches *Shane* as a most unusual film.

While the new screen on which the picture is being shown at the Music Hall is wider and higher than usual, in a ratio that slightly favors the width, the difference is barely apparent, except that some scenes appear trimmed at the bottom and the top. The greater size seems quite appropriate and unexceptional in the expanse of the Music Hall.

Charles Albright, Jr.
(1980)

Shane:
Magill's Survey
of Cinema Review

Shane
Released: 1953
Production: George Stevens for Paramount
Direction: George Stevens
Screenplay: A. B. Guthrie, Jr., with additional dialogue by Jack Sher; based on the novel of the same name by Jack Schaefer
Cinematography: Loyal Griggs (AA)
Editing: William Hornbeck and Tom McAdoo
Running time: 118 minutes
Principal characters
Shane............................... Alan Ladd
Marian Starrett ....Jean Arthur
Joe Starrett........................Van Heflin
Joey Starrett................ Brandon De Wilde
Wilson .... Jack Palance

Of the countless Westerns produced in Hollywood, *Shane* is among the most familiar and highly regarded. Its significance can be measured in terms of Hollywood's Western past, since *Shane* is a film that reflects upon the Westerns preceding it. It draws on the residue of this most enduring of film genres and abstracts its standard conventions, transforming them into myth. Given that many of the film's narrative events are seen through the eyes of a small boy, *Shane* further underscores the mythic status of the genre, suggesting its function as an outlet for the dreams and fantasies of youngsters.

The film's plot is deceptively simple. Shane (Alan Ladd), a mysterious, buckskin-clad loner, rides into a Wyoming valley during the late 1860s. He soon becomes a hired hand on the fledgling homestead of the Starrett family: Joe (Van Heflin), Marian (Jean Arthur), and young Joey (Brandon De Wilde). Shane is in fact a gunfighter who wants to change his ways; he hopes to settle down and start his own homestead. But Ryker, a cattle baron, intends to drive Starrett and the other homesteaders out of the valley, and Shane finds that he is being gradually drawn back into his past way of life. Because of Starrett's determined leadership, Ryker is unable to harass the homesteaders into leaving, so he hires Wilson (Jack Palance), a cold-blooded hired gun, to scare them out. After Wilson taunts, then easily kills one of the homesteaders in a one-sided gunfight, Starrett decides to put on his guns and stand up to Wilson and the Ryker bunch. Shane, however, knows that Starrett does not stand a chance against these seasoned killers, so he straps on his gun again. When Starrett insists on going, he and Shane wage a furious fistfight; Shane emerges victorious and rides off to meet the killers. In the town saloon, Shane outdraws and kills Wilson, as well as the Rykers. Though wounded, Shane rides out of the valley after indicating to Joey that he will never return.

Crucial to an understanding of *Shane* is its depiction of a mythic genre figure who tries to adapt to changing times by divesting himself of his heroic stature. The difficulty in making this transformation is first suggested when Shane trades in his buckskins for an outfit of drab workclothes. In these clothes, Shane enters a saloon, where he orders not the traditional shot of whiskey, but a bottle of soda pop. In the garb of a homesteader, Shane is taunted by one of the Ryker bunch. Since Shane wants to avoid trouble, he backs down from a fight, which leads the homesteaders to think him a coward. Wearing the same outfit, Shane eventually returns to the saloon, and with Starrett's help, bests the Rykers in a fistfight. The change of clothes allows Shane to initially "become" like a homesteader, but unlike them, Shane ultimately cannot back down from a fight.

Shane's relationship to the Starretts also points to him as one outside the locus of family-community-progress which they embody. While Joe likes Shane, and Joey worships him, Shane is nevertheless positioned as an outsider to the family unit. This is underscored by the unspoken love that he shares with Marian. Marian represents the nonheroic life style Shane can never attain, and their relationship is an idealized one. She is an insider while Shane is an outsider. The inside-outside duality is pointed up during a scene in which Shane stands outside in the rain while Marian is inside the Starrett house. The crosscutting between the two emphasizes the inside-outside relationship just as the gentle rendition of "Beautiful Dreamer" on the soundtrack at this point emphasizes the impossibility of Shane's transformation. When Shane finally goes to his quarters—which are, appropriately enough, away from the main house—Marian implies her love for Shane to Joey, telling him, "He'll be moving along one day and you'll be upset if you get to liking him too much." She then blows out a candle, causing the room to go dark. This suggests that her own attraction to Shane is as unattainable as his desire for her.

While Shane can never be a part of this family, he performs a heroic deed so that they—and the other homesteaders—can thrive in the valley. Before Shane rides off to meet Wilson, Marian asks, "Are you doing this just for me?" Shane replies, "For you—and Joe—and little Joey." As Shane rides off to the gunfight, he is again clad in his buckskins and, of course, is wearing a gun. Once again, his outsider status in relation to the family unit is suggested by editing: the Starretts are seen together in a single frame, while Shane rides off alone. Moreover, the ensuing long shots of Shane framed against the sky and mountains reaffirm his status as mythic figure.

Shane's relationship with Joey points to the Western genre as a source of preadolescent wish-fulfillment. This relationship is delineated in a number of ways. The lengthy fight in the saloon contains several cut-ins of Joey watching in fascination, as does the final gunfight. During the gunfight, Joey gets to realize his wish of participating in Shane's heroic actions, since he warns Shane that one of the Rykers is about to ambush him from upstairs, enabling Shane to kill the man. Prior to the climax, Joey gets to "be like" Shane by means of cutting on sound. During the saloon fight, after Shane lands a punch on the jaw of a Ryker henchman, a cut to Joey shows him biting hard on a candy stick. Here, the snapping sound of the bite replaces the sound of the punch.

Also crucial to an understanding of the film is the structuring opposition of civilization *versus* savagery that is a vital part of the generic structure of the Western. The valley town is not a thriving community but a few spread-out buildings and some tents. We see a disparate group of settlers (including an immigrant family and a family headed by a man who fought for the Confederacy), and the film posits that this cross-section holds the promise for a future—the transformation of a wilderness into a garden. The settlers are shown as nonviolent, and they are further ennobled by their harmonious relationship with the earth. During the scene in which they ride into town as a group, they are framed against the majestic mountains, the morning mist, and a sparkling brook. Moreover, the settlers clearly represent progress. This is suggested when Joe looks at a store catalogue from the East, and from his point of view we see the pages, full of appliances, dress suits, and so forth. The settlers, however, lack the ability to bring law to the savage land; they are ill-equipped to stop Ryker from transgressing nature. One homesteader notes that there is not a marshal within a hundred miles. The law, then, belongs to whoever has the fastest gun.

Within this opposition, Ryker and Shane, both of whom represent savagery, have no place in the advent of civilization. While Ryker is a villain, there are shades of gray to his character. He is the man who tamed the valley with his own sweat and blood. As he tells Starrett at one point, "We made this country. We found it and we made it." But Ryker's frontier dream has been perverted by his capitalistic greed, and Starrett's reply to his remark, "That ain't the way the government sees it," suggests that the homesteaders are sanctioned by culture and law. The film closely equates Starrett with democratic populism. This is especially suggested during the Independence Day celebration: the day honoring the establishment of the United States is also the anniversary date of the Starretts. During the celebration, the American flag is featured prominently.

While *Shane* clearly champions the populism represented by Starrett and the settlers, it also sadly concludes that there is no place for the rugged individualist within this new system. Finally, the film demonstrates that Ryker's kind of capitalist individualism violates law and community, while Shane's individualism enforces the principals of collective life. When Shane tells the cattle baron, "Your kind of days are over," Ryker replies, "My days? What about yours, gunfighter?" But Shane's next line, "The difference is I know it," stresses his own awareness of what he is. Shane, then, is the noble outlaw-savage who cannot be accommodated by civilization. It is he alone who is equipped to take effective action when words have proved to be inadequate.

In recent years, many revisionist critics have sought to devalue *Shane* because of its rigorous classicism. These critics argue that the "real" Hollywood Westerns have been made by once-slighted directors such as John Ford, Howard Hawks, Anthony Mann, and Budd Boetticher. While the great contribution made to the genre by these directors is incontestable, George Stevens's brief foray into a genre in which he had never worked (and never again worked) can be equated with the writers who came from the East to write about the frontier. Stevens takes the most familiar conventions of the West and stylizes them considerably. For him, the generic material becomes a means of glamorizing this most durable of Hollywood forms. This material also becomes a means of self-expression, and *Shane's* greatness is due in no small measure to Stevens's pictorial style and personal vision. Stevens himself has been devalued by revisionist critics, but he represents the best of the classical Hollywood cinema. Few directors used the close-up as effectively as Stevens, and the editing patterns linking close-ups of Shane, Marian, and Joey make the film genuinely touching and dramatically potent. This kind of editing recalls Stevens's great love stories, including *Swing Time* (1936), *Woman of the Year* (1942), *The More the Merrier* (1943), and *A Place in the Sun* (1951). After *Shane*, Stevens was weighted down by several elephantine spectacles which contain only flashes of his early brilliance. *Shane* is perhaps his last fully realized work. It is like those Stevens films in which a social misfit-outcast helps to make life better for someone who has a position within the social order, but who has certain problems which only the misfit can resolve. Notable among these films are *Vigil in the Night* (1940) and *The Talk of the Town* (1942). Other Stevens films detail the trials and tribulations of the social misfit-outcast in general, especially *Alice Adams* (1935), *A Damsel in Distress* (1937), *A Place in the Sun,* and *The Diary of Anne Frank* (1959).

Shane was made during the peak of Stevens's career, when the release of any film from him was considered an event (in this sense, Stevens was like Capra, Wilder, and Hitchcock). At the time of its release, *Shane* earned as much acclaim as any film of the 1950s. It was nominated for Academy Awards for best picture, best director, and best writing (screenplay). De Wilde's poignant performance was nominated for best supporting actor, as was Palance's menacing Wilson. Loyal Griggs received an Oscar for his breathtaking color cinematography. Stevens won the National Board of Review's best director award, and was also honored by the Director's Guild for quarterly directorial achievement. *Shane* was included on the ten best films of the year lists of the National Board of Review, *Time,* and the *New York Times.* The film's box office gross of eight million dollars made it the third biggest moneymaker of 1953, and even today, it is one of the most financially successful Westerns of all time.

Pauline Kael
(from *Kiss Kiss Bang Bang*, 1968)

Shane:
Review

Shane. Here's Galahad on the range, in one of those elaborately simple epics that important American directors love to make; superficially, this type of film is a Western, and thus salable, but those trained in the New Criticism will recognize it as the creation of a myth. You can start with the way Shane's horse canters or the Agincourt music or the knight's costume or at almost any other detail. The moviemakers put it there and we can find it all right, but it's academic on both sides. It's overplanned and uninspired; the Western was better before it became so self-importantly self-conscious. One trouble with this kind of mythmaking is that the myth is ready for the remainder counter by the time Hollywood takes it up. The enigmatic, pure-of-heart hero, Alan Ladd, defeats villains twice his size—e.g., the Prince of Darkness, Jack Palance. Ladd's chivalric purity is his motivation; his fighting technique (a secret weapon?) the enigma. With Van Heflin as the homesteader, Brandon De Wilde as the boy, Jean Arthur (in her last screen appearance to date) as the homesteader's wife, and Elisha Cook,

Jr., Edgar Buchanan, etc. Directed by George Stevens. Screenplay by A.B.Guthrie, Jr. Academy Award for cinematography (Loyal Griggs)—an award that must have seemed like a ghastly joke because Paramount, in order to take advantage of the new fashion for the wide screen, had mutilated the movie by cutting off the top and bottom of the entire picture. 1953, color.

James K. Folsom

Shane and *Hud:*
Two Stories
in Search of a Medium

Jack Schaefer's *Shane* (1949) and Larry McMurtry's *Horseman, Pass By* (1961) are two significant works of Western fiction. Successful books both, they reappeared as equally successful motion pictures—the first under the same title (1953), the second as *Hud* (1962).[1] Both movies faithfully followed the specific plots and general intent of the novels, unlike so many films—*The Big Sky* and *The Wonderful Country,* to mention two other Western novels so adapted—that too often bear little resemblance to their fictional sources aside from the same title. The faithful rendering of the novel by the motion picture based upon it in these two instances is partially attributable to the fact that both books are involved with thematic concerns that lend themselves to film treatment. Again this distinguishes them from many film versions of successful novels, which often center upon nothing more profound than the anecdotal interest of bizarre historical incident; or depend on the popular success of a colorful or notorious character (such as most film biographies, as well as films of a quasi-fictional character like *All the King's Men,* adapted from Robert Penn Warren's novel based on the life of Huey Long); or often solely upon the commercial desire to capitalize on the instant popularity of a successful book. In both *Shane* and *Horseman, Pass By,* however, the author's intent was to show the coming of age of a boyhood hero, a standard theme in both literature and films about the American West. In both books too, the boyhood hero must choose his way of life from among the various models of adult behavior that he sees around him and that are represented by the various characters in the novels—a method of fictional presentation admirably adapted to film.

More specifically, *Shane* and *Horseman, Pass By* lend themselves to film adaptation if only because they are short and fairly simple books, both with straightforward plot lines and relatively few characters. They do not, therefore, present the director with difficult and often paradoxical decisions of how best to preserve the author's "intent" when changing a novel to a film; or of how best to use the different techniques of cinema to achieve ends similar to a novel; or of the most satisfactory way to preserve the general character of an author's work while changing his particular artistic means in order to make the transition from printed page to screen. And most important, both novels relieve the director of the almost insoluble problem of how best to preserve the spirit of a sprawling "epic" novel, despite the inevitable distortion that cutting large sections of a complex book to manageable proportions for film treatment will produce. In the adaptation of neither *Shane* nor *Horseman, Pass By* was the film director faced with the problem of eliminating a large number of elements peripheral to the main story—as was, say, the director of the film version of James Jones's *From Here to Eternity;* or of the elimination of myriad subplots as in Dostoevski's *Brothers Karamazov;* or of the total suppression of almost entirely nonvisual chapters, like the cetolo-

gy chapters of Melville's *Moby Dick*. In general, then, whatever changes were made in the film version of the two
Western novels under discussion can be attributed to the
varying specific demands of two different media rather
than to some larger esthetic necessity to change the particular details of a book in order to preserve its general
character.

Yet the differing demands of the written and visual arts
did force a number of changes upon the directors of these
two films; and an analysis of the implications inherent in
these changes may be the best way to discuss at least some
of the differences between visual and written art forms—
differences of which we are all aware, however we may
gloss over them by referring offhandedly to films as "versions" of novels. Different versions they may be, but the
differences are very important: after all, Goethe's *Faust*
and Gounod's *Faust,* though from one point of view only
different versions of the same story, have far fewer points
of similarity than of difference. We all realize this, and nobody would pretend to criticize Gounod wholly from the
esthetic perspective of Goethe, knowing full well that the
operatic form demands certain changes even from a form
as closely related to it as traditional drama. But the heresy
persists that films can often best be understood, as well as
esthetically evaluated, in terms of the accuracy with which
they reflect the details of the fictional work on which they
are allegedly based, and of which they are presumably
faithful copies. Copies of books their film "versions" most
certainly are not; they are more like translations, attempts
to render the very personal and specific metaphors of one
language into the equally personal metaphors of a second.
And, one hopes, analysis of the metaphors of each language will give some insight into the points of difference
between them.

That the essential point of difference is not in the plot

becomes clear when we examine *Shane,* a novel whose plot was faithfully followed in the translation to film. The scene of both novel and film is Wyoming in 1889, and the plot of each is a descant upon the well-worn Western theme of the conflict between the arrogant cattle baron who claims ownership of the range and the homesteaders with whom he disputes possession. Both the novel and the film open with the arrival on the scene of Shane, a stranger who is just passing through and who stops at the homestead of Joe Starrett, leader of the homesteaders. In both novel and film Shane is a man with a past, a paradoxical figure famil-iar to readers of all kinds of Westerns—the gunfighter who would like to leave his guns behind. Joe Starrett per-suades Shane to stay in the valley, where the situation de-teriorates when Fletcher the cattle baron decides to force the homesteaders out. The homesteaders, under Star-rett's leadership, form a league for their own defense, and Fletcher retaliates by trying to drive Shane out of town. Shane beats up one of Fletcher's men, and in a rather in-credible scene he and Starrett beat up five others, after which Fletcher imports another gunfighter named Stark Wilson to finish the job for good. Wilson provokes a homesteader into a gunfight and kills him, and after this he, Fletcher, and two cowboys come to Starrett's ranch, where they try to break up the homesteaders' league through an unsuccessful attempt to buy off both Starrett and Shane. Ultimately, Shane has to face Wilson, whom he kills along with Fletcher, though he is himself badly in-jured in the gun battle; and at the end of the novel, as in the movie, he rides out of town as mysteriously as he came.

Particular changes between the book and the film are relatively few, and many of them are of specific rather than general significance. Among the more important of these specific changes is the fact that the statement of the conflict between the cattle baron and the homesteaders is insisted upon from the beginning of the film, while in the book it becomes of importance only relatively late. The reason is of interest, and perhaps not immediately evident. For in the book the characters of Joe Starrett and Shane can be roughed out through the retrospective memories of Bob Starrett, Joe's son and the narrator of the novel, while in the film the character of each man must be developed in terms not only of symbolic but of actual physical interaction between him and some other character who stands clearly as a foil to him. In the film, therefore, Fletcher—who very clearly represents values that are placed in specific opposition to those of Joe Starrett—is introduced early, while in the book he exists as a nebulous presence, mentioned but never seen, until the plot has gotten well under way. Similarly, Stark Wilson, Fletcher's hired gunfighter, who represents a set of values antithetical to Shane's, is introduced almost immediately in the film and placed in specific contrast to Shane.

The more interesting changes from novel to film, however, are those general ones that are almost entirely attributable to the differing demands of a verbal and a visual medium. First of all, in the film it is impossible for the boyhood narrator to be the controlling consciousness of the action to the same degree as was possible in the novel. The narrator of the events of the novel, Bob Starrett can only be the observer of them in the film. Rather than representing the controlling point of view, then, Bob becomes in the film only one among many characters, and a relatively minor character at that. Moreover, Shane himself changes in the film from the moral exemplum he was in the retrospective memory of the novel's boyhood narrator. He becomes a major character, visualized externally through his relationships with other characters rather than internally through Bob's nostalgic reflections upon his significance. Shane, then, does become the real focal point of the film as well as the titular hero of the book; he is important in his own right as a character rather than as a walking complex of character traits, which he logically remains in the novel.

For its need to define Shane and Joe Starrett in terms of visually acceptable opposites, the film version of *Shane* must pay a certain price in complexity. One important area of conflict in the novel is almost totally eliminated from the film—the problem of whether Bob's mother, Marian, should stay with Joe Starrett or follow Shane, with whom she is obviously infatuated. An unintegrated and relatively disappointing aspect of both novel and film, its presence in the book can be tolerated—if not exactly welcomed—because the retrospective point of view of Bob Starrett implies no necessary opposition between Shane and Joe Starrett, however much there must have been in fact and—more important—*must* be visually if the conflict is to be shown at all on the screen. In short, Bob Starrett's memory of both Shane and his father as good men simply will not work so straightforwardly in a film: for inevitably the conflict between the two, when seen rather than remembered, implies some sort of moral opposition, thus destroying the neat pattern of polarities in which each positive character has his negative foil in the evil gunfighter and the rapacious cattleman.

Briefly, the retrospective quality of the novel cannot be insisted upon quite so obviously in the film. While we will accept the conflict in the novel as a remembered conflict told us much later by a boyhood observer now himself arrived at maturity, we must accept the conflict in the film as happening in the immediate present, and watch the education of the youthful Bob Starrett taking place under our very eyes. Moreover, Bob in his film role as one among many characters cannot comment upon the meaning of the unfolding action as he could in the novel. In the film he must live through the experiences that he remembers in the novel.

Another important difference between novel and film is related to this same point. For the need to conceive the conflict in the film as immediate, as happening directly before our eyes, implies that we must be able to visualize the characters. In fact, however, much of the stylistic power inherent in the novel *Shane* depends upon the opposite need that one *not* see the people Bob Starrett remembers. Just as the novels' focus is retrospective, so are its characters not so much concrete human beings as memories, subjectively conceived, which are summoned up only before the mind's eye: the characters, and most particularly Shane himself, do not really appear in the novel in their own right but rather as subjectively recalled creations of the mind of the nostalgic narrator.

This personal view becomes clear upon examination of some of the written descriptions of Shane. When in the novel he first appears at the Starrett ranch, Bob describes him in terms purposefully both vague and general. What impresses Bob is the fact that the "newness" is gone from Shane's clothes, "yet a kind of magnificence" remains, accompanied by "a hint of men and manners alien to my limited boy's experience."[2] Much later in the novel, when Shane rides into town to face down Fletcher and Wilson, Bob describes him once more, and again the physical description of the man fades into its connotative associations. Now that he is no longer dressed in his farmer's clothes, Bob thinks, "he seemed again slender, almost slight," as he had when he had first ridden up to the Starrett ranch. Yet the change is seen primarily not in terms of observed physical appearance but rather of metaphorical descriptive connotations. "What had been seeming iron was again steel," Bob goes on. "The slenderness was that of a tempered blade and a razor edge was there." There is, a little later, "a catlike certainty in his every movement, a silent, inevitable deadliness," and as he rides off to face Wilson he is "tall and terrible there in the road, looming up gigantic in the mystic half-light"—not a man but a clearly visualized "symbol of all the dim, formless imaginings of danger and terror in the untested realm of human understanding."

Admittedly all this is a bit overdone, yet its purpose is clear enough. Schaefer hopes, through insistence upon these basically connotative descriptions, to make each reader build his own mental picture of Shane, who becomes visualized then not in actuality upon an external stage but retrospectively upon the internal landscape of the reader's mind. And this is an end which simply cannot be achieved in a film, where a character must be seen clearly in external terms.[3]

Schaefer's insistence upon this kind of retrospective and basically internalized description affects the action of the novel as well as the physical presentation of his characters. Since Shane himself is clearly stated to be a symbol of some of the formless aspects of the human spirit, his actions in the novel take on a moral and symbolic quality beyond their practical purpose. A clear example is a central symbolic scene of both novel and film in which Shane and Joe Starrett work together to pull a huge stump out of the ground. Just before the final effort Bob reflects that Shane is almost *willing* the stump out of the earth, and that his effort is at least as much a concentrated act of mental power as it is of physical force. Bob sees that "all of him, the whole man," is "pulsing" in an "incredible surge of power," noting that "you could fairly feel the fierce energy suddenly burning in him, pouring through him." Again this is acceptable, if somewhat overdone, as a fictional statement, especially in a novel in which we have been asked to create our own mental picture of Shane. But when one has to visualize the scene as it really happened rather than as someone remembers it, its entire character changes.

Shane and Joe Starrett become merely two men prosaical-
ly sweating and tugging at a large stump in a field.

A similar difference in mood can be found in two of
Shane's attributes, his horse and his clothes, both of which
were changed—somewhat to the detriment of the film—
from their novelistic source. Shane's horse, "moving with
a quiet sureness and power that made you think of Shane
himself," is clearly an extension of his rider, or better, an
embodiment of the power and ominousness Shane represents to the narrator of the novel looking back upon his
childhood through the mists of years. The point is clearly
made when Shane calls the animal before riding off to face
Fletcher and Wilson: "And the horse came out of the shadows at the far end of the pasture, its hooves making no
noise in the deep grass, a dark and powerful shape etched
in the moonlight." Esthetically, the description of the
horse is more pleasing than the vague sketches of Shane
himself; but the horse is just as difficult to visualize as his
master, and for precisely the same reason: he is not a flesh-
and-blood horse but a metaphorical statement of the ominous quality of "horseness," in precisely the same way that
Shane is not himself so much a character as a symbolic
statement of the "formless imaginings of danger and terror" in the human spirit.

Clearly such a horse cannot be found, and any attempt
to place him on the screen is, almost by definition, doomed
to failure. In fact the horse ridden by Shane in the film was
a very nice horse, a bright chestnut with four white stock-
ings and a comfortable single-foot road gait, but he impressed me more as an ideal child's horse than as a suitable
mount for a man like Shane. The point, of course, is that *no*
animal could have been a suitable mount for a man like
Shane, since Shane's horse is not an animal of flesh and
blood but a symbol.

Ironically, the other great change in Shane's attributes
from novel to film—the change in the clothing of the mo-

tion picture Shane—is also a visual change, and results in
one of the few points of real difference in intent between
film and novel. In the novel, what first impresses Bob a-
bout Shane is "his clothes." He wears "dark trousers
. . . tucked into tall boots . . . of a soft black leather," and
"a coat of the same dark material as the trousers." He has a
kerchief of "black silk" knotted around his neck and wears
a "plain black" hat—"unlike any hat" Bob "had ever seen."
The important things about Shane's clothes are their
strangeness and their dark color, both of which suggest
the strangeness and intangibility of Shane himself. In the
film, however, Shane wears a fringed buckskin shirt, and
the effect of ominousness is almost totally lost, since
Shane's clothes impress us not so much as those of a stranger as merely the work clothes of a character in another
line of work. Just as farmers wear overalls, we feel, so do
mountain men wear buckskins, and that is about the end of
it.

The difficulty, of course, is again a visual one, for it is
very hard indeed to present a character as ominous as the
Shane of the novel upon the screen without his becoming
threatening. In the novel we will accept Shane as powerful
but benevolent because Bob—who presumably knows—
tells us so; but when we actually have to *see* him as he is
rather than as he is seen through Bob's prejudiced
memories, his ominousness inevitably implies, at least in
visual terms, a certain malevolence. And the point is clearly, if unintentionally, made through the figure of Fletcher's gunfighter Stark Wilson, a character more important
in the film than in the novel, whose clothing in the film is
precisely that of Shane in the book. Dressed totally in black
and moving in a stylized fashion suggestive of his role as a
symbol rather than a character of flesh and blood, the film
Wilson (brilliantly played by Jack Palance) actually con-
veys many of the intangible qualities with which the novel
endows Shane. In short, the complex of characteristics

that the author of the novel can attribute to the benevolent
Shane inevitably implies, when visualized, the malevolent
Stark Wilson. Jack Schaefer, in sum, is able by controlling
the implications of his retrospective point of view, to im-
pute certain qualities to Shane's character which, when
seen, must appear as basically contradictory.

The different treatments of the same story in the novel
Horseman, Pass By and the film *Hud* also show clearly the
difficulty of translating the "mood" of a work of fiction into
film and the necessity imposed by a visual medium of having characters act as visible foils to each other. Once again
the film closely follows the plot of the novel, both in specific
incident and in general intent.[4] *Horseman, Pass By*, like
Shane, is remembered in retrospect through the eyes of
Lonnie, its now older boyhood observer, who reflects
upon the significance of a series of events that had happened on the ranch of his grandfather, Homer Bannon.
Homer, a man past eighty years old, his wife, and Hud, her
son by a former marriage, live on a ranch in Texas together with Lonnie and Halmea, the black cook and
housekeeper. At the beginning of the novel a dead heifer
has been discovered that turns out to be a victim of hoof-
and-mouth disease. Homer's cattle must all be destroyed
in order to halt the spread of the disease, and the reactions
of the characters in the novel to the worst disaster which
can strike a cattleman form both the conflict in the novel's
plot and the catalyst for Lonnie's transition to adulthood.

In a sense the differences between the two treatments of
the story are indicated by the change in title from *Horseman, Pass By* to *Hud*. Specifically, of course, the novel's title
is a direct reference to the self-epitaph with which Yeats
concludes his poem "Under Ben Bulben"—an epitaph
also fitting to Homer Bannon. The title is generally re-
levant too, especially to the fifth section of "Under Ben
Bulben," in which Yeats exhorts the Irish poets to cele-

brate native Irish themes rather than conventionally gen-
teel ones and, more specifically, "well made" themes of
"other days," of "heroic centuries" now past. Something
like this feeling is basic to the thematic structure of *Horseman, Pass By,* which is, as a recent critic perceptively points
out, a historic study of "the evolution of the Southwest
. . . embodied in . . . three central characters," all of
whom turn out to be different aspects of the "single image
of the cowboy"[5]—a figure which itself exists in an uncomfortable and inconsistent world composed partly of myth
and partly of reality. The point is nicely emphasized
through the name of the town near which the Bannon
ranch is located and where much of the novel's action takes
place. For the town is named Thalia after the Greek muse
of history and epic poetry.

This ambiguity inherent in the nature of "the West"—
that part of the American experience that we like, conventionally at least, to think of as having epic potentialities—
has been seen by many of the critics of the West as one
important reason for the failure of western themes to produce a literature of epic proportions. The West, it is
alleged, is simply too close to us in historic terms to be
viewed from what is conventionally considered to be an
epic perspective; the prosaic reality of the cowboy's life
intrudes involuntarily upon the mythic grandeur of the
epic story. Whether this objection is ultimately true is beside the point here, but it does point up one factor in the
"epic of the West" of which McMurtry is cognizant and of
which in *Horseman, Pass By* he makes considerable esthetic
use. For, to oversimplify, the adult world toward which
Lonnie yearns at the beginning of the story he conceives in
essentially heroic terms, a perspective that his experience
ultimately teaches him is a false and childish one. Neither
Hud nor Homer, however each may appear to the childhood observer, is wholly a walking embodiment of mythic-

al characteristics. Both are characters of flesh and blood, with problems conceived of in human rather than epic terms.

The film's difference from the novel, to return, is nicely exemplified by the change in title. For the motion picture concerns itself with Hud in a way the novel does not, Hud becoming if not the film's moral hero very definitely its focal character. Again the film has had to make specific the various generalized aspects of the novel's "single image" of the cowboy and to present them in terms of direct foils. Hence the values that in the novel are scattered among a number of characters, in the film are polarized between Hud and Homer Bannon, both of whom come to represent two distinct and mutually exclusive models for adult life. Rather than having a general view of the adult world as presented retrospectively through a number of characters, the film Lonnie must make a specific choice between two models who are conceived of as being directly opposed to one another. Though at the beginning Hud seems to Lonnie more attractive, by the end of the film Homer has replaced him as the desirable model.

This overly schematic analysis of *Hud* may give the quite erroneous impression that it is less subtle than *Horseman, Pass By*. Such is most emphatically not the case. The difference is, rather, that in the film subtlety is expressed through the nuances of conflict between the two major characters, Hud and Homer, while in the novel subtlety is expressed through proliferation of characters and—as in the novel *Shane*—through the retrospective musings of Lonnie himself upon the meaning of his own experience.

Horseman, Pass By is quite consciously conceived of as a mood piece, and McMurtry does a brilliantly effective job of presenting, through Lonnie's thoughts, the inchoate but very real yearnings of adolescence for something, it knows not what. In *Horseman, Pass By*, then, Lonnie's adolescent perspective can effectively be presented in terms of his yearnings for some kind of escape from the world in which he finds himself.

Although it is immediately clear what Lonnie wishes to escape *from*, it is not at all evident exactly what he wishes to escape *to;* nor in fact does he himself know. He expresses his yearnings in terms of sex and travel, two generalized metaphors which he sees embodied respectively in the figures of the cook Halmea and Jesse, one of the ranch hands. Quite the opposite is true of the symbolic pattern of *Hud,* in which, if only because we must see both Homer and Hud, we understand very clearly what Lonnie is drawn *toward,* and not so clearly what exactly he is reacting *against.* The respective endings of novel and film emphasize the point: for while the metaphor of the novel is of escape, that of the film becomes exile.

Again, the very real difference between the two versions of the story can best be seen by analyzing some of the changes from the novel made in the film. First of all is the fact that Halmea is changed in *Hud* from a black to a white woman, and Hud's rape of her, successful in *Horseman, Pass By,* is abortive in the film. Though this change originally may well have been prompted by nonesthetic considerations, it is nevertheless an effective one. The rape of Halmea in the novel is accomplished by Hud while Lonnie, who loves her, stands passively by. Though thematically this may make good sense, it is impossible to visualize except upon the screen of retrospective memory. In the novel Lonnie can tell us that this is what happened, without further explanation, and we accept his statement, though not without some mental reservations. But when the scene is actually presented to us we withhold our assent. When we must actually see the scene rather than having it reported to us, the basic improbability of the action becomes evident.

A more important change in the film is in the development of Hud's character. In the novel Hud's attractiveness to Lonnie as an image of successful sexuality is not really insisted upon until the rape of Halmea, while in the film this aspect of Hud's character is emphasized from the beginning. Early in *Hud* Lonnie is seen searching for Hud, whom he finds in the house of a married woman whose husband is away. The adolescent devil-may-care attractiveness of Hud to Lonnie is clear in this scene, which stands in clear symbolic contrast to the unattractive aspect of the same side of Hud as presented through the attempted rape of Halmea. In *Horseman, Pass By* the contrast can be, and is, more abstracted.

The necessity in the film to place Hud and Homer Bannon in direct contrast issues in one other really major change, the almost total omission of Jesse, the ranch hand. In *Hud* Jesse's role is reduced to that of a walk-on part, while in *Horseman, Pass By* he is a major character.

The reason behind the change is again visual. In the novel both Hud and Jesse act as direct comparisons to Homer. Hud's morality is placed in specific contrast to Homer's, in both novel and film, in terms of the two men's different reactions to the discovery of hoof-and-mouth disease in their cattle. After the initial shock has worn off, Homer realizes that the only moral choice open to him is to have his cattle slaughtered, and he accepts the necessity for the destruction of his entire herd. Hud, in contrast, proposes to Homer that they sell the cattle before the disease is diagnosed and the herd quarantined. If someone is "stupid enough to buy" the cattle, Hud sees no objection to selling them. In short, *caveat emptor*. "That ain't no way to get out of a tight," Homer says, and refuses.[6]

Jesse, in contrast, acts as a foil to Homer in terms of the theme of escape. For he has been everywhere, Lonnie thinks, and Lonnie's own yearnings for distant places are gratified by listening to Jesse talk of his experiences on the rodeo circuit. "Just hearing the names," Lonnie says, "was enough to make me restless."

Hud eliminates the theme of Lonnie's yearning for escape that is central to *Horseman, Pass By,* and therefore of necessity decreases Jesse's significance and eliminates the minor subplot of the Thalia rodeo and Jesse's failure to perform creditably at it. The need inherent in a visual medium to establish an explicit polarity between Hud and Homer is again the explanation. While in the novel both Hud and Jesse may act as contrasts to different aspects of Homer, in the film the distinction between Hud and Jesse must inevitably be blurred because of the fact that, since Homer must be visualized as a person, they must be seen in contrast to all of him rather than to specifically differentiated qualities of his character. Therefore Hud and Jesse, had they remained of equal importance in the film, would inevitably have become redundant rather than complements to each other. The difference between them, in short, which is of basic importance to the novel, would have appeared less striking on the screen than their overpowering similarity in terms of their not being Homer.

This point is perhaps best illustrated by a scene from the novel that was carried into the film almost intact. In both *Hud* and *Horseman, Pass By,* Homer keeps on his ranch three longhorn cattle in addition to his beef herd as a reminder of the old days. "Cattle like them make me feel like I'm in the cattle business," he says. These three longhorns must be destroyed with the rest of the herd, since they too are presumably infected with hoof-and-mouth disease.

In the novel, when the longhorns are being rounded up Jesse suggests to Homer that he let them go. "If the government wants 'em, let the government go find 'em," he says. Homer brushes off the suggestion by saying, "I don't know what to think yet"; but when the diagnosis of hoof-

and-mouth disease is confirmed he has these cattle killed along with the others. In the film, significantly, the suggestion to Homer is made not by Jesse but by Lonnie, and his remark to his grandfather that the longhorns ought to be let go is very clearly reminiscent of Hud, who has made almost exactly the same suggestion about how best to get rid of the infected herd. Again, the film has concentrated its effect rather than spreading it out over a number of characters, since visually the most important thing is not which particular character makes the suggestion but that the suggestion itself is one totally antithetical to Homer's own values. In the film Lonnie has received a direct lesson in terms of two diametrically opposed characters; in the novel, by contrast, the same opposition can be expressed without redundance by more than one character, if only because each character, if not seen, is visualized by the reader as representative of a more or less isolated point of view rather than as a person of flesh and blood, someone who stands in opposition to relatively specific qualities in Homer Bannon rather than to his entire character.

This necessity to condense all the foils to Homer in the character of Hud inevitably implies the one major change between novel and film—a total reversal of the ending. Lonnie learns, through the action of *Horseman, Pass By,* the futility of his own generalized longings for escape. The world, he discovers, when viewed with, in Yeats's phrase, "a cold eye," is not the romantic place he had thought it was at the beginning of the novel. Captive at the beginning of the story of the common adolescent belief that somewhere there must be more "life" than there is in one's own environment, Lonnie learns the truth symbolized by the name of the town—Thalia—where the story's action has taken place: that the stuff of life and history and epic poetry can be discovered in one's own surroundings if one has the intelligence to know where to look for it.

In the novel, then, Lonnie's education culminates in his acceptance of the world for what it is and his rejection of the unreal attitudes toward it he had held at the beginning of the story. In the novel's final scene, after Homer's death, Lonnie hitches a ride on a truck to visit a friend injured in the Thalia rodeo and taken to the hospital at Wichita Falls. For a while, Lonnie says, "I was tempted to do like Jesse once said: to lean back and let the truck take me as far as it was going." But his newly achieved maturity enables him to reject this temptation, and he decides to stop at Wichita Falls, see his friend, and then return to Thalia.

In *Hud* the ending is quite different. Here, Lonnie's newly won maturity has taught him not to accept the world as it is, but rather to see the validity of Homer's attitude toward life and to reject the tempting but ultimately immoral standpoint represented by Hud. Lonnie has, therefore, no choice but to leave the world dominated by Hud that the Bannon ranch has become after Homer's death; and so at the end of the film he sets out to make his own way in the great world he has rejected in the novel. While the ending of *Horseman, Pass By* showed Lonnie's new maturity by emphasizing his realization of the flimsiness of his adolescent longings for escape, the ending of *Hud* shows it in terms of his symbolic acceptance of Homer's attitude toward the world and his rejection of Hud's.

The major differences between the stories of Shane and Hud as they are presented on film or on the printed page are largely implicit in the very different points of view required by the two media. The primacy of vision in the film, though perhaps an obvious point, cannot be too strongly insisted upon. It results first of all in the necessity for an almost complete denial of both the retrospective mood and the nostalgic point of view upon which the fictional versions of both stories heavily rely. The internalization of the fictional point of view implied by the reminiscences of an older hero reflecting upon his past is simply impossible to achieve with either success or consistency upon film for two reasons: first of all, the narrator of the novel must inevitably become one among many characters in the film; and second, the action of the story when seen must be seen as occurring in the present.[7]

An equally important, and less obvious, difference between novel and film also follows from the primacy of vision implied by the latter. For although the phrase "cast of thousands" has become a cliché for describing the so-called "epic" film, in fact the necessity for externalization implicit in the film results in an overwhelming tendency to simplify by reducing the number of characters. Most of the cast of thousands are background characters whose function is analogous to the consciously generalized mood-painting used by the novelist as a way of establishing his setting.

For all their specific differences, however, both media have in common one basic attitude toward their material—an attitude that has been present in Americans' treatment of their epic since the West was first assumed to be the most significant factor in the American experience and the unique part of that experience which set it off from other lands and other peoples. This attitude comes ultimately from an environmentalist belief, inherent in primitivism, that man reflects in moral terms the physical nature of his environment. This belief, which is in fact nothing more than an assumption, is treated as though it were axiomatic for interpreting the materials of the great American epic. Whether, as with Natty Bumppo, the American hero directly reflects the glory of his environment or, as with Emerson's strictures upon New Hampshire, the comment that "the God who made New Hampshire/Taunted the lofty land/With little men" is ironic,[8] the importance of the analogy is never doubted. And the

Western film has absorbed this analogical comparison between man and his environment. In the film, Shane has
picked up, along with his other attributes, the quality of a
mountain spirit, representative of the brooding grandeur
of the Grand Tetons against which he is filmed, an analogy
specifically evoked by the mountain man's buckskin shirt
he wears and by the theme song of the film, "The Call of
the Faraway Hills." In *Hud* the analogue is more ironic, but
the bleak Texas landscape, the stark ranchhouse on the
Bannon ranch, and the ugly town of Thalia make much
the same symbolic point: for Hud expresses them exactly
as Shane reflects the mountains.

The great problem, then, shared by both the Western
film and Western fiction is the problem of presenting man
against the landscape. What is the landscape, first of all:
the beauty of the Grand Tetons or the ugliness of the Bannon ranch? And how does man stand against it: does he
stand *for* it, symbolizing in detail what it expresses in
general? Or does he stand *in contrast to* it, repudiating everything it represents? There are of course no simple
answers to these questions, all expressions of a basic ambiguity in the American identity; no answers, that is, except
for the statement of the metaphorical problem and of its
ritual solution.

Notes

1. The change to the title *Hud* was a decision made by Paramount Studios. See Larry McMurtry, *In a Narrow Grave: Essays on
Texas* (Austin, Texas: Encino Press, 1968), pp. 4ff for details.
McMurtry—or so at least he claims—had suggested the title
Coitus on Horseback, for no very good reason. The final title *Hud* is
a shortened form of Paramount's working title, *Hud Bannon
against the World.*

2. *Shane* (Boston: Houghton Mifflin, 1949). All further references are to this edition.

3. The interested reader who does not remember the film can test my point by searching out one of the illustrated editions of the novel and noting how different the pictures of both characters and events are from his own mental conceptions of them.

4. Indeed, McMurtry, who praises *Hud* at the expense of *Horseman, Pass By,* sees the weakness of the film in its too great faithfulness to the novel. See *In a Narrow Grave,* p. 17.

5. Thomas Landess, *Larry McMurtry* (Austin, Texas: Steck-Vaughn, 1969), pp. 10, 14. Landess's study of McMurtry is generally excellent, though his interpretation of certain aspects of *Horseman, Pass By*—notably the ending—differs from my own.

6. *Horseman, Pass By* (New York: Harper & Brothers, 1961). All further references are to this edition.

7. This is true, I think, even of films—unlike these two—that use technical variations of the flashback as ways of insisting upon a film's action having happened in the past. Such action, even when we are assured by such violations of point of view that it did actually happen in the past, nonetheless seems to me to be happening in the present.

8. "Ode Inscribed to W. H. Channing," lines 24–26.

Michael T. Marsden

Savior in the Saddle:
The Sagebrush
Testament

As Frederick Jackson Tur-
ner pointed out, the birth of a new land demanded the
simultaneous birth of a new culture, with its roots necessarily in the past, but its blossom in the timeless experience
of the ever-extending and never-ending frontier.[1] This
operative truth is acted out time and again as Western after Western unfolds on movie screens across this land. It is
logical, therefore, to suggest that notions of a Savior, a
Messiah, would have undergone a similar transformation
from the Christian Savior of almost nineteen hundred
years of European cultural refinement to a Christ e-
quipped to serve the essentially different spiritual needs
of a new and separate culture. Nowhere is this transformation more clearly seen than in the Western film.[2]

American heroes have a long tradition of serving as
the Redeemer. For the Puritans, the wilderness of their
Chosen Land was inhabited by devils, and these devils
could be driven out only by the strongest and worthiest of
men. If the land was to be settled, it had to be tamed and
purified. It is of this challenge that the American hero,

beginning with Daniel Boone, was born. And Boone's direct cultural descendant, the Western hero, became America's most permanent heroic creation, serving as Redeemer for generations of Americans.

However, it is interesting that, while criticism of the Western film has suggested the Savior-like nature of the Western hero, no extended treatment has been given to the divine, Savior-like qualities of this American creation. Harry Schein, for example, in an article entitled "The Olympian Cowboy," suggests that in the western landscape one can discern "an Olympian landscape model, the Rocky Mountains—saturated with divine morality."[3] A little later in that article he suggests that Shane is "an American saint . . . and sits at God's right hand."[4] But these suggestions are never explored. Martin Nussbaum, in his article "The 'Adult Western' As An American Art Form," argues that the gun is a symbol of divine intervention into the American landscape, but he never entertains the implications of this regarding the nature of the Western hero.[5]

It is my purpose here to establish several of the religious parallels that abound in Western film, and then to crystallize them into a statement regarding the religious nature of the Western hero. The West of the American imagination is the landscape for this study, not the West as it was, but the West, as John Ford would say, as it should have been.

It is practically a commonplace for people to refer to the Western gunfighter-hero as an American parallel to the medieval knight.[6] While such mediations seem appropriate and stimulate interest, there is a very real danger that they will cloud the issue of the particular and unique nature of the American Western hero; he is an American god, who in the name of a divinely ordered civilization carries a Colt .45. As Gary Cooper succinctly put it, the five bullets in the cylinder were for law and order, and the one in the chamber was for justice. The Western formula clearly implies that the Messiah of the New Testament was unacceptable to a land of savagery, harsh landscape, and purple sunsets. The West needed a Christ who could survive the Great American Desert, and for much longer than forty days, and who could show himself equal to the American challenge, whether real or imagined. And this Savior would have to be equal to the wishes and dreams of a suffering people who wished to be delivered from the concretized evil that plagued their lives. The people longed for a Christ who would ride in, deal effectively with evil, and dispense justice with a finality that would make the angels envious and a skill that John Cawelti, in his book *The Six-Gun Mystique,* likens to that of a surgeon.[7] But this Western Savior must, of necessity, bring with him all the trappings of a just and at times wrathful God, as in the Old Testament. He could not be the loving and forgiving and merciful Christ of the New Testament but must be, rather, a Christ who has been modified, changed by contact with the western experience. The lawlessness of the frontier required a strong sense of divine justice untempered with mercy. The coming of the Western hero is a kind of Second Coming of Christ, but ths time he wears the garb of the gunfighter, the only Savior the sagebrush, the wilderness, and the pure savagery of the West can accept.

A just God and a Savior, there is none besides me
(*Isaiah* 45:21)

The West of the American imagination needed a clean, swift, sure, and final justice in a lawless land infested by outlaws, Indians, and a hostile and threatening environment. The Western film mythology, from the very beginnings of film history, combined the best myths available to forge a viable and lasting mythology which, until recently with the release of anti-Westerns such as *Bad Company* (1972), *Soldier Blue* (1970), and *Dirty Little Billy* (1972), has remained intact, and would appear to be able to weather even the tumultuous filmic assaults being waged against it during the last decade.

Finally, in dealing with the nature of the Western hero, it seems fruitful to view him as a coming together of certain elements from the Old and the New Testaments, and to see through him the creation of a Sagebrush Testament with its own ethos.

> Behold the days come, saith the Lord, and I will raise
> up to David a just branch; and a King shall reign, and
> shall be wise; and shall execute a judgment and jus-
> tice in the earth. (*Jeremiah* 23:5)

In 1916 William S. Hart starred in and directed an allegorical Western entitled *Hell's Hinges*. Hart plays the role of Blaze Tracy, who, as one title says, represents a two-gun "embodiment of the best and the worst in the early west." As the film opens he embodies primarily the worst. We find him in league with Silk Miller, owner of the local saloon, aptly named the Palace of Joy. The town is awaiting the arrival of a rather weak and selfish young parson who has been sent by his bishop to establish a church in the wilderness and prove himself as a clergyman. God does not, however, abide in Hell's Hinges, a truth which the inexperienced parson and his lovely sister, Faith, must soon painfully face.

As Tracy first gazes at Faith, it is "one who is evil, looking for the first time on what is good." Later, Tracy, who was expected by the corrupt townspeople to take part in the elimination of the parson from Hell's Hinges, stands up for the clergyman and his congregation as they hold their first church service in a local barn. The dance-hall girls, rabble-rousers, and other nonbelievers decide to break up the ceremony by holding a dance on the same premises.

But Blaze Tracy's two guns convince them to allow the Sunday service to continue.

When the parson's sister, Faith, attempts to "convert" Blaze, he utters: "I reckon God ain't wantin' me much ma'am, but when I look at you, I feel I've been ridin' the wrong trail." He seeks out religion because Faith holds stock in it, and there must therefore be some value in it. When the parson is lured into the lead dance-hall girl's boudoir, plied with drink, and seduced, it is Blaze who tells a parable to the bewildered good townspeople, who are now a leaderless flock. He tells them, in a Christlike and kindly New Testament manner, about Arizona, a renowned cowboy roper who set off to rope a calf, but the rope failed him. Thus, he says, it was the instrument they counted on that failed them, not their faith.

The evil townspeople are so depraved that they conspire to burn down the newly erected church. So effective have they been in destroying the parson that he is first in line with a willing hand and a lighted torch. But, before he can act, he is killed by the remaining good people who will shed blood to protect their church. After considerable bloodshed, and while Blaze is away on an errand of mercy, the church is burned down. The few remaining good people are literally sent into the desert, to await the return of the Savior who will seek revenge for the destruction of the church and the death of the parson. Blaze, living up to his first name, guns down Silk Miller and turns the whole town into a living inferno. He gives Hell's Hinges a "crown of fire," and forcefully damns it to eternity. In short, Faith is helpless in the West unless she has two blazing guns to defend her. The Western Savior needs the confrontation with civilization (formal religion) to tame him, but he can easily arrive at heroic stature because of his essential goodness.

In *Hell's Hinges* there is the obvious, but nonetheless

effective illustration of the blending of certain divine qualities from the Old and New Testament to form a kind of Sagebrush Testament, which must of necessity result in the forging of a new Savior, who is of the sagebrush, but also superior to it.

The 1931 film *Cimarron*, the only Western ever to receive the Oscar for best picture, contains another powerful illustration of the essential transformation of Christianity through the American imagination in the Western. Yancy Cravat (Richard Dix) is an incurable wanderer who finds himself in Oklahoma as a consequence of the land rush into the Indian territory opened for settlement. In turn, he becomes a poet, gunfighter, lawyer, and editor and is successful at each. Being a leading citizen, he is bound to defend the forces of civilization over the forces of the lawless frontier. During one scene, in order to bring religion to the frontier, he himself preaches a sermon. He pulls out a Bible from his back pocket, and as he draws it forward it crosses the butt of his holstered gun as a warning to all who would attempt to usurp the forces of civilization. The saloon is his church, and instead of a crucifix in the background, there is the traditional saloon nude. Christ has come to the frontier, but he wears different garb and follows a new ethos, a modified ethos that was born of the confrontation with the land and savagery. In the middle of his sermon, Yancey Cravat uses his free hand to draw his sixgun and shoot down several unruly cowboys who are disrupting his preaching!

The Savior-like nature of the Western hero is nowhere more clearly manifested than in George Stevens's masterful *Shane* (1953). Alan Ladd at the beginning of the film moves slowly down the Grand Teton Mountains from the west. He is the new Christ, the frontier Christ, coming down from a western Olympus to help the cause of the farmers against the ranchers. We see Shane through the

eyes of America's future, young Joey Starrett, through
whom the tradition that Shane represents will be handed
down. Shane is the pearl-handled-gun-toting Messiah
who *can* save the endangered land from the forces of
lawlessness. It is not by accident that Joey's parents are
named Joe and Marion, standing in wait for the Messiah-
son who will deliver them. The suggestion by some critics
that Joey may well be dreaming the entire story seems to
work well here. For Shane is what Joey wants to become
and what Joe and Marion want their son to become. Shane
brings with him all the trappings of a wrathful God out of
the Old Testament—omniscience, swift judgment or justice, and an anger born of injustice. But that "wrath" is only
hinted at in the early parts of the film as some dangerous
undercurrent in the man. As the film opens, he has
attempted to hang up his guns, to live peacefully, kindly,
and gently. But experience proves that evil must be dealt
with directly, swiftly, and surely.

The Devil is personified in this film by the hired gunman, Jack Wilson (Jack Palance), who shoots down an innocent farmer to instill fear in the homesteaders. When
the farmers are burying their murdered compatriot and
are considering giving up the land, it is Shane who, in the
middle of a barren cemetery with the flimsy, false-fronted
town to his back, reminds them about what is at stake in this
epic struggle. He preaches his sermon on the mount effectively, and they depart reassured, determined, and u-
nified. Shane, however, by unwillingly but obediently accepting the burden of the homesteaders, sacrifices his
right to the good life. He was sent from the mountain to
perform a task of salvation, and although he struggles
mightily with his fate and wishes it were otherwise, he does
not, in his moment of truth, hesitate to shoulder the burden of being a savior. He, finally, plays the hand he has
been dealt.

But before he sacrifices himself he instructs Joey in the use of the gun. Martin Nussbaum has correctly observed that the gun is really a deus ex machina in the Western.[8] It is the "word" of the West, and must be understood and used correctly. The temptation is to limit one's interpretation of the gun to sexual suggestions, which are indeed clearly there in *Shane* as in other Westerns. Marion, for example, is both fascinated by the power Shane possesses through the gun and afraid of it. The Western hero must use the gun deliberately and sparingly so that, in the words of Judd in *Ride The High Country* (1962), he can "enter his house justified." Shane tells Marion and Joey that it is not the gun that is evil, but rather the way in which it is used. It is only a tool, he explains, neither good nor bad in itself. Shane leaves Joey instructed. And when Joey runs to town after Shane, watches over his hero, and finally warns him of the danger, he is found tested and true.

After the showdown, Shane, who incidentally has been wounded in the left side, and who is about to ride off into the mountains again, stops and lays his hand upon the head of young Joey, as if to consecrate him for the task ahead.[9] But this Messiah needs only one apostle, not twelve. For the Christianity of the American imagination, of the American Desert, is an individualistic one.

From *Shane* to the cynical "Dollars" films of the 1960s is a long leap, but the image of the Savior clings even to Eastwood's portrayal of the self-interested yet fated Messiah of a deserving few. In *Fistfull of Dollars* (1964 — American release 1967), Eastwood rides into a Southwestern town on a mule. He is shot at, poked fun at, and swings from a cross-like beam. The whole scene suggests a Palm Sunday in reverse. As a consequence of doing battle with the evil forces in the town, he receives a terrible beating including, appropriately, a wound on the hand. He seeks sanctuary in a coffin, and is reborn again to fight evil, seeming to be invulnerable to shots in the heart by wearing an armor breastplate. In a touching sequence, suggestive of the Holy Family's flight from Bethlehem to the desert, Eastwood frees a captive mother, her helpless husband, and their young son and sends them off into the desert to seek refuge. Eastwood, "the man with no name," like the heroes of American-made Westerns, brings justice (and mercy) to this evil-ridden society through violence.

Eastwood returned in 1973 as the "no name" character in a Western of his own creation, *High Plains Drifter,* in which he eschews traditional religion because it did not intervene when the town had bullwhipped the Marshal to death in its streets. He comes to the town to execute an elaborate but just revenge upon its inhabitants. While pushing aside the parson who speaks empty Christian platitudes, "No Name" dispenses justice with an appropriateness that defies parallels. The cowardly townsfolk are, for example, led to believe they can be made courageous under his leadership. He, however, trains them and leaves them, taking with him their supposed courage. Called a Guardian Angel by some, the Devil by others, he turns out to be their judge and, like God, allows men to work out their own destinies, trapping and destroying themselves. As a final insult, he has them paint the whole town red, suggesting the crown of fire so memorable from *Hell's Hinges,* and he even paints "Hell" over the town's name on the sign at the edge of the town.

Alejandro Jodorowsky, a South American director, has successfully employed the convention of the Sagebrush Savior in his ultraviolent and enigmatic film *El Topo* (1971). El Topo rides into the desert with his son, abandons him to his own devices, and seeks adventure in the Great Desert. After numerous violent experiences; he is shot by a woman companion, left for dead, and rescued by a tribe of cave-dwelling mutants who are kept in underground confinement by the neighboring townspeople. While living among these strange people, he becomes a

kind of pacifist Savior and eventually leads them to freedom from their confinement. But when they rush en
masse into the Mexican village, they are promptly slaughtered by the forces of evil. El Topo, seeing the slaughter,
grabs a rifle and, declaring in turn that he is Justice and
then God, consecrates the bullets with his words. He becomes the personification of violence, seemingly invulnerable to bullets himself. The film ends in a holocaust as El
Topo destroys the villains with his rifle and then immo-
lates himself, Buddhist monk fashion, in the middle of the
main street, etching forever in the minds of the viewers the
inevitability of justice through violence.

Films such as *El Topo* serve as illustrations of the viability
of the Savior convention, as the Western is adapted to the
cultural needs of other nations which seek to develop it as a
unique folk-pop art within their own cultural contexts and
thus reexamine it in that milieu.

Criticism of the Western film must take into account the
transformation of a Christian mythology as much as the
transformation of other cultural traditions. The Western
hero cannot simply be a Christ transported out of the New
Testament any more than he can be a slightly altered
medieval knight. For in the American imagination, the
New Testament message of love and mercy does not provide solutions any more than the American judicial system
does. The answer lies in divine intervention, through a
hero who combines the most useful qualities of the Old
Testament God and the New Testament Christ, to create a
Sagebrush Savior who is kind, yet strong; who is just, yet
firm. This hero is the only hero the Western can abide by in
a wilderness which is ever ready to snuff out civilization as
it weakly struggles to exist in flimsy wooden churches,
schools, and town halls, strung out like cross-bearing tele-
phone poles against the ever-widening horizon. The hero
must be superhuman, and he must, above all, be invulner-

able to the human weaknesses shared by those whom he must defend and protect. If he is to be the answer to the dreams and prayers of the troubled, he must ride tall, shoot straight, and remain eternally vigilant for the causes of right.

But in order to create the needed hero the Western had to borrow from numerous sources to form the truly viable and invulnerable Savior who rides in, provides a definite and final solution to the problem, and rides out as inevitably and often as our psyches dictate. He, like the Christian Messiah, must always be with us, ever ready to sweep down on the evil towns and destroy them so they can be rebuilt to house families and civilization and the dreams of men. He may exist only in the American imagination, but he has the will of a people to give him strength and their hearts to give him immortality.

Notes

1. *The Turner Thesis Concerning the Role of the Frontier in American History,* ed. George Rogers Taylor (Boston: D. C. Heath, 1956).

2. I should like to express my appreciation to Jack Nachbar for many hours of stimulating conversation on the topic of Western films, and for providing the catalystic conception that the Western hero was more of the Old Testament than the New Testament.

3. Harry Shein, "The Olympian Cowboy," *American Scholar,* 24 (Summer 1955): 317.

4. Ibid., p. 319.

5. Martin Nussbaum, "The 'Adult Western' As An American Art Form," *Folklore,* 70 (September 1959): 464.

6. See, for example, Joseph J. Waldmeir, "The Cowboy, The Knight, and Popular Taste," Southern Folklore Quarterly, 22, no. 3 (September 1958): 113–120.

7. John G. Cawelti, *The Six-Gun Mystique* (Bowling Green, Ohio: Bowling Green State University Popular Press, 1970), p. 59.

8. Nussbaum, p. 464.

9. Joey was, of course, played by Brandon de Wilde, who later starred in *Hud* as the teenage nephew of Hud who turned away in disgust from all that he represented. Brandon de Wilde died at the age of thirty-three, as did, in 1973, Carl B. Bradley, who played the Marlboro cowboy in a national advertising campaign. The author does not wish to suggest anything more than that such curiosities in light of the Christ parallels prove to be interesting musings for the imaginative.

Harry Schein
translation
from Swedish
by Ida M. Alcock

The Olympian Cowboy

When middlebrow people want to express their utter contempt for films, they often cite the "Western" as typical of the idiocy they wish to deprecate. Actually, the Western is the backbone, not the tail, of the art of the film.

The Western, for that matter, is much more than a film. It offers us the opportunity to experience the creation of folklore, to see how it grows and takes form. The roots of the mythology of Europe and the Far East are hidden in the past, and today can be only imperfectly reconstructed. But the white man's America is no older than the Gutenberg Bible. It attained economic independence and, therewith, cultural independence about the time the novel achieved its artistic and popular success. It is no accident that James Fenimore Cooper's work stands as America's first significant contribution to literature. It is just as natural that the film, at its very beginning, seized upon the Western motif. In the life span of less than one generation, it has developed from an apparently innocent, meaningless form into a rigidly patterned and conventional mythology, into one body of young America's folklore.

Of course, most of the Westerns of silent films were substantially sideshows performed by puppets. But somewhere between William S. Hart and Hopalong Cassidy, a change occurred. The simple, upright, and faithful cowboy was decked out more and more with silver spurs and guitars; he sang much and drank little; he never worried about women even while protecting them. Almost imperceptibly he was changing into an omnipotent father symbol whose young attendants consistently avoided heterosexual and other traps of an unmanly nature.

The child is father to the man. The Western of the days of the silent film already contained the material and the tendencies which, little by little, as the element of sound consolidated the form of the film, were deepened and rigidified. Folklore demands a rigid form. If one is to feel the power of the gods, repetition is required. It is precisely the rigid form of the Western which gives the contents mythological weight and significance. This requires a ritualistic handling, with a rigid cast of characters similar to that of the *commedia dell'arte* and a strict orthodoxy like that of the Japanese kabuki theater.

Several years ago, when the Swedish state film censorship bureau wished to justify its existence by showing what erotic and brutal shocks we have escaped because of the intervention of the censor, it was found that these consisted to a great extent of saloon fights in the Westerns. The similarities among these fights, taken from perhaps ten different films, were astounding: the same bar counter, the same supernumeraries, the same groupings, the same choreography in the fights themselves. And when the Czech puppet-film director Iri Trnka decided to produce a satire on American films, it was natural that he chose the Western. It was simple enough to use puppets instead of human beings to make the rigid form and strict convention appear grotesque.

The movement in a stereotype is as obvious as the ticking of a clock in an otherwise absolute silence. The postwar shifts in perspective which the Western underwent did not disturb the mythological stability, but gave it a profound meaning aside from its aesthetic value. The genre has produced several good and many bad films, but even the stuttering priest can speak about God. Naturally, the Western does not lack aesthetic interest; even in its role of nursery for American film directors it has a certain aesthetic significance. Moreover, the rigid form requires speed, action and movement and, in propitious circumstances, can contribute to a dramatic conclusion. In addition, it creates an enormous demand for freshness within the limitations of the stereotype, an aesthetic stimulus as good as any.

Also characteristic of the Western is the public's relationship to it. The desire to experience the same thing time after time implies on the part of the public a ritualistic passivity similar to that which one finds in a congregation at a divine service. It cannot be curiosity which drives the public to the Western; there is no wish for something different and unfamiliar, but a need for something old and well known. One can scarcely talk about escape from reality in the usual sense; it is a hypnotic condition rather than a complicated process of identification. The Western has the same bewitching strength as an incantation: the magic of repetition.

In the center stands the hero. He is always alone in the little community. He often lacks family and, not infrequently, is one of those exceptional human beings who seem never to have had a mother. Opposed to him are the bandits (there are always several) and their leader, an older, rich, often to all appearances respectable man in league with corrupt political bosses. The bandit, too, usually lacks a wife and only now and then does he have an unfortunate daughter. Finally, there is the little community itself—respectable, timid, and neutral in action.

The action often takes place in the period immediately

after the Civil War. In such cases, the hero is often a southern officer and his opponents are northerners. The struggle between these two elements is an epilogue to the war, often with a reversed outcome. Uncle Sam is like a father figure, powerful and hateful, but at the same time filled with guilt feelings toward the ravished southerners. Although the Western apparently takes revenge for the defeat of the South, the revenge is still illusory, a rebellious gesture which culminates in loyal submission and father-identification.

The hero is surrounded by a good woman and several bad saloon girls, who later either sing about love or dance the cancan. The good woman is usually a blonde and a specialist in making apple pie. The bad women are the kind one goes to bed with. Although the beds rarely appear in Western interiors, there is reason to assume that the saloon ladies are supposed to suggest those prostitutes who, during the enormous woman shortage of the eighteen-hundreds, were imported into the West and, through their kind actions, saw to it that not all the men shot one another to death. Of course, in more advanced films, the typical mixed figure appears: an apparently bad woman who seems to be on the side of the bandits but who gradually shows herself to be innocent and finally helpful in their destruction.

The hero's relationship to women is very subtle. He shields them without actually being involved. In more and more Westerns a direct enmity toward women is displayed. Sadism is directed most often toward the bad women, but now and then even toward the mixed type. *Duel in the Sun* offers the best example of this. Often a triangle drama appears (a woman and two men) which ends with the men becoming good friends and arriving at the realization that the woman is not worth having. In *The Outlaw*, the young man, after prolonged abuse, humiliates the woman by choosing, in a tossup between her and a fine horse, the horse. In a priceless homosexual castration fantasy, the father figure of the film shoots off the ear lobes of the young man when he dares to defend himself. The pistol in Westerns is by now accepted as a phallic symbol.

In a series of films, the weapon stands in the center of the action—a bowie knife, a Winchester rifle, a Colt revolver. He who owns the weapon is unconquerable. The good men are the rightful owners from whom the bad men are trying to steal potency. To own the weapon is much more important than to own the woman. It is important how one draws the weapon. Bad men draw it too often but too slowly. Like Casanova, they shoot in all directions without finding their mark. The hero, who defends family and home—as an institution—draws his weapon quickly. He shoots seldom, but never misses. As protector of the community, he cannot afford to be promiscuous. There must be an outcome of the shooting. A strong man is able to fire six shots without reloading.

So much for the rigid Western pattern, familiar even to the more occasional moviegoers. It may be of interest to determine what variations this pattern displays and particularly those tendencies that have been most pronounced since World War II. The question, in other words, is this: Is there a relation between America's politically dominant situation in the postwar period and a new arrangement of luminaries in its mythology?

Accepting the usual risks of generalization, one can speak of three basic elements in the Western: the symbolic, the psychological and the moral. If one bears in mind the fact that the Western is usually a mixture of these elements, it will not be too gross a simplification to discuss each of these factors separately.

It is said that Chaplin never had any inkling of his profundity until he began to read what various intellectuals wrote about him. Then he himself became intellectual. That is, of course, sheer nonsense. If, however, this kind of reasoning is applied to the symbolism of the Western, it probably has a certain correctness. In other words, the Western seems to have become conscious of its symbolic purport and, as a result of this consciousness, has become quite dreadfully symbolic.

That unconscious enmity toward women, formerly expressed more indirectly, with lip service paid to chivalry while actions denoted inner indifference (placing on a pedestal always implies humiliation), now finds stronger and more direct expression. The hatred of women has become so obvious that it must give rise to speculation. Their ill-treatment in a physical and often purely sadistic sense is an increasingly common element not only in the Western but also in other American films such as *Gilda*. An outstanding example is *Winchester 73*. And *Colt 45* is a symbolic parody of this motif. Not only must the pistol be regarded from a symbolic point of view—it goes off with a louder bang than the rifle—but the villain in the film has a favorite position, teetering on a chair, half sprawling, with his hands on his hips and the pistol profile following a naturalistic line. Even if this conscious smuggling in of symbols never can take in an artistically interested customs officer, it indicates an ambition to make more than a classical spectacle of the Western.

This ambition is made even clearer through the psychological element. Though Westerns are undoubtedly unpsychological for the most part, they have a predilection for dealing with the psychology of the villain. Even this is refreshing to an eye that yearns for some gray oases in the black and white desert.

Through trying to clarify the villain's behavior, the films muster a certain sympathy for him. He becomes a product of unfortunate circumstances, orphaned at an early age and brought up in a loveless milieu. He has, as a rule, suffered injustice and seeks revenge in a certain criminal but, in the deepest sense, forgivable way. Often, as stated before, he is a southern officer whose home was devastated. The villain, of course, must die, but as a rule he dies happy, in a redeeming self-sacrifice through which the blessedness of the final kiss acquires a charmingly melancholy background.

These psychological efforts can give rise to important thematic rearrangements. A few years ago two films were made about Jesse James—a legendary western figure who is well on the way to becoming America's Robin Hood. In one of these films, *The Great Missouri Raid,* the James brothers are formidable enemies, but chivalrous supermen of steel, dutiful toward their mother. They are, of course, southerners, and their enemy is a northern general modeled after a hateful Gestapo type. The film is very well made and belongs to the classical Western pattern. The other film, *I Shot Jesse James,* seems more unpretentious. It concerns a man who shot his best—and oldest—friend in the back in order to obtain amnesty for himself and be able to marry a saloon girl (compare Freud). The victim is the bandit sought by the law, the murderer the one who is protected by the law. The psychological complications caused by this rearrangement of boundaries between the territory of the villain and the hero are dealt with in two sections. The murderer is certainly free, but he is detested by public opinion. Even the girl is unkind enough not to trouble herself about him after the treachery which has been committed for her sake. The murderer, desiring to defy public opinion, accepts an offer from a traveling theatrical troupe to appear on the stage and show how he shot James in the back. In another part of the film, he forces a singer to render the ballad of the murder of Jesse James. Thus, as his crime is repeated again and again, the

murderer returns to the mental scene of the crime and
suffers an inner decay which leads to a new crime, this time
unprotected by the law.

I Shot Jesse James is not the only Western which sets
friend against friend. Very often the motif is family; now
and then brother stands against brother, father against
son. As a rule it is a woman who divides them. Something
like biblically elemental conflicts are deftly extracted
from, or themselves extract, a taken moral stand. When
form and conclusion are rigid, a fundamental moral problem can have some of the simple, primeval strength of the
drama of fate and thus prevent the repetitions from becoming mechanical.

These moral conflicts are undoubtedly the most interesting elements in the modern Western. They are evident in *The Gunfighter,* a very fine film with far from ordi-
nary psychological creativity, and in *High Noon,* until now
the genre's most outstanding artistic success.

The Gunfighter deals with a middle-aged and unglamo-
rized gunman. No one in the entire West can handle a gun
as he does. He is, therefore, challenged by all the young
fighting cocks who wish to take over his reputation for
being invincible. He is forced to kill them in self-defense.
He flees from his home, but his reputation is swifter than
his flight; he is always recognized, and the killing is repeated time after time. Though he is fed up to the gills with
it, there is always someone who will not leave him in peace.
Finally there comes a man who draws the gun a fraction of
a second more quickly than he. The gunfighter dies with
what is almost relief, but at the same time he is filled with
pity for his murderer: now it is *his* turn to take over this
reputation as the foremost gunman of the West, his fate to
kill and never to be able to flee from killing until he himself
is killed.

The Western's moral problem revolves around the
Fifth Commandment. One can understand that a country

traditionally pacifist but suddenly transformed into the strongest military power in the history of the world must begin to consider how, with good conscience, it can take life. In somewhat awkward situations it is always good to take shelter behind the lofty example of the mythological gods.

I see *High Noon* as having an urgent political message. The little community seems to be crippled with fear before the approaching villains; seems to be timid, neutral, and half-hearted, like the United Nations before the Soviet Union, China, and North Korea; moral courage is apparent only in the very American sheriff. He is newly married; he wants to have peace and quiet. But duty and the sense of justice come first, in spite of the fact that he must suddenly stand completely alone. Even his wife, who is a Quaker and opposed on principle to killing, wishes to leave him, and only at the last moment does she understand that her duty to justice is greater than her duty to God. The point is, of course, that pacifism is certainly a good thing, but that war in certain situations can be both moral and unavoidable.

High Noon, artistically, is the most convincing and, likewise, certainly the most honest explanation of American foreign policy. The mythological gods of the Western, who used to shoot unconcernedly, without any moral complications worth mentioning, are now grappling with moral problems and an ethical melancholy which could be called existentialist if they were not shared by Mr. Dulles.

This conscious symbolism, these psychological ambitions and moral statements of account give both color and relief to the mythological substratum. The anchor in realism, for example, in the historical characters like Billy the Kid and Jesse James, or in the more and more ambitious and thoroughly worked out descriptions of milieus, contribute to the creation of an impressive space before the footlights of the mythological scene. The native strength and possibilities of the Western are developed in the counterplay between American film production and American film critics. As witness thereof, take that farfetched but characteristic comparison between *High Noon* and *That Old Game about Everyman* of which Howard A. Burton is guilty in a recent number of *"The Quarterly of Film, Radio, and Television."* His puzzle certainly does not fit together, but one still discerns an Olympian landscape model, the Rocky Mountains—saturated with divine morality. Even satires on the Western, such as Bob Hope's *The Paleface*, indicate a growing consciousness of the genre's true function.

An awareness of the mythological element is thus found not only among talentless writers, but also among talented directors like George Stevens. According to a statement in the English film magazine *Sight and Sound,* he is reported to have expressed his desire to "enlarge" the Western legend and to have said that the pioneers presented in the Western fill the same role for the Americans as King Arthur and his knights hold in English mythology. In Stevens's film *Shane* that ambition is entirely realized. As a matter of fact, the film incorporates the complete historical development of the Western, including the protest against the father and the identification with the father. It is, to be sure, an imperfect attempt—but still an attempt—at synthesis of the classical pattern, enriched with the three modern variations: symbolic, psychological, moral.

A large and fertile valley in the West is ruled by a powerful and greedy cattleman. With the help of his myrmidons, he carries on a private war of attrition against a handful of farmers who are struggling to bring the grazing lands under cultivation. To one of these small farms Shane comes, dressed in romantic garb of leather, cartridge belt, and gun. He takes a job there, becomes good friends with the farmer, his wife, and their twelve-year-old boy, Joey.

Shane has a mysterious past; he has been a gunman who now is trying to begin a new and peaceful life. He manages, for the longest time, to avoid being provoked by the cattle-man's hirelings, but the terror of the farmers becomes un-bearable. When one of them is shot down by an imported murderer, the others are willing to give up and move away. No one dares to meet terror with terror. Then Shane takes off his blue work-clothes and puts on his old leather outfit. He gets out the gun which he hoped he had laid down forever, rides forth to the saloon, and kills the murderer. He has tried to begin a new life, but he has not succeeded. He has killed again and must ride away to the unknown from which he came.

Shane cannot, from an artistic point of view, be com-pared with *High Noon,* possibly because it has not an equal-ly emphasized main point. It deals, as a matter of fact, with two motifs: Shane and the little family, and Shane and the community versus the dictatorial cattleman and his band. But the film is obviously strongly influenced by *High Noon.* The tempo is equally slow and heavy with fate, the por-trayal of the milieu equally penetrating. The action is one unbroken loading of a charge up to the climax. This is un-usual for a Western, with its generally very rapid changes of scene.

Like the gunman in *The Gunfighter,* Shane is the man marked by fate, he whom the gods set out to kill. The dis-tance between him and Mr. Babbitt, the farmer, and the small-town dweller in *High Noon* is as great as the distance between Brooklyn and Korea. Only the woman lacks perception of the hovering air of fatefulness. She sees only what she can touch. Between Shane and her the atmos-phere is tense with fear and eroticism, but only her hus-band can give her security.

The really original element in *Shane* is the relationship between Shane and the little boy, Joey. Joey cherishes a boundless, completely hysterical admiration for Shane, for his skill with the pistol. He himself is still not permitted to play with loaded weapons, but they occupy his imagination. He smacks his lips to imitate the sound of shooting; he catches sight of game without being able to press after it; he shoots imaginary enemies with imaginary bullets. His confidence in Shane is upset a trifle when Shane knocks his father unconscious. However, when the boy understands that Shane has not robbed his father of life, but only of potency (Shane wants to prevent him, less experienced in the art of shooting, from risking his life, and takes away his pistol), the boy identifies himself completely with Shane. He follows him to the saloon, witnesses the battle, and afterward takes leave of Shane, prepared to become his heir.

Shane, more than any other Western hero, is a mythological figure. This is partly because the film sees him so much through the eyes of Joey, looking upward. Shane's entry is as godlike as his exit; it is a higher being who comes, driven by fate-impregnated compulsion, to fulfill his mission. Shane is more than Robin Hood, more than Cinderella's prince. He is a suffering god, whose noble and bitter fate it is to sacrifice himself for others.

Shane is distinguished by a realism seldom worked out so thoroughly in Westerns. The film takes the time to portray the people in the valley, their everyday lives, their little festivities. A series of impressionistically bold details gives the production a sensitive and fine-grained texture. Its world is familiar and close to reality. Only Shane is alien. He is not Zeus, who, disguised as a human being, visits the earth to cavort with its women, but an American saint, the cowboy who died in the Civil War and sits at God's right hand. He is a leather-bound angel with a gun, a mythological Boy Scout, always ready to keep the hands of true believers and the community unsullied by blood.

As a rule, of course, it is meaningless to discuss the degree of individual vision behind a work of art or a film with a mythological purport. Mythology rests on a collective foundation which also includes the creative artist.

When creative vision is expressed in the form of satire, it has quite obviously freed itself from the mythological substratum, but at the same time it strengthens the existence of that substratum—a puppet show which does not concern itself with the obvious is a paradox. As far as the Western is concerned, Bob Hope and the Marx Brothers demonstrate a blasphemous emancipation. Large sections of the American public, through television's mechanization of the Western, have become surfeited with the genre. Since *Shane* is neither mechanical nor satirical, it ought to be reckoned as the first offspring and, through Stevens's statement, the first "documented" offspring of the new vision.

The question remains: Is this newly awakened mythological vision going to sabotage mythology itself by dispelling the cloud which carefully used to conceal the summit of Olympus? It is not altogether certain, since vision in and of itself does not preclude piety. Probably, however, these films are going to have a more and more strongly motivated central idea, whereby the distance between the hero of the Western and the rest of its cast is going to increase in proportion to the square of its consciousness. Most interesting, though, will be the future attempts to cram more and more current morality into the mythological pattern. When Shane's little Joey grows up and gets ammunition, he is not going to lack a target worth shooting at.

Afterword

Jack Schaefer

A New Direction

Seven years ago this month, in this same state of Colorado, my fellow New Mexican, Frank Waters, received the same honor you are bestowing on me today. He spoke then in eloquent words about words, about the power and significance of words. He cited his personal realization of what a dangerous game he had been playing in writing words. In effect, he was advising all writers to be aware of, to be careful with, what they are doing when they are writing words.

When I read his address as printed in the Western Literature Association quarterly, I realized how pertinent his warning was to my own situation at the time. For almost forty years I had been playing the dangerous game without being particularly conscious of the dangers inherent in it.

I was appalled then, as I am now, at the sheer volume, the sheer bulk, the hundreds of thousands into the millions of words I had written. Though I like to say that I have had two careers and am trying a third, the three are really one, that of inflicting words upon a not-always-patient public.

For many years I was a newspaperman producing pro-
digious piles of copy seven days a week. By conservative
estimate I perpetrated, in addition to an array of news
items and publicity material for causes I considered
worthy, some scores of long feature articles, hundreds of
special columns, several thousand reviews of books and
films and plays and concerts, and a minimum of fifteen
thousand editorials. Then for even more years, though
slowed some in total output, I was guilty of causing gallons
of ink to be imprinted on reams of paper in the form of a
lengthening list of novels and short stories and magazine
articles. Even now I am again an addict of the dangerous
game. In process of making myself into an amateur natur-
alist, I have already published one unclassifiable book-
bound mass of words and am well into another—and can
excuse myself only by insisting that I am currently more
aware of the dangers lurking in the game.

For a perhaps more manageable metaphor I quote
James Branch Cabell, whom I have recently been reread-
ing. "While it is well enough to leave footprints on the
sands of time, it is even more important to make sure they
point in a commendable direction." Though I have no
absolute certainty that my mental compass now guides me
in a *commendable* direction, I do know that I have shifted
course and my footprints point in a *new* direction.

Attempting to explain that shift, I wrote in the introduction to my new book, my first in a full eight years, that I
had lost my innocence, had become ashamed of myself
and my species. That pleased me when I wrote it, seemed a
neat ploy in the playing with words. Actually it explains
nothing—and what else I wrote in that introduction explains only a small part of it. And so . . . I am grateful to the
WLA for inviting me to be here today because the necessity
of preparing this paper has pushed me into seeking to
define more accurately what I mean by innocence lost—

and into puzzling why, having lost innocence, I was unable for so long to make any more verbal footprints, however fleeting, in any direction at all. Herewith, then, a brief summary of my results, a sort of minor personal testament.

Ashamed of myself and my species. Of my species and of myself as a unit within it. My species. Order: Primates. Suborder: Anthropoidea. Family: Hominidae. Genus: Homo. Species ironically labeled *sapiens*.

Innocence lost . . . What was lost was the complacent assumption, brainwashed into me by background and education and culture and the myths we humans cherish about ourselves, that our species can be judged on the basis of a relatively few individuals, those few who do manage to attain a high level of decency in living or in admirable achievement. All too readily we rate our species, not by the norm of our kind and by our collective doings, but by the peak performances of selected individuals. Curiously, or rather typically, we rarely if ever apply such selectivity in judgment to any other species—only to our own, which, actually, as a species, somewhat resembles those of the ants and the termites in that the average individual achieves significance only as a member of a collective myriad multitude.

What replaced that assumption was a deepening conviction that my species, taken as a whole as in objective view it should be, is more ignoble than noble, more contemptible than admirable, is a dangerous evolutionary experiment, a menace to all important forms of life including itself on this spaceship earth.

What was lost, too, was the equally complacent assumption that just because my species now and again does in the whirl of the roulette wheel of the genetic gamble produce an admirable individual, the species as a whole will in time improve. What replaced that assumption was a strong suspicion that the odds are against any such advancement and that many long-range and continuing human activities, despite feeble efforts by some few in opposition, steadily increase those odds. I found myself unable to regard the expansion of my species from a few million around the world some two thousand years ago to a rapidly multiplying mass of four billion people who are on the whole no wiser and no more humane than their long-ago ancestors as representing any true progress in other than technological mastery of the environment and thus, in consequence, in destructive power.

Better players of the dangerous game than I have been have said this better than I can. Loren Eisley, for one, has noted that "the instruments of power, . . . always spread faster than the inventions of calm understanding, . . . have grown monstrous in our time. . . . Man is only beginning dimly to discern that the ultimate menace, the final interior zero, may lie in his own nature."

Again, Pogo's Walt Kelly has put it beautifully bluntly: "We have met the enemy and he is us."

In final effect, then, I began to believe that the faint footprints I had been making might not, probably did not, point in a commendable direction. When making them I had worn blinders like those used on draft horses in the days of my boyhood, stiff leather flaps which restricted vision to the road ahead and blocked out anything to either side which might distract the equine mind. My vision had been similarly restricted, focused narrowly in the writing of each new story on a few characters in a specific situation with blinders blocking consideration of the larger overall meaning of what those characters were doing and of the situation in which they were enmeshed.

Innocence lost, blinders gone, of course I could no longer write—certainly not as I had written before. How could I write another *Shane* with the same innocent attitude toward him, even though using again the device of the perspective of a hero-worshipping boy? Inevitably I would be troubled by realizing he was aiding the advance of settlement, giving his push to the accelerating onrush of the very civilization I find deserving of contempt. Oh, yes, I could claim he was also doing his bit to slow the push toward overpopulation by eliminating two potential begetters of progeny. But that is not the kind of solution to the population problem even I would recommend.

Or again, how could I write another story like that of "Hugo Kertchak," who built sheds and barns and houses strong against weather and time? While I could still admire him for his stubborn independence and insistence upon sound workmanship, inevitably I would be thinking that every time he built a new structure he was helping the farmer for whom he built it to destroy more of the habitat of other living creatures, to crowd them more toward eventual extinction.

Or again, how could I write another story like that of "Jeremy Rodock," who raised and trained horses for stagecoach lines? Though I could still admire him for devising a proper punishment for the villains who had crippled some of his horses, inevitably my view of him would be tainted by knowledge that he was a contributing part of the transportation craze of my kind which has led to the traffic-clogged superhighways of today.

Or yet again, how could I write any more articles praising the natural beauty and enchantment of my chosen Southwest? Inevitably bitterness would be there, bred by my understanding that Aldo Leopold was right when he wrote that the Southwest is a "wrecked landscape" and buttressed by my almost daily seeing or reading about current wrecking crews spreading the deadly blight.

But enough in that vein. However murkily put, perhaps

I have made my point, have explained why I could no longer attempt footprints in the same old direction. Why did it take me so long to attempt a new direction?

It might seem that nothing should have been easier than simply to reverse direction. After all, through much of my writing, particularly the later books, there had been hints that my innocence was waning, that almost unconsciously I had been turning around. Why not now, instead of in a sense celebrating as before various aspects and individuals of the western frontier, indulge in debunking, enjoy the cynical attitude, emphasize the evils of what has been done, the mistakes made, the wrong goals pursued? In my new frame of mind I thought there could not be too much of such writing. Yet, somehow, I could not add directly to it. I have worked out a theory of why I could not.

All responsible writers of fiction, whatever form their work takes, are reformers at heart. Whether aware of this or not, often not, they are dissatisfied with the world as it is and write about it as they believe it should be. Some are upbeat, almost automatically concentrate on the more decent aspects of existence, emphasize characters and actions they can admire. These take what can be called a positive approach. Others are downbeat, concentrate on the ills of the world, emphasize characters and actions they can despise. Theirs, with no prejudice in use of the adjective, is a negative approach. Both have the same ultimate purpose, to help a bit in remaking this sorry old world closer to their hearts' desires, the one group by showing their readers what should be admired and emulated, the other what should be despised and avoided. The difference between the two is really one of the basic differences, perhaps the basic difference, between what is generally called romanticism and what is generally known as realism. The truly great writer, of course, moves on beyond, melds the two approaches in an overall portrayal of the human condition. The rest of us addicts of the dangerous game may try to do the same, but inevitably we slip into an overbalance of one approach or the other.

There was no doubt which way I had slipped. From start to finish my free-lance writing, that of my second career, had been liberally flavored with romanticism—upbeat, romantic in attitude, however much I sought to be realistic in materials and in treatment of it. As Dorothy Johnson once pointed out, my fictional people were "affirmative people." Right. Almost invariably I had had them win victories for their personal decent principles even if only in death. For the most part, that is, my writing had rested comfortably on those complacent assumptions I have cited.

Now such people were lost to me, submerged for me in the mass of my contemptible species. But the effect of my congenital romanticism remained. I found it virtually impossible to write about the opposite kind of people even though they are in the majority in the species—and even though I could applaud those of my fellows who did write well and realistically about them.

In a sort of desperation, remembering a lifelong interest in natural history and with much pertinent material collected through the years already on my bookshelves, I began to consider and contemplate our fellow creatures who share with us humans the magic mystery of life. Call that a cop-out, if you wish, but to my surprise and exhilaration I found it a realm in which my mind and imagination could roam unfettered by the cynical pessimism of my opinion of my own lone species. Gradually, through experimental attempts, I discovered I could make a few new faint footprints in a new direction by writing about fellow mammals, helping them, I hoped, in their struggle for survival in this age of man's dominance and through them making comments on my own species.

The immediate result is *An American Bestiary*. Not a very deep footprint, but a beginning. For the next footprint defining the new direction I am concocting a collection of personal interviews, talks, conversations, discussions, arguments, with various fellow creatures. So doing I can offer information about them plus opinions of my own species as supposedly viewed from their differently angled perspectives.

Aha! I have found a way out of my dilemma! I can be downbeat, realistic, about my species, which I cannot admire much, by being upbeat about fellow creatures whom I can admire to a considerable extent.

But what happens? Now and again my own device turns back upon me. I am incurable. The brainwashing of my youth was too complete. Romanticism about my own species creeps in. Wrapped up in the dialogues going on in my own mind, I somehow, virtually inadvertently, let the romanticism creep in.

I am arguing with a Jaguar, who is a hard-headed self-sufficient realist, and a Puma, who is something of a philosopher and has an ingenious explanation of why he is. As experts in weaponry, in physical prowess, they have been condemning our human efficiency in developing artificial weapons to compensate for our personal lacks, an efficiency which has led to the ultimate obscenity, weapons so deadly that they cannot, at least should not, ever be used. Both have been damning mankind for viciousness, selfishness, arrogance, for becoming a cancerous growth in the earth's biosphere. And yet, says my Puma,

> You humans may represent an exaggeration of the mammalian mode of life which evolution's balancing mechanism will be forced to eliminate. But that possibility is tainted with cosmic injustice because the probable process, that of your own destruc-

tive capabilities turning back upon you, might well be
atomic blastings with their aftermath of radiation or
a slow strangulation as your other works render most
of the world uninhabitable. In either case the process
would have a terrible and unjust impact upon all the
rest of us. I prefer to ponder another possibility.
. . . Consider the fact that you humans are a relatively recent addition to the mammalian roster.
. . . While it is true that in evolutionary terms no life
form can be said to be finished unless or until it becomes extinct, in a relative sense perhaps you humans can be said to be unfinished, not really much
more than started, still in a sort of experimental
stage. Perhaps further evolution will not eliminate
you but instead will continue to develop you in ways
that will eliminate the necessity of eliminating you.

Or again, for one last glimmer: I am talking to a bat, a
small furry brown bat, who is actually more closely related
to us than most other mammals. He has been condemning
us humans for the terrible toll our insecticides are imposing on his kind. And yet he, more generous than I, seeks an
excuse for us, suggests that we let our inability to fly limit
our thinking, prevent us too often from letting the one
part of us which can fly, our thoughts, take wing and explore and assess in the realm of the possibilities beyond the
scope of one-level two-dimensional existence. The bat
says,

For my part, I have faith in you humans. The true
capacity of your intelligence is virtually unlimited.
How else could you relative newcomers to this
ancient earth . . . so quickly have become the dominant life form of the whole class? In a sense you are
still mere youngsters making the hasty unthinking
mistakes of youth. I have faith that in the long run

you will uphold the honor of the mammalian
brotherhood, will restore and maintain this world a
better homeland for all of us.

I am a hopeless case. Incurable. Despite all the downbeat conclusions to which my species sapience drives me, it
must be that my small furry flying friend, my bat, with his
ultimate faith in mankind, asserts the upbeat hope that
remains hiding somewhere intact within me.

A Brief Schaefer
Bibliography

1939–41 *The Movies and the People Who Make Them* (periodical). Vols. 1–3, no. 2. New Haven: Theatre Patrons, Inc.

1949   *Shane*. Boston: Houghton Mifflin.

1953   *The Big Range*. Boston: Houghton Mifflin.
The Canyon. Boston: Houghton Mifflin.
First Blood. Boston: Houghton Mifflin.

1954   *The Pioneers*. Boston: Houghton Mifflin.

1955   *Out West: An Anthology of Stories* (edited by Jack Schaefer). Boston: Houghton Mifflin.

1957   *Company of Cowards*. Boston: Houghton Mifflin.

1959   *The Kean Land, and Other Stories*. Boston: Houghton Mifflin.

1960   *Old Ramon*. Boston: Houghton Mifflin. Illustrated by Harold West.

1963   *The Great Endurance Horse Race*. Santa Fe: Stagecoach Press (limited ed.). Illustrated by Sol Baer Fielding.
Monte Walsh. Boston: Houghton Mifflin.
The Plainsmen. Boston: Houghton Mifflin. Illustrated by Lorence Bjorklund.

1964   *Stubby Pringle's Christmas.* Boston: Houghton
        Mifflin. Illustrated by Lorence Bjorklund.

1965   *Heroes without Glory: Some Goodmen of the Old West.*
        Boston: Houghton Mifflin.

1966   *Adolphe Francis Alphonse Bandelier.* Santa Fe:
        Press of the Territorian. Series of Western
        Americans, no. 7.

        Collected Stories. Boston: Houghton Mifflin. In-
        troduction by Winfield Townley Scott.

1967   *Mavericks.* Boston: Houghton Mifflin. Illus-
        trated by Lorence Bjorklund.

        New Mexico. New York: Coward McCann.

        The Short Novels of Jack Schaefer. Boston:
        Houghton Mifflin. Introduction by Dorothy M.
        Johnson.

1975   *An American Bestiary.* Boston: Houghton Mifflin.
        Foreword by James S. Findley. Illustrated by
        Linda K. Powell.

1978   *Conversations with a Pocket Gopher.* Santa Bar-
        bara, California: Capra. Illustrated by Irene
        Brady.

        Jack Schaefer and the American West. London:
        Longman. Selections, documentation, and
        photographs by C. E. J. Smith.